Unexpected Riches

DIANE GREENWOOD MUIR

Cover Design Photography: Maxim M. Muir

ISBN-13: 978-1530769797
ISBN-10: 1530769795

CONTENTS

ACKNOWLEDGMENTS

This year is going to be fun. I hinted at it in "Home for the Holidays," but Bellingwood is celebrating its sesquicentennial. The four books in 2016 will offer a glance at the deeper history of the community. Iowa's history is fascinating. I fall in love with the state every time I do any research.

Writing is a solitary business and I've discovered just how much solitude I need in order to write. Even the smallest distractions throw me off. That my family and friends still love me even though I hide so much means the world to me.

The team that helps me pull this book together is amazing. Rebecca reads each chapter as I write them – with horrible flaws, mistakes and continuity errors. She tells me how fun the story is, with no judgment. I would quit writing if she weren't here for me. My beta readers are so important to me. They edit, find continuity problems, point out unnecessary words / phrases / thoughts, catch strange grammar and are such a necessary part of my process. Thank you to: Linda Watson, Alice Stewart, Fran Neff, Max Muir, Edna Fleming, Linda Baker, Carol Greenwood, and Nancy Quist. Linda Baker also has been capturing the characters that I build and one of these days I will finally find a creative way to share her information with you.

Thank you to Judy Tew for reading the book after I've edited and before publication. She caught so many silly little errors I made that annoy a reader to no end. Y'all appreciate her, though you don't realize it.

Thank you for being part of this community. One of the most fun things about writing these books is getting to know all of you who read them. If you have a chance, find us on Facebook (facebook.com/pollygiller). If Bellingwood is a real place, this is where you'll find it.

CHAPTER ONE

Watching Rebecca and Beryl sit together under the small shelter, blankets wrapped around their legs and sketching the scene in front of them, gave Polly a warm and contented feeling deep down inside.

Today was colder than Beryl and Polly had hoped, but they'd waited long enough and Rebecca was desperate to be out and about with her mentor. Polly's job was to make sure they had blankets to keep them warm on the outside and thermoses of coffee and hot cocoa to warm them from the inside.

With a history of getting lost no matter how many times Beryl drove somewhere, Polly was more than glad to drive today. She began to believe that Beryl's worst problem was that she spent more time looking at her surroundings than focusing on where she was or where she was going. While they'd traveled, Beryl and Rebecca chattered about the things they saw and lamented that they didn't have time to draw it all.

Beryl's family owned property along the Des Moines River. A small shelter, just posts and a roof, stood at the end of a dirt lane, offering small comfort against the elements, but it was enough for

1

today. Tall black trees rose up - stark against the white snow and bright blue sky. At the edge of the riverbank, a row of walnut trees stood as sentries. Even Polly was taken in by the intricate shapes of the branches as they reached upward.

Once Rebecca and Beryl put pencil to paper, they were lost in the moment, ignoring Polly altogether. Polly put her hand on Rebecca's cheek to make sure she wasn't getting too cold. Her daughter's only response was a half-hearted brush-off, as if Polly were nothing more than an annoying fly.

The two artists had been planning this day out for weeks and every day after school, Rebecca checked the forecast on Polly's phone. Snow and messy weather had surprised them several times and the girl wanted today to be perfect.

Polly sat beside Rebecca and tucked a blanket around her legs. After a few minutes of sitting still and being quiet, she realized this wasn't going to work. Obiwan should have come with them. At least they could have chased each other around the meadow. She got up and walked back to the truck for a book. No, it was too cold to just sit and read and sitting inside the warm truck didn't seem fair.

"I'm going for a walk," she said out loud.

Neither Rebecca nor Beryl acknowledged her. Beryl was pointing at something on Rebecca's drawing and making swooping gestures with her fingers. Rebecca nodded enthusiastically and did something with her pencil.

"Get in the truck if you're cold," Polly said. "I left the key fob on the console. I'll be back."

Beryl lifted her hand and waved.

"I was so concerned about making them comfortable that I didn't even think about how bored I'd be," Polly muttered as she wandered off. "I deserve a medal for this. Wonder-Mom or something." She giggled. No one would ever give her a medal for that.

She found a deer trail and stopped to take pictures of roots and interesting rocks, fiddling with different settings on her camera. "I can be artsy, too," she said out loud. The world ignored her.

Polly thought about calling Henry and making him talk to her while she walked, but he was busy. Since she and Rebecca planned to be gone for the day, he and Heath went to work. They were gone before she got out of bed this morning and wouldn't return home until late afternoon. Polly was glad things were going so well for Henry's business, but she missed him and the busy season wasn't even here yet.

They hadn't done much in the Springer House since purchasing it. She had taken most of her friends through it at different times, but wasn't ready to talk about their future plans. There was still so much work ahead of them.

"Oh," she said quietly, as she realized that she should call Simon Gardner to help her decide what to do with things that were still there. A dumpster had already been filled with rotted draperies and curtains, shredded rugs, mattresses and box springs. She'd started clearing out the cupboards in the kitchen, surprised at the containers still on the shelves. The family really had pulled up roots and just walked out of the house.

Henry had removed plywood from windows that remained intact, allowing more light into the house as well as exposing the enormous amount of cleaning that was required. Polly spent a week tearing out spider webs and gaining control of most of the dust on the main level. What she really wanted was to get a good look at the furniture. Even though the upholstery was worthless, she couldn't bring herself to throw things out until she knew for certain they couldn't be restored. Little things caught her eye, such as the leaded glass inserts in the buffet and hutch in the dining room. Several chairs in the parlor had potential and the bedroom sets looked like they could be beautiful. But it would require work and she already knew how much Henry hated refinishing furniture.

When Henry had asked the realtor about the contents of the house, the woman had been taken aback, not expecting anyone to be interested in all of that junk. Some quick negotiations with the trust's lawyers brought back a reasonable price, which Henry and Polly were more than willing to pay.

Polly was desperate to start on renovations, but there were so many things that had to happen first. The original house plans had given them room dimensions and that started Polly's mind whirling. Once she had a better idea of what she wanted, she would sit down with her new architect friend, Sandy Davis.

"It's a good thing Henry told you that it would take a year or more," Polly said to herself. "Until you know what you want to do with it, nobody can get started."

She stumbled and stopped to look around. After walking through a wooded area, she'd come out into a clearing about the size of the corner garden at Sycamore House. A weathered wooden split rail fence stood in the middle, though it was mostly falling down.

"What's this?" she asked out loud. Polly had long ago given up worrying that she talked to herself.

She tramped across the snow, stepped over a downed fence rail, then paced along the inside of the fence to the other side and brushed snow off a tall stone. When she saw that it had been chiseled and shaped, she brushed away more snow and discovered she was standing in an old Carter family burial plot. Polly wondered if Beryl knew this was here.

Kicking snow out of the way and brushing more stones clear, she took pictures of what she found as she made her way around the plot and back to the place where she'd entered. There were at least twenty stones and Polly couldn't be sure that she'd uncovered them all.

As she cleared the area near where she'd entered, she realized that the ground around the last stone had recently been dug up. A thin dusting of snow covered loose dirt that had been arranged in an odd formation.

"That's weird. But it means that someone knows it's here," she said, wishing there was anybody else here to talk to.

Polly might have walked away from the cemetery, but then she realized that the streaks on the side of the stone were blood red. She began pushing at the loose dirt, terrified of what she might find, but knowing that she couldn't leave it alone.

She stopped when she felt something solid. Taking a deep breath, she lifted more dirt clods away and realized that she was looking at a frozen hand. This was not a century old set of bones, but a very recent death. It figured, didn't it?

Hoping she was still in Boone County, she took her phone out and dialed.

"Sheriff Merritt's phone. Who's calling, please?"

"You know who this is," Polly said to Aaron.

"Let's just call it amnesia. I haven't heard from you on this phone in several months. I thought you planned to find fewer bodies in twenty-sixteen," he said.

"They find me," she replied. "I have no control."

"Have you found someone?"

"I think so."

"What does that mean?" he asked.

"I found a hand."

He took in an audible breath. "Is it attached to a body?"

"Maybe. I'm not digging any further."

"Digging? It's buried?"

"In a cemetery."

"Polly," Aaron said patiently. She heard it in his voice. "You aren't supposed to go to cemeteries to find bodies. Everyone knows they're already there."

Polly shook her head in mock disgust. "Yeah, yeah, yeah. Have you ever been out to the old Carter family cemetery?"

She waited for him to say something. "Are you there?" she asked.

"Where are you?"

"I'm out at Beryl's family place. She and Rebecca are being artists and I took a walk."

"Of course you did. You need to stop going off by yourself." He sighed. "That's not true. I suppose you had to go off by yourself so you could find this. Tell me what you have."

"I walked through the woods to a clearing and there's an old family cemetery here. Then I noticed that one of the graves had been dug up, but rather than robbing it, I think they added somebody." She looked down. "And not very well, from the looks of it."

"Just one?"

"I think so. Do you know where I am?"

"I know where Beryl's place is. My kids and I fished there with her brothers. Wow, that's been a lot of years ago. But I didn't know about the cemetery. How long do you think the body's been there?"

It was Polly's turn to chuckle. "I have no idea. There was snow on it, but that's probably just from the last snowfall. Are you telling me I should take some criminal forensics classes?"

"No, no, no," he said. "Please no. You bring me enough business as it is. Go on back and warm up. You have to be frozen by now."

That was all it took for Polly to realize how cold her hands were. "Okay. We're at the shelter. You can find us there."

"Give me time to get everyone together. Is the cemetery difficult to get to?"

"Yeah. It won't be easy. I took a deer trail through the woods."

He sighed. "We'll be right there. Go get warm."

Polly took a few more photographs of the cemetery before heading back. It wasn't a long walk and this time as she looked up and around, she wondered about the trees. She'd read about orchards the early settlers had planted in Iowa as they domesticated the land. How much of this had been wide open prairie before settlers claimed it?

Coming out of the trees on the other side, she only had a short walk to the shelter. She looked up and grinned. The truck was running and both Beryl and Rebecca were inside.

"Where did you go?" Rebecca asked when Polly climbed up into the driver's seat.

Polly turned around and smiled. "I went to find a body."

"You did not," Beryl said.

"Yes I did."

Rebecca leaned forward and tapped Beryl's shoulder. "We should have guessed. She went off by herself, you know."

"On my family's land?" Beryl asked. "How did you know it would be there?"

Polly looked at her in surprise. "I didn't do it on purpose. I was bored and went for a walk. Did you realize there was an old cemetery back through those trees?"

"A cemetery?" Beryl thought for a moment. "I guess I knew it was there, but I haven't thought about it since I was a kid. When we were little and had family reunions out here, all of us kids ran the entire breadth of this place. Wasn't there a fence around it?"

Polly took her camera out and brought up the pictures she'd taken. "A lot of the fence has fallen down. I took pictures of the gravestones. Do you know who any of these people are?"

Beryl put her hand out for the camera and scrolled through the pictures. "Jedidiah Carter. That's the big stone here. Over on the other side is his brother, Cyrus." She smiled. "Believe it or not, they were two of the founding fathers of Bellingwood."

"That's really cool," Polly said. "These shouldn't be hidden away."

"It's not all *that* exciting," Beryl said. "Jedidiah was a horse thief and a gambler. He's my great, great, great whatever." She handed the camera back to Polly. "I come from a long line of scoundrels."

"I like you because you're a scoundrel." Both Rebecca and Polly mis-quoted Han Solo from Empire Strikes Back. They looked at each other and giggled.

"I never thought I'd get to say that to anyone," Polly said. "Nobody uses that word anymore to describe themselves."

"It described Jedidiah." Beryl smiled at them. "From everything I've been told, he was quite a character."

"What about his brother?" Rebecca asked.

Beryl turned in her seat. "Cyrus was a good man. He started the first bank in Bellingwood. He, Jedidiah, and another brother named Lester, came to Iowa from Chicago. Lester went on out west. He thought Iowa was too close to home and wanted to see what the wild west was all about. He ended up as a lawman in California, I think." She gave her head a quick shake. "I haven't thought about these old stories in years. My grandparents loved gathering all of us kids around when we got together. He was quite the story teller. Fifty years ago at the centennial, everybody in Bellingwood was interested in his stories. I should dig out those old centennial books and help myself remember. I was only a kid at the time. I'm sure I've forgotten most of what he told us."

"Your ancestors founded Bellingwood," Polly said. "That's really something."

"I don't think they did it so that we'd be impressed a hundred and fifty years later. They were just trying to put down roots. Well, and Jedidiah was trying to make some easy cash." Beryl raised her eyebrows. "He had a few descendants that thought that was the way to live. Must be in the blood. Probably a good thing I never had kids."

"Don't talk like that." Polly pushed her friend's arm off the console.

"These qualities run deep, you know." Beryl pointed back the way Polly had come. "A new body is back there?"

Polly nodded. "I called Aaron. He's on his way. Someone dug up one of the old graves and dropped a fresh body on top of it. They didn't bury it very deep because I was able to pull the dirt off the top. It was definitely not old bones."

"That old cemetery is going to get more attention now, I guess. Maybe I should call my brothers and talk to them about clearing a better path to it. We've never talked about doing anything out there. I think Melvin mows it once in a while." Beryl shuddered. "That's my favorite thing in the world."

"What?" Polly asked.

"Talking to my family. They're such a joy."

"Are you going to tell them it's a crime scene?"

Beryl cackled. "Oh, that will be a fun conversation. I can hardly wait." Then her face grew serious. "Crap. You don't suppose one of them could have killed someone. There aren't that many people who know where the cemetery is." Beryl's entire body drooped. "Oh, please say that it isn't true. They wouldn't. They couldn't. I don't like them very much, but they just couldn't."

"We know nothing right now," Polly said. "Heck, maybe Aaron

will even accuse you of being the murderer. But until we know who is buried there, don't do this to yourself."

"When you're right, you're right," Beryl said, looking back up the lane. "So we're waiting for Aaron? I've never been around when they come in for one of your body-finds. This is exciting." She turned around to Rebecca. "Are you excited?"

"It seems weird. Somebody died," Rebecca said.

Beryl nodded. "You're right, honey. I'm sorry. That was insensitive."

Rebecca tapped Beryl's shoulder. "I was just kidding you. It's too bad that someone died and I hope they find out what happened, but it's kinda cool to be here right now. I wish we could stay while they dig the person up and do all of that crime scene stuff."

"You're raising a weird child," Beryl said to Polly. She turned around to Rebecca. "You're a weird child. What happened to those days when kids were supposed to be seen and not heard?"

"Wasn't that when you were a little girl?" Rebecca asked. "Look how well that turned out."

Polly chuckled and Beryl threw her head back in laughter. "This one is going to be a trip," Beryl said. "It will be fun to be part of her life."

"Did you two get enough time in the out-of-doors today to satisfy your inner artists?" Polly asked.

Rebecca pushed her sketchbook between the two women and waggled it. "I got a lot done. Beryl said that this is the perfect stuff to draw because there isn't any color. It's all about the shadows and light. She's teaching me about the range of values and how…" Rebecca stopped and looked at Polly. "You don't care about that." She drew her finger along a branch. "And there are so many interesting shapes in the trees. Have you ever looked at how cool branches are? They are bumpy and smooth and wavy and curly. It was awesome."

"And very different than when they are full of leaves during the summer. We should come back out and do this again," Beryl said.

"Maybe for each season?" Rebecca asked.

"Absolutely. But I think we'll find another driver."

"Why?" Polly asked. "I brought blankets and coffee and hot cocoa. I'm a great driver."

"You find bodies," Rebecca said, deadpan. "We don't need any more bodies."

Aaron Merritt's SUV drove down the lane to the shelter. She rolled down the window when he approached her truck.

"Good afternoon, ladies. Fancy meeting you here."

"These are surprises that I don't like," Beryl said. "Who gave them permission to do this on my land?"

He shook his head. "I have no idea."

"Do you need me to take you to the spot?" Polly asked.

"I can probably find it from your footprints," he replied. "But if you've warmed up enough to take another walk, I'd appreciate it."

"Can I come?" Rebecca asked from the back seat.

Polly looked at Aaron and he looked back at her. "You're going to make me be the bad guy?"

"Not this time," Polly said to Rebecca.

Aaron looked in the truck at the girl. "If there is any evidence along the trail, we need to keep activity to a minimum. But the cemetery will still be there long after we've gone. You can see it another time."

"Okay," Rebecca said with a sigh. She slumped dramatically back in the seat, then sat back up. "Andrew isn't going to believe this. I can't wait to tell him. Can I use your phone and call?" she asked Polly.

"Fine. I'll be back in a minute." She handed her phone to Rebecca and got out of the truck. "You girls stay here. Don't wander off."

CHAPTER TWO

"How about you come in for a while." Beryl said when Polly parked in her driveway.

Polly turned the truck off. "Would you like us to come in?"

"I could make some fresh coffee," Beryl said. "Maybe put a little Irish in it."

Rebecca leaned forward. "Could we? I want to play with the kittens."

"Sure," Polly said with a nod. "We're in no hurry."

Beryl had grown quiet during their ride home; a rare occurrence.

When Polly glanced at her, the woman's face was drawn. "Are you okay?"

Beryl forced a smile. "I suppose. When you're faced with it, it's no laughing matter, is it?"

"Death?" Polly shook her head. "No, it really isn't."

"That's somebody's child in that grave. Someone who didn't expect them to die this early in their life." Beryl put her hand on the door handle and pulled it open. "I need some kitty snuggles, too."

Polly nodded to Rebecca to follow Beryl inside and pulled out her phone. She swiped a call open and waited.

"Hello, dear," Lydia said. "Aaron already called me. I'm in front of Andy's house and we'll be right over."

"To Beryl's? That's where we are."

"That's where we're coming. She's not doing as well as you expected, is she."

Beryl stood at the front door and looked back at Polly while Rebecca went inside. Polly waved.

"I have to go. She's waiting for me."

"Tell her to put on a big pot of coffee. We'll be right there." Lydia ended the call and Polly got out of the truck.

It still floored her that she was friends with these people. How had she gotten so fortunate? They would drop anything when one of the others needed support. Lydia, Beryl and Andy had been close friends for longer than Polly had been alive. That was something else she didn't understand. No one in her life had been around that long.

Beryl waved impatiently and Polly jumped down, closed the door, and walked to meet her.

"Was that the troops?" Beryl asked. "Did you tell them that I'm a pitiful wretch?"

Polly grinned. "I didn't have to say a word. Lydia was already at Andy's house."

"You know," Beryl said, "I was really looking forward to today. I wanted it to be perfect."

"Until I stumbled across a body, it was, wasn't it?"

"I suppose. And this will occupy my mind enough so I don't have to think about the other bad things." Her shoulders sagged a little as she led Polly to the kitchen.

"What else is going on?" Polly asked. "Can I help?"

Beryl shook her head as she took her heavy coat off and draped it across the back of a kitchen chair. "No. I'm being a silly cat-mom." She looked up and gave a wan smile as Rebecca came into the kitchen, carrying the kittens in her arms.

Rebecca held one of them out and Beryl cradled the little thing before pulling it up to her face to kiss its head. When she looked back at Polly, there were tears in her eyes.

"Oh honey," Polly said. "What's wrong?"

"Nothing's wrong. I'm just being overly emotional. I have to take them to see Doc Jackson on Monday. They'll spend the night before being neutered Tuesday morning. Then they have to sleep in a strange place without me and when they wake up, they'll be in pain." She buried her face in the kitten's back. "They won't know what's going on and they'll be scared."

"Everybody there will take great care of them," Polly said. "Marnie and Doc Jackson are wonderful."

Beryl huffed a breath. "You're asking me to be sensible about this. I know they'll be fine. I know they'll be back to normal in a week or so and this will all be behind them. I never promised that I was sane."

Rebecca held the other kitten out to Beryl. "Here. Maybe you need to hold both of them."

"I'm okay," Beryl said, smiling at the girl. "This comes and goes on a fairly regular basis. It's gone now. As long as I don't think about it too much, I function just fine. But I'll tell you right now, Tuesday afternoon can't get here soon enough. I just want it to be over and for them both to come out of surgery healthy and genderless. I'm open-minded that way, you know."

Polly chuckled. "You're a nut. Now, where's the coffee?"

"In the fridge." Beryl pointed at the refrigerator. "I'll let you make it if you give me your coat. Rebecca, take the kittens back downstairs. We'll be there in a few minutes." She handed Hem back to the girl, took Polly's coat, picked up her own, and left the room.

Polly remembered taking Leia in to be spayed. That had been a difficult day for her. Those little fuzz-balls wasted no time to stealing a piece of her heart. She gave her head a quick shake and opened the refrigerator door, then took out the coffee. Beryl's refrigerator was a hoot. Several different flavors of coffee, two half-empty bottles of wine, take-out containers, and a loaf of Sylvie's bread from the bakery. The doors were filled with condiments and bottles of ... Polly had no idea. She picked a jar up and looked at it. Pickled and spicy asparagus. Weird.

The crisper drawers were empty, a butter dish was half full, several jars of jams, two of which had never been opened, and blocks of cheese. She opened the freezer and wasn't surprised to see it filled with frozen dinners and even a couple of frozen pizzas. Polly was going to have to invite Beryl over for more homemade meals.

"Envy my selections?" Beryl asked in Polly's ear.

Polly jumped. "You snuck up on me."

"Well, you're *checking* up on me. You know I hate to cook."

"I guess I didn't realize it was this bad."

"It's this bad. Now come on. Make that coffee before Lydia shows up or she'll think we're sitting around here moping." Beryl filled the carafe with water and poured it into the coffee pot. "Give me the coffee. You're useless when you're spying on someone."

"I wasn't spying," Polly protested weakly. Yes, she was and she'd been caught.

"Like I haven't been through your kitchen and all of your bathrooms," Beryl said. "Now where do I keep those filters?"

Polly opened a drawer and Beryl laughed. "I'm teasing you. They're right here." She opened the cupboard above the coffee pot and there, sitting by themselves on the lower shelf, surrounded by absolutely nothing, were the filters.

"How do you not have any food in this house?" Polly asked and opened more cupboard doors. She found dishes, glasses and mugs, but nothing else.

Beryl opened one last door. "I have cereal. It just isn't that important to me. I won't cook unless someone twists my arm, so why fill the space with food I'll just have to throw away down the road."

"I suppose that makes sense. It's weird, though. My cupboards are packed full of things I might need someday."

The front doorbell rang and Polly stepped toward the kitchen door.

"It's Lydia. We don't need to show her in. She knows the way."

Beryl scooped coffee into the filter and flipped the switch. "There. At least it's brewing." She tapped Polly's shoulder. "And no moping. She'll know right away."

Beryl started toward the living room and turned back to Polly. "Don't tell them about me getting all stupid over those kittens, okay? Lydia doesn't understand and Andy thinks I'm already being ridiculous about them." She lowered her voice to a whisper. "That's what happens when you don't have animals around. You lose your soul."

Polly laughed and shook her head.

"Halloo," Lydia called out. "Where are you?"

Beryl stepped into the hallway. "We're in the kitchen. I made coffee. Did you bring the whiskey?"

Lydia stopped and put two totes on the floor and pulled her friend into a hug. "I'm so sorry about your day. Aaron called me."

"It didn't happen to me," Beryl said. "I'm alive. Whoever that poor soul is out there is the one who deserves your sympathy." She turned to Polly. "And maybe her. She did the finding."

"Don't you dare get all tough on me, Madame Softy," Lydia said. She reached down and grabbed up the totes again and scooted Beryl back into the kitchen.

Andy was right behind her carrying two more totes. They put them down on the tiny kitchen table and Lydia pointed at the lower cupboard next to the refrigerator. "Have you opened that one yet, Polly?"

Polly shook her head and stepped back. She pulled the cupboard door opened and chuckled. "You have plenty of whiskey. And everything else. Good heavens, woman, it's a full-fledged bar in here." She reached down. "Blackberry brandy? What's this about?"

"That goes in one of my favorite party drinks," Beryl said. She put her hands under her boobs and shook them. "I call 'em Hot Apple Knockers."

"Wait," Polly said with a snort. "What?"

"You heard me. Hot Apple Knockers. Don't be snorting at my knockers. They're all I've got."

"Do you shake your knockers when you serve these knockers?" Polly asked.

Beryl pursed her lips and then said, "That would be embarrassing. Why would I ever embarrass myself like that?"

Polly looked for help from Andy and Lydia and they both just looked at her with smiles on their faces. "No help?" she asked.

"There are thirty bottles of alcohol in that cabinet and you chose the blackberry brandy. You asked for it," Lydia said.

Andy pulled a baguette out of one of the totes. "Did you girls eat anything today? I know how this woman is when she's focused on her artwork. She loses all sense of time."

"And Polly isn't much better if she's finding bodies." Rebecca stood in the doorway. "I heard you come in. Hi there."

"Hello dear," Lydia said. "Did you find scenery to sketch before Polly did her thing?" She and Andy continued to empty the totes, filling the table and counter tops."

"Do you want to see what I did?" Rebecca asked.

"Of course," Lydia responded. She put a casserole dish in the refrigerator and closed the door. "I'll be back." She put her hand on Rebecca's back as they walked out.

"She's a good grandma," Beryl said.

"Did you find anything interesting to draw today?" Andy asked.

Beryl laughed. "You're a good grandma, too. And yes, we had fun with our pencils and I even snuck in a little charcoal training." She shook her head. "That girl is a natural artist. She's a joy to work with. I hope you plan to encourage her to do something with this."

"She can do whatever she wants," Polly said. "I want her to be a physicist or an astronaut, an artist or an actress. I just want her to always do her very best and find happiness."

Lydia's phone began to ring. Polly picked it up and saw that it was Aaron. She grinned and showed it to Beryl and Andy. "Should I?"

"If you don't, I will," Beryl said.

Polly swiped the call open. "Hello, sweet-ums, how are you?"

"Lydia?" Aaron asked, confusion evident in his voice.

"Oh, honey-bear, don't you know who this is?" Polly asked.

"Polly Giller, what are you doing on my wife's phone?"

She laughed. "We kidnapped her. She won't be allowed to leave until she's baked many goodies and hugged many necks."

"She's good at all of that," he said with a laugh. "Are you at Beryl's? Lydia was planning to go over there when I talked to her."

"They just got here with totes full of food. Lydia's looking at Rebecca's sketches from this morning."

Aaron grew serious. "I need to speak with Beryl. You're going to be there for a while?"

"Sure, what's up?" Polly walked out of the kitchen to the living room where she found Rebecca and Lydia on Beryl's sofa, flipping through the morning's sketchbook while May and Hem wrestled on the couch beside Rebecca.

"We have an identity of the man you found and I want to ask Beryl if she knows who it is. Don't say anything to her yet, though. You don't need to upset her. I'll do that."

"Sure. We'll be here," Polly said. "Did you want to talk to Lydia?"

"It's okay. Tell her I'm on my way and to save me something good to eat. I forgot to get lunch today."

"Got it. See ya." Polly reached over and handed the phone to Lydia. "That was Aaron. He's on his way here. There's something he wants to talk to Beryl about."

"Is everything okay?" Lydia asked.

"I think so."

Lydia stood up. "You are quite talented, Rebecca. This is beautiful."

"Thank you," Rebecca said. She flipped the sketchbook closed and then looked at Polly. "Did you want to see it?"

Polly tried to read her daughter. Rebecca didn't sound as if she wanted Polly to see what she'd drawn but was being polite because Lydia had seen it. "You know I love looking at what you do, but if you'd rather wait..." She let the sentence trail off.

"There are just a few things I want to touch up," Rebecca said. She put it down on the table in front of her and picked one of the kittens up. "They're a lot of fun when they're little like this. Look at her. She just melts into my arms."

Polly nodded. "You stay with them while we get things ready in the kitchen. If the doorbell rings, it's Aaron. I don't know if he'll let himself in or not."

"Is somebody in Beryl's family in trouble?" Rebecca asked.

"I don't know. We'll see what he says." Polly turned to go back to the kitchen, nearly tripping on Miss Kitty who had come down from upstairs to see what the commotion was.

"Hey there, Miss Kitty," Polly said. "How are things going with the kittens?"

If the cat had a response, Polly wasn't sure what it was, so she stepped around it a couple of times as they made their way out to the kitchen.

"There you are," Beryl said. "I'll bet you're hungry. Where have you been hiding?"

"Not talking to me?" Polly asked.

"Ptaw," Beryl huffed out with a laugh. "Were you hiding from us and feeling sorry for yourself because no one came looking? You have to announce the game of hide and seek with this group. We're too old to catch on to those subtle hints you young people throw out there." She picked Miss Kitty up and put her on the counter, then turned and winked at Polly with a wicked grin on her face.

"I don't know why you let those cats on the counter," Andy said.

"Right on cue," Beryl said. "Because the kittens will eat her food if it's on the floor. They can't climb up here yet, so she gets a meal in peace. And don't you forget, Missy, this is their house, not yours. Got it?"

Andy sighed. "That's why I bring these." She pulled a wipe from a plastic canister and wiped the kitchen table off.

Polly knew these women were friends, but was shocked at Andy's behavior in Beryl's kitchen.

It must have shown on her face because Beryl patted her arm. "Don't worry. I get her back every opportunity I can grab. She fusses over my cats and I fuss over her fussiness. Organization and cleanliness does not mean she's a better person than I am. It just means that she wastes her time on boring things." Beryl poked Andy in the arm. "Am I right or what?"

"A whole lot of what," Andy replied.

"Blah, blah, blah." Beryl opened the cupboard under the sink and took out a bag of cat food, then poured some into a small dish. In a split second, two small kittens were in the kitchen with them. One of them jumped up on a chair and then on to the table.

"Get down, you cat," Lydia said, trying to protect a plate of meat. The other jumped up on another chair and before it could climb onto the table, Polly snatched it up and tucked it into her arms.

"They have no manners yet," Beryl said, cackling like a madwoman. "You'll want to put the human food on the stove top. They aren't used to having all of those scents around."

Lydia gathered up the platter and was trying to wave the kitten away.

Polly chuckled and reached over to snag that one up with her other hand. "I've got them," she said. The first kitten was doing its best to wriggle out of her arms and back to the table, but Polly walked out of the kitchen and handed the two to Rebecca, who was coming down the hallway.

"They're creating chaos," Polly said. "Can you corral them?"

"We'll go downstairs. I'll put them in their room." She poked her head in the kitchen. "Is that okay, Beryl?"

Beryl was still laughing. "That's fine for now. Thank you, sweetie."

"Why didn't you do that in the first place?" Andy asked.

"Because it's a lot more fun watching you get frustrated over things you can't manage," Beryl said. "So there. I thought you two were supposed to be coming over to take care of me. How is harassing me about my kitties taking care of me?"

Andy looked properly chagrined. "I'm sorry. You're right. It's just a little more than I'm used to. It's your house and my rules don't apply."

"There ya go. Now you're talking my language," Beryl said. She put her arm around Andy's shoulder. "And I'm not mad at you. I could never be mad at you. You take better care of me than I do myself sometimes. So what's for lunch?"

"Sandwiches and I brought beef stew," Lydia said.

Beryl wrinkled her brow. "How did you whip together beef stew so fast? We weren't here long enough for you to do that."

"I was making up a pot for some neighbors, but you're more important. I'll take them something tomorrow." Lydia opened the lid of a crockpot she'd plugged into the wall.

"You're amazing," Polly said in awe. "Are you always cooking something?"

"I do enjoy myself in the kitchen. The best part of taking food to friends and neighbors is that I get to cook and then I don't have to eat it all." Lydia took a deep breath. "I didn't know what to do when my kids left home. Cooking for two is a lot different than cooking for seven plus all of the random friends that used to show up. I had to come up with a new plan. So I deliver food whenever I can. It makes me happy."

The front doorbell rang and Beryl glanced at them. "Who's that?"

"It's Aaron," Polly said.

Beryl grimaced. "Surely he doesn't think I had anything to do with that person's death, does he?"

Lydia was already weaving through them to the kitchen door so she could retrieve her husband.

"Are you here?" Aaron called out.

"Back here in the kitchen, honey," Lydia said. "Come on in."

"See," Beryl said in an aside to Polly. "They even let strangers into my house without asking permission."

CHAPTER THREE

"Everyone is here," Aaron said, coming into the kitchen. "This looks like trouble." He walked over to Beryl and put his hand on her shoulder. "I know Polly is used to dealing with death, but how are you doing?"

"I was a little shook up," she admitted, "but now I'm worried. Why are you here?"

Beryl's kitchen was too small for five people. Since Rebecca had come upstairs to see what was going on, the room had grown smaller and Polly felt as if she couldn't breathe.

She slid past Aaron into the hallway. "Too many people," she mumbled. It took three deep breaths to relax. She hadn't dealt with claustrophobia since being kidnapped by Joey Delancy. These people were her friends, but it didn't matter.

"I just need to speak with Beryl," Aaron said. "If the rest of you want to go out to the living room, we'll find you when we finish."

"Oh no you don't, Mister Sheriff-Man." Beryl pushed his shoulder. "If you have bad news for me, you know better than to take away my girlios. We'll all go to the living room." She pushed him again, this time toward the kitchen door.

Rebecca followed Polly out to the big living room, where every horizontal space was covered with a quilt or blanket, often in layers of two or three. The coffee table had a brightly colored quilt on it, covered by a second, denim quilt turned at forty-five degrees. The sofa had colorful blankets and quilts draped across the back, one over each arm and there were full-size, brightly colored quilted pillows at each end. Rugs of different shapes, sizes and colors were scattered across the carpeting. All of the plants, vases, and knick knacks had been either removed or put up high in the bookshelves. Beryl had done her best to kitty-proof the room.

This living room was still one of Polly's favorites. She'd never be able to pull off what Beryl had done. Even though it might seem cluttered to some, it was soft and comfortable and tastefully arranged. Maybe she just needed more quilts. If the ladies at the new shop downtown were serious about teaching her how to sew, she could create her own and fill the apartment.

Polly sat down at one end of the sofa and tugged on Rebecca's hand so the girl would sit beside her. Rebecca reached across Polly to grab a pillow and set it on their laps. She looked up and grinned, shrugging her shoulders. What a little nut.

After everyone sat down, Beryl put her hands in her lap and clasped them, rubbing one thumb on top of the other. "I'm ready. Spill the bad news."

Lydia was sitting on the sofa next to Beryl's chair and reached across the space to stroke her friend's arm. She looked worried.

Aaron sat on the coffee table in front of her and pulled a sealed and marked plastic bag out of his pocket. "This wallet belongs to the man we found in that grave. I want to know if he is a member of your family."

He passed it to Beryl and she creased her forehead as she looked at it. The wallet had been opened before being placed into the bag and Beryl stared at the driver's license.

"Ethan Carter," she said. "He has my maiden name, but I've never heard of him and he's from Taos, New Mexico. Nobody in any part of the family that I'm familiar with lives there."

She handed it over to Lydia, who glanced at it and passed it to Andy. After a quick look, Andy handed it to Polly. Aaron watched the transactions happen with a grin on his face.

Polly held the wallet so both she and Rebecca could look at the driver's license of Ethan Carter.

"You know," Beryl said, with no small amount of sarcasm in her voice, "there are thousands of Carters in the country who aren't related to me. Hell, there are probably thousands of Carters out there who are related to me, but I wouldn't recognize them if we met face to face in a mud puddle. Carters have been around for a long time. I have ancestors that lived in jolly old England and others that came from Scotland."

The picture on the driver's license was that of a young man, just about Polly's age, with jet black hair that curled around his ears and big, dark eyes. Ethan Carter was a good looking young man. How did he end up in Iowa? She poked her fingers in the plastic so she could look inside the wallet and saw that there was nearly two hundred and fifty dollars. So he wasn't killed for his money. There were credit cards, punch cards, and store reward cards, but no photographs that she could see.

"Was he married?" Polly asked.

Aaron shook his head. "No wedding ring, but that doesn't mean anything. Anita is checking the Taos area for family connections and missing person reports. We're just beginning our investigation. But I wanted to speak with you first, Beryl, just in case he was someone that you knew."

Beryl nodded and then swiped her hand across her forehead. "You had me really worried, you know. It's not fair to do that to an old lady." She crossed her legs. "I could have embarrassed myself."

Aaron chuckled and put his hand out for the wallet.

Polly directed Rebecca's eyes to the photograph and raised her eyebrows. Rebecca gave a slight nod and Polly reached across the table to put the package into Aaron's hand.

"What else do you know about him?" Polly asked. "He's not married. Was there a weapon or anything? Do you know how he was killed? Was that his blood on the gravestone? Has anyone reported an abandoned car with New Mexico plates? Do you have his cell phone? Anything?"

"No weapon," Aaron said. "We'll know more later." He looked over his shoulder at Polly. "But not later today. I don't know when the autopsy will be finished. There was no cell phone and as for an abandoned car with plates from New Mexico ... you're kidding, right?"

She shrugged. "I don't know. It's something I'd notice."

Beryl jumped to her feet. Everybody looked at her.

"What?" Lydia asked. "Are you okay?"

"My aunt. She's done a lot of genealogy for our family. I wonder how deep her information is." Beryl sat back down again. "Aw hell. She hates me and I don't want to talk to her anyway."

She reached forward and patted Aaron's knee. "I'm sorry if I got your hopes up."

"My hopes?" He was confused.

"Genealogy."

He shook his head, still not understanding.

Beryl chuckled. "You're telling me that you didn't follow my train of thought?"

Aaron laughed with her. "I guess not. What are you apologizing for? What am I hoping for?"

"If I can get hold of some of her genealogy charts, we might find out if this young man is part of another branch of my Carter family."

"I see," he said. "I suppose that's one way to investigate this."

She grinned. "Well, it's the way my mind worked it out. But it might take a few days. We aren't on the best speaking terms."

"Who isn't?" Andy asked. "You and your aunt?"

"No. Well, yes. Actually, me and all of the cousins on that side. They think I'm daft and I think they're redneck idiots. Not a bright bulb in the bunch."

"What did you do?" Lydia asked.

"I told them all to go rot in hell. It's been about twenty years now, but my feelings haven't changed." She huffed out a chuckle.

"Theirs might have, though. They are dumber than a pile of pea gravel and by now, they've probably forgotten everything." Beryl sported a wicked grin. "It really wasn't a fair fight. There were only six of them and one of me."

Lydia looked at Beryl in shock. "Why would you do something like that? They're family."

"You know my family." Beryl glared at Lydia. "But, it was a long time ago and they made me angry. I don't even remember what it was all about, but there were some nasty comments about my side of the family. Stupid hillbillies think they're better than the rest of the world. They don't even know what it means to be better than the rest of the world."

She'd wound herself up, rising off the chair. Lydia put her hand out and Beryl realized what she'd done. "Okay, okay. I can't talk about them. But if I have to talk to them, I will. Maybe I can find out if there's a link between this young man and my family." She turned to Aaron. "It does seem odd that a Carter was buried in our old Carter family plot, don't you think? That's a coincidence that even I recognize as just too much."

He nodded and laughed. "Makes sense to me. The genealogy idea is a good one. Especially if there is someone who has done a great deal of research. If you need me or one of my people to reach out to your aunt, just let me know. I'd like to see what she has."

"Come to think of it," Beryl said. "So would I. Maybe I could find an entirely different set of relatives that are at least tolerable to be around for short periods of time." She looked around the room. "Not that you all aren't my favorite family in the world."

~~~

Aaron left without eating, claiming that he was needed back at the office. Andy and Lydia went back out to the kitchen to finish preparing the food and Beryl leaned back in her chair.

She closed her eyes and took a deep breath. "I could really use a kitty snuggle," she muttered, more to herself than anyone else.

"Do you want me to let them out?" Rebecca asked.

Beryl opened her eyes and nodded toward the kitchen. "No, not while they're here. It's just too much chaos. But if you wouldn't mind going downstairs to play with them, at least I wouldn't worry that they're lonely."

Rebecca glanced at Polly, who nodded. "Wait," Polly said. "Take your sketchbook. Did you get a good look at that photograph?"

"Of course I did. That's what you wanted me to do, right?"

"You're a smart girl," Polly said. "See what you can do with it." She watched Rebecca head down the steps and then said, "I wish I could draw like she does. I always have."

"You do your own thing very well." Beryl's voice slurred as she relaxed, her body molding itself into the chair.

"Oh honey," Polly said. "You've had a rough day. Did you not sleep last night?"

Beryl opened her eyes again. "I was in the studio until about three. I have too much work to do. I'll be fine. Just let me rest my eyes for a minute."

Polly put one of the many blankets from the back of the couch over Beryl's lap. As she stood up to go to the kitchen, Beryl pulled it up around her shoulders and gave her a sleepy smile.

"We should leave," she said when she turned into the kitchen. She dropped into a chair across from Andy. "Beryl's exhausted."

"She'll be fine," Andy replied. "Just give her a few minutes to regroup. We're almost ready to serve lunch."

"I'm not kidding." Polly looked at Lydia for help. "She's asleep out there. She didn't sleep last night because she was working and then the emotions of all of this really took her out."

Lydia glanced around the room and without a word, started closing up plastic containers and replacing aluminum foil on dishes.

"What are you doing?" Andy said. "She'll kill us if we leave."

"I'd rather she kill us than wear her out any more. If I don't miss my guess, that woman is about to have one of Polly's crazy couple of weeks ahead of her."

"My what?" Polly asked with a laugh. Then she nodded. "You're right. Those weeks. I try not to make anyone else live through them. Do you think that young man is related to her?"

Lydia continued closing up containers while Andy stood up to put dishes and glasses away in the cupboard. Lydia glanced at Polly. "I suspect it's a very distant relation, but there will be some connection. There are going to be strangers in town and we all know how Beryl is with too much human interaction."

"It's bad," Andy acknowledged. "Very, very bad." She reached down into a tote and took out a marking pen and a plastic container of pre-cut labels.

"What are you doing?" Polly asked.

Andy looked at her with a sheepish grin. "You be nice. Beryl will be glad to have names and dates on these containers."

"Okay then." Polly held up a box of crackers. "Shall we label these as crackers or baked flat wheat toasted thingies?"

"Put them in the cupboard and leave me alone. This will only take a minute."

Polly tossed the box to Lydia, glad they were in close enough proximity to not have to worry about her awful throwing and catching arm. How she missed out on learning how to do that, she'd never know. That she couldn't do either was hilarious most of the time. With Henry, she didn't even bother trying any longer. He was never going to stop giving her trouble about it, so she might as well just own it and have fun. He'd tried a few times to help her learn how to see where she was throwing or what was coming at her, but she had a block about it.

"I'm going to get Rebecca," she said.

"Tell her to let the kittens out," Lydia said. "Beryl loves those little things and they'll do more to help her relax than we can."

Polly went back out into the living room and checked Beryl before heading downstairs. The woman had pulled her legs up and was leaning on the wing of the chair, sound asleep.

Tip-toeing down the steps to the basement, Polly followed the sound of Rebecca's voice to a back bedroom and opened the door.

"Careful, they'll get out," Rebecca cried.

"It's okay. We're going to leave. Lydia and Andy are cleaning up the kitchen."

Rebecca wrinkled her forehead. "Why?"

"Beryl is sleeping. We just need to get out of here and let her relax. It sounds like she didn't get much sleep last night and today's activities wore her out emotionally."

"Nobody really does death like you do," Rebecca said. She held out the sketch pad. "Is that close?"

Polly looked at the drawing Rebecca had done of the young man's driver's license. She'd captured him perfectly. "Weird question," Polly said. "Can you draw Beryl?"

Rebecca shrugged. "Yes. Why?"

"Look at this picture and then think about Beryl. Are they related?"

"Do you want me to do it now?" Rebecca asked.

"No. We'll wait until we get home. It's just a strange thought I had." She handed the sketchpad back to Rebecca. "Do you see anything?"

"Not right off," Rebecca said. "But I want to see what my hands do when I draw Beryl. Maybe I'll make the same nose or the chin or the eyes or something. I'll know it when I feel it."

"When you feel it?"

Rebecca stood up from the bed. "I know it sounds weird, but when I draw, I move my hand in certain ways. Do you know that your nose is similar to Henry's? When I drew Heath and Hayden, they had a lot of facial features that were exactly alike, but their cheeks are different. Heath has a wider face. When I drew their eyes, those were exactly the same and so are their lips and the way their nostrils look."

Polly nodded, accepting what Rebecca said, even if she didn't know how to assimilate the information. "Is that the way everyone draws?"

"I don't think so. Beryl says that she only really feels landscapes, not faces like I do. She even said that sometimes she can feel the colors that she paints. They mess with her emotions. Have you ever seen her cry when she paints?"

"No," Polly said. She put her arm around Rebecca's shoulders. "I don't think I've ever really watched her paint anything."

"It's kind of cool. She doesn't like having people around, though. She says it makes her feel all stilted and stuff."

"I get that." Polly looked around the room. "Kittens are gone?"

"They took off. They were wrestling when I got down here. Hopefully they'll just sleep now." Rebecca took Polly's hand. "They're really cute, but I like Luke and Leia. Sometimes they play, but they aren't always getting into trouble because they're curious about every single thing. They've experienced it all."

The two walked out into the basement. "You should have seen them when they were little," Polly said. "I thought they were going to drive Obiwan crazy. Fortunately, he was a puppy at the same time. But they were two against one and those two kittens had no idea that he was as big as he was."

"He's a good dog. He wouldn't hurt them," Rebecca said.

CHAPTER FOUR

"Now, what's this?" Sal asked, holding up an iridescent turquoise glass vase. "Keep or toss?" She pulled the top off the base and looked at it like it might bite her.

"Put that on the counter," Polly replied. "Mr. Gardner can tell me if it's worth anything."

Sal bent down from the top of her step ladder and carefully placed the vase among other glass pieces on the counter. "I can't believe a young woman collected all of these granny things. What was she thinking?"

"That she'd be a granny by now," Polly said with a laugh.

"Are you keeping any of this?" Sal asked. She held up a second, matching green vase."

Polly shook her head and shrugged. "I don't know. I have no idea what I'd do with it."

"People pay good money for these antiques. Mr. Gardner could make a great commission if he sold this stuff. Don't you think?" Sal held up a pair of pewter candlesticks. "I'd love these. Can I buy them from you?"

"Sure," Polly said. "You buy lunch and they're yours."

Sal laughed. "I already bought lunch."

"Then I guess they're yours," Polly replied. "Take them if you like them."

"I can't believe that poor girl collected so much stuff in just those few short years she was married," Sal said, climbing down and carrying the candlesticks over to an empty box. "It feels like my Mom's house and she has things from her parents and grandparents on top of all the things she's gotten over the years."

"From what I understand, the second wife's wedding gifts are here, too. And maybe Muriel had her own family's things."

"Why wouldn't anyone else have come in to get it? You said Muriel has brothers who are still alive. Wouldn't their families want these things?" Sal climbed back up and patted around the inside of the cabinet she'd been emptying.

Polly was glad to have her here. Her height made this part of the task that much easier. "The realtor called the family and they said that there wasn't anything here they wanted." She stood up and stretched. "Doesn't that sound weird?"

Sal laughed, a sad and angry sound. "It does. When my dad's mother died, it was ugly. Everybody thought they deserved even the silliest kitchen items. Dad walked away from it, though. He said that she'd given him everything she wanted him to have while she was still alive. He didn't want to fight about her things. He made Mom and one of his sisters really mad."

"Why's that?"

"His sister was mad because a sister-in-law was trying to take everything and she wanted Dad to step in and put his foot down."

Polly nodded. "And your mom?"

"She thought he should have gotten a few more memories for me. We really didn't get any of her china or crystal or paintings or even books. All of the things that I remembered using when I stayed with her were gone. I'll never see them again. But Dad couldn't do it. He just couldn't handle that fight. He said he'd rather still have a relationship with his brother. His sister finally got over being mad at him." Sal paused. "Maybe not. She still doesn't talk to us very often."

"Your dad sounds pretty smart about it all."

"Grandma's will split all of the money from her estate, but the things in her house weren't specified and no one was willing to put them up for auction. Mom got the money she wanted from Grandma..."

"Sal!" Polly scolded.

"What?" Sal asked. "When it came down to it, that's what she wanted the most. She didn't need any more clutter. They have two sets of china, a bunch of sets of crystal and more silver than they'll ever use. Their walls are filled with artwork and the furniture is exactly whatever Mom wants at the moment."

"No heirlooms?"

"Sure. There are some. Others are in storage." Sal nodded. "There are some nice pieces in the house. And I'm not really saying anything that Mom wouldn't agree with. She likes what she has and she likes money." She had climbed back down, moved the step stool and was patting around in the top shelf of a corner cupboard.

"What's this?" Sal pulled out a large envelope.

"I don't know," Polly said with a grin. "What is it?"

Sal climbed down and took it to an empty spot on a counter.

"This feels old," Polly whispered, touching the outer paper.

"Why are you whispering?" Sal asked, also in a whisper. "And you should open it."

Polly giggled. "I don't know. It just feels momentous."

"You weirdo," Sal said. "It's yours. Open it."

Polly had no idea what to expect. The pale green envelope was an odd size - at least twelve by eighteen inches. It was thick enough that there was more than a single piece of paper in it. She wasn't even certain that she should open it on her own. What if she damaged something important? "Maybe I should take it up to Mr. Gardner."

"It could be something silly," Sal said, handing her a knife. "Just open it."

"What do you think it might be?" Polly asked. "Just take a guess."

"It's big," Sal replied. "Maybe it's a collection of maps." She grinned. "Of Iowa in the early nineteen hundreds. And maybe the maps were drawn by Lewis and Clark."

"Uh huh. That makes so much sense."

"What's your guess?" Sal asked.

"Military orders or some kind of official certificates."

Sal put her hand down on the envelope. "So what you're telling me is that we have Schrödinger's cat in here. It's either something amazing or it's nothing at all, but as long as the envelope stays sealed, it could be either, both, or neither."

Polly looked at her sideways. "Physics from you?"

"I watch television and read books," Sal said, laughing. "Now are you going to open this envelope or am I going to have to poison your cat?"

"What?"

Sal shook her head in mock disgust. "Bad Schrödinger joke. Sorry. Just open the envelope."

Polly slid her finger into an open space on the flap and pushed it apart. The glue was practically non-existent after all these years. "Okay. That's done."

"You're killing me here," Sal said. "Open the damned envelope."

Taking a deep breath, Polly reached in and drew out a stack of papers. "Here," she said. "What's this?" And pushed a couple of newspapers across the counter to Sal.

"Newspapers. There's one from Chicago and a Boone News-Republican. They're from March of nineteen sixteen. What do you have?"

"I think it's a title to this house." Polly peered at the paper in front of her. "But it wasn't a house when they first built it."

Sal chuckled. "What do you mean it wasn't a house?"

"I think it was an inn or something. It was called the Bell House and there are some words here about occupancy."

"It's right here," Sal said. She'd flipped the Boone News-Republican over and on the lower half of the front page was a write-up about the opening of a lavish, new hotel in Bellingwood for those with extravagant taste and wealthy pockets. "Apparently, this wasn't meant to be a hotel for travelers." She skimmed down a few paragraphs. "Visiting professors to the State University who come from the East and West Coast will be welcomed into its plush rooms with entertainment brought in from as far away as Omaha and Kansas City."

"Wow," Polly said. "Why didn't we know about this before?"

Sal ran her finger across the photograph. "It was a beautiful building." She pointed to where the garage now sat. "That looks like stables and right behind it is another building. What do you suppose that was?"

Polly shook her head. "I don't know." She breathed out. "A hotel. I have to call Henry. He'll never believe this."

"I thought you said he found plans for the building."

"They were renovation plans that had been filed," Polly said. "Not what we originally thought, but at least they give us dimensions. I'd love to see what this place looked like when it was a hotel. I wonder if any interior pictures exist."

"So when did the Springers buy it?" Sal asked. "Were they the ones who turned it into a residence?"

"We haven't gotten the whole abstract," Polly said. "I don't have any of that information yet. But now I want to know." She tapped the issue of the Chicago Tribune. "Why do you suppose that was saved?"

Sal thumbed through the top corners of the pages. "There are so many bits and pieces of news in here it would take a full week to read it all. My goodness, but newspapers were different back then. This is so much more interesting than any newspaper I've ever read. It's like I'm holding a microcosm of the city in my hands."

"Look at this," Polly said, holding up the Boone paper. "Headline. *Young Englishman Comes to Iowa and Finds Love.*"

"No way."

"Yes way. *Mister Thomas Kenner arrived in central Iowa this week to pursue the heart of Miss Evaline Carter, the daughter of Frederick and Cicely Carter of Bellingwood. The two young people met while she was visiting her maternal grandparents in southern England. Mister Kenner, a farmer by trade, hopes to establish himself as a laborer on a local farm and would entertain enquiries from those who might be able to use a strong back and bright mind."*

"I wonder what ever happened to him," Sal mused. She pushed the Chicago Tribune back into the envelope.

Polly rubbed her forehead. "This boggles my mind. I don't know what to think about it. One hundred years ago this place was built to be a fancy hotel. Why did no one ever tell me?"

"Maybe because the whole haunted house thing took over," Sal said. "And how long was the hotel even open? Maybe no one knew what it was because it failed."

"Tomorrow I'm making Joss help me look for information in the library." Polly flipped the Boone News-Republican back over and put it back into the envelope. She allowed the title to fold back in on itself and slipped it in on top of the newspapers. "I wish they were open this evening, but I can wait until tomorrow."

"Is anyone in here?"

Polly and Sal both glanced at the back door.

"Come in," Polly called out. "We're in the kitchen."

"I just took the kittens..." Beryl stopped when she saw Sal standing with Polly. "I'm sorry. Did I interrupt something?"

"No," Sal said. "We were looking at some old papers I found in the top of the cupboard."

"Anything interesting?"

"Did you know this place was originally a hotel?" Polly asked.

Beryl cocked her head. "No, I never heard that. What did you find?"

"The original title and an old newspaper from Boone that talks about its opening. It was called the Bell House."

"That's probably the old Bell family. They were original founders, too. You know. Bell? Bellingwood?"

"Get out," Sal said.

Beryl laughed. "Nope. Not gonna. Yeah. Hiram Bell was a railroad man. Made a lot of money back in those days, you know. Railroad coming through Iowa right down there in Boone. He didn't want to live so close, so he came up north and helped start the town. There were several of those men who saw this little plot of land and thought they could make something of it."

"How did his name become part of the town's name?" Polly asked.

"He was the one with most of the money. Well, him and James Garwood - another railroad man." Beryl rubbed her chin. "If I remember my history, there were ten families that came up here and settled. By the mid eighteen-sixties, it wasn't that much of a risk. Iowa was a state, the Indians were no longer a threat and settlers were taming the land."

"You know a lot of history."

Beryl rolled her eyes. "Some. I grew up with it. Having an ancestor who was a founder made it a big deal. And since I was an impressionable kid when we had our centennial, at least a few of the stories stuck."

Polly took the Boone newspaper back out. "But that Hiram Bell would have been an old guy by nineteen sixteen," she said. "Do you think he opened the hotel?" She handed the paper to Beryl.

"The owner's name should have been in that article," Sal said. "I missed it."

"Uh huh, first line," Beryl said. "Franklin Bell, son of Hiram, one of Bellingwood's founders." She pointed at the sentence and Sal blushed.

"Look at the article down at the bottom of the page, in the corner," Polly said. "Relatives of yours?"

Beryl read through the article about Evaline Carter and Thomas Kenner. She smiled and handed the paper back to Polly. "Yes, they're family and I actually knew her. That's one of our family stories. But they never got married. He went back to England to fight in World War One and was killed before he could come back and marry her. She died an old maid in the early sixties."

"I wonder what she had to say about Muriel Springer killing herself when she thought her husband had died in World War Two," Polly said.

"She never said anything to me." Beryl handed the newspaper back to Polly. "I'd like a scan of that article sometime. Aunt Evaline never said much about Thomas, but when she did, she'd smile and get a faraway look in her eyes."

"Can you imagine someone falling so in love with you that they traveled across the ocean and half of the country to find you?" Sal asked. "And that was back before we had jets and fast cars. He really had to work for her."

"Then why would he go back?" Polly asked.

"Aunt Evaline said he couldn't let his fellow countrymen fight alone. He promised to return, but he had to go. It was important to him."

"They should have gotten married before he left."

Beryl nodded. "She regretted that they didn't. I have letters that he sent to her. He regretted it, too."

Polly put the newspaper back in the envelope. "What are you doing out today?"

"I just dropped the kittens off with Marnie at the vet's office." Beryl heaved a huge sigh. "I know they'll be okay tonight and I certainly don't want to have to fight with them to keep them out of food and water, so it's best this way, but I'm going to miss them."

Sal looked at the time on her phone. "Speaking of missing them. I have two little kiddos at home who are desperate to go outside." She chuckled. "Not that they love going out in the cold. Mark scoops the snow out of the yard for them. There's nothing sillier than watching a dachshund try to negotiate snowdrifts so they can pee. I try not to laugh at them, but sometimes I can't help myself. They're adorable."

She reached over to hug Polly. "I had fun today. Call me the next time you want help. This is a treasure trove of excitement."

"Don't forget your candlesticks," Polly said. She turned and picked up the box.

"I'll leave the box. Maybe I can put things in it the next time I'm here, but thanks for these. I can't wait to clean them up. They're beautiful."

"Thank you," Polly replied.

After the door closed behind Sal, Beryl looked around the kitchen. "The Springers really didn't take a thing with them when they left for Chicago, did they?"

"No. I'm going to have to ask Simon Gardner for help sorting through these things," Polly said. "I don't know what's worth keeping or what should be thrown in the trash."

"These are wild." Beryl picked up the turquoise vase that Sal had put on the counter. The top of the vase came off and Beryl flinched.

Polly grinned. "I think it was made that way. Do you want them?"

"They'd be kind of awesome in that front room, don't you think?" Beryl asked.

"Take them. I have newsprint over here. We can wrap them up."

"But what if they're worth money?"

"Please," Polly said with a scowl. "They make you smile. That's worth more than money."

Beryl put the vase back together and placed it on the counter. "Are you going to show me around? Do I have to beg for a tour?"

"I didn't realize you hadn't been here yet. Andy and Lydia saw it just after I bought it."

"I was in Boston, remember?"

Polly took Beryl's arm. "Come with me. We haven't done a thing because I'm still trying to figure out how to handle what was left here, but Henry says the floors are safe. He brought electricity in from outside because we don't know what's in the walls and I might start a fire."

Beryl smiled and followed Polly into the dining room. She ran her hand across the table and then looked at the doorways.

"How did this table get in here?" she asked.

"Henry says it must have been built in the room. The legs could come off, but he doesn't think they were made to ever come apart."

"So you're keeping it?"

Polly scratched her head. "It's a nice table and big enough for large family meals. I don't know why I wouldn't."

"Wow."

"You haven't seen the best thing yet," Polly said. "Follow me." She took Beryl through the other rooms on the main floor until they came to the foyer.

"What is that crazy thing?" Beryl asked.

"It's a fountain." Polly snapped her head up. "Do you suppose it was part of the hotel?"

"It wouldn't be the first thing I'd put into a home when I renovated it." Beryl walked around the fountain, looking into the nooks and crannies. "It would have been more interesting with a naked boy peeing water on the plants below."

"Whatever."

"Well it would. Are you keeping it?"

"I dunno. There are so many decisions we have to make. I get overwhelmed when I think about all of them."

"This can't be as big of a deal as renovating that school house."

"I was younger then and a whole lot more naive," Polly said. "I just kept pushing ahead because the only person I was responsible for was me. Nobody knew me or cared what I was doing. It didn't even occur to me that I was messing in the town's history. But here, it feels like every time I turn around there's something about the house that came from a different time in Bellingwood's past. And everyone is paying attention to what I'm doing."

"We were all paying attention when you renovated Sycamore House," Beryl said quietly. "Trust me, we were paying very close attention."

"But I didn't know it then. Now people stop me when I'm buying groceries and ask if we're going to have an open house or whether the ghost is bothering me."

"It's the life of a celebrity." Beryl poked Polly's arm. "Now show me the rooms upstairs."

CHAPTER FIVE

Polly walked into Sweet Beans Tuesday afternoon, desperate for more caffeine. She'd spent the morning in Story City working through paperwork for taxes. Her accountant, Steve Cook, had offered her a cup of coffee, but it was horrible, bitter stuff and she'd stopped drinking it halfway through.

"Hey there, Ms. Giller." Skylar Morris finished wiping down a table and went behind the counter. "Your regular?"

"Yes please," she said. "Make it a large." Polly pointed at a plate behind the glass. "What's that?"

"It rocks," he replied. "Mrs. Donovan said she was given the recipe by a little old lady down south."

Polly grinned at him. "What is it?"

"Old Lady Cake." He glanced up and winked. "I'm not kidding. It's a Dutch recipe. It has all of those Christmas flavors in it and anise for a kick."

"Then I want a piece of that, too." Polly glanced around the room and saw Elise sitting in a booth, peering at her computer. "Wave at me when it's ready."

"I got 'cha," he said.

Polly walked across the room and stood at the table, waiting for Elise to look up. When it didn't happen, she coughed and put her hand on the edge of the table.

"Oh!" Elise jumped in her seat and then relaxed. "I'm sorry. I was concentrating."

"I shouldn't have bothered you."

Elise grimaced. "No, I'm always like this. If you didn't bother me, I'd never come out of my head." She scooted to the edge of the bench with a startled look on her face. "Will you excuse me? I didn't realize I needed to go to the bathroom."

Polly watched her friend run away. "Nice to know you're glad to see me," she muttered. The coffee shop was quiet, so she sat down across from where Elise had been sitting.

"Here you go," Sky said, putting Polly's coffee and the plate in front of her. "I barely warmed the cake up. You'll love it."

"Thanks." The scent of cloves and nutmeg filled the air and Polly took a bite. He was right. It was terrific. She blew on the coffee before taking a sip. It was the perfect temperature. Skylar knew how to take care of her. Polly turned around to catch his eye and waved to thank him.

"I'm so sorry," Elise said as she slipped back into the booth. "I don't even know how long I've been here. What time is it?"

"One thirty. No classes today?"

"Not until this evening." Elise pulled out her phone. "Speaking of that, I need to set an alarm. If I don't remind myself to go to class, I'm worse than my students at being forgetful."

"We haven't seen much of you. How are things going?"

Elise tapped a few keys and closed her laptop. "Oh Polly, I'm having the best time. I'd forgotten what it was like to be around people who are as smart as or smarter than me. I don't have to make an effort to come up with conversation. There's always something interesting to talk about. It's so much fun to be able to talk about Ramanujan's formula and not..." She looked at Polly and grinned. "Get that face."

Polly laughed. "You mean the face that asks who is Ramanujan and why should I care about his formula?"

"That's the one."

"Should I care?" Polly asked.

"Nah. It's a crazy math thing." Elise picked up her mug and looked at it. "I'm empty. I should probably stop. What are you eating?"

Polly cut a piece of the cake and pushed it to the edge of her plate. "Try it. It's all cinnamony and yummy."

"I want one of those chocolate cupcakes with the cream filling that Sylvie makes. I'll be right back." Elise jumped up and then sat back down and reached for her purse and the cup. "Now I'll be right back."

"Maybe something without caffeine?" Polly said.

"I'm a little high."

Polly sat back and took another drink of her coffee. She hadn't seen Elise this animated in a long time.

"Just one more cup," Elise said, sitting back down. "Then I'll stop. I can't believe you put a coffee shop in Bellingwood just for me."

"Yep. We were psychic and knew you were moving back to town," Polly said. "I'm surprised to find you here, though."

"Because you think I'm at Sycamore House in my room?"

"Or at your office on campus."

Elise nodded. "I'm trying to be better. Nobody bothers me here and I can participate in society from afar. I really like Camille, too. She said that she's going to introduce me to some of her family one of these days. I'll bet she has some gorgeous cousins."

"You're interested in meeting men?" Polly's eyes grew big. "Who are you and what did you do with Elise?"

"I told you. I'm trying." Elise looked out of the booth, behind Polly and waved. "There she is. Hi, Camille."

Polly waited for Camille to join them before looking up.

"Hello, Polly," Camille said. "How do you like Sylvie's Old Lady Cake?"

"It's very good."

Camille motioned to Elise to move over and the girl actually pushed her computer out of the way and scooted toward the wall.

"I got it," Camille said to Elise. "We close in two weeks." She turned back to Polly. "I found a house and I'm buying it."

Polly sat back and put her hands on the table in front of her. "You bought a house? Here in Bellingwood?"

"It's a cute little house out on Hickory. I saw the sign go up last week and I jumped on it."

Polly creased her brows. "Hickory? Isn't that the road that goes into Secret Woods?"

Camille nodded.

"The pretty little white house on the corner?"

"That's the one. The last owner spent a lot of time fixing it up and it's just perfect." She turned back to Elise. "You'll love it."

"I can't wait. I've never done anything like this before. A house and a yard. Maybe a dog or a cat."

"One of each," Camille said.

"Wait," Polly said. "You're both moving out of Sycamore House and in with each other?"

Camille shrugged. "It's really the only way I can swing it and still have a life. I need a roommate. We'll have fun together."

Polly looked at Elise.

"The rent is perfect and it isn't in a building full of people," Elise said. "I hated living in an apartment. All of those people. Tromping around upstairs when I was trying to think, parties at whatever hour in the middle of the night." She lowered her voice. "And the sex. The girl above me was loud. I'd be embarrassed to be that loud and know that other people heard me."

"Did you ever say anything to her?" Polly asked.

Elise screwed her face up in shock. "Me? Say anything?" She laughed. "Uhhh, no. I bought a pair of noise canceling headphones."

"So you're going to be roommates," Polly said. "Are you sure about this?"

The two young women nodded enthusiastically as they looked at each other and then back to Polly.

"Can I make a recommendation?"

"Sure," Camille said.

"Give yourselves a six month or one-year limit and then revisit it."

Camille turned to Elise. "That makes sense. If something happened, in a year, I'd be fine doing the mortgage on my own."

"And I could find my own place after living here for a year." Elise looked at Polly. "But I don't know why you think this is a bad idea."

Polly shook her head. "No, I'm sorry. I think it's great, but I can't imagine putting two independent adults in the same house. You guys don't live the same way. You'll have different ideas of how to clean and when to clean. Do you know how you're going to split food costs? And what if one of you is always cold while the other one wants it to be freezing in the summer? Do you have separate bathrooms? Who owns the furniture? And what about when one of you wants to study in front of the television while the other one wants to watch a movie?"

The two young women looked at each other and nodded.

"We'll handle it," Camille said. "We just have to talk."

Elise looked over her glasses at Polly. "Don't you say it," she said.

"What?" Camille asked.

"I won't talk about things. I just let them happen around me and never say a word."

"We'll figure it out," Camille reassured her. "Don't worry."

"She says I'm not supposed to worry," Elise said to Polly. "And it will be nice to be in a real house again." She put her hand up. "Not that living at Sycamore House hasn't been wonderful. It really has and I can never thank you enough for putting up with me, but I'll have my own address and I can decorate my space with my own things."

Polly smiled and nodded. "You two will have a ball." She gave Camille an ornery grin. "There's a bedroom for your mother when she visits?"

"Oh," Camille said with a shudder. "Since we're so close to Sycamore Inn, I might just rent her a room there. That way she doesn't drive me nuts."

"She's a lovely lady," Elise said. "I like her very much."

"You've met Camille's mother?" Polly had no idea any of this had happened.

"We went to Omaha two weeks ago," Elise said. "I met her family."

"You met her family? The big family?" Polly was flabbergasted. Elise *was* changing.

"No," Camille said. "Just my family. My little brother played in a band at church. We went over on Saturday night and then came back Sunday afternoon. There was going to be a big family dinner, but I knew Elise couldn't do that." She shrugged. "But she wasn't busy and we were talking and the next thing we knew I was driving, she was riding, and we were in Omaha."

Polly put her hand on the table and reached across to Elise. "I'm so proud of you."

"I know, right?" Elise said. She patted Polly's hand and then patted Camille's arm. "Camille is good for me. She doesn't know how bad I was, so she doesn't let me get away with my fears."

"Well, I'm sorry I said anything negative about the two of you living together," Polly said. "I should have kept my mouth shut."

"It's okay." Elise reached over and patted Polly's hand again. "You're a worry wart and can't help yourself. We love that about you."

Polly laughed. "It sounds like you can talk about some things."

"Just with people I trust," Elise said. Her face flushed. "And now I've embarrassed myself."

"Don't ever be embarrassed about teasing me," Polly said. "I can take it." She glanced up at the doorbell ringing. This would be a terrible place for her to work, she was distracted by everything that happened around her.

"Joss," Polly said. "I'm over here." She turned to Elise. "You've met Joss, right?"

"She's the librarian, right?" Elise whispered.

"Yes."

"I was in there a few times looking for a quiet place to work." She picked up her coffee. "They don't serve this, though."

"How are you ladies?" Joss asked, standing at the table's edge.

"My tenants are moving out," Polly said. "Camille is buying a house and Elise is moving in with her."

"That's wonderful," Joss said. "Congratulations." She opened her mouth to say something more and then shook her head.

"What's up?" Polly asked.

"I was about to make a snide comment about buying a house rather than building one. But I don't need to rain on your parade today. I'm grumpy."

Polly stood up. "Let's take you and your grumpy self to another table. These two are celebrating and I was already a grey cloud in their sunny day."

" It was good advice, Polly," Camille said.

Polly bent back over. "I'm very happy for both of you. Let me know what we can do to help you move and we'll be there." She reached over and took Elise's hand. "I'm so happy." She picked up her coffee cup and plate and followed Joss back to the counter.

"Another one?" Sky asked Polly.

"Just plain coffee now," she said.

He drew off a mug and handed it to her. "Your regular, Mrs. Mikkels?"

Joss rolled her eyes at him. "How old am I?" She stuck her tongue out at Polly. "He refuses to call me by my first name. Drives me nuts."

"Everybody calls you Mrs. Mikkels," he protested.

"Whatever. When you call me Joss, your tip will get bigger." She winked at Polly and dropped a penny in the tip jar.

"Thank you, Joss," Skylar said, with only a hint of petulance.

"Haha. There you go," she said and followed the penny with two dollar bills. "Stick. Carrot."

"I'll bring your coffee to you," he said, laughing.

"What's going on with the house?" Polly asked as they walked to their table.

"Just more decisions about things that Nate refuses to participate in. If Henry weren't helping us, I'm pretty sure I'd have drop-kicked my husband clear back to Indiana."

"You know he probably doesn't care what you choose."

"I just want him to have an opinion," Joss protested.

Polly laughed. "But what if it's the wrong opinion? He's been married to you long enough to know how to handle you."

"Apparently not," Joss said with a snarl. "Even if it's wrong, at least it's something and it can give me a clue as to what we are doing."

"Do you really need him?"

"I guess not. Henry helped me this morning when I was having a fit about doors. We got through it. He's patient. You're lucky."

"Yes I am. And next year, this will all be nothing more than a memory and you will be happy in a beautiful new home."

"With just me and the kids."

"Because you'll have drop-kicked him to another state?"

Joss laughed. "Exactly." She looked up at Sky when he put her drink down in front of her and smiled. "Thank you."

"Any time, Mrs. Mikkels." He gave her a wry grin as he walked away.

"That kid is wonderful," Joss said.

Polly nodded. "I like him. He gets along with everyone." She took a drink of coffee and waited while Joss got through the initial moment of bliss with her own coffee. "Better?"

"Much." Joss put the cup back on the table and tapped the top. "Without this, there would be scores of crying children who would refuse to ever return to the library. What are you up to this afternoon?"

"Going to the library," Polly said. "I'll stand between you and the children."

"You're kidding, right?"

"No." Polly sat back in her chair. "I want to look through some of the Bellingwood history. Sal and I found something yesterday while we were cleaning out the kitchen over at the Springer House." She stopped and thought. "I have to quit calling it that. I'm not sure what to call it, but it's our place now."

Joss sat silent for a few moments and then drummed her fingers on the table. "Well?"

"Well what?"

"Well, what did you find yesterday?"

"Oh," Polly said with a laugh. "I'm sorry. Sal was clearing out one of the kitchen cabinets and found a big envelope in it with old newspapers and a title. The son of one of the founders of Bellingwood built that place as an exclusive inn. It wasn't always a residence."

"And this is the first you've heard of it?"

"We haven't gotten the full abstract yet, so yes. I want to look for old pictures of the inn. Nobody's ever talked about it, so I don't think it was in existence very long."

"The Bellingwood history section has been active lately."

"The sesquicentennial committee?"

"Mostly them."

"If I'm right, that inn was built in nineteen sixteen. That would make the building a hundred years old."

"Then you should do an open house this summer," Joss said.

"Oh no," Polly said. "Henry would absolutely kill me if I brought that up. He'd kill me." She thought a moment. "Dead. I'd be wholly and completely dead." Then a grin crept across her face. "But it would be really cool. We wouldn't have to be finished with the place. Just enough so that people could go through it and set aside all of the memories of it being a haunted house. If we cleaned up the yard, we could put tables out and the town could come over for a picnic."

"Henry wouldn't have to be involved in fixing up the yard, would he?"

Polly shook her head. "No. I could ask Eliseo to help me figure out what to do and then hire Andrew and Rebecca and their friends to help me do the work. And if Henry told me what needed to be done to clean up the..." She stopped. "No. That won't work either."

"What?"

"I was thinking about fixing up the outside of the house, but Henry has to rip that solarium off and re-build the porches. He'd kill me."

"You really should talk to him before you decide that he's going to kill you," Joss said.

"You know that's funny coming from you, don't you?"

"Because of the whole Nate not helping thing?"

"Uh huh."

"You and Henry are different. You work on projects together all the time. I don't work on cars and apparently Nate doesn't work on the house." Joss checked the time. "I should get moving. The doors need to be open for my early-birds."

"Here's your coffee to go," Skylar said, coming up behind Polly. He handed the cup to Joss. "Just made it fresh."

"You're my hero even if you don't know what to call me." Joss pressed money into his hand. "Thank you. I'll see you tomorrow."

"Coming?" she asked Polly.

"I'm right behind you."

CHAPTER SIX

"Oh my, what's all this?" Henry asked when he walked into the dining room.

"Research," Polly said. "Dinner's in there." She nodded at the kitchen.

Henry bent over and kissed her cheek. "Sorry we're late."

"I told you earlier not to worry about it." Polly sat back, stretched her arms up, and pulled him down for another kiss.

"This is the difference between being a kid with parents who've been married for fifteen years and a kid who has to put up with practically newlyweds," Rebecca said with mock disdain. "Will you two quit it? We're not supposed to see that stuff. We're still innocent."

Henry reached over and ruffled her hair. "Uh huh. What did we miss for dinner?"

"We made tacos," Rebecca said and jumped out of her seat. "Let me help you. I cut up all of the veggies. All you have to do is heat up the meat and warm up tortillas." She got close to Henry and made a face while holding her nose, then turned to Heath. "Do you smell as bad as he does?"

"What?" Henry asked. "Don't like the smell of paint and varnish?"

"You stink. You should take a shower."

"Rebecca," Polly scolded. "They've worked a long day."

Henry laughed. "A shower it is." He ruffled Rebecca's hair again and she brushed his hand away. "Will you warm up our supper?"

Rebecca lowered her head. "Sorry. Yeah. I'll do it." She glanced over at Heath, who was grinning. "Sorry."

"I wasn't stuck inside. I don't smell bad," he said.

Polly turned to look at him.

"But I'll take a shower anyway," he said. "And I'll hurry."

"That wasn't very nice," Polly said to Rebecca after they'd left the dining room.

"I know. I said I was sorry."

"Okay." Polly stood up and pushed the books and papers to the far end of the table. "Go ahead and heat up the meat in the pan. Do you remember how I warmed up the tortillas?"

Rebecca nodded and pulled paper towels off the roll. "Shouldn't I wait until they're back?"

"Sure. Hand plates and silverware to me," Polly said.

The two had dinner on the table when Henry and Heath came back into the dining room.

"We made a lot because Polly thought you would be really hungry," Rebecca said, putting the warmed tortillas between Henry and Heath. "And there's cake and ice cream, too. We waited for you on that."

"Thank you," Henry said. "This looks great." He pointed at the pile of books at the other end of the table. "You never told me what you're working on?"

"Look at this," Rebecca picked up her sketchbook, flipped through some pages and handed it to Henry.

"This looks like the Springer House without the solarium."

"We're not calling it that anymore," she said. "It's the Bell House."

He looked up at Polly, who nodded in agreement.

"I've learned so much in the last couple of days," Polly said. "It all started when Sal found this in the top of the corner kitchen cupboard while we were cleaning." She picked up the envelope, sat down beside him and pulled out the title and newspapers. "I couldn't figure out why they'd saved an old Chicago Tribune, but after spending time with it today, I discovered an ad in there for the Bell House in Bellingwood, Iowa." She flipped the Boone News-Republican over so he could see the article. "Did you know about this?"

He read and ate for a few minutes. Polly made another taco and put it on his plate. He picked it up and finished it while she made a third for him.

Henry chuckled. "What are you doing?"

"You were busy reading and eating. I was keeping the cycle going," she said.

"I'm not doing that for you," Rebecca said to Heath. "You're on your own."

With a mouth full of food, he nodded and tried to form a word, then looked guiltily at Polly and swallowed. "I got this. So what's that all about?"

"That old house used to be a fancy hotel," Rebecca said. "It was built by the son of Bellingwood's founder. You know, Bell? Bellingwood?"

"Who's the *ing* and the *wood*?" he asked and reached for the bowl of taco meat.

Polly picked it up and handed it to him. "I think the 'wood' is a man named Garwood. He was another one of the founding fathers." She tapped a black leather-bound book. "Beryl's ancestors were part of that group and then some other names that I don't recognize. I've been reading all about the early days, but nobody knew that the Springer House used to be a hotel."

She dug through the pile and pulled out a colorful booklet. "This was printed at the centennial and there's no mention of the place." Polly laughed. "Here's a picture of little Lydia at the centennial parade in her prairie bonnet. How cute is she?"

Henry flipped through some of the pages. "I've never seen

this." He chuckled. "All of these people were just kids. Look," he said. "Here are the Gardner boys on a float for the bank."

"Will there be a parade this summer?" Rebecca asked.

"I'm sure there will," Polly said. "They're going to tie it all in with Bellingwood Days. Jeff says it's going to be a busy couple of weeks." She pointed at the date on the Boone newspaper. "Bell House was built in nineteen-sixteen. We're going to have to do something fun to celebrate its hundredth birthday."

Henry nodded.

"Maybe an open house so people can forget about it being haunted and think about it as part of the history of Bellingwood," she blurted out.

He nodded again as he filled another tortilla. Then he laughed and looked at her. "An open house? This summer?"

She giggled. "Maybe?"

He looked at Heath and Rebecca, then back to Polly. "You said that in front of them so I wouldn't react."

"Maybe?" Her eyes darted back and forth. "Am I dead?"

"No, not dead," he said with a laugh. "We'll talk about this later."

Rebecca said, "She's dead."

Henry pointed at the pile of books again. "What else did you find?"

"Well, I was looking for more pictures of the Bell House."

"And?"

"I didn't find anything other than what's in that newspaper. But I think the place was a huge failure. It was supposed to be a posh hotel for wealthy people who came out here for the railroad, but they were too far away from Boone. And then World War One started the next year and as far as I can tell, it just closed down."

"That's probably why it's not in the published history of the town," Henry said. "But still, it would have been interesting. Weird. Whatever happened to the young man who built it?"

"I haven't found that either. He was the last Bell to live in Bellingwood. The hotel closed and there's nothing about him leaving town or dying. He just disappeared."

Henry glanced over at Heath. "Oh no," he said. "It's a mystery. A hundred-year-old mystery, but if Polly finds old bones in the house, she'll find a way to solve it."

She swatted at him. "Stop it."

"He's not in the cemetery?" Henry asked. "There's a whole Bell plot there."

Polly took out another booklet. "Joss told me I could have all of this stuff for two days, so I'm desperately trying to absorb it all." She flipped through pages of photographs of gravestones. "Here they are. Hiram and Susanna. Then there is a Leona who lived for three years and a William who died in nineteen eighteen. Do you suppose he was killed in the war?"

Henry nodded. "Probably. What was the name of the son who built the house?"

"Franklin," she said. "And he's not in here anywhere."

"Have you found lists of Bellingwood residents who fought in the war?" Henry asked.

Polly slumped back in her chair. "Seriously? No. I didn't think it was that important."

He shrugged and laughed. "I just wondered. You were doing all of this work."

"Leave me alone." She sat forward and pointed at the article about Evaline Watson. "That was Beryl's aunt or something. She died in the sixties. Beryl remembers her."

"That makes sense," Henry said. "There would be a lot of people in town who knew folks that had lived during the early part of the century."

"It's weird to think of how much history has been lost," Polly said. "Someone knew what happened to Franklin Bell, but we don't even know who to ask or how to find out the information. He's just lost to us now."

"My great-grandfather fought in that war," Heath said quietly. "I never knew him, but Mom said he and his brother went together, and he was the only one who came back." He shook his head. "I'm glad I don't have to go fight in a war. It seems so stupid to get sent to a foreign country just so you can die."

"There were a lot of men and women who were proud to serve," Henry replied. "Their country called and they responded."

"That's not what I meant," he said. "In the history books, it just didn't feel like they had a choice. They were drafted and had to go."

"There are still a lot of men around today who were drafted to serve in the Viet Nam war," Henry said. "They're proud, too. They did what they were called to do even when it cost them everything. And those men didn't get very much respect when they came back to the United States."

"I didn't mean anything," Heath said.

Henry patted his arm. "I know you didn't. Just be careful what you say in public." He smiled. "We all know that Eliseo sacrificed a lot in a war because his scars are all over his body. But there are other men and women in town with scars that are on the inside because of sacrifices they made. They're very proud of their service and we should always honor them."

"Yes sir," Heath replied. "I'm sorry."

Henry took Heath's arm and made him look up. "It's okay. This is a safe place. It's your home." He looked at Rebecca. "This is where you should learn about these things. I'm not upset with you. Okay?"

Rebecca nodded. "So..." She drew the word out. "Cake and ice cream?"

"That sounds perfect," Polly said, laughing. She got up, walked around the table and hugged Heath's shoulders. "Do you want another taco before I put things away?"

"I'm done," he said and handed her his plate.

Polly looked at Henry and he responded with a small nod.

"Rebecca," she said. "We're taking the dogs out for one last walk before we have ice cream. We'll let the boys have a few minutes for their dinners to settle."

"But," Rebecca started to protest, but looked at Polly's stern face. "Fine. I'll get my coat."

The dogs were more than ready for a trip outside and ran for the tree line as soon as Polly opened the door.

"Is Henry yelling at Heath?" Rebecca asked.

Polly drew Rebecca in for a hug. The cold and wind forced them to stay inside the garage. "Not at all. He's just going to try to fix it. Heath hasn't had anyone around to help him learn how to respond properly to the world. His aunt and uncle just let him exist and now that there are course corrections for his life, it's difficult. He's embarrassed and feels bad that he might have upset Henry. They need to work it out on their own."

"How did you guys get so smart about raising kids?"

"That's funny," Polly said. "We just want to treat you like we want to be treated. A lot of love, a whole lot of respect and then some more love."

The door opening behind her made both of them jump. Two dogs went hurtling past them and into the back yard.

"Hi Polly," Doug Randall said. He grinned when he saw Rebecca in front of her. "Hi there."

"Dog duty tonight?" Polly asked.

"Billy and Rachel are at some family thing of Rachel's in Boone." He laughed. "They had to get all dressed up and everything." Doug rubbed his hands together. "It's cold out here."

Rebecca pointed at the dogs. "And they love it. Look at them running in the snow."

"They're dogs," Polly said, pulling Rebecca in tighter to hold onto the girl's extra body heat. "Where are you working now?" she asked Doug.

"Jerry has us on an apartment job in Ames. I can't believe how many are going up over there. Where do all these people come from?"

"I don't know," Polly said. "But Henry likes those jobs, too. They're good money and the work is straightforward."

"But it's cold in the winter," he said. "I heard you found another dead body last weekend. Anybody from around here?"

"Nah. From New Mexico," Polly replied. "But the last name was Carter. And that's Beryl's maiden name."

He rubbed his hands up and down his arms and jumped in place. "Do you think they're related?"

"We don't know. It was out on her property." Polly glanced at him. "Why aren't you wearing a heavier coat?"

"Because I wasn't going to come out and talk to anybody, I was just going to let them run and call them back in a few minutes." Doug edged his way back to the door up to his apartment.

"Go," Polly said. "You're freezing."

"I'll be right back." He ran to the door and was gone.

"He's funny," Rebecca said. "Is he ever going to get a girlfriend?"

Polly laughed. "I don't know. He must not be ready for one. Sometimes people take longer than others to decide they want to be in a relationship."

"Oh, I understand that," Rebecca said, her voice full of passion. "Relationships are hard work. He should wait as long as he wants."

"Trouble with Andrew?"

She sighed. "It was so much easier when we were just friends. He wants to sit with me at lunch all the time and the other day, he tried to hold my hand when we were walking home from school. I had stuff in my hands!"

"What did you say to him?"

"That I had stuff in my hands!"

"Maybe you should break up if it's that hard to be in a relationship."

Rebecca pulled away and turned on Polly, crossing her arms in front of her. "I don't want to break up with him," she said. "I like him. I just want him to be normal and not all this lovey dovey stuff. Why doesn't he get that?"

"Maybe he's just as confused as to why you aren't more like him." Polly reached for Rebecca and pulled her back in. She missed the warmth.

"I thought you'd be all against that lovey dovey stuff."

"Holding hands? Sitting beside each other at lunch? That's the fun stuff and it doesn't get you into trouble with me. If you and Andrew are going together, that's part of it. It isn't like I'm naive about being in junior high. I was there once, myself."

"Yeah, but that was decades ago," Rebecca said.

Polly started to protest and realized that at least two decades had passed. "Thanks. Now I feel really old."

"I'm getting cold."

"Obiwan! Han!" Polly called. "You do know that if we move into the Bell House, we'll have a fenced in back yard and can just let them go outside without watching them."

"That would be awesome," Rebecca said. "Obiwan! Han! Come here!"

The two dogs sauntered toward them, Doug's dogs not far behind. Big Jack ran up and nipped at Han's neck, barked and ran away. The two chased off toward the driveway.

"Hey!" Polly yelled.

Rebecca put her hands over her ears. "That was loud."

"Oops. Sorry." Polly stepped away from her out of the garage. "Han. Jack. Come." She clicked her teeth and Han stopped in his tracks. "Come," she said again. Han turned to the bigger dog and walked toward her.

"Sorry about that," Doug said. "I didn't mean to leave you. The phone rang."

"Anybody interesting?" Polly asked. She put her hand down to pat Han's head. "Good boy."

"Nah." He opened the door that led up to his apartment and his dogs shook themselves before going inside.

"You're not telling me what I want to know," Polly said with a grin. She opened the door to Sycamore House and Rebecca stepped inside, waiting for their dogs to follow.

Doug turned around and gave Polly an evil smile. "I guess I'm not."

He stepped inside his doorway and she put her hand out to catch him. "That's not fair," she said.

"Life's not fair." He laughed out loud and pulled the door shut.

Polly shut the garage door and then stepped into the main building. "He's a rotten, horrible person."

"Because you want to know something?"

"Yes. If you ever do that to me, I'll do cruel and despicable things back to you," Polly threatened.

Rebecca opened the door up to their apartment and the dogs ran up in front of them. "Oh I know. I know."

Henry and Heath were in the media room with the television on when they got upstairs.

"You took long enough," Henry said. "We almost had ice cream without you."

"That would have been a dreadful mistake," Polly said. "Heath, any homework?"

He shook his head. "Nothing. I did it all at school." When she looked at him, he put his hands up. "I swear. I did it all."

"Okay. Ice cream for you?"

"Yes please."

She looked at the kitchen. "Thanks for cleaning up, guys."

"We set up the bowls. All you have to do is scoop," Henry said.

Sure enough, four bowls were prepared with cake already in them.

"What are we watching?" Polly asked.

"*Shannara Chronicles* is just about on," Heath replied.

Polly grinned. She'd made such a big deal about watching the show when it started in January that they'd all sat down with her. When Heath expressed interest, she took the first book in Terry Brooks' series off the shelf and handed it to him. He found the next books on his own.

CHAPTER SEVEN

Living near a coffee shop was dangerous, but Polly could hardly keep herself away. What made it even worse was that it was just down the street from the elementary school. Dropping Rebecca off on cold days led to temptation and she generally caved in to it.

When she walked in, Polly was surprised to see Lydia at a table by herself.

"Good morning, dear," Lydia said.

"Good morning to you," Polly replied. "What are you doing here so early?"

"We have an emergency."

Polly chuckled. "An emergency that requires coffee?"

Lydia looked back toward the bakery. "No. Muffins. I'm waiting for the next batch to come out."

"What's the emergency?" Polly waved at Camille behind the counter. She and a new employee were waiting on several customers. Polly was in no hurry.

"Beryl called in a complete panic an hour ago," Lydia said. "I didn't have time to bake, so Sylvie is taking care of us."

"What's wrong with Beryl?"

Lydia smiled. "Her brothers are at her house." She looked at her watch. "Just about now."

Polly sat back in her chair and crossed her arms. "Beryl Watson's brothers showed up at her house early in the morning. When did they tell her they were coming?"

"The poor girl got an email from Melvin. He and Harold needed to speak with her."

"At nine o'clock in the morning. It couldn't wait until later in the day," Polly said.

Lydia nodded. "The worst thing is that the email arrived at six o'clock this morning."

"At least they didn't show up on her doorstep with no notice."

"They knew what they were doing," Lydia said through gritted teeth. "Those boys have no respect for their sister."

Beryl rarely talked about her family and Polly had never met her brothers. It was hard to imagine that they didn't have anything to do with her. No, once Polly thought about it, that wasn't hard to imagine at all. Most people in Bellingwood didn't have much to do with Beryl. She was her own person and lived her own life, seemingly oblivious to what others thought.

"What are they like?" Polly blurted out.

"Melvin is just like his father. When he was younger, he drove a propane truck. Good honest work. He has two daughters who married men a lot like their daddy. I don't know what they do. Harold worked as a welder down in Boone until he had to stop. Then he went to work for the county roads department. I think he retired a couple of years ago. He and Pat had six kids and between them, they have at least twenty grandkids and there might even be a couple of great-grandkids by now."

"And Beryl isn't involved in any of their lives? None of them want to be associated with a famous artist?"

Lydia smiled a sad smile. "She tried when her nieces and nephews were young. She'd go to Christmas parties and attempted to go to their school events, but I think she embarrassed her brothers because she wasn't bland like they were." Lydia sniffed. "She even dressed down for them, but the poor woman doesn't own plain navy blue or brown anything. Then one day she realized that nobody had told her when school events were happening. She was invited to their weddings, but the kids didn't know her any longer. She'd never been allowed to be part of their lives once they were through elementary school. Beryl sent gifts - she still does. She goes to weddings and if there is a public event like a baptism at church or a graduation, she's always there."

"Wow," Polly said. "She's better than me. I've never attempted to get involved in Uncle Will's kids' lives."

"He's not your brother, though," Lydia replied. "It was his responsibility to be involved in your life. Not only was he not involved, but he blatantly told your father that he wanted nothing to do with you. It's a little different."

"I suppose. But this has to be hard on Beryl."

"It is. And the thing that just raises my ire is that those damned brothers of hers still think that after all of that, they have a right to disrespect her." Lydia pulled her right hand into a fist and shook it. "If she'd just let me at 'em one time. I'd give those boys a piece of my mind."

Polly chuckled. "Beryl always gives people a piece of her mind. I can't believe she doesn't say anything to her brothers."

"Isn't it funny," Lydia said. "After all these years, she's afraid that they'll cut her off completely from their families." She snarled. "Like they haven't already. But at least it's still amicable and Beryl desperately wants it to stay that way. She'll put up with anything from them."

Camille came over to the table with a box and a cup. "I went ahead and made your regular, Polly," she said. "Is that what you wanted?"

Polly took the cup from her and held it against her chest. "It's exactly what I wanted. Thank you."

"Sylvie says she didn't put any poison in the muffins." Camille put the box down in front of Lydia.

"Rats," Lydia said. "Just a little to make them feel sick to their stomachs?"

Camille laughed. "Not this week."

"Tell her thank you." Lydia pressed some bills into Camille's hand. "Thank you very much."

"This isn't necessary," Camille said. "You've already paid us."

"I just paid for Polly's coffee and a little extra. You took care of me today and I appreciate it."

Polly smiled up at Camille and shrugged. "You try to fight with her. It's a losing battle."

"Then I'll say thank you." Camille patted Polly's shoulder and walked away, picking up mugs from a table whose occupants had just left.

Lydia looked down at the box in front of her. "It's time to enter the fray. I can think of a thousand things I'd rather do with Beryl today." She looked at Polly, pleading in her eyes. "Do you want to come with me?"

Polly took a slow sip from her cup. "What's in it for me?" she asked.

"My undying love and one of Sylvie's muffins?"

"You already love me and I know the baker," Polly said.

Lydia put her hand over her mouth and coughed. "I'm coming down with something and I should send you over with this food."

"Why don't you want to do this?"

"Were you not listening?" Lydia scowled at Polly. "Beryl has insensitive brothers who are mean to her."

"It can't be that bad. But of course I'll go with you. I don't have anything important to do this morning. The research on Bell House can wait."

"Bell House?" Lydia asked. She stood up and took her coat up from the back of her chair.

"I haven't had a chance to tell you yet," Polly said. "We found an old title to the house. The original title. The son of one of Bellingwood's founders originally built the Springer House as an inn. It's one hundred years old this year."

Lydia smiled. "Are you going to celebrate that with the sesquicentennial?"

"Maybe," Polly said. "It all depends on whether or not Henry can find time in his schedule to do the renovation work. We'll do something this summer but I'm not sure what it will be."

She waved goodbye to Camille as they walked out the front door.

"I'll see you there," Lydia said. "And don't you dare drive off and leave me. I'm counting on you now, you know."

"Got it. Straight to Beryl's house and no detours." Polly climbed in her truck, took her phone out of her pocket, and dialed.

"You have a better offer, don't you?" Jeff Lindsay asked.

She was perplexed. "What?"

"You aren't coming into the office this morning. I know you, you're a slacker."

"Why, yes I am," she said with a laugh. "I did think to call and let you know, though."

"Spending the morning at the Springer House?"

"Bell House," she corrected. "No. I'm going over to Beryl's for a while. If you need me, though, call."

"I'll let Stephanie know," Jeff said. "I'll be out most of the day. Maybe I'll see you tomorrow."

"Okay." Polly backed out of the parking space and drove the few blocks to Beryl's house.

Two pickup trucks were parked in Beryl's driveway, so Polly pulled in behind Lydia's Jeep in front of the house. She was immediately transported back to the days when they'd rebuilt Beryl's studio. Neighbors were upset at the extra traffic. She inadvertently turned around and glanced back at Larry Storey's house. He'd made sure that Polly knew how offensive the extra vehicles were around Beryl's house.

There he was, peeking out of his front window. He'd pulled the curtain back to see the activity.

Polly got out and walked around the back of her truck, looked up again and waved at him before going to the front door. The poor man waved back, then left the window altogether.

She put her hand up to knock, but Lydia was right there and opened the door. "Polly Giller," Lydia said. "It's good to see you. What brings you out today?"

"Ummm..." Polly was at a loss.

"That's wonderful," Lydia said. "I'm sure Beryl would like you to meet her brothers. Come on in."

Polly followed Lydia into the living room and hugged Beryl when the woman jumped out of her seat and rushed over to her. "How are you this morning?" Polly asked.

Beryl nodded. "I'm fine. Let me introduce you to my brothers. Melvin, this is Polly Giller. She owns Sycamore House and the Sycamore Inn."

The older of the two men stood up. He'd lost most all of his hair. What was left was white and thin. He was a big man, mostly in the belly. His well-worn blue jeans barely stayed up. Polly knew she shouldn't notice that he had no butt to hold them in place, but she did and he didn't.

He'd stood to shake her hand. "This is our brother, Harold."

Harold looked a lot like his brother. Not quite as big, but still a large man. He wore a flannel shirt over a t-shirt that was tucked into his jeans. The hat on the table had to have been his because there was still a crease in the little bit of hair he had left on his head.

Because there wasn't much room beside his brother, he didn't stand and Polly reached over to shake his hand.

"It's nice to meet you both," she said.

One little grey cat was alert on the chair Beryl had just left. "Where's the other one?" Polly asked.

"I'll pick her up this morning after we're finished," Beryl said. "Hem came home with me last night." She gestured to the kitchen. "Would you like some coffee?"

Polly looked at the mugs on the table and glanced at Lydia who gave her a surreptitious nod. "I'd love some. But I can get it."

Beryl looked at her brothers. "I'll be right back. Help yourself to the muffins. They're made by the best baker in town." She pushed Polly ahead of her, scooting her toward the kitchen. Once they crested the threshold, she whispered. "I'm so glad you two are here."

"What's going on?" Polly asked.

"They're asking me questions about that young man that was

killed. I told them to call the sheriff, but they want to hear it from me. I don't know what to tell them. I've been so busy that I haven't called my aunt about the genealogy and I don't have any answers. Aaron hasn't told me anything new. What am I supposed to say?"

"Say that," Lydia said. "What do they want from you?"

"Answers. They're upset that I didn't call anyone on Saturday when it happened. How was I to know that they required a phone call from me? Am I a mind-reader?"

Lydia patted Beryl's arm. "Calm down. If you don't have information for them, then that's all there is to it. They made a trip for nothing."

"Not for nothing," Beryl said. "You brought muffins. They got a free breakfast."

"Those two men are your brothers?" Polly asked.

Beryl cackled. "I love you, Polly Giller. You know the best things to say." She took down two mugs and poured coffee into them. Then she opened the lower cupboard and pulled out a brown bottle. "Want some Irish cream in there?"

"No," Lydia said. "I'm not starting my day out by getting drunk."

"You're no fun." Beryl stuck her tongue out and put the bottle back into the cupboard. She handed the mugs to Lydia and Polly. "Shall we?"

They followed her back to the living room and sat down in chairs opposite the sofa.

"Muffin?" Beryl asked Polly, reaching for the bakery box.

"No, I'm fine," Polly replied. "I had breakfast this morning."

Lydia waved her off as well.

Melvin and Harold watched the interplay in confusion.

"Did you have plans this morning, Beryl?" Melvin asked.

"No, why?"

"Your friends are here when we're trying to discuss family matters."

Beryl took a deep, measured breath before looking at him. "What family matters are we discussing?"

"That dead boy in our historical family plot," Harold said. As if he realized that he'd said something out loud, he shook his head quickly and shut his mouth.

"Polly was the one who found that poor boy," Beryl said.

Harold nodded. "We've heard about her."

Beryl shook her head. "What is there to discuss? Is he someone you know? I know he was a Carter, but I don't know what family he's from."

"One of those West Coast Carters," Melvin said with derision.

She chuckled. "We have West Coast Carters?"

"Must be from that branch that moved out there," he mumbled.

"A hundred and fifty years ago? You think you can tell that he's a descendant of Lester Carter?" she asked.

"Who else would it be?"

"Where does your Mary live?" Beryl degenerated to sarcasm. She'd given up being nice about this.

"Tennessee," Harold answered.

"What if she'd moved to any state west of Colorado? Would you assume that she was a descendant of Lester?" Beryl kept pushing them. This didn't sound like someone who was scared of her brothers. "What if one of Cyrus's descendants had moved out there? It could be anyone or it could be someone who isn't related to us at all."

"Well, what does the sheriff say about him?" Melvin asked. "He's her husband," he nodded at Lydia, "and your friend. Surely you can get some information from him. It happened on our land!" He sat forward as he worked himself up.

Beryl glanced at Lydia.

"My husband is investigating the death," Lydia said. "But murder investigations take time. They are looking for the young man's family and trying to understand why he was killed, much less buried in your family plot."

"It's a historical plot," Harold repeated. "No one is buried there nowadays."

Lydia nodded in understanding. "As soon as your sister knows something, I'm certain that she'll let you know. If this young man is part of your extended family, I'm also certain that she would be glad for assistance from both of your families in welcoming his family to Iowa. They will need a great deal of love and care in this terrible time."

Beryl looked at Lydia, gulping back laughter. She turned back to her brothers. "I would be glad of your help. You have larger homes than I do."

"You can afford to put them up at the hotel," Melvin said.

"If that's what you'd like me to do, I will," Beryl replied. "Lydia was just recommending that we be hospitable."

"Do either of you have any information about the early families of Bellingwood?" Polly asked. "Are there any documents, pictures or other items that might have been handed down to you? Things that weren't copied for the centennial?"

Harold looked at his brother. "You have papa's things."

"I haven't been through any of those boxes in years," Melvin said. He turned to Polly. "Why do you ask? What does that have to do with any of this?"

"It just seems to me that if this young man is from another branch of the family and you have old information, we might be able to find something that connects it all." Polly shrugged. "And besides, since the sesquicentennial is coming up this summer, the planning committee will probably want as much information as they can get. I just purchased the Springer House and discovered that it was built in nineteen sixteen as an inn. The son of Hiram Bell built it. There's got to be more information about those early years if we can just get people to open up their old trunks, scrapbooks and files."

Melvin nodded, thinking about what she said. "I could dig those out." He looked at his sister. "But I don't have time to look through them."

"I'd love to do that," Beryl said. "I'd love it."

"Come on out and pick them up. Give me a day or two to bring the boxes out of the closet."

"Thank you," she gushed. "I had no idea you still had those boxes."

"It's just old papers and pictures, but if you find something that the town would like to have, give it to them." Melvin put his hand on his brother's knee and pushed himself to a standing position. "We should go now and leave you three to do whatever you were planning to do. Come on, Brother."

Melvin stepped away from the chair and Harold stood up. "Thank you for the coffee, Beryl. It was nice to see you. Pat says I should ask you to Sunday dinner some one of these days. It's mostly just the two of us, but sometimes the kids are home."

"I'd love to come," Beryl said. She waved at Polly and Lydia to stay seated and followed her brothers to the front door.

Polly took a deep breath and relaxed. "That was interesting."

"They did better than expected," Lydia said. "Melvin even got nice there toward the end." She grinned at Polly. "Must be because there was a pretty girl in the room."

The front door thudded closed and Beryl let out a shrill howl as she came back to the living room. "What in the world was that all about?"

"I think you're supposed to call Aaron and get the scoop before you talk to your brothers again," Polly said.

Beryl scowled. "Bet my little pink ass."

"Will you go get the boxes from your brother?"

"Maybe." Beryl sat back down in her chair, scooping little Hem into her arms. "If you go with me."

Lydia and Polly looked at each other, trying to decide which one of them she was talking to.

"You're both going with me. Then I'll take you out to lunch somewhere fancy." Beryl stroked Hem's head. "Please?"

CHAPTER EIGHT

"Look at this, Miss Giller." Tommy Garwood waved frantically from the back of the classroom.

"Yes, Tommy," she said. "Please stand if you would like to speak."

The young boy stood up beside his desk and put his hand up, "Miss Giller?"

"Go ahead, Tommy. What is so important that you feel you must interrupt reading time?"

"The sheriff and his deputy just rode past. Do you think there might have been another bank robbery?"

She sighed and pointed back to his desk. "Tom Garwood, if you spent your time reading rather than looking out the window, you'd find that your exam scores would significantly increase."

"But Miss Giller," he protested. "Everybody is heading toward town. Just look outside."

Polly glanced at the window and saw that he was correct. There was quite a commotion on the street going past the schoolhouse. Iowa wasn't the Old West any longer. Bellingwood was civilized now.

"You all stay where you are," she commanded. As she strode toward the back of the room, Polly stopped to press Tommy Garwood back into his seat. "That includes you."

Polly stopped in the doorway at the back of the room and took her cloak from the hook on the wall. She turned back to the class. "Miss Heater, you are in charge while I step out. Class, I expect that you will all listen to her and remain quiet. Understood?"

Twenty-five sets of wide eyes looked at her while their heads nodded in unison. Polly threw her cloak across her shoulders, buttoned it at the neck and drew on the gloves that she'd stuffed in its pockets this morning. She rushed out the front door of the schoolhouse and stopped the first person who walked past her.

"What's happening?"

"There's a gunfight in front of the bank," the young man said.

Polly stepped back, shaken at his words. While she stood there, two men on horses flew past, one turning in his saddle to shoot at whoever was following them. She was dumbfounded. How could this be happening in Bellingwood, Iowa?

In moments, the sheriff rode past again, his gun raised and pointed at the two who were fleeing. The crowd that had gathered to watch the excitement surged toward her and Polly attempted to get back to the safety of the steps of her schoolhouse. She tripped and slammed down on the ice-cold, snow packed ground.

"Polly!" She heard a familiar voice as she was lifted from the ground and she tried to focus on their face.

"Polly! Are you okay?"

"What?" Polly finally shook herself awake and found that Henry was holding her in his arms. "What are you doing?" she asked.

"Look around," he said.

She tentatively took in her surroundings and realized that they were on the floor of her bedroom. "What happened?" She had a good idea what had happened and felt a little embarrassed by the whole thing.

"I have no idea how you did it," he said, "but you fell out of bed. Are you okay?"

Polly laughed out loud and couldn't stop herself from chuckling. "I fell out of bed? How?"

He pulled her in for a hug and then let her go. "I told you, I don't know. But it might have something to do with those critters who demand that they deserve most of our bed. I felt you pull a blanket away from me and the next thing I knew there was a thud and you were gone."

"You got here really fast," she said. "I didn't even have time to..." Polly stopped talking and thought about her dream. "You got over to my side really fast."

"You didn't have time to what?" he asked.

"Nothing, I guess. I was having a weird dream about being a teacher in a one-room schoolhouse. There were bank robbers shooting at the sheriff. Everybody was riding horses or walking. I tried to get back into the school where I'd be safe, but I tripped and fell down." She rubbed the side of her head. "And I bumped my head."

"Bank robbers on horseback?" Henry smiled at her. "You've spent way too much time reading about Bellingwood's history." He stood up and held out his hand. "Did you hurt yourself?"

Polly took the proffered hand and let him pull her to her feet. "I think I'm fine. That was weird. The last time I fell out of bed I had to have been in elementary school. And I kinda did that on purpose."

He looked at her sideways. "You fell out of bed on purpose? You were a strange child. Why would you do that?"

"All of my friends told stories of how they fell out of bed. I couldn't figure out why they would want to do that, but one year it seemed like it was happening all the time. So I set myself a trap. I slept clear on the edge of the bed, just to see if I could fall out. The first night I didn't, so I moved even closer the next night. It took three nights before I finally hit the floor. I woke up and my butt hurt. I decided that was stupid, so I didn't do it again."

"Did your parents know what you were doing?"

Polly shook her head. "They didn't even know that it happened and I wasn't about to tell them. I didn't even tell my friends at school." She sat down on the bed and pushed one of the cats back into the middle. "Unless those animals were pushing me, I still don't understand why I fell off tonight. I don't toss and turn that badly, do I?"

Henry walked to the bathroom. "Not since those trials got over last fall. You're back to your regular sleep-like-the-dead sleep."

"Did you do this to me?" Polly asked the animals. "Because I don't want to worry about doing this ever again." She rubbed her hand down Leia's back. "If you fall off the bed, you wake up enough to get your front paws down first. From now on, you get the outside."

Obiwan wriggled his way across the bed toward her.

"And you," she said. "I thought you were supposed to be my protector. How could you let that happen?" Polly bent over and kissed the top of his head. "I still love you," she whispered. "I still love all of you."

Henry came back out with a glass of water in his hand. "Drink?"

"No," Polly said with a half laugh. "At the rate I'm going tonight, I could very easily wet the bed. What in the heck?"

"Let it go," he said. "It was just one of those things." He drained the glass and opened the door of his bedside table and put it on the shelf. They'd learned to keep those types of things out of the reach of the animals.

Henry sat down on the bed, then turned to her. "But I think that maybe you should tuck up close to me for the rest of the night. Let the animals and me keep you where you belong."

Once they were settled, he switched the light off and turned to wrap his arms around Polly. She scooted into the protection of his body and slowed her breathing, trying to relax again.

"It was a strange dream," she said. "I wonder why I was a teacher."

"Because you love your kids," he replied. "So was Aaron Merritt the sheriff?"

Polly nodded. "Yes, he was. I can't wait to tell him that I saw him riding through town on horseback."

Henry chuckled. "With guns blazing. That would have been a sight to see."

~~~

"I should have a phone of my own," Rebecca announced at breakfast the next morning.

Polly glanced at Henry and then sat down at the table. "Oh you should? What makes you say that?"

"I've been thinking about this and since all of my friends have phones, I could keep in touch with them. This is how we communicate, you know." Rebecca held up her index finger. Before anyone could interrupt, she held up a second finger. "I would always be able to let you know where I am and what I'm doing." The third finger flipped up. "If I was in trouble, I could call for help." When she raised her fourth finger, she hesitated. "You'd always know where I was with the GPS thing on there." By the time Rebecca flipped her thumb up, she had lost ground. "It would be educational. I could look things up in a hurry and never be without information."

"I see," Polly said. She turned to Henry. "Do you have anything you want to say?"

He chuckled and backed away into the kitchen. "I'm just going to pour another cup of coffee and watch. Heath, do you want more toast?"

Heath stood up. "Nah. I'm going to get my stuff and get out of here. I told Jason that I'd pick him up at his house. Eliseo's working early and has to be gone for a while this morning." He leaned over to Rebecca. "Good luck with this."

"Chicken. I thought you had my back," she said.

"Uh huh." Heath took off before she could corner him any further.

"Don't say anything now," Rebecca said. "I want you to take some time to think about this. No rash decisions or anything."

"Oh honey," Polly replied. "There isn't anything rash about my decision. The answer is no."

"But why?" Rebecca whined. "I gave you well thought-out reasons why I should have one. The least you can do is give me a thought-out response."

Polly chuckled. "First of all. I don't owe you anything, much less a response to your whining. But secondly, if you'd slow your roll, I have plenty of good reasons for not giving you a cell phone right now."

Rebecca slumped back in her chair and crossed her arms over her chest. "I'm not getting a cell phone. That's all that matters. Everything else is just blah, blah, blah."

Henry's phone rang. He looked at the number and flipped it open. "Hayden? Is everything okay?"

Both Polly and Rebecca looked up at him. He listened for a moment and then nodded to them that things were fine. "Sure," he said. "I can make time today. Lunch?" Henry walked away into his office as he continued to talk.

"What's that about?" Rebecca asked.

"I'm not sure. But Henry will tell me later." Polly sat forward. "However, you and I aren't finished with this conversation. Don't you dare ask a question like this and then get nasty about my response without giving me an opportunity to talk about it with you."

"It doesn't matter. The answer is no and you're always in charge."

Polly felt herself starting to seethe. This girl was as sweet and wonderful as they came, but when she didn't get her way she had a tendency to slide off the cliff into raging adolescent rottenness.

She took a long, slow deep breath and shut her eyes. Part of her wanted Rebecca to run away to her room and head for school so she wouldn't have to confront the beast. Maybe if she kept her eyes closed long enough that would happen.

"Yes," Polly said. "I am in charge and I'm working on not screaming at you for your bad behavior right now. You're going to want to walk away from me for a minute."

Rebecca stood up and headed for the dining room. "*You* could have walked away," she muttered.

Polly let her go, even though every fiber of her being wanted to yank her back into the seat and read her the riot act at the top of her lungs. Tears squirted out of her eyes. She loved Rebecca so much and to have her act so disrespectfully incensed Polly. She dropped her head into her hands and tried to shut the world away.

"Are you okay?" Henry asked. He put his hand on her back. "Where did Rebecca go?"

"I don't know and I don't care right now. That little shit."

"She didn't like your answer?"

"No and she didn't want to hear why I gave her that answer." Polly shook her head and wiped tears out of her eyes. "What's going on with Hayden?"

"He's fine." Henry sat down at the table beside her. "It's actually kind of cool."

"What's that?"

"He wants me to talk to him about his future. He's been applying to medical schools and responses are starting to come back. He told me he isn't sure what to do next."

"And he wants you to help him figure it out? That's awesome."

Henry leaned in. "I don't have any idea what I'll say, but if all he needs to do is have someone listen while he talks through it, I can be that person." He took her hand. "I don't know how to describe the feelings I'm having right now. The boy doesn't realize that I'd walk through fire for him and when he asks me for anything, I'll give it to him."

"This is what it's always going to be like, isn't it," Polly said, her eyes filling with tears again. "We want to toss one in a snow drift and another one makes us so happy we can't describe it."

"I'll be honest," Henry said. "He could ask me for the money to pay for medical school today and I'd figure out how to find it."

Polly laughed. "Then I hope he's not that bold."

"Me too." He jumped up. "I'd better get going so I can make sure everyone has plenty to do just in case lunch goes long."

"Call when you're done, will you?"

He nodded. "I'll try." Henry walked back over to the table and tipped her head up so he could kiss her lips. "And remember I love you. We've talked about Rebecca and the phone and you made the right decision. You're the mama. She's the daughter. You're the boss."

"That's what she keeps saying," Polly said. "In derogatory tones."

"Whether she likes it or not, it's her reality. Be strong. You've taken down stronger men than her."

Polly shook her head. "I'm not sure about that. I do believe this is going to be a battle of wills for the rest of our lives."

"I'm putting my money on you." He smiled. "I'll talk to you later."

Polly watched him walk through his office and took another drink of coffee. She was absolutely going to treat herself to something fancy to drink at Sweet Beans before heading over to the other house this morning. She deserved it.

That made her laugh. She didn't deserve anything. Oh well.

"Come on, Rebecca," she called out. "It's time for you to go to school now. Do you want to walk or would you like me to drop you off on my way over to Bell House?"

Polly waited a few minutes and decided to go look for her daughter. She had no memory of this much drama when she was Rebecca's age, but wondered if it would have been different had her mother still been alive. Her dad wouldn't put up with it and Polly never felt comfortable talking back to Mary since she wasn't really family. If her father had ever heard her do something like that, he would have had her head.

"Rebecca? It's time to get moving." Polly walked through the living room to the closed door on the other side. She knocked twice. "Rebecca?"

There was no answer and Polly knocked again. "Rebecca, I'm coming in." She opened the door and looked into the room. Rebecca was huddled in a corner, her arms wrapped around her knees and her head down.

"Honey, it's time to go to school. You need to go wash your face."

"I'm sorry," Rebecca said.

"Thank you. It's going to be fine." Polly stood in the doorway and waited.

Rebecca looked up at her with a tear-streaked face. "I'm a terrible daughter. I'm so sorry. Please don't hate me."

"Honey, I will never hate you. I promise. Now stand up and pull yourself together. We'll talk about this tonight."

"But I was so mean." Rebecca burst into another round of sobbing.

Between the drama and the little rebellions, Polly wasn't sure Rebecca would make it through her junior high and high school years. She wanted to roll her eyes, but thought that might escalate things further.

"Yes you were," Polly responded.

Those words brought Rebecca's head up and she looked at Polly in shock. "You agree?"

"I do. It's time to get past this, though. Stand up and get moving."

"You don't hate me?"

"Honey, I've told you over and over again that I can never hate you. I love you no matter how you behave. Now I'm not going to say it again. Stand up. Right now."

Rebecca finally stood up. She stopped in front of the mirror on her dresser and looked at herself. "I'm a mess. Can I skip first period?"

"No. You can go wash your face with some cool water," Polly said. "You'll be fine."

"Okay." Rebecca heaved a big sigh, picked her backpack up and carried it out of the bedroom, then dropped it on the sofa before going into the bathroom.

Polly flipped off the bedroom light and sat on the back of the same sofa to wait for the girl to re-emerge. How in the world did parents live through these years? Everything could be going along just wonderfully and then out of the blue, the entire world fell apart. She chuckled, wishing there was a safe word she could use to just tap out of the situation.

"I'm ready." Rebecca came out of the bathroom, her head down and her hair pulled in front of her face.

"I'll drive you. Get your coat," Polly said. "I have your backpack."

When they got into the truck, Rebecca buckled in and then looked over at Polly. "What's my punishment this time?"

Polly laughed. "Your bedroom is a terrible mess and your bathroom needs some attention."

"I was afraid of that. When will I ever learn?"

This was the normal Rebecca. Polly felt relief. At least she'd be able to have a good day in school. "I'm not sure," Polly said. "Part of me hopes this is the last time it ever happens, but another part of me appreciates that your bathroom will get scrubbed down on a regular basis."

"Polly!" Rebecca protested.

She chuckled. "You're the one who asked." Polly reached over and lightly squeezed Rebecca's leg. "I love you and it's all going to work out. You're growing up just fine and I'm proud of who you are."

"Even when I sulk?"

"Even then."

"I'm not getting a phone this year, am I?"

Polly shook her head. "No, but like I said, we'll talk about it tonight." She pulled up in front of the school. "Now let this go and have a good day. Remember that I love you, okay?"

"Okay. I love you, too."

CHAPTER NINE

"Yes, I'm addicted to coffee," Polly muttered as she drove away from the elementary school. "I might have a problem." Her phone rang and she chuckled at herself.

"Hello, Grey. How are you this morning?"

"Fine, thank you, but I'm afraid that I am in need of your assistance. Are you too busy to spend time at the inn today?"

Polly made a quick turn. "Of course not. What's wrong?"

"It would appear that our young man fell into something he shouldn't have and was transported to the hospital last night," Grey said. "I must see him and find out what has happened."

"Our young man?"

"Young Denis. I thought he was achieving a great many goals, but my ecstasy over his progress dimmed my sight. He overdosed last night."

"Oh no!" Polly cried. "Will he be okay?"

"I fear this will set him back, but to hold out hope is to stand against the gods."

Polly felt like she was in a foreign film and needed subtitles. She tried again. "Will he live?"

"Why yes," Grey said. "Of course he will. And they will release him from the hospital just as soon as his mother and I discuss his options."

She took a deep breath. "What was that about hope and the gods?"

Grey chuckled. "When we hope, we stand and shake our fists at the gods. The tales of the ancient Greek gods were told so humanity understood who tormented them. They released evil upon evil into the world when Pandora opened her box. One of the gods - likely Zeus - placed hope inside that box and it remains there so we can continue in the face of tragedy. We must remember that we have survived and the Greek gods have long since surrendered to the erosion of time."

"I'm parking right now," Polly said. "I'll be right in." She closed her phone and looked down at what she was wearing. She'd dressed to work at the Bell House. Her jeans and sweatshirt were clean, but not professional.

Grey came out from behind the counter. "Thank you so much for doing this. I won't be gone all day."

"Take the time that you need," she said. "I'll see if someone can bring better clothes for me to wear. I'm not dressed for this."

"You look fine, but we do have Sycamore House t-shirts behind the counter," Grey said.

"What happened last night?"

He shook his head. "I don't know yet. His mother called in a state of great distress this morning. She'd been at the hospital with him all night. The other tenants of his home returned after an evening out and found him on the inside stoop. When they couldn't rouse him, they called 9-1-1. I will get the rest of the story today, I'm certain." Grey took Polly's hand. "I'm grateful for the freedom to help this family. Today, his mother needs me as much as does Denis. A child's problems are never solely his."

"What about her other children?" Polly asked.

Grey turned as he walked to the front door. "I believe that she also called Evelyn Morrow. Poor Leslie doesn't have enough friends in her life, so she relies on the help she has used in the past." He opened the door. "I will call you later to let you know how things are progressing."

"Give them my best," Polly said. She puffed air out of her lips, buzzing them as she did so. There went her morning coffee. At least the hotel's coffee would be fresh. Grey always made sure of that. She poured a cup and went behind the counter, scrounging through the cupboards for the shirts Grey mentioned. One of those would certainly look better than the sloppy thing she had on now.

After changing into a light grey t-shirt, Polly woke the computer and looked at the guest list. Two were scheduled to leave today, but had already paid for their rooms and she didn't expect to see them. She saw three reservations scheduled and five other rooms were occupied. Polly scrolled through the names, recognizing two as belonging to families in Bellingwood. It was nice to be part of their lives, offering a place for guests to stay so they didn't have the stress of extra people in their homes.

The front lobby of Sycamore Inn was clean and neat, leaving nothing for Polly to do. This was going to get old in a hurry. A game show was playing on the television, but that didn't interest her. She didn't spend time watching television during the day. Once she got started on that, she'd never get anything done.

Her research on Bellingwood's history was still sitting on the dining room table at home. A lot of good that was. But when all else failed, at least she could read. Polly chuckled. All of those books on shelves in her home and she was thankful to have access to the world's library on her cell phone.

Her dad would have loved this. He adored gadgets of all kinds, but was so frugal that they were usually three or four generations old by the time he finally gave in and bought one. He had jumped right into Macintosh computers, though. When she emptied his house, she found an old one in the attic. People told her that it would make a great fish aquarium, but she didn't have time for that and it had been taken to Goodwill.

He'd made sure she had what she needed for school. That was probably to justify his need for the newest and best thing. He'd gotten a Palm Pilot when people were moving away from them and was frustrated at its limitations, even though it was more powerful than anything he'd ever carried. He would have been on the forefront of GPS planting had he stayed on the farm.

Yes, he would have loved being able to access any book he desired. Polly smiled at memories of him sitting in his chair in the living room, the light on over his shoulder and a book in his hands. Sometimes it fell into his lap as he took a short nap - resting his eyes before moving on to the next chapter. He'd never admit to falling asleep. Whatever book he was reading in the living room stayed in the living room. He had another stack of books beside his bed. He told Polly that those were there to put him to sleep. She wondered if he ever finished War and Peace. It had been in that stack as long as she could remember.

Polly looked up at the sound of the front door opening. "Hello. Welcome to Bellingwood. How can I help you?"

"Do you have a room available this morning?" the young woman asked. "I drove all night and I'm dead tired."

"We sure do," Polly said.

They worked through the process of securing a room and Polly didn't think anything of the woman's name until she offered her home address in Taos, New Mexico.

"Carter?" Polly asked.

The young woman nodded, her eyes weary and red. "You've heard?"

Polly continued typing. "The man who was killed?"

"He was my brother. I told him not to come up here. I just knew something terrible would happen to him."

"Did the sheriff's office contact you?" Polly asked.

"I'm meeting with them later today, but first I need sleep and a shower. Is there a good place to eat lunch in town?"

"Yes, there is," Polly said. She wasn't sure whether or not to tell the young woman who she was. She glanced at the registration information. Natalie Carter. "Should we call you Natalie?"

"Just Tallie," the young woman replied. "Everybody calls me Tallie."

"I'm Polly Giller."

Tallie's head shot up. "You're the one who found Ethan's body."

Polly blinked. "I am. I'm surprised the deputy or whoever you talked to, gave you my name."

"He didn't," Tallie said. "I stopped for gas before coming here and the girl behind the counter was talking about it. I didn't tell her who I was, but she told me everything. Did you really find him in a Carter cemetery?"

"Yes," Polly said. "The cemetery is old and holds the remains of two of the founders of Bellingwood."

Tallie shook her head in disgust. "He was really looking for it, then. I told him it was a fool's errand, but he didn't want to listen to me. He only saw stars and unicorns. Nothing ever comes easy or free, right?"

"Looking for what?"

"The Carter treasure. Don't tell me you've never heard about it. Surely there are Carters around here who know what old man Jedidiah did."

Polly wasn't sure what to say. "Jedidiah Carter? There's treasure? We don't know anything about this. You have to tell me what you know!" She grinned at Tallie Carter, realizing the girl had no idea what was going on in her head. "I'm sorry. It's just that I'm friends with Beryl Watson. She's a descendant of Jedidiah Carter and she's never said anything about this."

Tallie nodded. "My great, great, great, whatever grandfather was his brother, Lester."

"We wondered," Polly said. "Beryl is certain that since there are so many Carters in the world, your brother couldn't possibly be related to her."

"I'd like to meet her. Do you think that would be possible?"

"Possible is an understatement," Polly replied. "Beryl's best friend is the sheriff's wife. That should make things go a lot more smoothly for you."

"Small towns, huh?" Tallie said with a knowing grin. "Taos is about twice the size of Bellingwood. Everybody knows everybody. I get it."

"Beryl won't be able to wait to meet you, but I can hold her off while you get some sleep. I've put you in room fourteen behind me here." Polly pointed to the back of the building. "It should be quiet enough."

Tallie turned her wrist to look at a watch. "I'll set my alarm, but if you don't see me by one o'clock, would you mind calling my room? I'm supposed to be in Boone at three o'clock and I need to eat something first."

"Of course I will," Polly said. "It's nice to meet you." She picked up one of Sycamore House's brochures and scratched her cell phone number on it. "This is how you can reach me. I own both of these places. If you need anything, just call."

"Small towns." Tallie smiled, picked up her bag and walked back out of the lobby.

Polly barely waited a heartbeat after the girl had cleared the front door and dialed her phone. "Pick up, pick up, pick up," she muttered as the call rang and rang.

"Hello, my friend," Beryl said. "I'm sitting on my sofa with two snuggly kittens, doing my best to keep them quiet so they don't rip their stitches. I'll need a few bottles of wine when this siege is over. They're happy they both lived through their ordeal. All they want to do is play with each other. But Doctor Jackson said I'm supposed to keep them quiet. Does he not have kittens in his life? How in the hell am I supposed to do that? It's not like I'm the boss of them or anything. Where did he go to veterinarian school? It's like he lost all sense of reality when he got his diploma."

Polly had been tapping her fingers while Beryl worked through her monologue. Finally, she couldn't stand it. "Beryl. Stop talking."

Beryl laughed. "Well, that's rude. Why did you call me if you didn't want to hear all about my escapades with the kittens? They've become my whole life these days, you know. And it isn't like I didn't have a full and complete life before they got here. I don't have time to be distracted by two more fuzzy things, but here they are and I can't give them up now. They love me too much and they rely on me for their whole existence. I'm their jungle gym, their warm spot in the middle of the night, I make sure they have food and water and for god's sake, why didn't someone tell me that three cats made that much poop? It's like a perpetual motion poop factory in here. It never ends."

"Seriously, Beryl. Shut up."

"Okay. Shutting up. Why did you call me?"

"Because Ethan Carter is related to you and his sister just showed up at Sycamore Inn. She wants to meet you."

"Why didn't you tell me that in the first place?" Beryl asked.

Polly sighed. "I don't know. Because I'm mean, I guess."

"Yes you are. Now tell me everything." Before Polly could speak, Beryl asked. "How come you know she's at Sycamore Inn?"

"I'm working here this morning for Grey. He has something else going on and I offered to help."

"That makes sense. Now why are you still holding out on me? Talk to me, woman!"

"Aaron's office reached her yesterday."

"He what?" Beryl cried. "Whoops. Sorry. I just woke up the kittens. It's okay, little ones. Go back to sleep." In a much quieter voice, she repeated herself. "He what? He knew that there was a sister and didn't tell us? I'm going to have his head for this one. Anyway, go on."

"She drove all night because she's going to meet with him this afternoon."

"The poor girl. I hope they don't make her identify the body. His wallet was there. That should be enough. Maybe she'd rather stay at my house. No, that wouldn't work right now. The kittens and I are sleeping in the guest room downstairs while they recuperate. That way they can't tear through the house like they usually do. It's bad enough as it is." She giggled. "Sorry. Go on."

"So, she's meeting with someone in Boone today and apparently there's a treasure that her brother was looking for up here."

"A treasure? In Bellingwood? That's ridiculous."

Polly smiled at her friend. "That's what she said, too. But her brother believed it was here and she thinks he was killed because of it."

"I should probably ask what her name is," Beryl said.

"Natalie Carter."

"That's a beautiful name."

"But people call her Tallie."

"I like that even better. Now, how did you find out that they're related to me?" Beryl yelped. "Stop that. Come back here, you little brat. Just a second, Polly. May escaped and she's the one I'm worried about."

Polly sat back down in the chair and laughed. This was the craziest conversation she'd had with Beryl in a long time. Until those kittens got past this crisis in her world, she was going to be quite distracted. Polly needed to remember to thank Elise for taking care of Leia for the first couple of days after the kitten had been spayed, even if she'd run away in the middle of it. With all of the chaos during those days, Polly hadn't had time to worry about whether or not the kitten was going to be okay. Leia had just sucked it up and lived through it.

"I'm back," Beryl said. "They're in their bedroom now. Can't trust them at all. No jumping, no running, no biting, no fun. Remind me to never do this again."

Polly huffed a laugh. "Bet me. You'll do it again in a heartbeat if you fall in love with another animal."

"I'm done with that. Three cats are more than enough for one old lady. Now, what else do you know?"

"Not very much," Polly said. "She's a descendant of Lester Carter and knows about Jedidiah and Bellingwood. The poor girl drove all night to get here and was completely exhausted, so I gave her a room and I'm supposed to call her at one o'clock. She wants to get some lunch before heading down to Boone to meet with Aaron."

"That poor girl isn't meeting with him today. I'll take care of that right now," Beryl declared. "Do you think she'd like to meet me for lunch? I'd bring Lydia and you should come too. What could Aaron say to that?"

"I don't think he'd be able to say very much," Polly replied. "But I'm not sure if I can go. I promised Grey I would stay here until he got back and I don't know how long that will take."

"Call him and ask," Beryl said. "You have to eat sometime. Surely he won't be gone all day."

"Not this time," Polly said. "But if you have lunch with Tallie and I can't be there, you'll just have to tell me about it later."

Beryl thought about it. "We could do that, but I don't want to. You've been part of this since the beginning. You should know what's going on. Especially if we're going to go on a treasure hunt. You find everything."

"I only find dead bodies."

"And cars and camera equipment last time. You're our finder. Hush up, in there. Quit your whining."

"What?"

"They're going to be the death of me, Polly. Why did I let you talk me into this?"

"Into the kittens? Not my fault. And oh, by the way. You found them. I didn't."

"Please let me blame you. It makes it easier on my soul when I'm mad at them."

"Nope. Not taking that responsibility."

"Hush up. I'll be in to pick you up in a minute. You will not die in there. It's a big room and everything you need is there. Shhh!"

"Everything but you and Miss Kitty," Polly said.

"That little May makes more noise than any cat I've ever known. Especially when she isn't getting what she wants. Quite the persistent little creature."

"She's good for you."

"Uh huh. Whatever. My productivity has decreased significantly since they got here. I'm blaming you for that, too."

"It has not," Polly scolded. "I know better."

"You're a worthless friend. Will you give Tallie my phone number when you talk to her next? I can't wait to meet her. This could be a lot of fun."

"She just lost her brother, Beryl."

Beryl's voice fell. "I know that. I'm sorry. I promise to be good."

"I'll tell her. Now go give your kittens some love."

"They never get enough. They're going to suck me dry, you know."

"Good-bye, Beryl. I love you. Did that fill you up a little bit?"

"Of course it did, you silly girl. Tell her to call me and I'm calling Lydia as soon as we hang up. She won't have to meet with Aaron today unless she really wants to. She's with family now."

"Got it. Be good."

CHAPTER TEN

Polly didn't need to worry about getting away from the hotel for lunch. Aaron insisted on speaking with Tallie Carter. He needed answers and she needed to come to grips with the reality of losing her brother. Try as Beryl might, she wasn't able to change things at the sheriff's office.

It was a good thing, too. Grey called, quite concerned that he was taking up too much of Polly's day, but didn't feel that he should leave the family. Denis was going to be admitted into a facility in Fort Dodge for thirty days. It was obvious by the tone of Grey's voice that he felt he had failed the young man, yet at the same time, he knew that Denis's life was the boy's own responsibility. Polly didn't want to ask about Leslie Sutworth. She was fragile on her best days.

They needed to find someone to help at the inn. Though he hadn't said anything yet, Grey was an integral part of Denis's rehabilitation. Traveling from Bellingwood to Fort Dodge on a regular basis would be time-consuming. Her employees were part of her family and when one member needed support, the rest would step up.

Polly picked up the phone to call Tallie Carter's room at one o'clock when a tall, good-looking older man came in the front door.

"Good afternoon," she said. "I'm Polly Giller. Do you have a reservation?"

"You should find it under Darien Blackstone," he said, smiling at her.

Polly had to look down before she giggled out loud. She was ashamed of herself. His British accent and that beautiful name were almost too much for her to handle. She steeled herself while pulling his information up on the computer. "It's right here. I see you've stayed with us before. Friends or family in town?"

He continued to smile. "You could say so. I understand you are the owner?"

"I am," she said. "How did you know?"

"I've heard things about Polly Giller." He put his hand up. "All good things, though. Mr. Greyson was to assign room fifteen to me. I prefer the larger accommodations since I will be in town for several days. Is it available?"

Polly nodded. The information was already in his file. "Certainly." She swiped a pass card for him and slipped it into an envelope. "Have we met before?" she asked.

"Not formally, but it is good to meet you today," he replied. "I look forward to seeing you again." With that, he picked up the portfolio he'd set down on the counter top and turned to leave.

She watched him walk away, trying to recall where she'd met him before. Surely she'd remember someone as attractive as him, but she had no memory of someone with a British accent. She looked at the time and grabbed up the phone to dial Tallie's room.

It only rang once before the girl answered. "Hello?"

"I'm sorry to be late calling you, Tallie. This is Polly Giller at the front desk."

"That's okay. I've been up long enough to take a wonderfully hot shower. If I come up to the front desk will you point me in the way of some lunch?"

"I'd love to. See you in a bit."

Polly hung up and dialed Beryl's number again.

"Hello again," Beryl said. "What have you got for me this time?"

"Tallie is going to be here in just a few minutes for directions to the diner. Do you want to do something this evening with all of us? I'd be glad to invite her over to Sycamore House and cook a meal for everyone."

Beryl hesitated.

"If this makes you nervous," Polly said, "we can wait until later. It was just a thought."

"That's not it. I have plans." Beryl sighed. "This really couldn't have happened at a worse time, could it?"

"I don't think that death usually picks good times to happen," Polly said.

"That was terribly selfish of me. I'm sorry. There are just so many things going on right now. How am I supposed to balance it all?"

Polly laughed. "You've been balancing life for quite a few years. Is it really that out of control today?"

"It's these damned cats," Beryl said. "They put unreasonable expectations on me and don't know any better. What in the world am I supposed to do about that?"

"They're cats, Beryl. They'll figure it out."

"But what if they're lonely and miss me when I'm gone?"

"They will be lonely and they will miss you. Where are you going?"

"Just out."

That made Polly laugh out loud. "They'll get over it. They have each other and they have Miss Kitty. Now quit obsessing."

"You don't know what it's like."

"Really?" Polly asked. "I don't?"

"Shut up."

"Should I ask what your plans are for tonight?"

Beryl snickered. "You can ask, but I probably won't tell you."

"That's not very nice. You know everything about me," Polly said. "Do you have a secret love life..." She stopped talking, realizing where she'd seen Darien Blackstone before. "He's here."

"What are you talking about, crazy girl?"

"Darien Blackstone. I just met him. That's the man you wouldn't introduce to me six months ago when we saw you at Davey's. I just checked him into the inn."

The phone went dead in Polly's hand and she stared at it, a wicked grin on her face. When you don't know what to say, maybe the best thing is to say nothing. Polly thought about calling Beryl back, but decided to leave it alone. Beryl would feel guilty about hanging up on her and find a way to make it up to Polly. As for Tallie, they'd come up with a time when everyone could gather.

Polly waited. If she was going to spend many days here at the hotel, she'd need a better way to manage her time. There had to be something more she could do to keep herself occupied. She left the counter and dug around under the counters in the lobby until she found cleaning cloths. Grey had probably already wiped down the counters and table tops, but Polly assumed there wasn't any such thing as too clean. She took books off the shelves and dusted, not finding much to be concerned about.

The front doorbell rang as Tallie Carter walked in, saw Polly by the fireplace and smiled. "This is a lovely place. The fire makes this room very cozy."

"I like restoring old buildings," Polly said. "The hotel was a good decision. Are you ready for directions to the diner?"

"Didn't I see it downtown?" Tallie asked. She smiled, a little embarrassed. "I drove around before I came here, just to get my bearings. It's strange to drive into a town that you've heard about as part of your long-past history and not find dirt roads and cowboys on horseback drawing their guns."

Polly laughed. "In Iowa? You're further out west than we are."

"I know, but that's all we really knew of Bellingwood. Lester left his brothers here to start a town when Iowa was still only about twenty years old. That's a long time ago. And now the town is all modern and normal. You even have a fancy coffee shop."

"You should stop in there sometime. A friend of mine runs the bakery," Polly said. "She's amazing."

"Maybe tomorrow morning I'll go up for coffee. Could I buy you a cup? You're the only person I've met so far."

"I'd love to meet you up there. How long are you planning to stay in town?"

Tallie shrugged. "I'm flexible since I'm an artist. I finished two commissions last week and everything else can wait until I get back. But I brought my travel kit just in case I find something that desperately needs to be captured."

"You're an artist." Polly shook her head. "So Beryl Watson's name wasn't familiar to you?"

Tallie creased her brow and thought. "No, I don't think so."

"Well, she's our local artist and is rather well known, especially on the East Coast." Polly looked up and chuckled. "I think Beryl always wondered where the artistic talent came from in her family. Apparently, it flitted around the generations."

"Now I can't wait to meet her. I wish I didn't have this meeting today. It would be so fun to talk to her."

"You need to get this over with first. Beryl's a crazy, wonderful person and I think you'll love her."

Tallie looked at her watch. "I'd better hurry so I can eat before driving down to Boone. Will you be here when I come back?"

"I doubt it," Polly said, shaking her head. "However, if you'd like to have dinner with my family, we'd love to have you."

"No. Not tonight. It's been a long twenty-four hours and if I'm going to be worthwhile, I need sleep. I do my best work with at least nine hours of sleep." Tallie laughed. "Like you needed to know that. I'll talk to you tomorrow."

Polly watched her leave and turned back to her dusting. Her phone buzzed with a text and she stopped to take it out of her pocket.

"*I'm sorry for hanging up on you, but ...*" It was from Beryl.

"*That's okay,*" Polly texted back. "*I have new, fun information about Tallie Carter that I'll keep to myself until you're ready to actually talk to me again. Enjoy your secret plans.*"

There, that should mess with the woman. Polly grinned as she held the phone in her hand, waiting for it to ring.

"*You're a mean girl, Polly Giller,*" Beryl texted back. "*I'm not ready to talk to you yet because I don't want to answer your questions today. We'll wait til tomorrow for the showdown.*"

Polly read the text twice more. She didn't want things to go this way, so she dialed Beryl's number.

"I told you I'm not ready to talk."

"And I'm not going to ask you any questions," Polly said. "Your business is your business. I'm sorry if I taunted and upset you."

Beryl took a breath. "Thank you."

"But I do want you to know that Tallie Carter is an artist. I didn't ask what medium or anything like that, but when she told me that, you just had to know."

"Oh sweetie, that's wonderful. I'm looking her up online as soon as I get off the phone. I just knew there had to be more of us out there somewhere."

"You might have found your long lost sister," Polly said. "What's so interesting is that I think that branch of Carters knows more about Bellingwood's history than you all do about them. She said that she's heard about Bellingwood. How crazy is that?"

"If you have to work at the hotel tomorrow, we're coming over for coffee and breakfast," Beryl said. "I won't be able to wait much longer to hear about what she knows and I'm not mean enough to keep you out of this loop, too."

Polly opened her mouth to say something about Darien Blackstone being in the vicinity, but thought better of it. "I'd love that. When Grey comes back, I'll find out for certain what my schedule will be and let you know."

"Thanks for calling," Beryl said. "And I *am* sorry that I went away so abruptly."

"You owe me."

"Yes I do, my sweet girl. Yes, I do."

Polly smiled as she hung up. People played too many games and messed up too many relationships. She didn't have time for that silliness.

The fire was inviting and she sat down in a chair so she could see the front door. There were plenty of books on the shelves.

Maybe one would interest her. She chuckled. Walls were made for shelves and shelves were made for books. Every place she touched had bookshelves lining the walls. It almost felt like nirvana.

Grey had done the same thing Sal did when she filled the shelves at Sweet Beans. He'd gone to thrift stores and picked up boxes of books, then brought them back and sorted through them to fill these shelves. There were signs in all of the shelves inviting people to take books with them to their rooms, on their travels, and to leave books they had finished reading. The turnover wasn't immense, but some took advantage of the library and moved books back and forth.

A well-read copy of Sherlock Holmes stuck out at Polly. She took the book back to the chair, sat down and put her feet up on the ottoman. The first thing she wanted to have fixed at Bell House was the fireplaces. Well, after the floors and electricity, plumbing, new walls and everything else. But she did want to have fireplaces again. This was fantastic. The animals would love curling up on the floor in front of a roaring fire in the middle of winter.

Polly flipped through the pages until she came to "The Sign of the Four" and her phone rang.

Still looking at the book, she swiped the call open, "Hello?"

"Polly?"

"Henry, I'm sorry. I wasn't paying attention. How was lunch?"

"It was interesting."

That set her back. She closed the book and put it on the table beside her. "What does that mean? Is everything okay?"

"I'm sorry. Yes, everything is great. It was just interesting to listen to him talk about what he's done and what he needs to do if he's going to do all he wants to do with his life. This boy has big plans. Certainly a lot bigger than playing basketball."

She chuckled "I assumed that was only for the scholarship."

"You're right. He's already taken the MCATs and has applied to medical schools around the country. Now he needs to start making decisions about where he wants to go."

"And that's what he wanted to talk to you about? He wants help making a decision?"

"That's part of it. But the reason he wants help making a decision is because he's worried about his brother. If he leaves the state, he's worried that Heath will fall apart again."

"Where is he thinking about going?"

"He's looking at Pennsylvania and even Mayo in Rochester."

"To be a doctor, right? Med school?"

"Well, we talked about that. He wants to do research, too. His advisor told him that he doesn't need a medical degree to do research, but his mom always talked about him growing up to be a doctor. How's he supposed to fight that compulsion?"

Polly sighed. "His mom would feel horrible if she thought that her death pushed him along a path he didn't want to go. If she were still alive she'd encourage him to follow his heart. Her dreams and plans for him would expand to fit his desires."

"I didn't have the heart to say those things. Maybe you could talk to him." He paused. "The thing is, there is an excellent program at Iowa State and they've already expressed an interest in him."

"But there's no med school, right?"

"Right."

"You know, I'd like to think we wouldn't be stupid in the things we say to our kids, but just when we think we're encouraging them, they will probably interpret it incorrectly and we'll end up pushing them down a path they aren't interested in taking."

"Raising kids isn't going to be easy," Henry responded. "I'm glad you're doing this with me. So what have you been up to today?"

"Just hanging out at the inn and meeting the sister of the young man whose body I found. She's an artist, just like Beryl and yes, they're related - by a long distance, but they're related. And then, I met the man that was with Beryl at Davey's last summer. His name is Darien Blackstone."

"What?" Henry asked. "What man?"

"Don't you remember? She came into Davey's with a man and wouldn't introduce me to him? I called Lydia and she wouldn't tell me anything either?"

He laughed. "I have no memory of this. So is this a boyfriend?"

"How can you not remember?"

"I don't know," he said, still laughing. "It wasn't important. If Beryl didn't introduce him to us, then it was no big deal."

"But it was a huge deal to me."

"I see that," Henry said. "Who is he, then?"

"I don't know." Even though she was alone, Polly pushed her lower lip out in a pout. "He has a cool British accent and is really good looking. But Beryl hung up on me when I tried to ask about him."

"She what?"

"I know, right? She hung up on me and wouldn't talk about him."

"That is a little strange. Now that you've met him, what are you going to do?"

"Nothing. I told Beryl I'd be good. It's going to kill me, but until she's ready to tell me who he is to her, I have to be a good girl."

"That will kill you. Should I bring home ice cream sandwiches tonight to rescue you from yourself?"

"Maybe. It never hurts."

CHAPTER ELEVEN

"Let me have it!" Rebecca yelled. "He took my pen."

"Did not. You dropped it. It's mine now." Heath held the pen over his head and out of her reach, dancing around the table where they were doing homework after supper.

"Give me my pen," she demanded.

"Not gonna. You were drawing funny pictures of me. You can't have it back." He lowered the pen and waved it in front of Rebecca's face. "Possession is nine-tenths of the law." With that, he raised his hand again and took off for the other side of the table.

"Polly!" Rebecca's voice turned to a whine. "Tell him to give me back my pen."

Polly spoke under her breath. "Give her back her pen."

Henry laughed as the two of them watched from chairs in the media room.

Han and Obiwan had run to the dining room at the first sounds of excitement and were up on their back legs, trying to get in on the action.

"You're going to have to clean the bathroom," Rebecca said. "If I have to when I'm in trouble, it's your turn this time."

"I'm not in trouble," he taunted.

She ran after him, jumped up and grabbed his arm, ripping his shirt when she came back down.

Rebecca froze. "Sorry," she said. "Have you told Polly about it yet?"

Heath grabbed his shirt with the other hand, wrapped it around his forearm, dropped the pen on the table and ran to his bedroom.

Polly and Henry got to the dining room after he'd shut his door.

"What was that about?" Polly asked.

"He has a huge scar on his arm. Did he tell you about it yet?"

Polly shook her head. "You go back to work." She picked the pen up and handed it to Rebecca. "And thanks for playing with him tonight. That was pretty great."

"Yeah, up to the point where I ripped his shirt and freaked him out. I didn't mean to do anything wrong."

"I know you didn't. You were fine. It was fun to see him loosen up a little." Polly took Henry's hand. "Will you come with me?"

He nodded and the two of them walked across the living room. Polly knocked on Heath's door. "Heath, honey. Can we come in?"

"Go away."

"Not gonna," she said. "I don't have to be anywhere tonight, so I can stand here for a long time talking to you. You're aware of my tenacity, right?"

"Please just go away."

"Nope. You and I have been down this road before. I always win, remember?" Polly grinned at Henry when they heard footsteps approach the door.

Heath pulled it open and went back over to his bed to sit down. He'd changed his shirt, covering his forearm. "I'm sorry I caused trouble tonight. I shouldn't have teased Rebecca."

"You were just fine," Henry said. "There isn't enough teasing and playing in this house. That's not why we're here."

Polly sat down on the bed beside Heath and put her hand on his arm. "Let me see it," she said softly.

Pulling the sleeve up, he exposed the long, ugly scar on his forearm.

"What happened, Heath?" she asked.

"I cut it."

"On what?"

"Glass."

She traced the raised skin of the scar. "And no one thought to take you to the emergency room?"

"Nobody else knew about it. They didn't care."

"Who didn't care?" Polly asked. "Your aunt and uncle."

"Yeah. Them. And Ladd. He made me do it. Told me that a little blood couldn't hurt me."

"You cut yourself for Ladd?" Henry was livid.

"No. Not like that," Heath said. "I broke the window at the shoe store so we could get in. Ladd made me and then told me to suck it up."

Henry gulped. "Crap. You could have cut something important."

"I was fine." Heath shrugged. "I bandaged it with old t-shirts and stuff. I had to steal some antibiotic cream from my aunt. I knew I had to keep it clean, too, so it wouldn't get infected."

Polly wrapped her arm around his. "Does your brother know?"

"He just found out. He was mad at me for not telling him. He said he would have fixed me up if I'd have called him, but that was last summer. He wasn't going to come all the way back to Bellingwood just because I cut myself. And then he would have asked how I did it and things would have been a big mess."

"Oh honey," Polly said. "I'm so sorry you had to deal with this alone. It breaks my heart." She wrapped her arm around his shoulder. "Sometimes I wish we would have known you before all of this bad stuff happened to you. I would have asked you to be part of my family a long time ago."

When Heath didn't pull away, Polly continued to hold on to him. Little by little he relaxed into her until he finally sagged against her shoulder. She looked at Henry, not knowing where to go next, but desperately not wanting the moment to end.

Henry pulled a desk chair out and sat down in front of them. "I had lunch with your brother today. He wanted to talk to me about his future college plans."

Heath lifted his head, but didn't move away from Polly. "He respects you." After a pause, he continued. "So do I."

"I think the world of both of you," Henry said. "Hayden also wanted to talk about your future, especially if he goes to grad school out of state."

"I don't know what I want to do. He keeps trying to get me interested in things, but I just don't have a clue."

"Your grades have been pretty good this year," Polly said.

She felt Heath chuckle against her.

"That's because of Rebecca," he said. "She thinks she's the boss of me."

"I think she is, too," Polly replied. "But with grades like you're making right now, that will help when it comes to applying to colleges." She tapped his shoulder. "Shouldn't you be taking the ACTs this spring?"

Heath shrugged.

"Have you done anything about it?"

He shook his head.

Polly squeezed his shoulder. "You do know that when I walk out of this room, I'm looking up the dates online and then we'll have a different discussion, right?"

That elicited a grunt.

Henry laughed at them. "Son, you might as well give up. She's going nowhere."

At those words, Heath took in a halting breath and Polly turned to look at him. Tears had filled his eyes and he was trying to stop them from flowing.

"What's wrong?" Polly asked.

"It's nuh-nuh-nothing," he stammered.

Polly wanted to pull him into her lap, but he was too big. "Oh honey, I'm not going anywhere. I promise."

"Mom and Dad were supposed to still be here, too," he said and sobs wracked his body.

Henry leaned forward and put his hand on Heath's knee. "I'm so sorry. Of course you don't want to hear those words from us."

"It's okay. It just hit me," Heath said, gathering himself back together.

"Sometimes when we lose people we love, somebody else shows up to take care of us," Rebecca said from the doorway. "It might take longer than we think it should. I didn't have to wait as long as you did, but just because your parents died and my Mom died, doesn't mean that Polly and Henry are going to die." She put her foot inside the room. "Can I come in?"

Heath nodded at her and Rebecca ran across the room and hopped up beside him. She patted Polly's hand. "You made him cry. He never cries."

"I cry," Heath said, glaring at her. "Just never when there are people around. I thought you were doing your homework with your special pen."

Rebecca patted the bed and first Han, then Obiwan jumped up and circled around behind their people. Obiwan pushed his muzzle between the two kids. "I finished my homework, but you have more to do. I checked. And if you're going to have to take the ACTs, you'd better get studying on that stuff, too. No low scores for you."

Heath pulled gently away from Polly and she released him, then took his arm back in hers.

~~~

"Having a family is pretty awesome," Polly said.

Henry wrapped his arms around her and pulled her in tight. The cats were sleeping in Rebecca's room and Han had made his nest on Heath's bed, leaving Obiwan as the only four-legged creature in their bed. "You say that now when everybody is communicating and letting you love them."

She laughed. "You mean as opposed to when I want to clamp Rebecca's mouth shut and dump water on Heath's sullen head?"

"Yeah. That."

"Even then it's pretty nice," she said. "I wouldn't trade this for anything."

"Neither would I," Henry replied. "But then I get to do this, too." He ran his hand up her side.

Polly snuggled in and kissed him, then hissed when her phone rang. "What in the hell?" She rolled away and picked it up from the bedside table. It had to be an emergency for Grey to be calling her at this hour.

"Grey?" she asked.

"I've already called 9-1-1," he said, "but someone shot into two of the rooms in the back."

"Which two?" Polly already had an inkling and dreaded what he had to say.

"Fourteen and fifteen," he replied. "I heard shots ring out, but I'm pretty certain I also heard a car. It's over, so I feel as if we're safe. I'm already out the door, heading for their back doors."

Polly jumped out of bed and said, "Shots were fired at the hotel. I think it's in those two rooms I rented today. Grey's called the police. I have to go." She reached down for her jeans on the floor.

Henry leaped up as well. "Then so do I."

"Tell the kids," she said. "I'm staying on the phone with Grey."

"Miss Carter?" Grey called out. "Mr. Blackstone? Are you here? Are you okay?"

Polly waited, her heart pounding in her chest. It felt like it took forever before he spoke again.

"They're both okay," Grey said, his breathing shallow and his voice raspy.

"I'm the manager, Alistair Greyson," he said out loud. "Come with me into the main building. Hurry."

"Polly," he said. "I'm going to hang up and take care of them. Will I see you soon?"

"As soon as Henry and I can get out of here." She slipped a sweatshirt over her head and pulled a pair of boots on.

Henry came back and sat down on the bed to lace his shoes. "I talked to Heath and Rebecca. Told them to stay here and try to sleep; that we'd tell them what we knew in the morning." He looked up at Polly. "Rebecca wanted to go with us."

"Of course she did," Polly said. "She's as curious as I am."

"I'm ready," he said. "Do we need anything?"

"No. Let's just go." Polly put her hand on Obiwan's head. "Find Heath. You're staying here, too."

He sat in the doorway and watched them leave.

"Shooting in Bellingwood?" Polly asked. "At our hotel?"

Henry climbed into the driver's side of his truck. "It isn't the first time. The place tends to attract it, I guess."

"That's just creepy. Do you ever think your life would have been quieter if you'd married someone else?"

He laughed out loud. "Absolutely. But it wouldn't have been nearly as interesting."

They followed a police car into the parking lot of the hotel. Grey was outside, guiding guests who were coming out of their rooms into the main lobby. Two more police cars blocked the entrances to the hotel, their lights flashing, but sirens silent.

The police chief, Ken Wallers, approached Polly and Henry when they got out of their truck. "What's going on here tonight?" he asked.

"I don't know," Polly said. "I got the same call you did, that shots had been fired in the back. It doesn't seem like any of the guests were hurt, though. Grey said the guests from the two rooms that were shot at are okay. I think they're already inside here."

"I'll speak with him, then," Ken said. "I'd like him to introduce me to the guests."

Polly walked with Ken. "I was actually the one who checked them in today. You'll want me there to do the introductions." She put her hand on his arm. "The young woman is in town to claim her brother's body. Her name is Natalie Carter."

Ken stopped. "Aaron's case? The murder?"

Polly nodded.

"We'll do the paperwork tonight, but I'll bring him in on it tomorrow. And the other gentleman?"

"He's associated with Beryl Watson as well," Polly said. "But I'm not sure how. I don't think it has anything to do with the rest of this, though."

"So our local artist-in-residence is smack dab in the middle," he said with a grin. "She's a pip, that one. I believe that I'll be glad to pass it all off to Aaron. Just a minute. I want to give Bert some instructions."

Ken stepped away from Polly and strode across the parking lot to Bert Bradford, one of his officers.

"Are you calling Beryl tonight?" Henry asked her.

She grimaced. "Ain't no way. Can you imagine having her show up with all of this going on?"

"But she'll probably be angry with you for not letting her in on the fun."

"That's fine with me," Polly said. "It's better for her to get her beauty sleep."

Ken came back and they walked in the front door. Several of the guests jumped out of their chairs, asking questions about what was happening and if they were safe.

"Ladies and gentlemen," Ken said. "My officers are going to speak with each of you. They will get basic information and ask if you saw or heard anything that can help us learn the identity of the person who used a gun here tonight. Since only two rooms were targeted, it is our assumption that everyone else is quite safe." He looked around the room. "That is, unless you give us a reason why you might not be safe here in Bellingwood. We will be on site as we investigate and an officer will remain here throughout the rest of the night. Be assured that your safety is our priority."

He beckoned to Polly and Henry, who led him past the front counter and into Grey's apartment, where Tallie Carter and Darien Blackstone were seated at the kitchen table.

Grey took Polly's hand. "I'll see to our other guests. Thanks for coming over."

"Of course," she replied. Polly stepped into the kitchen and stood beside Tallie Carter. "Tallie, Mr. Blackstone, this is

Bellingwood's police chief, Ken Wallers. I can't imagine what you must be feeling right now, but he has some questions for you."

Tallie Carter's face was ashen. She shivered under a blanket wrapped around her body. The room was warm enough that she couldn't be cold, so it had to be shock. Darien Blackstone sat quietly with his hands clasped together on top of the table. He was fully dressed in comfortable slacks and a polo shirt. Neither had any signs of wounds and for that Polly was grateful.

"Henry and I will let you have some privacy," she said to Ken and turned to leave the room.

"Please stay, Polly," Tallie said, reaching her hand out. "I don't want to be alone right now."

"Of course I'll stay," Polly replied. She looked at Ken and he nodded.

Henry stepped back so Polly and Ken could be seated at the table.

"Did either of you see or hear anything before the shooting began?" Ken asked. "Anything at all that could point us to who might have done this?"

Tallie looked at the man across the table from her and shook her head. "I was in the bathroom, soaking in the tub. It's been a long couple of days and all I wanted was to read and relax before falling asleep. I heard the sound and started to get up and then I realized what it was. I cowered inside the tub until I heard Mr. Greyson calling my name, then I grabbed my clothes, put them on and came out. He led us here as fast as I could walk." She shivered. "I haven't stopped shaking."

Polly put her arm around the girl, trying to hold her tight enough to stop the fear from taking over.

"And you, Mr. Blackstone?" Ken asked.

"I heard a car drive in, but didn't think anything of it, this being a hotel and all. I might have thought that it was another guest coming in for the evening, but then I heard gun shots and to be honest, I didn't move. I'm lucky that the chair I was sitting in was far from a window. I don't know that I would have had sense enough to duck out of the way. Why would someone shoot at me?

I don't live in a world where people shoot at me or mine."

"I'm afraid we all live in a world where this is a possibility," Ken said. "Not even Bellingwood is safe any longer." He scrawled a few notes in his pad and took a deep breath. "I'm sure you have other rooms available tonight, Polly?"

"I do, but maybe they should come over to Sycamore House. The addition is open and I'm sure both would feel safer there."

Darien Blackstone put his hand up. "I can make other arrangements. I just need to make a quick phone call. I assume I'm free to go as I please?"

"Yes," Ken said. "Are you leaving Bellingwood soon?"

"I planned to be here for several days. My accommodations have just been adjusted, but that will work out."

Polly leaned forward. "Are you calling Beryl?"

He smiled at her. "I was planning to."

One of Ken's officers stepped in and said something into his ear. Ken nodded and said, "I'm afraid that we can't let you take your vehicles tonight, but would be glad to transport you wherever you would like to go."

"We'll take Tallie with us," Polly said. "I can drive you to Beryl's house if you like, Mr. Blackstone."

"You have enough to handle with all of this." His sweeping gesture encompassed the inn and he turned to Ken. "I would appreciate the ride. I assume I can gather my things from the room?"

Ken thought for a moment. "Take what you need. I'll send an officer with you. Miss Carter, your room took the most damage. Are there things in there that you can't live without tonight?"

"Maybe just some clean clothes," she said. "I unpacked everything into the drawers this afternoon, but I don't want to go back in there."

"I can do that for you," Polly said. She stood up. "And I'll get your things out of the bathroom. Do you have your phone with you?"

Tallie held it up. "The charger is on the desk. Can you grab that, too?"

"Of course." Polly followed Bert Bradford and Darien Blackstone out the back door and they crossed the yard to the two empty rooms. The shooter had done a bang-up job. Windows were shattered and curtains hung at odd angles, blowing in the night breeze. The two cars parked outside of the hotel in front of the rooms had taken bullets. Polly was certain that it had something to do with Tallie's brother, but why would they have wasted bullets on two rooms?

She went into Tallie's room and glanced around. The shots hadn't hit the bed or the chair or any of the furniture. It was as if the person was shooting out windows just for effect.

"Bert?" she called out.

"Yes, Miss Giller." He stood outside, between the two rooms.

"Is there anything I shouldn't take?"

"Anything in the drawers or the bathroom is good to go."

Polly opened the closet and took down a pillow from the shelf and removed the case. That would have to do for now. She shoved Tallie's clothes into the case, emptying the drawers, then went into the bathroom and filled the girl's toiletry case with things on the sink. She glanced around, picked up the phone charger and walked back out. She opened the bag, showing Bert what she'd taken and he nodded and smiled.

Tallie wasn't going to spend the rest of the night in the addition. Polly decided as she walked back to Grey's apartment that she and Henry would make room in their home tonight. The girl had dealt with far too much already; she might as well be safe with other people around. They had plenty of sofa space and as long as Tallie wasn't allergic to dogs or cats, everyone would be fine.

CHAPTER TWELVE

As soon as they could, Henry, Polly and Tallie headed back to Sycamore House. While Polly and Grey lined up accommodations in Boone and Ames for guests who weren't comfortable staying at the inn, Tallie had curled up in a chair in front of the fireplace. When Polly found her, she was sound asleep, all of the worry and stress erased from her face.

"There might be a couple of happy dogs at the top of the steps," Polly warned Tallie. "There isn't a single mean bone in their body. They'll simply want to lick you."

The girl smiled. "I miss my dog. She's staying with friends."

"What kind do you have?"

"She's a mongrel named Stella." Tallie hung back while Henry opened the door to the upstairs apartment.

Polly went up first and he gestured for Tallie to go ahead. True to form, Han and Obiwan were standing on the top landing, wagging their tails so fast that their bottoms shook with happiness.

"Come on in, Tallie." Polly pointed to the bathroom off Henry's office. "That will be yours. The kids have their own in the main

110

part of the house. You can sleep on this sofa." She stopped in the media room. "If you'd rather sleep on an air bed, we have a nice one and can get it out for you."

"This will be wonderful." Tallie sat down and moaned as she relaxed into the couch. "This will be great."

"I'll get pillows and blankets," Henry said.

Polly sat in the chair beside Tallie. "How are you?"

"I don't know," Tallie replied. "Did someone really just try to kill me? Or was I just in the wrong room?"

"It will be interesting to see what the police make of it," Polly said. "From what I understand though, they weren't trying to kill you."

"If I'd been walking in the room, the bullets would have hit me." Tallie shook her head. "I don't know what to think. Why? I only came up here to get Ethan. I didn't want him to be a nobody after he died." Her breath caught in her throat and Tallie held her breath. When she composed herself, she turned at a sound.

"These should work," Henry said. He handed Polly a sheet.

"Stand up a minute," Polly said and shook the sheet out. She and Henry draped it across the seat of the sofa, tucking it around the cushions. She opened a second sheet and tucked it in at one end and folded it back, then waited for Henry to place two pillows at the other end."

"Did you watch that show that talked about never sleeping with your head near the door?" Tallie asked.

Polly grinned. "Yes I did. I'd never thought about it before that, but I always make sure that I can see the door. There are plenty of blankets on the back of the sofa and here in a stack behind this table. Use as many or as few as you like."

Han jumped up on the chair that Polly had vacated and was tentatively putting his paw on the end of the sofa.

"Down, Han," Henry said, pointing to the floor. "We'll keep him in our room."

"It's really okay," Tallie said. "I wouldn't mind if they stayed with me, but I'm afraid I'm too wired to sleep."

"This place is locked up tighter than a drum," Polly said. "We're at the back of the house - nowhere near a road. Nobody can get in and no one will hurt you."

Tallie sat down on the sofa and patted the edge, inviting Obiwan to jump up. He obeyed and put his head under her hand. "Do you think he'd stay with me tonight?" she asked.

"That's Obiwan," Polly said. "The other boy is Han. Obiwan will stay for a while. I have no idea where he'll end up. We get up early in the morning, especially since tomorrow is a school day. I might have you move into Rebecca's room if you want to sleep late."

"Will you leave the light on in the bathroom?" Tallie asked.

"Honey, you can leave any light on that you want," Polly said. "Feel free to watch television, raid the fridge, anything. Make yourself comfortable and at home. Tomorrow's another day."

"Thank you both. It's weird that I just drove into town and am staying in a stranger's house tonight, isn't it?"

Henry chuckled. "This is Bellingwood and one of the first people you met was my Polly. Weird is just another word for normal around here. Get some sleep and we'll see you in the morning." He put his arm around Polly's waist and gave her a gentle push toward the living room.

"Goodnight, Tallie," she said.

They were almost in their room when they heard a small voice. "Polly?"

Polly looked at Henry and smiled. "Little Miss is up. You go on in. I'll be right there." She pivoted to head for Rebecca's room and rapped on the door. "Yes?"

"Is everything okay?"

"It's fine. We have a guest staying on the sofa in the media room. Her name is Tallie. You can meet her in the morning."

"Is she nice?"

"She's very nice. Now go back to sleep."

"Okay. Goodnight."

Polly pulled the door to within an inch of being closed. If the cats wanted to roam, they could push it open the rest of the way. She yawned and went into their bedroom.

Henry came out of the bathroom. "This is going to be a short night. Tomorrow will be rough."

"Thanks for being there tonight," Polly said.

"I wouldn't have missed it for the world. So what do you think is going on?"

Polly stripped her clothes back off and realized that she was still wearing her nightgown under the sweatshirt. She giggled. "I'm all ready for bed."

"Come snuggle with me until we fall asleep." Henry turned the overhead light off and crossed the room.

They climbed into bed and returned to the position they'd been in when the night began. Polly kissed his lips. "I don't know what's going on. Tallie said something about Jedidiah's treasure. If they're looking for treasure from one hundred and fifty years ago, they have to have some information as to where it is. I don't know why they'd attack her, though."

"Maybe because she's Ethan Carter's sister," Henry said.

"Whatever." A yawn wrenched Polly's mouth wide open.

"That's my sexy girl," he said with a laugh.

"Whatever," she repeated.

~~~

When Polly and Henry got up the next morning, they found Rebecca in the media room with Tallie. Rebecca had a sketch pad and was showing the older girl some of the things she'd been working on with Beryl.

Tallie stopped Rebecca. "That's Ethan," she said.

Rebecca darted a look at Polly. "You know him?"

Tallie just nodded.

"Do you want it?" Rebecca pulled the sheet out.

"Thank you. That's really nice."

Heath came stumbling into the dining room and pulled up short when he realized a stranger was in his house. He glanced at Polly in the kitchen, looked at Tallie and then back to Polly, lifting his shoulders in a question.

"Tallie," Polly called out. "This is Heath. Heath, Tallie Carter. She stayed with us last night after the trouble at the inn."

"What kind of trouble?" he asked.

"Gunshots, police and scared guests trouble." Henry patted him on the shoulder. "Put your coat on and come outside with me and the dogs. I'll tell you all about it."

Rebecca came into the kitchen. "Can I stay home today?"

"Ummm." Polly furrowed her brow. "Are you sick?"

"No, but I could spend the day with Tallie while you went to work."

Polly laughed and handed Rebecca a bowl filled with oranges, grapefruit and bananas. She nodded to the dining room table. "You'll have to do better than that."

"It was worth a try," Rebecca said, dramatically slumping her shoulders. She dragged her feet across the floor as she walked to the dining room.

"Absolutely." Polly followed Rebecca out, carrying a stack of plates and silverware. As they headed back into the kitchen, Polly put her hand on Rebecca's shoulder. "Tallie is the sister of the young man that I found out at Beryl's place last Saturday."

Rebecca's eyes got big and her mouth opened into an "O" shape. She looked at Tallie, who was drawing something. "She doesn't act like someone whose brother just died. I'm glad I gave her the picture."

"She's probably still in shock," Polly said. "Her hotel room was shot at last night. That's why she's here."

"I'd take the first bus out of town." Rebecca lifted glasses down and carried them to the peninsula. "That's a lot. So she's related to Mrs. Watson, too?"

"It seems like Beryl has a lot of family we're getting to know these days," Polly said.

The sound of paws scrambling across the floor alerted everyone to the fact that the dogs had returned. Polly had already put their food down and made sure she was out of their way.

Heath nodded at Tallie as he walked through, then turned for his bedroom.

"He's changing his shirt," Henry said quietly, tilting his head toward Tallie.

Polly grinned and was glad that Rebecca had missed that interaction. The two kids were great friends, but she wasn't yet sure how much teasing Heath could take. For that matter, she wasn't even sure how much Rebecca might dish out.

"Here," she said, flipping a cupboard door open. "Put the cereal out."

He scowled. "Cereal?"

"And breakfast sandwiches," she said, placating him. "I'll fill you up before you have to go work your poor fingers to the bone."

Henry leaned in and kissed her cheek. "You're so good to me."

"Tell Heath to hurry." Polly looked up. "Tallie and Rebecca, breakfast is just about ready. Come on over."

When Heath came back into the dining room, he'd radically changed his appearance. At least for a school morning, he had. His hair was neatly brushed and he was wearing a long-sleeve shirt tucked into his jeans, rather than his normal t-shirt under a plaid flannel shirt or sweatshirt.

"Wow," Rebecca said. "Polly needs to invite pretty girls to spend the night more often. You clean up nice."

Polly was about to interrupt, but Heath simply flipped Rebecca's hair up. "Be careful, little sis. You never know what I'll say in front of your boyfriend."

Rebecca opened her mouth, looked around at everyone, then shut it and sat down.

The oven timer dinged and Polly pulled out the last of the items to make breakfast sandwiches: English muffin halves - some buttered and others with melted cheese. She slid them onto a platter and took them to the table. "Bacon or sausage. Your choice." She took the lid off a dish. "Eggs are here. There's plenty of everything. Help yourselves."

She didn't make this very often, but when she did, Polly liked to make plenty of extras to assemble leftovers for another day. They came in handy when everyone was running late and all she had time for was popping something in the microwave.

"How long are you staying in Bellingwood?" Rebecca asked Tallie.

The girl shook her head. "I don't know. I only came up to get Ethan's remains and find out what the police were doing."

Heath had been just about to take a bite and stopped. "You're related to him?"

"His sister," Tallie said. "But since someone shot at my room and messed up my car, I guess I'll be here for a while." She stopped what she was doing. "I don't want to stay at the hotel, though. No offense. The room was really nice."

"I understand," Polly said. "We have some rooms on the other side of the house here. You can look at those and see if one would be okay. There are always other options."

"She could stay in my room with me," Rebecca said. "It's almost the weekend, so I don't have to go to bed early every night."

"I can't put you out," Tallie said. "Maybe I'll just get a hotel room in Boone."

Polly smiled. "No reason to make any quick decisions. Things always work out if we give them time.

Henry looked up at the clock on the wall. "I need to move. Can I take one of these with me?"

"Of course?" Polly looked at him in confusion. "When have I ever stopped you from taking food?"

He laughed. "Didn't want you to run out since we have a guest."

"We'll be fine," Polly said. "You get your stuff and I'll make a to-go package for you. More coffee?"

She assembled two more sandwiches for him, wrapped them in paper towels and poured coffee into a thermos. Henry came back through and she stood up to walk him to the back door.

"This is pretty awesome service," he said, stopping at the top of the steps.

"And don't you forget it, big boy. You owe me for last night."

It was his turn to look at her in confusion. Polly reached up and kissed him, wrapping her arms around his neck. She deepened the kiss and then broke away.

"Ohhhh," was all he could say.

"Like I told you, you owe me."

He grinned. "I'll pay. I'll pay. Is Tallie spending another night?"

"We'll see. I'd like her to stay with Beryl, but if that strange man is spending nights there, it's probably not an option. But I have all day to work on it."

"And that means you will have a great plan before the night arrives." Henry took the coffee and sandwiches from her and bent over to get another kiss. "Thank you."

She winked. "Thank *you*! I'll see you later." Polly watched him go down the steps and then turned back to the dining room.

"Heath says he can be late today if you want him to take me to school," Rebecca said.

Polly looked at the two of them and waited for the explanation.

"Jason is riding down with his buddy, Scar," Heath said. "They have something due this morning. If Rebecca leaves five minutes early, I have plenty of time. It's just that parking sucks, but I don't mind."

"Take your scarf if you have to walk across the parking lot," Polly said.

He gave her an agreeable nod and she chuckled. "Scarf will stay in the truck?"

"You're funny," Rebecca said. "I can't get away with that. She watches me all the way."

Polly sat back down. "You two finish up and get moving. Tallie, do you need more sleep before the day starts? I'm sure Beryl will want to meet you and once you start down that path, it will take a while."

"I'm pretty awake right now," Tallie said. "I keep thinking about that coffee shop. A caramel mocha coffee sounds wonderful." She glanced at the cup of coffee in front of her. "Not that this wasn't great." Tallie sat back in her chair. "I just keep walking into it. I'm sorry. I'm not usually this awkward."

"You're fine. Let me call Beryl and see what time she can meet us." Polly smiled as she thought about it. "You might as well take a nap, though. Beryl is not a morning person."

Rebecca looked at Tallie, put her hand over her own mouth and faked a yawn. She waited until Tallie couldn't help herself and yawned. "There," Rebecca said. "I got you started. Yawn a couple more times and then you'll start feeling sleepy."

Tallie chuckled. "You're kind of funny."

"She's a real riot," Heath said, standing up. "You about ready to go, short stuff?"

"Don't you be calling me names, lunkhead," Rebecca retorted. She stood to follow him, then turned back to Polly and Tallie. "You gotta keep these boys in line. It was nice to meet you, Tallie. I hope I'll see you later."

"I'm sure you will," Tallie replied. "I'll be around town for a few more days. Your artwork is really good. You should be proud of what you're doing. I hope you keep up with it."

"Me too," Rebecca said. "Thanks." She went into the living room and they listened as she crossed to her bedroom.

"She is really good," Tallie repeated.

Polly nodded. "She's been working with Beryl. She's gotten better, but I think most of all, it's given her confidence to try anything. I'm pretty proud of her."

Rebecca and Heath went through and waved as they left by the back door.

"You haven't eaten much," Polly said. "Can I make something different for you?"

"No," Tallie said. "I just don't feel like it. The thought of food makes me queasy."

Polly grinned. "Just a second. I might have the perfect thing." She went to the freezer, took out a small container and returned to the table. "Frozen chocolate chip cookies. They're the perfect antidote for stress and shock. Sugar and chocolate. What more could a girl want? Dunk 'em in your coffee."

"I've never done that before."

"That's just a sad state of affairs. Now is a great time to start." Polly pushed the container in front of Tallie. "You try one while I clean up. Are you sure you don't want anything more to eat?"

"This will be enough," Tallie said. "Can I help?"

"Nope. You're my guest." Polly leaned back and stretched to reach a box of small plastic bags. "I'm going to assemble the rest of these sandwiches to put into the freezer anyway. After that, all I have to do is fill the dishwasher and I'm done. Maybe by then you'll be ready to sleep. I'll spend some time in the office and let you know when we're meeting Beryl. Sound good?"

Tallie took a deep breath and blew air out of her mouth, puffing her cheeks. "I suppose so. I slept okay last night, but it wasn't very long. This has been a really weird week. I feel like things are never going to get back to normal."

"I know that feeling," Polly said. "But trust me, they always do. Either that or we adjust to the new normal. You're going to be fine."

CHAPTER THIRTEEN

Yawning at the sight of Tallie asleep on the sofa, wrapped around the two dogs, Polly shook herself. She needed to go down to the office.

"We haven't seen you for a while," Jeff Lyndsay said when she walked into the office.

Polly stuck her lower lip out. "Sorry. I'm a bad owner."

"Yes you are." He followed her into her office, shut the door and sat down. "Tell me what happened at the inn last night. Do we have a problem?"

"I don't think so," she said. "It probably has something to do with Ethan Carter, the young man I found on Saturday. His sister was staying in one of the rooms that was shot up."

He frowned at her. "Where is she now?"

"In our apartment."

"Is that safe?"

Polly chuckled. "As safe as anywhere else. The only way anyone could have known she was at the inn was by her car. I don't know where it is right now, but as long as it isn't parked here, they won't know she's with us." She nodded. "I thought about asking Beryl to take her in."

"That would put both of them in danger."

"Exactly. I don't know what to do. Henry's fine with her staying at our place, but we just don't have a lot of room up there."

Jeff chuckled. "You have the entire upper level of a school and it's not enough room. How funny is that."

"Not funny," Polly replied. "It's weird. Have you talked to Grey this morning?"

"Luckily the windows that were shot out are on the back side of the building. No one will see the damage unless they deliberately drive that way. He won't rent rooms back there until the windows are replaced and things look normal again. Before the police left at whatever ungodly hour they finished, they helped cover the windows to keep wildlife out. I've already talked to Henry. He's ordering the windows and doors. As soon as Chief Wallers gives me permission, those two rooms will be put back to normal."

"Wow," Polly said. "Thanks."

"It never surprises me," Jeff said.

"What?"

"The things you come up with to make my job interesting."

"I didn't do this! You can't blame me."

He laughed. "You're the one who found that poor boy's body. If you hadn't done that, his sister wouldn't have come to town and our hotel wouldn't have been the subject of a drive-by shooting."

"You're trying to make me feel guilty." Polly put her head in her hands.

"Can we talk about installing video surveillance out there?"

She looked up at him and frowned. "I guess."

Jeff sat forward. "No argument."

"I can't argue about this. We have to keep our guests safe. Dang, I'm tired."

"You had a short night. Do you want coffee or would you like me to close your blinds and turn the lights off when I leave?"

Polly yawned. "I'll be fine. I'm going up to Sweet Beans with Tallie later this morning. Don't worry about me."

"If you need anything, you know my number," Jeff said. When

he got to her door, he flipped the light off and pulled the door closed quietly behind him.

She dropped her hands and head to the desk and shut her eyes. "Just for a few minutes. Then I'll call Beryl."

~~~

It felt like only a few minutes had passed when Polly jolted awake. The dream was already fading, but she'd been back in early Bellingwood. This time she'd been a clerk at the local hotel when gangsters came through on their horses, shooting up the town. They'd ridden past and shot out windows, knocking plants off tables and even shattering one of the kerosene lamps sitting on the counter. She'd been in the process of patting out the small fire when something woke her up.

She tried to place the annoying sound, finally realizing it was her cell phone, but Polly couldn't find the silly thing. It had to be around here somewhere. Buzzing in the back pocket of her jeans drove through the foggy mist in her brain and she pulled the phone out.

Polly swiped the phone open. She'd been asleep for forty-five minutes. That was longer than she'd intended, but at least it was another forty-five minutes she could add to the sleep tally for the night.

Sure enough, the call was from Beryl. Polly re-dialed and waited as it rang.

"Is your ass dragging as much as mine is?" Beryl asked. "That was a hell of a night. Are you okay?"

"Good morning to you," Polly said.

"Yeah, yeah, yeah. What's up with my family and friends getting shot at?"

"They're your family and friends. You tell me."

"I certainly don't know what to think. I understand that you took young Miss Tallie back to your house last night. How is she?"

"Oh Beryl, I think she's fine. I left her upstairs with my animals to get some more sleep and I'm in my office. The poor girl has been through so much this week. But I promised to contact you and see if we could meet at Sweet Beans. Do you have time this morning?"

"Of course I do."

"What about your friend? Is he staying at your house? You can bring him along, if you'd like."

Beryl released a deep sigh. "Not today."

"You're going to have to tell us who he is. Curiosity is going to reach new heights for me."

"I know," Beryl said. "This isn't easy for me. But I promise to tell you everything when I'm ready."

"Okay. I shouldn't push. Do you want to invite Lydia and Andy to meet us for coffee, too?"

"I'll call them," Beryl said. "But Polly, I can't wait to see you. There's so much to tell!"

"About what?"

"About what I found! You won't believe it."

Polly smiled. "Then I can't wait ... and you're mean for teasing me that way."

"I practice, you know," Beryl said. "See you later. Tra la!"

Polly went back upstairs to wake Tallie. The girl was already awake, fully dressed and curled up under a blanket on the sofa with both cats in her lap.

"How long have you been up?" Polly asked.

"Not long. Did you reach Mrs. Watson?"

"Yes, and we're meeting her and a couple of other friends at the coffee shop. Do you have anything else you need to do this morning?"

Tallie shook her head. "I have to make an appointment with the funeral home to take care of Ethan, but the sheriff said they weren't releasing his body yet. Otherwise, nothing." She stopped. "Oh, I probably need to find out what's happening with my car. I have to get the windows replaced."

"And you'll want to get it detailed so that the glass is cleaned out of there. I'm sure that someone from the police will talk to you later today. All of the answers will come."

"I didn't do anything wrong," Tallie said, her voice tinged with a whine. "And now I have to spend money to get my life back together. It's not fair."

"I tell Rebecca that life isn't fair. But that doesn't help you at all, does it."

Tallie shook her head. "It's all Ethan's fault. I told him it was stupid."

"As much as I want to know what's going on," Polly interrupted her, "I think it would be best to save the story for Beryl. She'd kill me if I got this information first."

"Sorry."

"I understand that you're frustrated and want to talk about it." Polly looked at her. "Do you have other family back home?"

"Yes," Tallie said, nodding. "Mom and Dad live in Albuquerque."

"And they sent you up here to deal with your brother's death?" Polly put her hand out. "I'm sorry. It's none of my business. That was insensitive of me."

"It's okay. They can't leave home. Mom and Dad own a restaurant and then there's my sister, Beth. She lives with them." Tallie took a deep breath. "They can't leave her and she doesn't travel very well."

"I'm sorry," Polly said. "I didn't mean to pry."

"It's really no problem. I would have told you about them anyway, but it just hadn't come up yet. I'm not ashamed or anything. It's just sometimes difficult to explain."

~~~

Polly and Tallie walked into Sweet Beans, fully expecting to arrive before anyone else, but to Polly's surprise, her friends were already at a table.

"Hurry over here, girls," Beryl called out, standing and waving at them.

"Tallie Carter, this crazy woman is Beryl Watson," Polly said. "Beside her is Lydia Merritt and this is Andy Saner."

Andy looked over her glasses at Polly.

"What?" Polly asked.

The woman laughed. "I've been married for a while now, Polly. It's Specek."

"And I'm Sylvie Donovan." Sylvie slid into a seat next to Lydia.

Polly took a breath and smiled. "These are the first friends I found in Bellingwood." She sat beside Andy and gestured to the last empty chair. "I guess I should rephrase that because they found me. Everyone, this is Tallie Carter. She's Ethan's sister."

Sylvie touched Tallie's shoulder. "We are so sorry for your loss."

"Yes we are, dear," Lydia said. "If there is anything we can do to make your stay in Bellingwood more comfortable, we want to do it."

"Yeah," Beryl said mockingly. "We'll shoot up your car and hotel room just to make sure you fall in love with our little town. If that isn't enough, I'm sure we can come up with something better. Maybe we can steal your first-born, too."

"Beryl, stop it," Andy said. She swatted at Beryl.

"I'm okay," Tallie said. "Polly and her family took care of me last night, but I wish I knew who did it."

"We all do," Lydia interrupted. "Aaron wasn't happy to get that phone call this morning. He and Ken..."

"Chief Wallers," Polly whispered to Tallie."

Lydia nodded and smiled. "Anyway, he and Ken are working together on this."

Tallie looked at Polly. "Aaron? Sheriff Merritt?" Her eyes grew big. "Oh. I get it."

"Yeah," Beryl said. "We stay friends with his wife just in case he tosses us in the clink. Someone has to be around to bail us out. Especially Polly. She's bad news, you know."

Polly stood up. "I haven't had enough caffeine yet to deal with the likes of you, ma'am. Tallie, what did you want?"

"Let me get it," Tallie said. "I owe you for taking me in last night."

"No you don't."

Tallie made a stopping motion with her hand. "Let me. Sit back down. I assume they know your regular drink here?"

The other four women at the table started giggling and Polly spun on them. "Stop it."

As one, they shook their heads no. Beryl was the first to speak. "Nobody ever tells you that you can't pay. That was terrific. And yes, Tallie, they know Polly's regular drink. She says thank you, by the way. Now sit your butt down, girlie."

Polly frowned at her.

"Yes. I meant you. Sit down."

Polly sat back down and scratched her head while Tallie walked to the counter. "What just happened here?"

"You got served," Lydia said. "We all know she wouldn't have gotten away with it if you two had been alone, but it was fun to watch you flounder."

"You guys are awful. The poor girl lost her brother, drove all the way to Iowa and then had her room shot up. I could have bought a cup of coffee for her."

Sylvie put her hand on the table in front of Polly and leaned forward. "Do we want snacks? I have some things in the bakery that aren't pretty enough to be on display."

"That would be wonderful," Andy said. "May I help you?"

"No, that's fine. I'll be right back." Sylvie greeted a few customers on her way to the back room.

"This is nice," Lydia said. "All of us having coffee together. We should do it more often."

"Polly's up here all the time from what I hear," Beryl said. "All we need to do is drop in and we'll find her."

"Where do you hear that?" Polly asked. "I am not. I've been working at the Bell House and yesterday I worked at the hotel." She dropped her shoulders. "That was awful. I didn't get to come up here at all. I had to drink black coffee all day long."

Tallie put a drink down in front of her. "You didn't tell me they wouldn't charge me for yours. I gave the lady a big tip."

"Polly owns the bakery here and one of her best friends owns the coffee shop," Andy said.

"Do you own everything in town?" Tallie asked.

"Pretty much," Beryl said. "We're all worried that we're going to have to become tenant farmers just to eke out our existence."

Before Polly could respond, Sylvie placed a platter filled with muffins, scones and tarts in the middle of the table.

"Those don't look like mistakes," Lydia said. "They look wonderful."

Sylvie shrugged. "Some of them are lopsided and others didn't fit in the display. Enjoy."

"Enough chit chat," Beryl said. She shook her hands in front of her. "I have things that I need to tell you all and questions that Tallie might be able to answer. Eat your food and be quiet, okay?"

Lydia lifted a tote bag into her lap. "Pay no attention to the crazy rude lady," she said to Tallie. "Beryl's just excited."

"You bet I'm excited. I put on my big girl pants and went over to Melvin's house to get those boxes of family stuff. I started digging into them last night. Nobody has ever thrown things away. There are so many stories in here, I'm nearly busting at the seams," Beryl said. She reached into the tote bag and drew out an old, old magazine, then placed it on the table and opened it.

"Isn't this great?" she asked.

Polly nodded. "I suppose so. What am I looking at?"

"The story, you ninny."

"You want me to read it?"

Beryl huffed out a breath and rolled her eyes. "No. Just look at the author's name."

"Duke Leo Dorchester." Polly looked around to see if she was missing something. Nobody was responding. "Who is that?"

Beryl tapped the author's name several times. "That's Pearl Carter. She was Jedidiah's daughter." She reached back into the tote on Lydia's lap. "She was an authoress, but because no one thought women could do anything worthwhile, the stories she wrote were submitted and sold under a pen name." She spread photos out on the table. "That's Pearl with her father, Jedidiah."

Polly picked up the photo that Beryl indicated and passed it to Tallie.

"This picture is of the three brothers before Lester left for the West Coast. Jedidiah is on the left, Cyrus in the middle and Lester is on the right," Beryl pushed another picture to Polly. "This is Cyrus standing in front of his bank. I can't believe I have all of these things. I had no idea."

"Weren't these used during the centennial?" Andy asked.

Beryl glared at her. "That was fifty years ago. I was too young to know what we had." She took a book out of the tote, opened it and pointed to the handwritten list of numbers in columns. "I think this was Pearl's account book. There are notes all the way through about how she spent her money. That old Jedidiah was a gambler and a thief. She kept paying his debts." Beryl flipped a page. "And look at this. She writes about giving her checks to her uncle so he could make the deposit in Duke Dorchester's name. What a riot!"

"This is pretty cool," Polly said. "I can't believe you have all of this history. I know practically nothing about my family."

"My family has this kind of stuff too," Tallie said. "We have letters that Cyrus sent to Lester."

"You do? I'd love to see those sometime. We should scan things and exchange them." Beryl nearly lifted out of her seat she was so excited.

"There's a series of them where Cyrus is frustrated with his brother." Tallie nodded as she flipped through the pages of Pearl's book. "He wrote about Pearl paying her father's debts. I think he was a horse thief, too." She put the book down and slid it to Sylvie. "I'm pretty sure he robbed the bank."

Beryl had been about to say something and she stopped. "He robbed his brother's bank?" She took a breath. "Wait. Don't go anywhere. Don't say anything." Beryl took the tote out of Lydia's lap and dumped it on the table in front of her, then riffled through the papers until she pulled out a very old newspaper article. "Here it is. This was the article about the robbery, but it didn't say who the thief was. Just that they got gold."

"Hah," Polly said. "I wonder if they ever got it back. If Cyrus knew his brother stole it, surely he could force him to return it."

Tallie held her hand out for the article and Beryl handed it to her. "The letters never mentioned the gold being returned. They searched everywhere for that gold and didn't find it. Cyrus was angry because Jedidiah caused the family so much pain."

"What do you suppose happened to it?" Lydia asked.

"Cyrus thought he buried it and passed away before things died down enough for him to dig it up and spend it."

"He buried it?" Beryl asked. "Where?"

"Somewhere around Bellingwood," Tallie said. She put the article back into the center of the table. "That's why Ethan came up here. He thought he had an idea where he might find Jedidiah's gold."

"No kidding," Beryl said. "Well doesn't that just take the cake. Buried treasure in Bellingwood. How did he know where to look?"

Tallie shook her head. "I'm not sure. A few cousins looked through the letters at Thanksgiving and laughed about how funny it would be if it were really true. Ethan was elected to come up here and look around, just to see if there was any possibility it being true. He'd done a little research about the land that Jedidiah and Cyrus Carter owned and planned to look through abstracts to see if there was any other land with their name on it."

"Why didn't he ask for help from one of us?" Beryl asked.

"I don't know," Tallie said with a shrug. "I doubt that he even thought about Jedidiah's or Cyrus's descendants still living here. It really was just a lark. And then," she sighed, "it wasn't."

Sylvie spoke quietly. "Do you think one of those cousins came up with him? Maybe they're involved in his death."

"I don't know," Tallie said. "The whole thing got really big, really fast. Pretty soon everyone was talking about it. But Ethan never told us that someone else was here with him. As far as we knew, he came by himself."

"Did you tell all of this to Aaron?" Polly asked.

"Most of it. He knows about the treasure hunt."

Beryl looked at her. "Have you talked to any of these cousins since Thanksgiving?"

"No. I thought it all was absurd and told Ethan to just let it go." She shook her head. "And you know how it is with family. Once a year whether you want to or not and then if you never talk to them again, it's too soon. Thanksgiving, weddings and funerals are about all we do anymore."

"Most families don't even do Thanksgiving," Polly said.

"Tallie Carter?"

Everybody turned at the voice calling Tallie's name.

"Elise?" Polly said, standing up.

"Is it really you, Tallie?"

Tallie looked at Polly in confusion and then stood up and waited for Elise to join them. "Debra? What are you doing in Bellingwood?"

Polly took Elise's arm. "Debra, is it?"

CHAPTER FOURTEEN

"So, how do you know Tallie?" Polly asked Elise, pulling another chair over to the table.

Elise looked at the group, at Tallie and then Polly. "I. Uhhh. I."

"Dad introduced us. She used to eat at their restaurant all the time," Tallie said. "Debra bought two of my paintings." She looked at Elise. "I didn't know you'd left Albuquerque."

"Tallie is a very talented artist," Elise said. "I haven't unpacked any of my things from that time yet. It's all still in storage." She turned to the counter. "I should get my coffee and..." Elise turned back to the front door. "No, I should just go. It was nice to see you all."

Polly caught up to her. "Hey. You don't need to run off. It's okay."

"But she doesn't know who I am."

"A professor?"

"No, that I was hiding. What's she doing here anyway?" Elise shook herself. "This is just too strange. I can't even think."

"Slow down. It's okay. Tallie came up because her brother Ethan was killed. You know, the body I found? And she's some very far detached shirt tail relation of Beryl's. They're talking about family connections from when Bellingwood was founded. You're safe."

"That's all?"

Polly took her arm. "That's all. It's a crazy coincidence that you two both ended up here, but how wonderful for you to meet someone again from that life. Right?"

"Right," Elise said, clearly not ready to accept it. "She and Beryl are related?"

"I know! Can you believe it?"

Elise glanced at the table. "That's a lot of people."

"You know everyone," Polly said. "And it's interesting stuff. Tallie and Beryl are talking about a bank robbery and treasure. It might be buried around Bellingwood somewhere."

"Just for a little while." Elise let Polly take her arm and lead her to the table. "I'm sorry," she said.

Tallie patted the chair and said, "How did you get to Bellingwood and did I hear Polly call you Elise?"

"It's a long story," Elise replied. "Maybe sometime later. But yes, they know me in Bellingwood as Elise. You might as well call me that."

"Crazy." Tallie blinked her eyes. "Somehow I feel as if I've been transported into a story and I've lost control of it. I meet Beryl and find out that Jedidiah was her ancestor. Then out of the blue, someone I knew in New Mexico is here with a different name. Is it always like this in Bellingwood?"

Lydia laughed out loud. "Not until Polly moved in. We blame all of our interesting tales on her. Bellingwood was quiet and boring until she bought that old schoolhouse. We turned into the most fascinating place in the region. She finds dead bodies, drags us into wild mysteries, and now we're looking at a treasure hunt."

"We are not," Polly said, as firmly as she could. "We are not getting caught up in this. Ethan Carter was killed and then Tallie was shot at." She glared at Lydia. "Your husband would be mad at me if we did something as crazy as that. And besides, we don't even know where to start."

"Ethan's body was found at the family cemetery," Beryl said. "We should start looking there."

Andy shook her head. "That doesn't make any sense. That cemetery didn't exist when Jedidiah was alive. He would have hidden the gold some place that he could easily put his hands on it. Or at least some place that made sense to him." She pointed at the stack of things Beryl had put on the table. "Is there any record of the land that he or Cyrus owned?"

"Not in here," Beryl said. "This is only a few of the things that I got from my brother. I started looking through the first box last night." She stared at Polly, daring her to say anything. "And then I was interrupted, so I put the rest aside."

Polly looked away. She wasn't going to tell Beryl's secrets even though she had no idea what the woman was hiding.

"Maybe we should have a party at your house," Sylvie said. "I'm up for one of those. We can go through the boxes and see if there's anything more in them."

Beryl shook her head. "I can't right now. I'm sorry."

"What do you mean you can't? Is your house a mess? You know that we don't care." Lydia turned concerned eyes to her friend. "Have the kittens wrecked things? It's okay. All of that can be replaced."

"How many boxes do you have?" Polly asked.

Beryl's face had grown more and more drawn as Lydia pressed, but she smiled at Polly. "Three more and a big leather satchel filled with photographs. You have to realize that our family saved everything."

"Do you want to pack them up and bring them over to Sycamore House? We can spread out on the conference room table."

"I could do that. Maybe not tonight, but tomorrow night." Beryl looked at Tallie. "How long are you staying in Bellingwood?"

Tallie shrugged. "People keep asking me that. I don't know. I don't want to leave without Ethan, but I didn't think about how long it would take before the sheriff released his body to be cremated."

Polly sighed. "I can't believe we're doing this. Lydia, if your husband dumps me in a snowbank, it's your fault."

"Not mine," Lydia said. "Andy's. She's the one who wants to see land records."

"Hey," Andy exclaimed. Then she smiled. "You're right. I do. But doesn't this sound interesting? I'll do some digging at the library this afternoon while I'm there."

"Okay then," Polly said. "We're having a party at Sycamore House tomorrow night."

"I have another copy of the letters between Cyrus and Lester," Tallie said quietly. "I don't know what happened to Ethan's set, but when we got the call that he'd been killed, I thought maybe someone here could help me figure out why."

"Has Aaron said anything about finding Ethan's things yet?" Polly asked Lydia.

Lydia smiled. "Not to me, but that isn't surprising. You should be the one to ask him. He tells you more about the cases he's working on than he does me."

"Do we know if Cyrus's bank continued through the years?" Sylvie asked. "If it still exists, they might have some historical information, too."

Beryl sat back. "I should know this. It would have been part of the centennial." She started cackling. "Don't you just want to laugh at the craziness of this? Me! Part of an exciting Bellingwood history." She could barely contain herself. "All of those prissy little old ladies who think I'm beneath them and I'm about to prove them absolutely right. My great, great whatever grandfather robbed the bank. His daughter wrote stories under a pseudonym and we've only just begun to dig. I'm bringing bottles and bottles of wine tomorrow night. You'd better have your menfolk around to help unload my car, Miss Polly."

"Since your room was shot up at the hotel, where are you staying, Tallie?" Lydia asked.

"I don't know," Tallie said. "I spent the night at Polly's, but I can't do that to her family very long." She let out a breath. "I don't even have a car right now. I just don't want to think about it."

Polly finally came to a decision. "You can stay in the addition of Sycamore House. Elise is in one of the upstairs rooms and Camille is in the other, leaving the two downstairs rooms available. Since your car won't be parked out front, no one will know you're there. You'll be as safe as anywhere."

"That has to be really expensive," Tallie said.

"No more so than the room at the hotel," Polly said. "We'll work it out."

Andy was the first to stand up. "If I'm doing research at the library, I want to start now," she said. "I'll bring ..." Andy paused and looked at Sylvie. "It seems ridiculous to offer cookies or anything baked with this girl involved."

Sylvie shook her head. "Stop it. Bring whatever you want. Why don't I make ..."

"No," Lydia interrupted. "You bake and work all day in a kitchen. You take tomorrow night off. I'll make an enchilada casserole. Andy, you bring a vegetable side or salad. Polly, you've got dessert and Beryl is bringing wine." She looked at Elise and Tallie. "You both are more than welcome to eat with us. There is always too much food."

"If I can use a microwave, I have a great recipe for queso," Tallie said.

Elise smiled. "I won't be able to come, though this all sounds insanely exciting. I have to teach a class."

Sylvie dropped her hands on the table. "I'm bringing a loaf of my sourdough bread. Do you want to argue with me?" She grinned at Lydia.

"Nope. Not today." Lydia reached over and hugged her. "Do you remember that party we had at Beryl's house? You went to so much work with those amazing little dessert treats. And now look at you and all of this. I'm so proud." She stood up. "I need to take off, too, but I'm looking forward to spending time with you all tomorrow night. This is more fun than it should be."

"I should get back to work," Sylvie said, standing up. "There haven't been any explosions from the kitchen or desperate pleas for attention." She paused for effect. "Yet."

Beryl sat back as her friends left. "It's just us'ns now."

"That's a little scary," Polly said. Then she turned to Elise. "So ... Debra?"

"It was one of my identities," Elise said. "We had to change it twice because they thought I'd been compromised. I spent quite a bit of time in a little town between Taos and Albuquerque."

"There was some hot guy that you showed up with every once in a while," Tallie said. "What happened to him?"

Polly smirked. "Hot guy?"

Elise shook her head, her face flushed with embarrassment. "It was just the marshal. No big deal."

Tallie touched Elise's arm. "You really have to tell me what's going on. Were you in witness protection or something?"

"Yes and I'm glad to tell you about it." Elise looked up at the clock. "But I need to leave. I was going to spend this time preparing for my next class."

"I'm sorry," Polly said.

" Don't be sorry," Elise replied with a laugh. "It's fun to get caught up in someone else's mystery. But if I hurry, I can duck into my office for some last minute prep time. These kids keep me on my toes."

"Dun, dun, dun." Beryl intoned, leaning forward. "And then there were three."

"You really connected with Pearl Carter, didn't you," Polly said.

Beryl nodded. "To think that there was an independent young woman all those years ago who didn't fit into normal expectations of society. Why, I'll bet she even wore long pants when she worked outside. Such scandal!"

"It's interesting that she's also named for a gemstone." Polly creased her forehead. "How did your parents come up with your name?"

"There was another Beryl Carter. She was a great aunt of my dad's." Beryl shook her head. "I think I have a strange family. Is yours this odd, Tallie?"

"Probably. Aren't everybody's families a little odd?" Tallie smiled. "My dad's family is big. He's in the middle of nine and his father had six brothers and sisters. I have thirty-five first cousins so it's chaos when we all get together."

"You still do that?" Beryl asked.

"Every Thanksgiving. No debate. Grandma put her foot down and doesn't put up with much argument. The only way you can get out of Thanksgiving dinner is if you are in the hospital. Even then, she expects a doctor's note."

"I guess it keeps you all in touch with each other," Polly said.

Tallie rolled her eyes. "Whether we like it or not. Actually, we're pretty close. Everybody lives in the Southwest. A few families ended up in Texas and Oklahoma, but when Grandma expects us to show up, we just do."

"Did you ever contact your aunt about that family tree information?" Polly asked Beryl.

"I called her," Beryl said. "She got all judgmental about me finally paying attention to family history. Like everybody in the world wants to dig into the past. Some people do and that's great. But she more or less told me that it wasn't fair of me to benefit from all of her work if I wasn't going to participate in the work."

"I'm pretty sure that is exactly opposite of the purpose of genealogists," Polly said. "They do it because they love the search and once they put the puzzle pieces together, it's fun to share."

Beryl dropped her head and banged it twice on the table. "I'm going to visit her tomorrow. Does anyone want to ride over to Boxholm with me?"

"I will," Tallie said. "I'd love to spend the day with you."

"You would?" Beryl popped up. "That would take the pressure off. She couldn't be mean to me in front of you." She grimaced. "What am I saying? Yes, she could. She actually told my father that I was a disappointment to the family because I didn't have kids. When my second husband died, she implied that I killed him because I wasn't a good enough wife." Beryl heaved a sigh. "Family is really difficult."

"Why would anyone be that cruel?" Polly asked.

"I think families get worse as we get older. We grow farther and farther apart, living our own lives. The connections are harder to find." Beryl looked at Tallie. "You're fortunate that your grandmother insists on gathering you all together. Every year you reconnect, if only for a few hours. Now tell me more about your brother, Ethan. What kind of boy was he?"

So much had happened since Tallie arrived, Polly hadn't taken time to ask this question. Part of it was that she wasn't sure if Tallie was ready to talk about him, but the girl lit up when Beryl asked.

"He's great." Tallie stopped. "He was great. It still seems unreal. I know that I'm here because he died, so it isn't like I expect him to call me or show up on my doorstep. But..." Her voice trailed off.

"I can't imagine," Beryl said. She changed the subject and pushed forward. "Your parents own a restaurant and you have another sister?"

"That's Beth. She's the oldest, but something happened when she was born. She looks normal and can talk and interact with people, but for her it's overwhelming to be alone in the world. She can't make good decisions. Her IQ is low and she trusts everyone. She can't manage money or even know when to take a shower. But she's sweet and if you suggest the right things to do, she does them. Mom and Dad love having her at home. They redid the basement so it's like a little apartment. Beth has cupboards, a sink and a small refrigerator in the kitchen. She decorated her own living room and bedroom. It's really girly. All pinks and purples."

"It's great that your parents can take care of her."

"Beth works at the restaurant and makes some money so she can go to the movies with friends and our cousins. That's one of the nice things about having a big family around. They don't mind being her social outlet." Tallie nodded. "Ethan and I used to talk about who would get Beth when Mom and Dad died. I guess it's me now. We always used to say that we'd all move back into the house someday. If I ever get married, my husband better be prepared to help me take care of my family."

"If you ever get married, he'll know long before the wedding day what your family is like," Beryl said. "It sounds like you have a pretty good one."

"So you never had any kids?" Tallie asked.

"No. I love my nieces and nephews, but it just wasn't where I wanted my life to go," Beryl said.

"Me either! Mom doesn't understand that. If I meet the right guy, I'd happily get married, but I don't want to hurry into having children. I have too many things to do." Tallie slumped again. "Ethan wanted a big family. He couldn't wait to meet a girl who wanted a bunch of kids. He loved going to all of the family gatherings and he was like the king of the cousins."

"Was he the oldest?" Polly asked. "No, you said Beth was the oldest in your family."

"Not at all. Dad's in the middle of the crowd of aunts and uncles and we're pretty much in the middle of the ages of our cousins. There are cousins a lot older than us. But Ethan was a natural leader. He always did his own thing and if anyone else wanted to join him, that was great. The thing was, when he was just a little kid, all of the cousins waited to find out what he was going to do before starting games and stuff. If Ethan wanted to do it, then everyone wanted to do it."

"Was it Ethan's idea to look for the gold?"

"Absolutely," Tallie said. "He reached out to the first cousins and some of our second cousins, asking if anybody had information about Lester Carter coming from Iowa to the Southwest. He'd had the idea when he was in college and started collecting tidbits here and there. It was really a lark, but he thought it would be fun to go back for an anthropology degree and do a research project on the movement of the Carters from England to the American colonies and then to the Southwest. Coming up here to look for the gold was going to be fun, but at some point, he would have started looking for descendants of Jedidiah and Cyrus. It fascinated him."

Tallie pointed at the pile of information Beryl had brought. "I think this is interesting, but I have no desire to assemble it all so that it shows the family's progression. Ethan would have come unglued with all of this. Now there's no one who cares about this like that."

Beryl listened and nodded while Tallie spoke. She glanced at Polly and took a loud breath.

Polly opened her mouth to ask what she was thinking and Beryl shot out of her seat. "I need to get home to the kittens. I've left them alone too long already. Tallie, can you be ready to go at ten o'clock tomorrow? I'll pick you up at Polly's back door."

"You can really do this trip alone?" Polly asked.

Beryl sat back down. "I don't know." She chuckled and looked at Tallie. "I get lost a lot."

"I'm good with a map." Tallie held up her phone. "And we can use GPS to find where we're going. I'll be your navigator."

"See?" Beryl said. "We're all set." She stacked the papers and photographs into a pile and slid them back into the tote bag. "Would you like to take this with you?" she asked Tallie.

"I'd love to. Thanks. And then it will already be there tomorrow night. You won't have to carry it in."

"Fabulous." Beryl flung a deep green cape around her shoulders. "And now I must be off. I have places to go, people to see and things to do." She bent over and kissed Polly's forehead. "Take care of her tonight. I want her in one piece when I get there tomorrow."

"On it," Polly said.

They watched Beryl flutter out of the coffee shop and Tallie smiled. "She's something else."

"Beryl was pretty tame today," Polly said. "When she drinks wine tomorrow night, you might meet a different woman."

"Do you want another coffee?"

Polly rapped her empty glass on the table. "I'd better not. Two in one day is very bad for me."

"Oh come on. I'm buying." Tallie laughed at her own joke.

"Maybe I'll pick up some muffins for breakfast tomorrow. You go ahead and get your coffee, though."

Tallie walked away while Polly picked up the litter on the table. She carried it to the trash can by the counter and waited while Tallie and Camille chatted about coffee, then stepped aside to make a phone call.

"Hello Polly," Grey said. "How's your guest?"

"She's good. How are things over there?"

"The windows will be repaired tomorrow morning and then the girls and I will clean out the rooms and make better decisions on what repairs will be needed."

"You'll call Henry, right?"

"I've already spoken to him today. He stopped by a few hours ago, but the police were still working at the hotel."

"Will you need me to watch the front desk?" she asked.

"That's very kind of you, but they're moving Denis to Fort Dodge this afternoon and he will be unavailable to me for the first two days. I'm certain that Jeff and I can work something out by then."

"Let me know. I'm glad to help."

"Thank you, Polly," Grey said. "And now I must depart. There are three canines in desperate need of a walk."

She had Camille box up a selection of muffins and a loaf of cinnamon bread. Having a bakery in town was almost too decadent.

Tallie pressed another cup of coffee into Polly's hands. "If you really don't want it now, you should put it in the freezer."

"You're horrible," Polly said and took a drink. It was perfect. "But thank you."

CHAPTER FIFTEEN

Waiting for the kids to get home from school gave Polly time to make cookies. She pulled a baking sheet out of the oven and smiled as Kayla, Rebecca and Andrew crossed the street. Rebecca's scarf was trailing behind her and she watched Kayla pick it up twice, trying to get Rebecca's attention, but the girl was too caught up in her conversation with Andrew. Her hands were flying as she spoke, and as they got closer, Polly saw Rebecca's face was flush with excitement. Kayla finally just yanked the scarf off Rebecca, garnering a quick glance, but nothing more.

She put a plate of cookies on the counter and waited. "They're almost here," she said to Han and Obiwan. As soon as the words were out of her mouth, Obiwan ran out of the kitchen, Han following right behind him.

"I still don't care what you think," Rebecca declared when she came in the front door. "I'm not putting a wizard in that alley. It's stupid. He'd blast everything in sight and end the story."

"But it's my story ..." Andrew protested.

"Wrong. It's our story. You can't recover from this. I've said so over and over."

"I can too. Maybe there's a vampire on a fire escape that he didn't see. It can drop a cauldron on his head and knock him out so everyone can escape."

Rebecca puffed a breath out between her lips. "Like *that* would happen." She dropped her backpack on the floor beside the table.

"How long have they been like this?" Polly asked Kayla.

"All. Day. Long." Kayla put her backpack down. "I'm so tired of this comic book." She slipped out of her jacket and placed it on top of the backpack. "I'm going back downstairs to say hi to Stephanie. She was on the phone when we came in."

"Just a minute," Polly said, taking a plastic container out. She filled it with warm cookies and snapped the top on. "Take her these. We'll see you later."

Kayla ran back out of the kitchen and Polly tuned back into the argument.

Rebecca sat down at the table, her coat still on, and opened her backpack. She took out a sketchbook and flipped it open, then jammed her finger at an open spot on the page. "You have to come up with something other than the wizard. I'm not going to do it."

"Why are you being so stubborn?" Andrew asked.

"Because that's who she is," Polly interrupted. "The two of you keep your coats on and take the dogs out. I want you to pay attention to Obiwan and Han while you're outside, do you hear me? It's time to talk about a different angle for your story if you can't agree on this one. Don't fight losing battles."

"But she won't listen to me," he protested.

"I'm hearing that," Polly said. "Your friend went downstairs to spend time with her sister because you aren't involving her in what you're doing. You haven't said hello to me or even greeted the animals that are so happy to see you. Figure this out and become the kids I love before I have to do something radical."

He slumped and shook his head. "I never win when there are more girls than boys around. Come on, Han. Let's go outside."

At the magic word, both dogs ran for the back of the house. Andrew zipped his coat back up and walked away from the table, but Rebecca didn't move.

"Get going, little girl," Polly said. "He doesn't have to do this alone."

"Does he really think he never wins?"

"Yep. Boys always do. It's okay. He still loves you. Now go."

"Maybe I shouldn't be so hard on him."

"Then go apologize for acting that way. But Rebecca, if you really believe in something, don't change your mind."

Rebecca smiled. "Got it. Be nice, but be strong."

"That's my girl."

Polly sat down at the table to wait for the next batch of cookies to come out of the oven and flipped through the pages of Rebecca's sketchbook. She had no idea what story the kids were working on. Vampires dripped blood from their lips while holding down innocent, doe-eyed young girls. Werewolves stood over gory carcasses with entrails strewn everywhere. She laughed out loud. Where in the world had they gotten these ideas? Then she turned a page and discovered a hero who looked remarkably like Polly. The woman stood across a chasm filled with demonic looking faces; their hands reaching up, but never quite far enough. The staff she held was planted firmly in the ground. Where she'd walked, the world had knit back together and the demons in the chasm all wore looks of terror.

She shut the book with a grin, thrilled that they were having such fun using their imaginations. Her phone rang. She took it out of her pocket. Heath should be on his way home. Maybe he needed extra time tonight.

"Hey there," she said.

"Is this Polly?" a young girl's voice asked.

"Yes it is. Who's this?"

"It's Libby, and Heath's been hurt really bad. You have to come."

She was on her feet and heading for the back door before she could even speak. "Where are you?"

"We're down at Seven Oaks. It's all my fault."

Polly grabbed her coat and hit the back steps at a run. "What's all your fault?"

"We left school early and came out here just to talk since Mom never lets us be together."

"Okay, okay. What happened?"

Polly slammed her fist on the garage door button and ran for her truck. Her heart was racing and she couldn't think other than to get to the recreation area south of Boone.

"We went for a walk and these guys started harassing me. Heath told them to shut up and then they jumped him and beat him up. One of them cut him real bad."

"Just a minute. Don't go anywhere." Polly rolled the passenger window down and yelled. "Rebecca! Andrew! I'm leaving."

"Where are you going?" Rebecca asked, coming to the truck.

"Heath's been hurt. I'm heading to Boone. I'll let you know what's going on. Take the dogs inside."

"I want to come," Rebecca said.

Polly shook her head. "No. Please just go inside and let me deal with this. Take care of things here."

The kids backed away from the truck and she headed out. "Okay, I'm back. Have you called anyone else for help?"

"Who am I supposed to call?" Libby asked. "We're not supposed to be here."

"Does Heath need an ambulance?"

"I don't know. He won't talk to me."

"Oh god," Polly said. "Are you outside in the cold?"

"He has his coat on."

"Is he bleeding?"

"Yeah," Libby replied. "I told you that one of the guys cut him with a knife."

"Where did they cut him?"

"On his arm and his face. They kicked him a lot. In the head and in his stomach."

Polly wanted to vomit. She could barely function. "Tell me exactly where you are, Libby. I need to find you."

"Come through town to Highway Thirty."

"I know where Seven Oaks is," Polly snapped. "Where are you when I get there?"

"Well, we're not really there. We're across the highway. Heath said he knew where some trails were and we could have some privacy."

Polly's patience was nearly gone. "So you aren't at Seven Oaks?"

"Well, kinda." Libby stopped. "Wait. He's waking up. Heath. Are you okay? I called Polly."

"Libby?" Polly asked. When the girl didn't respond, she said her name again. "Libby!"

"Polly?"

She nearly collapsed with relief at Heath's voice. "Where are you? I'm on my way."

"I'm sorry. I didn't think anything like this would happen."

"I know you didn't. Just tell me where you are." Polly stopped at a light in town and tapped her toes impatiently on the gas pedal.

"It's a gravel road before you get to Seven Oaks. The truck is just off the highway. I'm so sorry."

"Sorries come later," Polly said. "Right now I want to make sure you're taken care of. Where are you once I find your truck?"

"We didn't go very far before we were jumped. Just north and east a little bit. Let me look." He groaned and Polly's heart broke.

"I can't get up to look around. They really took me down, Polly." His words slurred and she cringed.

"Don't move. Don't move at all. Let me talk to Libby."

"Yes Polly?" the girl asked.

"Make sure he's warm. I'll be there in a few minutes. If you have to take your coat off, do it. Rip your shirt if you need to so that you can stop the bleeding."

"I put my scarf on his face. I didn't want to take it back off. But it's getting really red."

"That's good. What about his arm?"

"His coat is around it. I can't get a good look."

"Okay. I'm hanging up to call 9-1-1. But I'll be there before they are. Don't you leave him. When I drive in, I'm going to yell. Just yell back and I'll find you, okay?"

"Okay."

Polly hung up and dialed the emergency number, her fingers shaking on the phone. She gave them the general location and what she knew of the incident. After hanging up, she turned west onto the highway and made one more phone call.

"Polly, don't tell me," Aaron said.

"No. It's not a body, but Heath was hurt. He's south of Boone and I'm headed his way."

"Just a second," Aaron replied, then came right back. "I see the call just came in. What happened?"

"They tell me that they were attacked by some boys. I don't have the whole story yet."

"I'm on my way. Take care of your boy and we'll figure this out."

Polly slowed, looking for the turnoff and Heath's truck. She breathed a sigh of relief when she found it the first time. Pulling into the access, she honked the horn several times, reached into the back seat for the dog's blankets and towels, got out and looked for a trail that led east.

"Libby? Heath?" she called and waited, cursing at the sound of traffic on the highway. "Libby!" Polly screamed the name, darting in and out of several trailheads leading off to the east. She stopped and thought. Heath hadn't said anything about more than one trail. It had to be the first one. Polly jogged back to the trail and ran down it, yelling their names. Finally, she heard them.

"Polly! We're here."

She was close and forced her legs to pump faster, then rounded a slight bend and pulled to a stop. Heath was crumpled in on himself, his head in Libby's lap. The girl face was streaked with tears as she huddled over him.

"Polly, you found us," Libby said through sobs that threatened to choke her.

"I'm here. Sheriff Merritt and the EMTs will be here soon." Polly knelt down beside the two, placing the blankets and towels beside Libby. He'd been cut more than just on his arm and his face. Too much blood. "Libby, I need you to stop crying and help me." Polly stood up, paced to the other side of the trail, took a deep breath and steeled herself. This was way too much blood for her.

"What should I do?" Libby asked.

"Cover him with those blankets. I have to look at his arm." Polly steeled herself and opened the slash on Heath's coat. The gash on his arm was no longer flowing. She wasn't sure whether or not she had the stomach to tie a tourniquet. Polly pressed a towel against it and cringed when Heath flinched.

"Heath, honey. Wake up. I'm here," she said.

"Polly?"

"Don't move. The ambulance is on its way. Just stay still."

"I'm cold."

"I know you are. We have blankets on you and as soon as the EMTs get here, they'll put you in a warm ambulance. You're going to be okay." The words came out of her mouth and Polly silently prayed, "God, please let him be okay."

"It hurts to breathe," he said.

Polly hoped it was nothing more than some bruised ribs. "I'm so sorry, Heath."

"My fault," he murmured.

She heard the sirens wailing in the distance and stood up. "I'm going out to show them how to get here."

"Don't leave us," Libby wailed.

"Libby, I have to bring them in so they'll get here as fast as possible. We don't want them to spend extra time searching for you, right?"

"But I'm scared. You can't leave."

Polly put her hand on Libby's shoulder. "It will be only for a few minutes."

"No. Don't go."

"I'm leaving. I know you're scared, but you have to suck it up." Polly put her fingers under Libby's chin and brought the girl's face up to look her in the eyes. "This isn't about you. It's about Heath."

Libby closed her eyes. "Okay," she said. Tears streamed from her eyes again and Polly jogged back out until she could see the entrance. She didn't have to wait long for the ambulance and another vehicle from the fire department to pull in. Two young men jumped out and walked up to her. "Miss Giller?"

"He's back here," she said.

"Show us." They followed her along the trail and rushed to Heath's side when they rounded the bend. One of the young men helped Libby extricate herself from Heath and knelt over the young man. Libby walked to Polly, but held back as she got close.

"It's okay," Polly said. "I'm not angry with you at all. Come here."

The girl wrapped her arms around Polly's waist. "I'm so scared."

"Do you know who did this?"

Libby looked at the ground.

"Libby. The Sheriff is going to be here and will ask the same questions. Do you know who did this?"

"No." She shook her head and pressed herself closer to Polly.

"You're sure?"

The girl nodded silently.

~~~

Polly sat in her truck outside the Emergency Room entrance. Libby had called her mother after worrying over what she would say. There just came a point when she had to admit that she'd been with Heath. Aaron had talked to Libby for quite a while, trying to discover who it was that had assaulted them on the trail, but she continued to insist she didn't know.

Now that the excitement was dying down, Polly took a breath and realized she needed to make some calls. Libby was huddled in on herself in the passenger seat. Even though Polly had the truck running to make sure there was plenty of heat, the girl hadn't stopped shivering until they'd reached the Boone hospital.

She swiped the first call opened and felt her muscles relax when Henry answered. "What's up?" he asked. "Need me to grab pizza on the way home?"

Polly was so glad to hear his voice she felt her throat close up and tears threaten. "Yeah. Pizza," she said.

"Polly, what's wrong?"

"I'm in Boone at the hospital."

"What happened?" he demanded.

"I'm fine. But Heath got beat up. The ambulance brought him here and I'm sitting in my truck with Libby. I figure it will take a few minutes for them to get things going and I wanted to talk to you."

"Have you been in to sign papers?"

"Yeah. I already did that. Libby's mom is coming to get her."

"Are you telling me that you don't want to talk about it with her in the truck."

"I knew you would understand," Polly gushed. "I love you."

"What do you want me to do?"

"I bolted out of there when Libby called. Rebecca doesn't know where I went."

"Okay," he said. "I've pulled over to think. What do you want to do tonight?"

"I don't know," Polly replied. "If they keep Heath overnight, I'm staying with him. I don't want him to ever think he's alone again."

"I get that. Tell you what. As soon as Kayla and Andrew leave, Rebecca and I will come down to be with you."

"That's not necessary."

"Polly, I love you, but we're a family. We're a strange family, but we are still a family. It will kill Rebecca not to be able to see Heath. Her imagination will conjure up gruesome images and a terrible tale. It's better for her to just spend some time with him. Have you called Hayden?"

"Not yet. I wanted to call you first. And we need to pick Heath's truck up."

"Let me ask Eliseo if he can ride down with us. We'll get that taken care of tonight, too. You just be with our boy and make sure he knows he isn't alone."

"I will. Henry," Polly said. "I have to go. I think Libby's mom is here."

"Stay in touch and we'll be there later on."

Polly swiped the call closed and put her phone on the console between the seats. "That's your mom, right?" she asked Libby.

"She's going to kill me."

"I doubt it. She'll be as glad as I am that you two are safe."

Libby gathered up her backpack and opened the truck door.

"Libby!" her mother said, coming around her car. "Are you really okay? Nobody hurt you?"

"I'm fine, Mom. Can we just go home?"

"I told you that you weren't supposed to be dating anyone. What do you think you were doing?"

"We were just talking, Mom. It was nothing."

"I don't know whether to be angry or relieved. Get in the car. I want to have a word with Ms. Giller."

Now Polly was nervous. An angry mother was never a good thing. She got out of the truck and walked around the front to greet the woman.

Libby's mother slammed the passenger door shut after her daughter got in and stepped up to Polly. "I told her that she wasn't supposed to be dating and now I find that not only have they been seeing each other behind my back, they're even skipping school. I'm terribly sorry that Heath was hurt, but if I were to choose any boy for Libby to spend her life with, it wouldn't be him. He may act like a nice boy, but we all know that he has problems. I don't care what you have to do. Keep him away from my daughter."

Polly reached out to try to stop the woman, but before she could say anything, Libby's mother spun on her heels, walked back around the car, got in, slammed her door and drove off.

"Wow," Polly said. "No good deed and all. And to think he went out of his way for not only Libby, but I seem to recall him rescuing you when your car broke down." She slapped the truck. "Bitch."

Walking toward the hospital, Polly took her phone back out. She didn't want to make this call, but Hayden had to know.

CHAPTER SIXTEEN

It frustrated both Aaron and Polly that they couldn't get a straight answer from Heath about who had beat him up. He insisted that he didn't know, but evaded any direct questions about their descriptions or how many boys there were.

She hadn't slept at all on the chair beside Heath throughout the night and they were waiting this morning for final paperwork to come in so they could leave the hospital.

Hayden had a basketball game this evening, but had ducked out last night with his coach's permission to come see Heath. Even he couldn't get Heath to admit that he knew his attackers.

Rebecca was shocked at the abuse poor Heath had taken, but her curiosity got the better of her and she asked him about every single bruise and scrape, inquiring about how they'd happened and how much they still hurt after several hours had passed.

Henry. Well, Henry had been silent while they were at the hospital last night. Polly knew he'd been shaken by the event. If he hated feeling helpless when *she* was attacked, this was nearly impossible for him to handle. Henry had leapt into this parenting thing with his heart wide open and his protective nature knew no bounds when it came to his kids. Heath was his son now and nobody got to do this and get away with it. She hoped that a night's sleep would help him be calmer about the whole thing.

After Heath got settled at home, Henry and Nate were going to Hayden's basketball game in Ames. Polly wanted to cancel the party this evening with her friends, but when Heath heard her talking to Lydia on the phone, he'd put his hand out asking her to listen to him. Rebecca would be home with him and Polly would just be downstairs. Lydia insisted on taking care of dessert so Polly had nothing to worry about.

Sylvie surprised them by actually taking a Saturday night off until she told them that the wedding reception at Sycamore House was just a small group. There was no music or dancing, just a light dinner, and they planned to be out by six o'clock.

The nurse came in with a clipboard and papers for Polly to sign. "Are you ready to go home, Heath?" the young woman asked.

"Yes, ma'am. Thank you." He clutched the teddy bear that Rebecca had given him. She'd decorated it with a bandage on the arm and another on its cheek.

"I'll bet you are too," she said to Polly. "Those chairs aren't very comfortable for sleeping."

"We'll all be glad for our own beds tonight."

With additional help from the nursing staff, Heath climbed into the cab of Polly's truck and after she pulled the seatbelt around him, he leaned back. "I'm glad we're going home," he said.

"Me too. Do you want anything before we leave Boone?"

He turned to her. "Like what?"

"I don't know. Ice cream at Dairy Queen?"

Heath laughed and then clutched himself. "Don't do that to me."

"It was a serious question," she said.

"If you want ice cream, go ahead. I don't feel like it."

Polly grinned. "Is there something else you'd rather have?"

"McDonald's?"

"Are you kidding me? Of course I'll take you to McDonald's."

"Polly," Heath said. "I'm really sorry."

"It isn't your fault. You don't have to apologize for getting beaten up. Especially when you were standing up for someone else."

"But I should have known better."

"Could you really have changed the outcome?" she asked.

He reached up and ran his hand through his hair, flinched and sat back again in the seat. "I don't know."

"I'm giving you a pass today," Polly said. "But you and I are going to have a serious sit-down. There's something you aren't telling me and I'd hope you know me well enough by now to realize that won't fly."

"Mmmph."

She smiled. "But you have a day's respite. I'm too exhausted to fight through this with you and you have to be a wreck."

"I'm okay."

"Yes, I understand how that works. You're the big tough boy and nothing can hurt you. I'm glad that you let me come take care of you yesterday."

He glanced at her and tilted his head.

"If you could have moved, would you have tried to get out of there on your own?"

"Of course."

"That's what I mean. I'm glad you allowed me to help. We didn't know if you had broken ribs or internal bleeding, or how badly you'd been kicked in the head. There were so many things that could have been a problem if you'd tried to move."

"But I couldn't."

She laughed and sang, "Will it go 'round in circles."

"You're weird."

"It's my best thing." Polly turned the radio on. "I'm so glad you're okay and we're heading home. We'll deal with the rest another day. Today you relax and recuperate."

~~~

"We've got this, Polly," Rebecca said. "Go take a nap. Heath's in good hands." She smirked at Heath and rubbed her hands together. "We'll take very good care of him."

The boy was exhausted from climbing up the steps and dealing with the animals. He shook his head, moaned and leaned back on the sofa.

"Let him sleep, too," Polly said. "You know how hospitals are. They're in checking on the patient every few hours. Nobody sleeps."

He gave her a grateful nod.

"We will. Now go." Rebecca made a shooing motion. "If he needs anything I'm right here. Andrew and I will just be at the table working on our comic book. We won't bother him at all."

"No arguing," Polly said. "Promise?"

"We worked that all out last night. Of course we also had to clean up the horrible mess you made when you walked out of here and left cookies in the oven."

"Whoops!" Polly laughed. "You must have done a good job. I don't smell burned chocolate at all."

"They were only a little burned," Andrew said. "We smelled them when we came back upstairs. Rebecca and I baked the rest of the cookies, too." He swatted at Rebecca. "It wasn't that bad."

Polly walked behind the couch and stroked Heath's forehead, pushing back his hair. The bandage on his cheek made him look so broken. "Rest. I'm glad you're here and safe. I'll check on you before I go downstairs. And please don't give Rebecca too much trouble."

Heath smiled and a tear formed in his eye. "Thank you for coming to help me."

She bent over and kissed his forehead. "You're welcome. I will always come for you. I promise."

Before she saw any more tears or started crying herself, Polly left the room. The cats followed, weaving in and out of her legs. Obiwan dashed for her room and jumped on the bed before she got there.

Henry was at Mikkels' new house, working on something that

needed to be finished before more crews came in on Monday. He'd asked if she needed help getting Heath home, promising that he'd be there in minutes if necessary, but they'd made it without extra help.

Polly sat down on the bed, texted Henry to tell him they were home and settled in, and that she was lying down for a nap. Before her head hit the pillow, it occurred to her that this might be another opportunity to call on Evelyn Morrow for help. It would make Polly feel better if Evelyn stopped by just to assure her that Heath was recuperating. Maybe she could even talk Evelyn into changing some of his bandages. Avoiding that would be worth nearly anything.

She slid her legs under the sheets, luxuriating in the feeling of finally being able to stretch out. Turning over on her side, she felt Obiwan lie down against her back and she reached out to stroke his fur. Luke curled up in front of her belly and Leia found a place on Polly's pillow. She was so tired that she felt none of her usual claustrophobia, but relaxed at the warmth and purrs surrounding her.

~~~

"Polly, honey. Are you ready to wake up?"

She found herself unable to move with animals packed in around her. "Move it," she muttered.

Henry picked Leia up off the pillow and deposited her on a ledge of the cat tree, while Polly made a valiant attempt to push Luke far enough away so she could twist and turn in the bed.

"Help?" she asked, pleading with Henry.

He laughed and reached in for the big cat, then planted him beside his sister. They wrapped up together on the ledge and ignored their humans.

Polly fumbled for her phone. "What time is it?"

"Four thirty. I didn't know if you needed to do anything for your evening with the girls tonight. If not, I'm sorry I woke you up so early."

"No. This is great," she said. "I've had a good nap. How's Heath?"

"Sound asleep on the sofa. Rebecca tiptoes over to check on him and then skitters back to the table so she doesn't wake him. That poor boy looks so small and young. I talked to his brother earlier today and he's coming home after the game tonight."

Polly sat up and rubbed Obiwan's back. "I'm glad. We'll take care of both of them tomorrow."

"He has late classes on Monday, so I told him to just plan on spending a couple of nights here."

"Thanks," she said, reaching out her hand. She scooted Obiwan over so Henry could sit on the edge of the bed. "I'm a little worried about leaving Heath alone this evening. With you in Ames and me..." Polly grinned. "I'm being ridiculous, aren't I?"

"Yes you are. You'll be downstairs and Andrew will be here with Rebecca. If they need you, one can run down and find you."

"I'm glad you're going to the game."

"Heath and I always have a good time together and I'd rather take him." Henry let out a breath. "We had a short conversation about me staying home tonight, but it's important to him that his brother has family at as many games as possible."

"Hayden likes having you there, too," Polly said.

"It's a strange feeling," Henry said, stroking the top of her hand with his thumb.

"What's that?"

"This family thing. Polly, last night I was so angry that someone hurt Heath, I didn't know what to do. Fortunately, Rebecca chattered about the silliest things at school while we drove down. When I saw him in that hospital bed, all beat up and having trouble breathing, I wanted to..." He took a breath. "I don't know what I wanted to do. I thought you were the only person that raised those protective instincts in me."

Polly sat forward and wrapped herself around him. "You make me so happy."

Henry chuckled and pulled back. "Because I want to do unthinkable things to people who hurt my family?"

"Well, yes. That," she said. "We all know you won't lose control, but that you want to protect our family sends a little thrill through me. You are such a good man."

"How much of a little thrill?" he asked, winking at her.

Her eyes darted to the bedroom door and then she sat back. "Andrew's here."

"I'll shut the door. They're busy in the dining room."

"We can't do that," Polly whispered. "Not in the middle of the day when everybody is awake. They'll know we're in here messing around."

Henry curled his upper lip. "I missed out on all of those years before kids came into our lives."

"Go tell them that you're going to take a nap," she whispered.

"Really?"

Polly lifted her shoulder and smiled as seductively as she could. She ran her finger around the collar of her shirt, pulling it down so he could see a little skin.

"I'll be right back," he said and jumped up, startling the cats.

In a few moments, he was back in the room, kicking off his shoes as he pushed the door closed. "What brought this on?" he asked.

"You are so amazing and I love you," Polly said, pulling her shirt over her head.

"And?"

"That has to be enough," she said. "But it also helps that I've finally relaxed after the stress of worrying about Heath. I missed you last night, too."

"The animals tried to make up for you being gone, but it just isn't the same," he said. Henry pulled her back down into the bed beside him and kissed her. "I missed this, too."

~~~

"Don't hesitate to come get me if you need anything," Polly said.

"What could we possibly need?" Rebecca asked. "You've gone

over everything four times and Heath has already had his medication. He's going to be pretty much out of it for the next few hours. You made way too much food for the three of us, especially since Heath doesn't feel like eating. We have his phone with both yours and Henry's numbers on speed dial." She looked at Andrew. "What am I missing?"

He grinned.

"Oh, of course!" she said. "You'll be right downstairs."

"Precocious brat," Polly said.

Heath had moved into his bedroom with Henry's help. Polly made sure he had water and cookies and fruit in containers on his bedside table. His cell phone was within easy reach and she'd even given him a small brass bell so he wouldn't have to summon up the strength to yell for help. Rebecca and Andrew were under strict orders to not have the television up too loud.

It occurred to Polly as she put her hand on the front door handle that she should warn Andrew and Rebecca to be good. She was leaving them alone in the house with no supervision and in the stress of the last day, she hadn't connected the dots on that one. Polly had been very careful over the last few months to make sure that there was always a third person with them. It was usually Kayla, but even Heath was conscripted from time to time. Tonight would be the first time they were truly alone since she'd caught them last fall. She could only be thankful that it hadn't been more of a problem.

A little voice in her head reminded Polly that they were junior high kids and this couldn't have been the first time they'd been alone. They were smart enough to make a way. Polly took a deep breath. She was certain that she wasn't cut out to be a mom of kids older than nine or ten years old. This other stuff was high stress.

She took one last look at Heath's bedroom. Just one more check on him. Polly walked across the living room and pushed his door open enough so she could look in. He was propped up in the bed, his head tilted to one side on the pillows. His eyes were closed and though it was obvious everything ached, he was as peaceful as possible.

"Polly?" he asked. "Are you still here?"

"Sorry. I was just checking on you before I left. Do you need anything?"

"I'm okay."

She walked on in. "Are you sure?"

Heath nodded and flinched. He touched the bandage on his face. "I was just thinking about this. Is it going to leave a scar?"

"We have an appointment with the plastic surgeon who took care of you. He did a really nice job. Yes, there will be a scar, but it will fade."

"Why would they cut my face?" he asked.

"I don't know, honey. Maybe they hated your good looks." She brushed a few stray hairs off his forehead.

"That's a laugh. It will cut into my modeling career, though."

"Are you going to tell me who did this to you?"

He turned his head to look away from her. "I told you I don't know who it was."

Polly slipped her fingers into his hand. "And I told you that we weren't done with this conversation. You can't look me in the eyes when you say that, which tells me there's more to the story. I won't stop until I find out."

"But you said we'd do it tomorrow or another day," he said.

"That's right. I did." Polly laughed and squeezed his hand. "My bad."

"Is Henry mad at me?"

She looked at him. "No. Why do you ask?"

"He hasn't said very much today. It's like he doesn't want to talk to me."

"You two have gotten pretty close, haven't you?"

"I really like him. He's cool."

Polly smiled. "Yes he is. I doubt that he even realizes he isn't talking to you. He doesn't know how to fix this. I haven't seen him this angry since the last time I got myself into trouble. He's patient and lets us live our own lives, knowing that sometimes we forget to ask for help. But when somebody else tries to hurt us, he wants to jump in and stop it. The problem is, since we don't know who hurt you, Henry can't confront them. And just about the time he's ready to deal with it, somebody from the sheriff's department or the police shows up and he has to step back." She chuckled. "I test his patience on a regular basis and now he's got more people in his life that will do that, too. If he's acting upset, it's because he couldn't stop what happened to you last night."

"I didn't mean to upset him."

"It's part of being in a family," Polly said. "Tomorrow will be a lot more normal. Hayden will be here; we'll all stay in and have a good day together. You'll see."

"Thanks for taking care of me," he said. "And for staying at the hospital last night."

She reached up and touched his good cheek. "You're our son now, Heath Harvey. And we love you." Polly patted his shoulder. "And now I'm going to get out of here before I make us both weepy. Try to get some rest and don't forget to ring the bell if you need anything." She snickered. "Hmmm, let's see."

Polly rang the little brass bell and waited. It didn't take long for the sound of Rebecca's feet in the living room to reach Heath's door.

"What are you still doing here?" she asked. "And why are you ringing the bell?"

"Just checking," Polly said. "You have a really good response time."

"So it was nothing?"

"Yep."

Rebecca put her hands on her hips. "You know the story about the boy who cried wolf, don't you

"I didn't do it," Heath protested. "It was her idea."

"You have people coming to a party in your house," Rebecca said, scolding Polly. "You should be down there to greet them."

"Yes ma'am," Polly said. She touched Heath's hand and smiled at him. "I'd hug you, but I don't want to hurt anything."

"Thank you," he whispered.

CHAPTER SEVENTEEN

"There you are," Polly said to Tallie as they met in front of the Sycamore House office. They'd moved Tallie into the back downstairs room yesterday. "How was your day with Beryl?"

Tallie laughed and rolled her eyes to the top of her head. "She's a riot. I want to be like her when I grow up."

"Did you get lost?"

"So many times." Tallie laughed uproariously. She finally took a breath. "I would tell her to turn right and she'd keep going straight so we had to turn around. Then we drove around and around before she finally had the courage to drive up to her aunt's house. And what an old biddy that woman was."

"Really bad?" Polly asked.

"But Beryl handled her. It was awesome. She had a purpose and she was going to make sure we got out of there with what she wanted. We have to take everything back soon, so when Beryl comes with the stuff, we were hoping to use your photocopier. Aunt Mildred said that we had better not lose anything or put coffee cups on it or draw pretty pictures on any of her pages. And oh, we dare not get them out of order."

Polly turned the photocopier on. "Dare not?"

"That's what she said. 'Don't you dare get these out of order. I've spent fifty years compiling this information and if you mess it up, there will be hell to pay.'" Tallie's voice changed to mimic an old lady's command. "The first thing Beryl did when we got into the car was shuffle two of the folders around. Then she asked me if I wanted to do anything to them. I decided it would be better if I didn't. I get to leave town and never deal with that old biddy again."

"Beryl won't want to deal with her ever again either. What time did you get home?"

"We were all over," Tallie said. "I was afraid I'd never see Bellingwood again. Beryl had us in Boone, in Webster City and when we ended up in Fort Dodge, I begged her to let me drive."

"Holy cow," Polly said.

"I know! We went to this great place in Fort Dodge, though. It's an old drive-in. She told me I had to eat the pork tenderloin because it was your favorite sandwich. I've never heard of anything like that."

Polly smiled. "Good for her. Did you like it?"

"It was good."

"So. Not your favorite sandwich?"

"It was good. But I couldn't finish it. She made me have ice cream, too."

"She made you?"

Tallie smiled. "I couldn't say no. If I spend much time with you people, I'm going to gain ten pounds before I get home."

"It will all be worth it," Polly said. "I promise."

"Who's that?" Tallie asked, looking out into the hallway.

Polly turned around. "Eliseo. Just a second." She stepped out of the office. "Eliseo, could you come in here a minute?"

His eyes were the only part of his face that showed his smile, but they were very expressive and lit up in greeting. "Certainly."

"Eliseo Aquila, this is Tallie Carter. She's staying in the back room on the first level. Tallie, this is Eliseo. He's my everything here. He takes care of the grounds and the large animals."

He put his hand out and Tallie shook it. "Nice to meet you," she said. "I love watching the horses play in the snow. The big one was rolling in mud this afternoon. I'll bet you love cleaning that up."

"As long as they're happy," he said. "I have plenty of help to brush them down. Welcome to Bellingwood. If there's anything I can do to make your stay more comfortable, please let me know."

She nodded and watched as he walked back into the auditorium. "What happened?"

"He was in Desert Storm."

"Oh," Tallie said. "One of my cousins was killed in Afghanistan and another lost his legs in Iraq." She dropped her head. "I'll never understand war, but I guess I understand the need to stand up for what's right. He seems like a good man."

"He's wonderful," Polly said. "I couldn't do what I do here without him."

"And Sylvie? Did I understand that she works here as well as at the bakery?"

"She's our head chef. She's in charge of anything that has to do with food - the receptions and meetings here as well as our catering. She's putting together a good team. We have another girl who works here full-time. Rachel will be around during the week."

"I met her when I came back this afternoon," Tallie smiled over Polly's shoulder.

"Hello," Sylvie said. "How are you? I can't believe you had to spend the night at the hospital."

Tallie looked at Polly in concern.

"Not me," Polly said. "My son was beaten pretty badly. But he's upstairs in bed now. They don't keep them in the hospital very long, that's for sure."

"Do you know who did this to him?" Sylvie asked.

Polly shook her head. "No. He's not saying. But I've informed him that the conversation isn't over yet, so he'd better figure out a different story." She looked at the clock on the wall. "Where is everyone? I thought I was going to be late."

Sylvie looked back toward the kitchen. "They should be coming through. Beryl caught Eliseo and asked for a handcart to bring everything in. Lydia and Andy are finishing up a few things in the kitchen. I thought we could leave all of the food in there."

"Or we could eat at the kitchen table," Polly said. "No reason to carry things back and forth." She chuckled. "For that matter, let's just spread out the work on that big table. That way we can eat all night."

Tallie moaned. "You're killing me."

"Come on. Let's stop them before they move all of the boxes too far in," Polly said. She took Sylvie's arm. "I left the two kids upstairs alone and didn't threaten them with their lives if they got out of hand."

Sylvie grinned. "Andrew is so scared of you and Henry, it's funny. He's promised me that he won't do anything. But if Rebecca ever starts something, I don't think he has much control."

"That poor boy," Polly said. "He's got no hope."

"Eliseo," Sylvie said, stopping the man in his tracks. "We're going to just take everything to the kitchen. No need traipsing through the whole building with this. Do you mind?"

He nodded. "Of course. Go ahead, I'll put this wherever you'd like."

Lydia looked up when they walked in. "Hello there. We were just finishing things up here." She watched Eliseo follow Sylvie to the back of the kitchen. "What are we doing?"

"We're going to meet in here," Polly said. "It's just as comfortable and we have access to food and wine all night long."

"Fabulous!" Beryl said, coming in from the storage room. "I'm ready to start on the wine. Did you get a delivery today?"

Sylvie nodded and pointed to the refrigerator. "The whites are already chilling." She turned to Tallie. "We have a winery in town and I'm pretty sure Beryl is their best customer. When she calls, they deliver."

"Don't be that way," Beryl said. "He told me he was bringing over a delivery for the wedding reception anyway." She smiled and hugged herself. "But they are the sweetest boys."

"The corkscrew is already on the counter," Sylvie said. "And you know where the glasses are."

Beryl snatched up the corkscrew and headed for the cooler. "If I get too smashed tonight..." She spun around. "And after the day I've had, being smashed is a great remedy. Anyway, if I get too smashed tonight, will you open up the other room for me?"

She leaned against Polly until Polly had to shift her weight so the two didn't fall over.

"I will make sure you are well taken care of," Polly said. "But maybe we start with dinner instead of drinking this evening. The food is already out on the counter."

"Party pooper." Beryl smooched Polly's cheek. "But I still love you."

Eliseo said something quietly to Sylvie and Beryl swooped in. "Are you making plans for later? Because a drunken Sylvie is a fun Sylvie."

"No," Sylvie said. "He asked me if I'd like him to take Jason out for dinner. And Eliseo, I already told Jason that I'd have dinner ready at home for him, Scar and Kent, but if you want to spend more time with them, it's fine with me. Thank you."

"Will you need help putting these boxes back into your car this evening, Mrs. Watson?" Eliseo asked.

"Heavens no," Beryl said. "If I'm too drunk to drive, I'm not taking them home and if I'm not too drunk to go home by myself, that's just too bad. I don't know what to do with it all anyway."

"We'll keep it here until you are ready to store it," Polly said.

"That might be a while. If I don't miss my guess, we're going to want some of these things for the sesquicentennial celebration this summer."

"Then I'll ask Jeff to put them in a safe place until the committee needs the information."

"But it's a jumble," Beryl protested.

Polly laughed. "What in the world do you want me to do with it, then?"

"Damn it girl," Beryl said. "I don't know. Just quit being so helpful."

Lydia handed Beryl a plate. "You need to eat something."

Beryl scowled. "No, I don't. You should have seen the food that Tallie made me eat today. She wouldn't let me leave Fort Dodge until I'd burst the seams of my pants. And I don't wear those damned skinny jeans either. I have plenty of room for these old chicken legs."

Tallie's eyes grew big as she looked around the room.

"I'm leaving now," Eliseo said as he made his way to the kitchen door. "If you need me, let me know."

"Run for your life," Polly said. "We'll try not to need you."

"Since the menfolk have gone, we might as well get this party started," Beryl said. "Last one to the table has to drink first and fast."

Nobody moved.

"I'm not kidding," she said. "Move it. Move it. Move it. Get your food on. We're not wasting time this evening. Too much to do." She gave Polly a push. "Go, go, go, go, go."

"What got into you?" Polly asked, allowing Beryl to push her toward the counter.

"I don't know," Beryl said. "It was a rough and weird day and I'm just thankful to be among friends."

The meal ended up being a much bigger deal than Polly had expected. Of course, Lydia had made fabulous chicken enchiladas, topped with melted cheesy goodness. She'd also brought a dish of Spanish rice and wasn't telling anyone what she'd ended up creating for dessert. Andy had made a Mexican corn salad with colorful bits of red onions, black beans, red and green peppers and then had sprinkled fresh basil leaves on top. She'd also brought a corn casserole, still hot from the oven. Tallie's queso dip and bowls of tortilla chips were moved from the counter to the table and Sylvie took a basket of sourdough rolls out of the warm oven.

They pushed all of the boxes and totes to the far end of the table and after everyone had taken a seat, Beryl stood up again, holding out her glass of wine. "A toast," she said. "To old friends and new, to memories we share, those we make, and stories we uncover."

"Hear, hear," the women said and tapped their glasses together before taking a drink.

The room grew quiet as they took their first bites of food.

Lydia was the first to speak. "I haven't had a chance to talk to you yet, Polly. How's your boy?"

"He hurts. When I found them last night, I was pretty scared for him." Then she laughed. "But you know me and blood. There doesn't have to be a lot of it to freak me out. And there was plenty."

"What in the hell?" Beryl asked.

"Heath was beat up by some boys last night. He was with his ..." Polly took a breath. "With a girl he knows, and apparently some boys were harassing her. He stepped in to stand up for the girl and they thrashed him. One of the boys cut his face and his arm; they kicked him and beat him. I can't believe he wasn't hurt worse than he was."

"And he doesn't know who did it?" Andy asked. "That's what Lydia said."

Polly shook her head. "He says he doesn't. But I don't believe him. We'll have further discussions about this when he's not quite so sorry-looking."

"Do you think it was those boys he got in trouble with last summer?" Sylvie asked.

"I hope not." Polly's shoulders slumped. "I'd hate to think that he'd started up with them again and was lying to me. That would destroy everything we've been building. I don't want to start all over again."

"Don't worry until you know for sure," Lydia said. "Your imagination will create much worse scenarios than reality will deliver. He's trying really hard to be part of your family. Hold on to that."

Polly nodded and sighed.

"Is Henry staying with him tonight?" Sylvie asked. "I thought I saw his truck leave."

"He's in Ames tonight with Nate Mikkels watching Hayden play ball."

Andy's eyes grew wide. "I can't believe you aren't upstairs hovering over him. I would be."

Polly looked around the table and gulped. "Should I be? Am I a terrible mom? Rebecca and Andrew are with him. He took a painkiller before I came downstairs and I figure he'd sleep most of the evening."

"Leave her alone," Lydia said, scowling at Andy. "You're just fine. You aren't the hovering kind of a mama and that's okay. You're close enough to take care of any problem that comes up and we all know that Rebecca adores him and will do any hovering that needs to be done."

"I've felt a little guilty about it," Polly said. "Henry told me not to worry and I really wanted to be here with you tonight."

"You shouldn't worry at all," Lydia said.

Polly relaxed. Lydia was her stabilizing force. Most of the time she felt confident in the decisions she made regarding Rebecca and Heath, but when something fell apart, Polly couldn't help but wonder if she'd missed something and it was really her fault.

"Enough," Beryl said. "This isn't helping her."

"What about you?" Lydia asked. "How was your day?"

"Oh lawd," Beryl said, fanning herself. "I'z plum wore out from all the excitement."

They looked at Tallie, who glanced at the ceiling.

"What happened?" Sylvie asked.

Andy smiled. "I'll bet they got lost."

Tallie burst out laughing.

"That's a yes," Andy said.

"So lost," Tallie agreed. "We were all over the place."

"But that was after we went to Aunt Mildred's house and were treated like twelve-year-old reprobates," Beryl said. "You wouldn't have known that I was a sixty-year-old woman who spent my entire adult life earning my own way. Oh no, she was dreadfully afraid that I might wrinkle one of her precious pages of information. And Tallie wasn't any safer. Because, you know, she's from New Mexico where all of those hippies live."

Tallie laughed. "She isn't wrong."

"But the old biddy insinuated that you all sit around smoking peyote in sweat lodges," Beryl said. She stood up. "I'm opening another bottle. Tell me I'm not drinking alone."

"Did you get any interesting information?" Lydia asked.

"I think so," Beryl said. "We have a lot of family tree charts. She traced as much as possible of all three brothers. Even Tallie's dad is listed." She brought a fresh bottle from the cooler. "We'll have to dig into it. Of course," she said, rolling her eyes, "we need to make copies first. Wouldn't want to damage her precious papers."

Tallie put her hand up. "I can do that after we eat while you look at some of the other things Beryl has."

"I found some interesting things at the library," Andy said. "The Carters claimed a lot of land around the area when they got here in the eighteen-sixties. And this morning I stopped at both of the banks to see which one might have been here the longest."

"It was the County Bank," Beryl said.

Andy looked at her and stuck her tongue out. "Yes it was. It was founded as the Bellingwood National Bank in 1867 by Cyrus Carter, Hiram Bell, Philip Downs, Leonard Adams, Howard Roberts and Caleb Stone." She had ticked them off with her fingers. "Whew, I made myself memorize those names."

"Is it the same building?" Beryl asked.

Andy shook her head. "No. Don't you remember back when we were kids? The bank was on the corner downtown and then they put up this new building so it would be more modern. They put that drive-through in, too."

Beryl poured another glass of wine. "Don't mind me. I'm not paying attention."

"Don't you get too messed up," Polly said. "We have a lot of work ahead of us tonight and I'm not going to do your work for you while you're sprawled across the papers all passed out and stuff."

"Can I at least drink until I'm finished complaining about nasty Aunt Mildred?" Beryl asked.

Polly laughed. "How old is that woman anyway?"

"The old biddy is close to ninety. I can't believe she's still hanging on. This one is too mean to die." Beryl snickered and then laughed because she'd snorted. "If God's waiting for her to get nice before she shows up at the pearly gates, it's a good thing he has eternity. Knowing her, she'll bounce back and forth between heaven and hell, because I think she's meaner than the devil."

"Beryl," Lydia said, using her best mother-voice.

"You don't know her. I think even you would want to trip her as she walked past you."

"She's your family."

"Yeah. Like we all don't have family members that we'd rather not claim. Don't give me that. She's a mean, dried-up old bitch who hasn't had the sense to just die."

"Beryl Watson!" Lydia said. "Stop it."

"But I'm not ready to stop it. I had to voluntarily spend time with that old witch today. I put on my best smile and my nicest, kindest face and walked into her lair. If she'd been a dragon, I'd be dragon kibble by now. Trust me." Beryl looked at Tallie. "Help me out, here. You met the woman. She's awful, right?"

"She was pretty acerbic," Tallie said.

"See. Asher. Asker. Asser. Oh whatever the hell word she used," Beryl said. "Aunt Mildred is mean. So there."

CHAPTER EIGHTEEN

Happy to clean up, Lydia and Sylvie insisted that the others dig into the boxes while they worked. Tallie offered to take the papers from Beryl's Aunt Mildred into the office and make copies, assuring Polly that she was familiar with the machine.

"Before we start," Andy said, "we should make a plan."

"Here she goes," Beryl moaned. "I haven't even lifted the top off the first box and she's ready to put labels on it. Tell me you didn't bring your label maker. That would just be embarrassing." Beryl huffed. "I'd be embarrassed for you."

Andy grinned at her friend. "You can get all huffy if you like, but these papers and pictures are too important to leave unorganized. I have felt tip pens, file folders and blank labels. We might as well make some sense of things now. Remember, only touch things once if you want to be efficient."

Beryl tapped the top of the box three times and smirked. "I'm going to need more wine for this."

"It seems to me," Andy said loudly as Beryl walked to the cooler, "that we should set up stations for different decades. If there is really over a hundred years' worth of information, we could be overwhelmed by data from the mid-twentieth century. We don't need that tonight, but it might be important another time." She opened the plastic carryall tote she'd brought in and took out a stack of three-by-five cards and a roll of tape. "I've already written out the decades on these. If you don't mind, I'll tape them up around the room. We can sort to that level first."

Beryl waggled her hand at Andy. "Do whatever you want. I'm digging for gold."

"Where do *you* want to begin?" Polly asked Beryl.

"I have absolutely no idea," Beryl whispered. "I'm so overwhelmed by this, I want to cry. If Andy weren't here to take care of me, I'd just pitch it all in the trash bin."

"Top box it is, then," Polly said, choking back laughter.

"What?" Andy asked from across the room.

"We're just trying to figure out if the boxes have any order to them. I remember my granddad and Aunt Evaline packing these boxes up," Beryl said. "I was young, but they were trying to organize their memories. Uncle Jessup had died. Yeah," she said. "It was right after his funeral. They didn't want any more memories to escape, so they sat down and wrote names on pictures and put notes in books and things. Poor Melvin. He's the oldest. Granddad sat him down and told him that he would have to take care of these things; they'd be important someday."

She scowled. "I don't know if Melvin ever moved the boxes, though. They were stuck in the back of Mom and Dad's closet. After they moved into town and he took their home, he probably never looked at them again. His poor stupid kids don't know what kind of heritage they have because he never talked about it."

"You mean a bank robber and gambler?" Tallie asked as she came over to the table.

Beryl chuckled. "Well, yeah."

"Look at this," Tallie said and put a slip of paper down in front of Beryl.

"What is it?"

"It wasn't there earlier today when your Aunt Mildred packed up these boxes."

Beryl picked the paper up, turned it upside down and then back up, flipped it around and pursed her lips. "This notepaper is from my desk, but it's not my handwriting. How did it get in there?"

"I don't know," Tallie said with a shrug. "I have no idea what those numbers mean either."

Polly chuckled. "A series of numbers. Television investigators would tell us that if it isn't a phone number it's probably latitude and longitude."

"Ah ha," Beryl said. "The secret location of the gold treasure."

Tallie produced a sheaf of papers. "Or it could be page numbers. Your aunt numbered each page in her chart and that note was tucked inside the cover."

Beryl gave her a sideways look. "You're a party pooper. Okay. Let's look through these pages and see what we can find." Then she slapped her hand down on the table. "But who in the heck went through this..." She stopped. "Ohhh. Well, damn it all to hell."

"What?" Lydia asked.

"Nothing," Beryl said. Her hands curled into fists, crumpling the paper between her fingers. She took a deep breath, looked at what she had done and slowly unclenched her fingers, dropping the paper back onto the table. With deliberate movements, she smoothed it out and handed it to Polly. "Why don't you go through these. I need to step out and regain my composure. I'll be back." Beryl grabbed up her purse and walked out to the garage.

"What was that all about?" Sylvie asked.

Polly shook her head. "Why don't you all start on the boxes and I'll sort through these pages."

"I'm going back to the copy machine," Tallie said. She chuckled. "Aunt Mildred didn't know about all of these boxes of history. She would have been apoplectic if she thought Beryl was holding out on her."

"Are you composed?" Andy asked.

Polly looked up to see Beryl stalk back in, her face red and frustration washing across her.

"What's up?" Polly asked.

"My composure has left the building," Beryl said.

"Literally?"

"Literally. No answer." She looked at her watch. "It's not even nine o'clock." Beryl's eyes grew big. "The kittens!"

Andy shook her head. "What about the kittens? They're fine. You leave them alone all the time."

"Not when it's the first week after they had surgery." Beryl stamped around the prep table. "I can't believe this. What is going on in my world? I'm a good person."

Polly put the papers down on the table and stood up. She took Beryl's arm and led her out of the kitchen. "We'll be right back," she said over her shoulder.

She opened the door to the auditorium and flipped a light on. "What's going on?"

"That man was supposed to watch the kittens tonight for me. He's not answering his cell or the house phone. And Polly, he's the only person other than me who had access to the things I brought back from Aunt Mildred's house. He's involved in all of this. I just know it." Beryl kicked at the wall. "I'm an idiot."

"Who is he?" Polly asked.

"I'm so embarrassed I don't want to tell you. I should have known he was up to something. Nobody that nice just drops into my life." She sagged against the wall that she'd just kicked. "After all of these years, I just wanted somebody to treat me like family. That's all. Just one person."

"Oh honey," Polly said. She reached over and took Beryl's hand. "Tell me what happened."

"I don't know where to begin."

"Do you really not want to tell Lydia and Andy about this?"

Beryl snarled. "They already think I'm a pathetic old fool. They have their perfect lives with their kids and grandkids. They will never understand what it's like to be on the outside looking in and wondering why nobody loves you."

Polly couldn't help it as tears filled her eyes. "Oh Beryl, but the thing is, we love you so much."

"It doesn't matter to me most of the time," Beryl said, "But sometimes it's hard to accept that my own family doesn't have time for me unless I'm doing something for them. And even then, as soon as they get what they want from me, they're off and running away."

"Beryl?"

They turned around to see Lydia standing in the doorway.

"Don't come in here," Beryl said. "I don't want you to hear all of this."

"I'm going to hear all of this whether you tell me now or you tell me later," Lydia said. "Let's just get it out now."

"You'll use this against me someday when you think I'm not doing what I should be doing."

"Come on, Beryl. You know that isn't true."

"No I don't," Beryl said with a pout.

Lydia closed the distance and pulled Beryl into a tight hug. The older woman sobbed and sobbed on Lydia's shoulder.

"That happens a lot to you, doesn't it," Polly said.

"What does, dear?"

"People cry on you."

"She has that mama-effect," Beryl said, snorting back tears.

Lydia stepped back. "We're your best friends in the world. Come in and tell us what's been going on."

Polly nodded. "It's time to tell the whole story, don't you think?"

"You know?" Lydia asked.

"No," Polly said. "I'm just starting to make some assumptions. It's her story to tell."

Beryl let Lydia lead her back into the kitchen. Sylvie and Andy looked up from stacks of things they held in their hands as they walked around the room.

"What's going on?" Andy asked. She put her pile down and stopped Beryl before she could get past. "Are you okay, honey?" Andy reached up and brushed tears from Beryl's cheeks. "Who made you cry? You aren't mad at me for organizing. You know I can't help myself."

Beryl smiled and took Andy's fingers into her own. "No. I'm so grateful for what you do, even though I insist on teasing you about it."

"That's what I thought," Andy said. "Now, who's making you cry?"

"Come on over and bring more wine," Beryl said. "I need to tell you what's been going on in my life the last few months."

"Is it a man?" Sylvie asked.

Beryl nodded and then held her glass out so Polly could refill it. "Yes, it's a man, but it isn't what you think."

"Damn," Polly muttered.

"What does that mean?" Beryl asked with a smile.

"Well, he's gorgeous and speaks with a British accent and he ..." Polly stopped and looked into Beryl's eyes. "Whoops."

"Yes. Whoops," Beryl said. "Exactly."

"What?" Andy asked.

"I need to go backwards to last spring," Beryl said. She lifted her hands and rotated them in small circles. "Have we all taken the trip?"

Lydia rolled her eyes. "Go on."

"Last spring, out of the blue, I got a phone call from a man in England. He was looking for a half-sister of his. Me."

Andy sat back. "You have a half-brother?"

Beryl pointed her long finger at Andy. "Be quiet while I'm telling this story or I'll lose my nerve."

"Okay." Andy looked properly chagrined.

"He told me that my father had been there on business." Beryl looked around. "Yes, my father traveled a lot in the sixties. It makes sense that he was there." She stopped. "Crap. It just hit me that he went back there to spend time with..." She shook her head. "That's beside the point. Apparently he and Mom worked out whatever it was. Anyway, Dad met a young woman who worked at the office where he spent a great deal of time when he was in London. And they had an affair. And she had a son. And Dad was in his life when he was a child, but then she met someone and Dad just quit being around. But even though that other man adopted him, Darien always knew that his biological father lived in the middle of the United States.

"His mother died last winter and as he was going through her things, he found notes about Dad and there were a few newspaper articles about me and my artwork. So he called me."

"How did you react?" Lydia asked.

"Honestly?" Beryl said. "My first thought was that he was trying to come up with a way for his life to be my responsibility and was going to ask for money. I was polite, but when I got off the phone, I figured it was a hoax and I'd never hear from him again. I hadn't said much. I didn't want to say very much."

Sylvie quietly asked. "What did that make you think of your Dad?"

"He's been gone long enough that, though I was shocked, what could I do? I couldn't yell at him and he was really good to Mom after this affair ended. I don't think she ever knew anything." Beryl shook her head. "Who am I kidding? It took about three weeks for me to calm down about the whole thing, but that feels like it was forever ago now. I dealt with it."

"Did he call again?" Andy asked.

"About a month later. He apologized for hitting me with all of that information and asked if we could chat online. He had some pictures he wanted to show me that would prove Dad had been around and he wondered if I had any fun pictures I could share with him. He told me how much he loved his father, but wanted to know more about his heritage. That went on for a few months." Beryl smiled, a sad smile. "It was so much fun. As we talked, it felt like I had another brother. One that wanted to hear about my life, who wanted to be proud of what I'd done. He always complimented my artwork. He was interested in the things I was working on and the places I traveled. And it wasn't threatening at all. It was wonderful."

Andy put her hand on Beryl's "What did he think about the rest of your family?"

"Well, that all came later," Beryl said. "He knew there were two other brothers, but I told him that I wasn't ready to break the news to them that Daddy had been unfaithful. And as I described them to him, he understood that and said that maybe someday they'd be able to meet him, but just having me in his life was enough. See, he was an only child. And since I feel like I am alone, we had so many things in common."

"You aren't alone," Lydia said. "You have us."

"But you have your own families," Beryl responded. She gave her head a quick shake. "That's not what this is about. Anyway, we talked all summer long and he mentioned that now that he had Dad's name and some of the other family names, he would do research in England about our ancestors. There are plenty of Carters, but you know, they all have to come from somewhere. Even without Aunt Mildred's research," she pointed at the papers in front of Polly, "I had information about Jedidiah's parents and grandparents who came over here from England. With that, Darien started digging."

"That has to be great information," Polly said.

Beryl scowled. "Yes it does. So anyway, we talked and chatted online and on the telephone." She paused. "And then one day, he mentioned that he wanted to come to Bellingwood to meet me. I didn't know what to think. I didn't want to tell anyone about him just yet. I was barely managing the fact that Dad had another son out there. What would I do if he ran into my brothers and wanted to introduce himself? And how was I going to hide him from all of you? But he pressed and pleaded and we finally set a date for him to come. He promised to just be in town for a couple of days and would stay at a hotel in Ames."

"I can't believe you took him to Davey's," Polly said.

Lydia looked at her, "Was that the night you called me?"

Polly nodded. "Uh huh. You ignored me. I knew something was up, but I just figured that Beryl was out on a date and nobody wanted to tell me about it. And then you never said anything and I thought that maybe I was losing my mind."

"We'd been all over the area that day," Beryl said. "We were starving and since it was so late when he brought me back to town, I didn't want to have to go down to Ames and then drive back. I knew where Andy and Lydia were that night, because I'd checked. They were the only people I wouldn't be able to blow off if they saw us together."

"You did check," Lydia said. "At the time I thought it was weird that you called me, but I got busy with other things."

Beryl nodded. "I couldn't believe that Polly didn't press it, but she had so much to deal with that week. Darien flew out the next day and we went back to having conversations online. Just after the first of the year, though, he asked about coming back to see me again. We set it up for this week. He said that he'd been doing more research into our family and had some fun things he wanted to show me. This time he said that he wanted to really get to know Bellingwood, especially since our family had been so integral in its early days. He was absolutely fascinated by our history."

"I loved every minute of this," Beryl said, shaking her head. "I couldn't believe someone was finally listening to my memories and talked about people that I'd only heard stories of when I was a kid." She looked around the table. "You guys just don't understand what it's like to be alone in the world. Even when you have family around." Beryl turned to look at Polly. "I'm sorry. You probably do know what it's like."

"It's okay," Polly said. "We have very different lives. But speaking of family, doesn't Darien have a wife or kids or anything?"

"He sure does," Beryl replied. "A very nice wife and two sons." She smiled that sad smile again. "I had so much fun sending them Christmas gifts. They called me that afternoon. Well, afternoon their time. We had a video chat while they showed me all of their gifts and thanked me for the things I'd sent. Girls, it felt like I was in a family again." She put her head in her hands.

"What's wrong, dear?" Lydia asked.

"His sweet family. If he's involved in this, what's that going to do to them?"

"Involved in what?"

Beryl looked up, her jaw set. "When I told him about Ethan's death, he wasn't shocked or surprised. He didn't ask many questions about it. Now that I think about it, it's like he already knew it had happened. He didn't even try to fake it. When his room got shot up, he wasn't upset about that either. He just took it in stride."

"Maybe he's got that British stiff upper lip thing going," Sylvie said.

"I don't think so," Beryl said. "He knows more about this search for the gold than he's letting on. Please tell me that it isn't an extreme coincidence that he's here during the same time as Tallie's brother was here."

Polly glanced around to see if Tallie was anywhere near. "You don't think he had anything to do with Ethan's death, do you?"

"I hope not," Beryl replied. "But he knows something." She sighed. "He encouraged me to go out to the studio this afternoon when we got back. Said he'd had fun with the kittens all day and was just going to take a nap on the sofa. So I went. That's probably when he started digging through the things Aunt Mildred sent with me."

"Now tell us why you're so upset with him tonight?" Lydia asked.

"Because he's not answering his phone. And I gave him a bunch of cash today." Her shoulders slumped.

"You what?" Andy was livid.

"There were some things he wanted to do and he wondered if I would collect some cash for him. He wrote me a check." She tried to smile. "You know they spell that with a 'q-u-e' right?"

"Have you tried to cash the check yet?"

"No," Beryl said. "Since it's international, I'll take it in on Monday. They have to wait for funds to clear before it goes into my account."

"Well, how much was it?"

"Andy," Lydia said softly. "Don't."

"But he might be stealing from her."

Lydia nodded. "That's not your business. It's Beryl's."

"It was five hundred dollars," Beryl said. "It won't break me."

"But it gives him freedom to move around without leaving a

paper trail," Sylvie said. When everyone looked at her, she laughed. "Law enforcement always finds people by tracking their credit cards. If he wants to be off the grid, he needs cash."

"What's he doing about a car if his was shot up?" Polly asked.

"We dealt with that yesterday," Beryl replied. "He'd taken out insurance, so they'll handle it after the police are finished. He rented another car."

"You ladies aren't getting much done in here," Tallie said, causing everyone to turn and look at her. "What? I'm done with my part." She realized they were still looking. "What's wrong? Something bad happened, didn't it. Did you find something?"

Polly stood up and walked over to her. "Tallie, did a British guy ever call you or your brother and ask about your family's history?"

Tallie put the stack of copied papers onto the counter. Slowly nodding, she walked with Polly across the room. "Now that you mention it, I think somebody did. Yeah. That's right. Ethan thought it was cool that a guy from England might have information about the Carters before they came to America. He was telling everybody about it at Thanksgiving. I can't believe I forgot." She grimaced. "I didn't pay much attention to him. Why?"

"We think it's the man who was in the room next to yours at the hotel," Polly said. "He's a relative of Beryl's."

"Really?" Tallie said. "That crazy! We were right next door to each other and didn't even know it?"

"Do you have any idea whether or not your brother told him about the letters?" Polly asked.

Tallie grinned. "Probably. He told everybody. Ethan would have thought that was cool."

Everyone jumped at the sound of a door opening. Polly stood up, on guard. The main doors should have all been locked down when Eliseo left.

She relaxed when Henry walked into the kitchen.

"What do we have here?" He looked at the empty wine bottles. "You've only done a little damage. I was expecting it to be much, much worse."

"How was the game?" Polly asked him.

"We won. Hayden's a good ball handler. Have you talked to the kids upstairs? How's Heath?"

Polly looked guiltily around the room at her friends. "I assume everything is okay. But I haven't checked. We kind of got busy here."

He chuckled. "Of course you did. Hayden should be here after a bit. I'll make sure they're all still alive upstairs."

"I'm a horrible mom," Polly said, sitting back down. "I can't believe I forgot about them."

"No you're not, dear." Lydia reached over and rubbed her shoulders. "You're just fine."

Beryl looked at the clock on the wall. "Damn it. I can't stay here any longer. If he isn't there to take care of my kitties, I don't know how they're doing." She glared at Andy. "Don't you dare give me any trouble about that, either."

"I won't. I promise," Andy said. "But what should we do with all of this?"

Polly looked around. They hadn't unpacked that much yet. "Pack it back up and I'll ask Hayden and Henry to haul it into my office tomorrow. We'll deal with it another day."

"That's good," Tallie said, dropping into a chair. "I'm beat. Tell me I don't have anything to do tomorrow."

"If that jerk has left my house, I might invite you to come stay with me," Beryl said. "I'd love to have you, but with him there, I wasn't ready to add someone else."

Tallie glanced at Polly, who smiled and nodded. " I'd love that," she said. "And I'd love to see your kitties." Then she took a breath. "And your studio. I really want to spend time in your studio."

Beryl nodded. "We'll have lunch and go from there."

"What if he's still there and his phone was just off?" Andy asked.

"Then he's moving to a hotel room," Beryl said firmly. "I'm done with him." She smiled. "Unless he can prove that he's an innocent bystander. Okay girls, let's clean this mess up. I have kitties who need their mama."

CHAPTER NINETEEN

By the time Polly woke up Sunday morning, breakfast had already been started. Whenever Hayden came to visit, she made sure to have plenty of breakfast food in the house. He loved cooking for them.

She'd come upstairs last night to find Rebecca and Andrew sound asleep on the couches in the living room, with Heath's door open wide so they could hear if he needed them. Heath was awake and watching something on his phone when she walked in. They'd talked for a few minutes about his pain and the fact that Hayden would be there soon, then she woke the kids and sent Andrew downstairs to his mother. Henry took the dogs out for a last walk and when he came back upstairs, Hayden was with him. He'd been nice enough, but it was obvious that all he wanted to do was see his brother.

Heath wanted to be part of the activity, so after she made sure he had his pain medication, they'd pulled chairs into his bedroom and stayed up talking. Polly had finally insisted that it was time to sleep, so they blew up the air bed for Hayden and she sent Rebecca to bed.

She rolled over in bed and stretched her legs, pushing against Luke's dead weight. The dogs were gone from the room, meaning Henry had gotten up and taken them out. For a man who hadn't grown up with pets, he loved these animals. The door to her bedroom was open just enough that she could hear voices in the house. What a wonderful way to spend a Sunday morning. It was hard to believe that this was her family. After the conversation with her friends last night, Polly realized that she didn't feel what Beryl felt. She'd grown up as an only child, with no real cousins or relatives so she'd made her family from within her circle of friends. Mary Shore, the woman who raised Polly after her mother died was as much family as anyone. Her husband, Sylvester, had worked for Polly's dad as long as she could remember. There was never a Christmas or holiday when they weren't at her family's table.

Sal was like Polly's sister. They spit and spat at each other, but that didn't change how they felt about the other one. And now that Polly lived in Bellingwood, her family had exploded. It was wonderful, but it was interesting that Beryl didn't approach her friendships that way. The poor woman had been burned too many times by the people who should have supported her. It made no sense to Polly that they couldn't see how absolutely intriguing and fascinating Beryl was. She also couldn't understand that they didn't see just how much Beryl needed them.

Polly looked up at the tap on her door.

"Come on in, Rebecca. I'm surprised to see you up and moving this morning," Polly said.

"Breakfast is ready any time." Rebecca walked in and handed a cup of coffee to her. "Do you want pancakes?"

"This is amazing service," Polly said. "Thank you. Now what is it you want?"

"Nothing. Hayden told me to bring it in when I woke you up."

"Hayden is a good boy. Give me three minutes to put some clothes on and I'll be right there."

Rebecca headed for the door and turned around. "So. Pancakes?"

"Yes please."

Polly waited for Rebecca to shut the door and dashed around getting ready for the day. As she pulled her bra on, she laughed. There once was a time when she didn't have to abuse herself like that on Sundays. Henry hadn't cared. Actually, Henry had enjoyed it. But those days were long gone. She sighed and picked up her phone and found that she had a text from Beryl asking if she could bring Tallie over to her house for lunch. Polly was welcome to eat with them.

"*Of course I will,*" Polly texted back. "*Were you alone last night?*"

Beryl must have been waiting by the phone because she responded right away. "*He's gone. Everything of his is out of the house.*"

"*Did you cry when you got home?*"

"*Leave me alone.*"

Polly smiled. She was glad Tallie was here this week. Beryl had too much family that didn't express love very well.

No wonder it was so difficult for her. The last week had reminded Beryl that her family just couldn't bring themselves to care. The rest of the time, she ignored them. On the other hand, Tallie was a great young woman and she seemed to handle Beryl as well as any of the woman's friends.

When she opened the door, she saw Heath propped up on a couch. Polly sat down on the coffee table in front of him. "How are you feeling this morning?"

"I'm better," he said.

"Really better or I-have-happy-drugs-in-me better?"

He started to laugh, clutched his stomach and said, "Don't do that. I'll be okay."

"I know you'll be okay. You're a strong young man. Are we all eating out here this morning?"

Heath swung one leg to the floor. "I said I'd go to the dining room when they were ready."

Polly glanced at the dining room. "Stop right there. Let me guess. Hayden and Henry figured you could probably make it, right?"

"Yeah."

"Yeah. Well, no. You stay still. We'll eat here where you can be comfortable." She stood up and shook her head. "Men and boys. Such idiots."

"It's okay," Heath said, but he didn't make any further attempts to get off the couch.

"Sit," she commanded with a grin. "Stay."

Polly strode out into the kitchen. "We're eating in the living room. You two are nuts if you think I'm going to let that poor boy sit up at the table."

Hayden turned around from the stove. "He said he'd be okay."

"He'd be miserable," she said. "We can pamper him this morning."

"I tried to tell them," Rebecca whispered.

"It's fine. Start carrying out the things from the dining room table." Polly walked into the kitchen and gave Hayden a hug. "It's good to see you. Congratulations on your game last night."

He lifted his arm up and around, then pulled her tight. "Thanks. And thanks for taking care of Heath. Has he talked to you yet?"

"No," she said, stepping back. "But he will. The poor boy is probably nervous. I told him he had until today." She chuckled. "We'll see, though. My day is getting busy, so it might wait until tomorrow."

"Let me know if I need to sit on him."

Polly looked around. "Where's Henry?"

"Right here," Henry said, coming in from his office. He watched Rebecca carry milk and juice into the living room and gave Polly a guilty look. "We made a bad decision?"

"We're just making a new one," she said. "Would you get the TV tray tables?"

He nodded and went on in to the living room. The tables were stored in one of the big closets he'd built after they were married. If they moved into the Bell House, Polly knew she'd miss this place, but having plenty of space to spread out and easily store her things would be such a relief. Having extra bedrooms for guests and family would be even better. She chuckled inside. Creating this immense apartment was supposed to give her plenty of room, but before she knew it, she'd spread her family into the space. No matter how big of a house she had, Polly worried that it might never be enough. And to be honest, that sounded pretty good.

~~~

Beryl had texted back that Tallie wanted to do a late lunch - maybe around two o'clock. She and Rebecca cleaned up after breakfast, giggling at the sounds of laughter and then Heath's moans, coming from the living room. After a quick shower, Polly joined them until it was time to leave.

Tallie met her in the kitchen and they headed for Polly's truck.

"How did you sleep?" Polly asked.

"It was wonderful. That's a beautiful room and the view is incredible. I can't imagine waking up every single morning to the horses and donkeys and that beautiful back yard."

"Sycamore House is idyllic most of the time."

"Debra and I..." Tallie stopped and shook her head. "Sorry. Elise. That's going to take some getting used to. Anyway, we went up to the coffee shop for breakfast. It's so strange seeing someone I know from home all the way up here."

"Elise invited you to go to breakfast with her?"

"No. I was in the kitchen looking for leftovers from last night when I heard her walking around." Tallie grinned. "She's kind of shy."

"Yes she is. Good for you for catching her. What was she like when you knew her?"

"Still really shy. She liked to be alone, but she was so nice to Beth. I think she went to the restaurant a lot more often because Beth was there. Whenever Debra..." Tallie stopped. "I'm sorry."

"Don't be. I get it. Go on."

"Whenever..." Tallie paused. "Elise came in, Mom let Beth stop what she was doing. Elise invited Beth to sit with her and they talked about everything. It was weird, though. Elise would write these mathematical equations out on a placemat and Beth was fascinated by them. She'd watch Elise create the entire thing and then draw her fingers through the patterns like it made sense to her."

"Maybe it did."

Tallie blinked. "It could have. Beth was sad when Elise told us she was leaving town. I'm not sure how I'll tell her that I got to see her again. It won't make sense to her."

"How did she take the news of Ethan's death?"

"She cries a lot. I think she understands."

"Have you talked to her since you came up here?"

"Not about Ethan," Tallie said, shaking her head. "We talk about other things, though. I've taken pictures so she can see where I've traveled. We put a map on the wall for her and Mom prints out the pictures I take so Beth can pin them to the map. She needs help, but I highlighted the route I was driving and circled the names of the big cities."

"That's so much fun," Polly said. "She's lucky to have you all."

"Honestly, we're lucky to have her. We know she's different, but we wouldn't want it to be any other way. She's just Beth."

Polly pulled into Beryl's driveway. "You're going to love this house."

"Come in, come in," Beryl called from her front door as they exited the truck. "I've been waiting for hours and hours."

"She's kidding," Polly said to Tallie. "She knew what time we were arriving."

"But I *have* been waiting. I've been cooking and cleaning just for you."

Polly lifted her eyebrows. "Cooking?"

"Someone cooked it," Beryl said, stepping back as they entered. "Let's just leave it at that."

"Stop," Polly said, reaching out to touch Tallie's arm. "You have to start here. It's probably my favorite room in any house I've been in." She led Tallie into Beryl's front room.

"Did you paint this?" Tallie asked, looking at the arrangement of paintings on the wall. She peered at the signature. "Oh my, you did. This is incredible. I could look at these detail pieces for hours."

Beryl smiled and took a seat in one of the wing chairs. She crossed her legs and before long, a small grey kitten had found her and was on her lap.

"Every time I come over, I want time to take it in," Polly said. "But I never get to. There is always something else happening."

"You can come over any time," Beryl said. "You know I'd love that."

Polly nodded. "You're right. It's not like you're a famous artist who needs time in her studio or anything. What you really need is people bothering you at all hours of the day."

"I'd leave you alone in here while I worked."

"No you wouldn't," Polly scolded. "You'd feel like you had to take care of me."

Beryl stood up, holding the kitten in her arms. "You two spend as much time as you'd like. Little May and I will see what her brother and the old lady are doing." She turned around when she got to the door. "I'm serious. We're in no hurry. I'm glad you like my work."

"I didn't look," Tallie said. "Did she do the big tree at Sycamore House?"

"It was a building-warming, Christmas gift my first year," Polly said. "I can't believe she did that for me."

"Look at these intricate details." Tallie reached up to touch a tiny squirrel. "This one's just a baby."

"Maybe this is the mother over here," Polly said.

Tallie stepped away. "Would she ever take on a student? I'd give anything to study with her."

"She'd love that. Beryl works with Rebecca and I know of at least two other girls who were her students. They were in high school, so I don't know if she's ever taught anyone other than beginners. But you should ask."

They walked into the living room and Tallie stopped again. "This is cool," she said. "So comfortable."

"Peel back one layer and there are still five or six more," Polly said.

"Blankets?"

Polly chuckled. "And rugs on the floor, pillows scattered everywhere." She pointed to the other end of the room. "And look, now cat toys and scratching posts. Smart woman."

"Are you girls done?" Beryl asked.

"For now."

"Then come on downstairs. I've set us up there." She grinned. "It's closer to the kitty toys. That way I can keep them occupied while we eat. They still haven't learned all of their manners. If one jumps up on the table near you, please don't hesitate to pick it up and put it on the floor. I'll give it a firm 'no,' but they need to know what's polite and what's not."

Beryl had decorated the table with shades of browns and golds. Two vases were filled with daisies and cattails carved from wood. The petals were exquisite.

"Where did you find these?" Polly asked, touching a delicate wooden daisy petal.

"It was years ago. I picked them up in a tiny grocery store in Kentucky. Some of the locals made them and I thought they were fun. I probably gave too much, but the area was poverty stricken and a few extra dollars of mine wouldn't hurt me and might help the artist."

Lunch was simple: sandwiches, a tossed salad and a savory vegetable soup.

"This is perfect," Tallie said. "I've eaten so much since coming into town I feel really guilty."

"Did we find anything out last night?" Beryl asked Polly. "All of that data and information and we spent more time listening to me complain about my horrible family than we did digging into the story."

"I flipped through some of the pages that Tallie copied. The page numbers that he'd written down were mostly from the Lester Carter line. In fact," Polly nodded at Tallie. "One of the pages was your family."

"If he had already talked to Ethan and more than likely some of the others out there, why was he going through the genealogy?" Beryl asked. "He already knew their names. And surely they've already put together all of the information that they were going to find from the letters."

"Think about it," Tallie said. "Our family had those letters and you have those boxes of things that your grandpa and Aunt Evaline collected. We can't be the only ones with pieces of history. Ethan assumed there was more out there, but he started out just looking for family stuff, not clues to a treasure. He wanted pictures and things like that. The whole treasure thing was an unexpected fluke."

"Do you think there is even treasure to be found?" Polly asked.

Beryl rolled her eyes heavenward. "It's ridiculousness at its prettiest. Of course there isn't. Think about it. Pearl had been bailing her father out for years. She and Cyrus communicated about her finances on a regular basis, so don't you think that he would have talked to her about that gold after Jedidiah died? If anyone knew where he hid it, Pearl would have known. Ten to one, she found it, returned it to her uncle's bank and the whole episode was finished."

Polly looked at Tallie. "But you didn't find a letter from Cyrus to Lester that the situation had been resolved."

"I don't think so. I can look again. They're in my room back at Sycamore House." She pursed her lips. "What about relatives from Cyrus's line. What if they have any information from that time? Are they still around here?"

Beryl snagged May when she jumped up, snuggled her, said "No" before putting the cat back on the floor. "I wouldn't know them from Adam. And the charts are still at Sycamore House."

"By now it's tucked into my office," Polly said. "Henry and Hayden said they'd take care of it."

"Would you like to stay here while you're in town?" Beryl asked Tallie. "I'd let you have that room over there. I moved back upstairs when that jerk Brit came in. You'd have the run of the whole basement. Well, except for the kittens. They're everywhere.

Your own bathroom and the little bar kitchen here. There's the television and I do have Wi-Fi."

"I hate to put you out," Tallie said. "I know you work at all hours and don't want to be the reason you feel you have to sneak around in your own house."

"Don't be silly. I can sneak out to the studio any time. I'd love to have you."

Tallie looked at Polly.

Polly desperately wanted to tell her to please say yes. Tallie hadn't been in the kitchen last night when Beryl exposed her soul to her friends, but this girl was the closest thing to family Beryl had around. "We can drive back and get your things."

"And that tote of Aunt Mildred's papers," Beryl said. "I thought about that last night and was glad Tallie left it in the office. At least that was locked up. I don't know how I'd explain it to the old hag if something happened to her precious, precious charts. Use a scanner, old lady."

"Then I'd love to."

"Good," Beryl said, her face lighting up into a smile. "If you wouldn't mind, maybe we could go through that genealogy chart this afternoon and find some names we can give Aaron."

"What?" Polly asked.

"I got to thinking about it. He's looking for Carters in the towns around here. But there are other family names he should be looking for, too. Tallie would know which of her cousins were the most interested in what Ethan was doing. We can make a list of names for Aaron and then he'll have something to start with. We can also research Cyrus's descendants. Maybe they live close by and have more historical documents we can look at." She stood up, snatching May from the top of the table again. "And I want to see that information that Andy gathered about land owned by the Carters when Bellingwood started. Maybe there's something there."

Polly smiled as Beryl paced back and forth, carrying the kitten. "Do you want help?"

"No. That's okay. We can go through the rest of it later." Beryl spun around. "Maybe I'll promise Andy another trip to Spain if she just sorts it and deals with it."

"She'd love that," Polly said.

"I know. It's really her thing." Beryl sat back down and put the kitten on the floor, then leaned in toward Tallie. "Would you like me to ride back to Sycamore House and help you?"

"You want to do this right now?"

"Are you finished eating? You stopped a long time ago," Beryl said.

"Yes."

"Polly?"

Polly pushed her plate back "Of course. This was terrific."

"I'd serve dessert, but I know you have plenty of sweet stuff at your house and I want to get started on this with Tallie. Do you mind?"

"No, not at all. Shall we take the food upstairs?"

"Oh yes, so the kittens don't get into it." She picked Hem up and put him on the floor. "Miss Kitty spoiled me. She is so polite. All of this kitten training is for the birds. They're getting better, but my goodness, they ignore me when they don't want to be good."

Hem jumped back up to the table and Polly grabbed him. She put him on the floor and picked up her plate and the tray of meat and cheese. "They did very well for a while. We took too long. Let's get going."

CHAPTER TWENTY

Everyone was finally where they belonged by five o'clock and Polly only had a short time before meeting her friends at Pizzazz for their regular Sunday night gathering. After crazy weekends like this, she was often tempted to push the group into meeting once a month, but nobody wanted to give up this time they got away from all of their responsibilities.

The dogs rushed to the top of the steps to greet her and she sat down, nuzzling Obiwan's neck. "It's good to see you, bud. Will you let me rest here for a minute?" She wrapped her arms around him and he sat still as she relaxed against his body.

"Polly?"

She startled, having nearly fallen asleep, even though it was just a split second later.

"What are you doing?" Henry asked, standing over her.

Maybe it had been longer than a split second.

"Just taking a breath."

He reached out so she could take his hand while standing up. "Did you get everyone settled?"

"Tallie is at Beryl's and those two are in love with each other.

By the time I finally dropped them back off, they didn't know whether to talk about their favorite brands of oil paints and brushes or all of the family history they share. I'm so glad Beryl has found her. How's Heath?"

"He's asleep in his room. Hayden left about an hour ago to visit a friend here in town."

"And Rebecca?"

"She hovered over Heath all day. As soon as he went into his room, the poor girl crashed on the living room sofa."

Polly smiled, but yawned in the middle of it.

"You need a nap, too," he said.

Polly yawned again. "But a real nap. Not one of those happy naps. And only forty-five minutes so I can be mostly alert for supper tonight."

"You're still going? You have to be exhausted." Henry stopped her in the doorway to the media room. "Have you stopped moving at all this weekend?"

"I'm fine. And I want to go. Nobody needs me to help them or fix something or figure out a mystery. I just get to eat pizza and see my friends."

"If you're sure."

"Do you mind if I take a quick nap? I kind of left you with all the responsibility around here today."

He chuckled. "I watched television and napped on the couch. It hasn't been too difficult. In fact, I should probably spend some time in my office. You go sleep."

"Wake me if you don't see me in time."

Henry kissed her cheek and gave her a gentle push out the door. When she got to her room, she collapsed on the bed and waited for the rush of animals to end. Once they were settled, she turned over on her side, wrapped her arm around Obiwan, tugged him in close and felt herself relax.

~~~

The sky was gray as she stood beside an open grave,

surrounded by people she couldn't identify. A young woman dressed in a long black dress and holding a black parasol stood across from her, reading from a book. Polly assumed it was a Bible, but couldn't understand the words coming from the young woman's mouth. Six men carrying a coffin trudged up the hill, marching in time to a song being hummed by the gathered crowd. Polly tried to hum along, but found she didn't know the tune.

She tried to step back, but the people behind her were a solid wall. As she peered into the grave, Polly was surprised to see a flat wooden box at the bottom. There was plenty of open land here, why would they bury a second body on top of the first? She looked back at the pallbearers and saw another set of young men, marching toward them with a second coffin. That must be the way things were done here. Dig one deep grave and fill it with all of the dead family members.

Polly looked around for ropes, trying to understand how they planned to lower the coffins into the ever deepening grave. She looked up as the first pall bearers arrived. They walked around the side of the grave, pushing her away, then tipped the coffin in and let it fall. Polly heard a strange sound and looked over the shoulders of one young man to see glittering gold flutter to the floor of the grave. The second bearers arrived and when the first young men wouldn't move, they put the coffin down on the ground and walked away.

The young woman opened the coffin and people began pouring out of it, filling the hillside. She knew she was looking at all of the Carters that had ever been born and found herself looking for the two that she knew, Beryl and Tallie. She thought maybe one of them was at the back of the crowd, but no one would let her through so she could reach them.

~~~

"Polly wake up," Henry said.
She blew air out of her mouth. "That was frustrating."
"Were you dreaming?"

"I was standing at a gravesite. It was just weird. I saw the gold and all of the Carters. I was trying to find Beryl and Tallie, but no one would let me get to them."

"That does sound weird. Heath and Rebecca are awake and Hayden is back."

"Okay?"

"Well, just so you knew where everyone was when you came out. You were sleeping pretty hard in here."

She crooked her finger at him. "Come here, baby."

Henry bent over and kissed her. "I love you, too. You'd better get moving if you don't want to be late. Rebecca and I have decided that we're doing takeout from Davey's tonight. We don't want pizza and we don't want to cook."

"I'm sorry," Polly said.

"For what?"

"For not cooking a good supper for you."

"That's right." Henry nodded as he walked to the door. "You're a horrible wife and mother and should be ashamed of yourself. It would be helpful if there was somebody we could report you to."

Polly flung a pillow at him, but it landed just beyond the bed.

"I'll let you pick that up," he said and laughed as he left the room.

The dream continued to haunt Polly as she washed her face and cleaned up for the evening. She hated having odd images hover at the edge of her consciousness. She didn't think for a minute that it had anything to do with reality. It was one thing to find dead bodies, but Polly knew for a fact that she wasn't psychic. No, she didn't think the gold was buried in that old cemetery. Andy had explained that one away. She'd just been so surrounded by all of the information about Beryl's family, it was trying to sort itself out while she slept.

"Hey there, you look better," she said to Heath once she stepped into the living room.

Heath was propped up on the sofa, but for the first time since Friday, his face didn't look like he was trying to hold back the pain. "I am better," he said.

Polly brushed her fingers on his cheek. "That's great. A few days away from school and you'll be back to normal in no time."

"I don't have to go to school tomorrow?"

She snorted. "No, honey. You don't."

His face lit up. "Hear that, Hayden? I'll be here all day tomorrow while you're home." He looked back at Polly, concern replacing his relief.

"I'm in no hurry," she said. "We have time. As for tonight, you're going to have fun without me. I'm gone unless you need something."

"We've got this," Rebecca said. She followed Polly through the house. When they got to Henry's office, she tugged on Polly's sleeve. "He's worried, you know."

"About what?"

"About you guys making him leave."

Polly wrinkled her forehead. "Why would he think we'd do that?"

"That's what Hayden and I told him. But he knows he wasn't supposed to have anybody else in his truck and he wasn't supposed to be with Libby and there's something about those boys who beat him up."

"I know there is," Polly said. "But we aren't about to abandon him because he screwed up. He's a kid for heaven's sake. That's what you do." She sighed. "That's what we all do."

Rebecca startled Polly by grabbing her into a hug. "You're so cool."

Polly wrapped her arms around the girl. "Stay here a minute," she said, releasing Rebecca. She ran back into the living room, bent over Heath and whispered in his ear. "I love you. You can't do anything bad enough to make me stop doing that or not want you to be part of my family. Now quit worrying."

Without waiting for a response, Polly turned and left the room. Rebecca was still standing in the doorway.

"What did you do?" she asked.

"Told Heath to quit worrying. Now have a good evening and I'll see you later."

"You're still cool, you know," Rebecca said.

Polly laughed. "We'll see if you believe that in a few years."

She was a few minutes later than usual getting to Pizzazz and nearly everyone was there. Sal waved at Polly when she walked in the front door and pointed to the chair beside her.

"I have your soda already," Sal said. "We were worried you wouldn't be able to come with everything that's going on. But since you didn't text any of us..."

Polly smiled and hugged Sal's shoulders. "I wasn't missing this. It's been a weird weekend. Hopefully tomorrow things will start settling down again. I haven't been back to the Bell House since early last week and there's so much to do before Henry can get started."

"You should let us come help you," Joss said.

"I'd love for any of you to come any time," Polly responded. "But honestly, I feel like I'm getting to know the old house. I'm making friends with it."

Sylvie laughed out loud. "First it's a haunted house, now Polly's insisting that it be her friend. What's next?"

Polly sneered at her. "You never know. Maybe it will grow its own food and weave its own fabric." She threw her hand in the air. "Oh, I don't know what I'm talking about. I took a nap before coming up here and had the weirdest dream about a grave and gold and people coming out of a coffin. It's still hovering right here." She tapped her forehead.

"I hate those," Sal said. "And I especially hate those nightmares that come back over and over. I used to dream about a grave, too." She shuddered. "It was in a clearing in the middle of a forest. I knew that it was mine, but thank goodness it was always empty. I woke up night after night shaken because I'd found myself in that same place again."

"That's kind of creepy," Camille said, sitting forward. "Mine was about trying to walk up a really icy hill. I'd start and then slide back down. Every time I'd get almost to the top, I'd lose my footing and slide to the bottom again. But I haven't had that dream since I was a kid."

"Mine happened when I was young, too," Sal said. "I thought I'd never lose that dream, but one day I realized I hadn't had it for years." She shivered again. "Weird."

"Hello," Sandy Davis said, dropping into a chair beside Joss. "Sorry I'm late. I couldn't find my keys."

"How's Benji doing with the baby this week?" Joss asked.

"So much better. I tell you what, getting out every week has really forced him to get comfortable being a hands-on dad. I didn't realize how much I was stopping him from getting involved with everything." Sandy smiled at them all. "Thank you for letting me be part of this. Not only do I get some sanity, but you're teaching me to do this right."

Sylvie laughed and looked around the table. "How weird is that? You, Joss and I are the only ones who raised babies."

"And I haven't been doing it for very long," Joss said. "I feel like every day is a new opportunity to discover things I probably should have known yesterday."

"Like what?" Sandy asked.

"Oh, yesterday I turned my back for a second to put dishes in the dishwasher and when I turned around, Cooper and Sophie were painting each other with the butter. It was in their hair and all over their clothes." She sighed. "We got to have another bath and the butter now goes into the refrigerator." She grimaced. "Because once they learn a trick that makes Mom crazy, they'll do it again and again, just to see if I react the same way each time."

"Mine was lipstick," Sylvie said. "You might notice that I never wear it. I got out of the habit because it wasn't safe in the hands of my boys. One day I came home after working all day. Jason was maybe five and Andrew wasn't quite two. I collapsed on the couch and before I knew it, they had painted themselves and colored the back of the recliner. Andrew was coloring the bottom of his feet when I got to them."

"What did you do?"

I dropped Jason into a bath. He was lucky I didn't spank his little bottom. He knew better, but Andrew had found a couple of tubes of my lipstick and Jason thought it would be fun."

"This is why I'm very happy with bringing older kids into my family," Polly said.

"You just wait," Sylvie retorted. "You'll get yours someday."

Polly held up a cross she made with her index fingers. "Stay away from me with that talk. I like it that all of you young chickadees are having babies."

"Young chickadees?" Sal asked.

"Yeah. Like them." Polly waved her fingers at Sandy and Joss. "You know, not me in my old age here."

Sal frowned at her. "We're only thirty-five."

"You may be thirty-five, but after this weekend, I feel like I'm in my..." Polly looked at Sylvie, who was giving her an "I dare you" look. "I feel like I'm in my early fifties or something."

Sal relaxed and Polly glanced at her, wondering what that was about.

"How are things with Heath?" Joss asked.

"He's doing good tonight." Polly grinned. "He felt much better when I told him he didn't have to go to school for a few days."

Sandy peered at her. "What happened to Heath?"

"Somebody beat him up Friday night. Heath stepped in to protect a girl he was with. A few bruised ribs and some good cuts from a knife." Polly shook her head. "I don't know that I've been that scared for someone else in a long time. He was a mess."

"Do you know who it was?"

"Not yet. Heath insists he doesn't know them, but Boone isn't that big and he's been going to school there for three years. We aren't finished with the conversation."

Their regular waitress, Bri, stepped in, carrying two pizzas. Everybody moved things to make room and she put them in the middle of the table. "It's good to see you all here at the same time this week," she said. "Can I get anything else?"

Sal held up her hand and Bri nodded. "I'll be right back."

"What was that?" Polly asked.

"Nothing," Sal said. "You'll see."

They passed plates back and forth, filling them with pizza and soon chatter died down as they ate.

"When do you think your house is going to be ready?" Sandy asked Joss.

Joss mumbled something, then pointed to her mouth.

"Sorry," Sandy giggled.

"Nate says we'll be in by mid-April, but Henry thinks it's more like May," Joss said, after swallowing. "All I know is that I want to get our house on the market so that once I move out, I don't have to think about it again. But oh dear lord, I don't want to pack and clean things."

"Hah," Polly said. "Your house is so clean and orderly, all you'll have to do is slide things into boxes and they'll find their own transportation. They wouldn't dare disobey you."

"That would be nice, but with Sophie and Cooper underfoot, packing will be the death of me. When we get closer, Mom said she'd help with the kids."

"I'll help you pack," Polly said.

"Me too," Camille said. "I can't wait to see the inside of that beautiful home you're building."

Sandy nodded and put her hand up. "I'll be there."

Bri stepped back in and put plastic champagne glasses in front of everyone, filled with something bubbly. Another waitress handed her a final glass that she gave to Sal.

"What's this?" Polly asked.

"I have an announcement," Sal said. She put her head down and took a deep breath, then looked back up. "I'm not sure how to say this, so I'm just going to put it out there. I'm pregnant."

Polly slowly turned to look at her friend. "You're going to have a baby?"

"That's generally what happens at the end of being pregnant," Sal responded.

Polly looked at the glass in front of her and then back at Sal. "A baby?"

"Uh huh. Now pick up that glass and make a toast before I think that you believe it's a bad idea."

"It's great," Polly said. Her mind was still a little fuzzy from the announcement, but she picked the glass up and raised it high. "I'm so happy for you, Sal. Here's to an exciting new life you're about to lead."

"Hear, hear," the other women said, raising their glasses.

Polly took a sip. "Hey, this is the real thing. We're really celebrating."

"Mine's not, of course," Sal said. "But yes, we're celebrating."

They peppered Sal with questions until she put her hand up. "Let me fix this for you," she said. "I found out around Thanksgiving and told Mark at Christmas, just in case everything fell apart." She glared at Polly. "Because thirty-five is old, you know. I'm keeping the baby and we're really happy about this. We talked about getting married, but we'll probably elope. I haven't told my parents." She sighed. "Because I'm just not ready for that. We're going to fly out to see them so Mom doesn't have a heart attack on the phone. Now that the first trimester is over and the baby is healthy, I'm ready to tell people. So I'm telling you."

"Look at her," Sylvie said, pointing at Polly.

The rest of them laughed.

"What?" Polly said.

"You're crying."

"Shut up." Polly put her glass down and turned so she could hug her friend. "I'm so damned happy for you."

Sal whispered. "I never thought it would be me. I always thought you'd have babies and I'd be an old maid."

"I don't want babies and you could never be an old maid," Polly said.

"We have to have a baby shower at the coffee shop," Camille said. "Ohhh, everyone is going to be so excited about this." She rubbed her hands together. "I love babies."

Polly snickered. "Maybe your mom will move to Bellingwood so she can help you."

"Now *you* shut up," Sal said. "That's the most horrible curse you could wish upon anyone. Well, everyone in Bellingwood at least. We want to keep her as far away from here as possible. Maybe I won't tell her anything ever and she'll continue to believe that I'm going to move back to Boston and pick up my old life."

"Have you had morning sickness?" Sandy asked.

Sal moaned. "It's just been the worst. But I couldn't tell anybody since I didn't want you to know. Poor Mark has been wonderful."

"Do his parents know?" Polly asked.

"Not yet." She glanced at the kitchen. "I suppose they will now. Dylan will find out from Bri and then he'll tell his wife and she'll probably call her mother."

"Maybe Mark better call his sister and tell her to be quiet until you can spill the beans," Sylvie said.

"Whatever," Sal said with a shrug. "I wanted to tell you before the whole world knew. Now we tell everyone else."

Polly hugged her again. "I am so glad you're going to be here in Bellingwood for this. We're going to have a blast."

"Maybe Rebecca can babysit when I need a shopping fix?" Sal asked.

"She'd love it." Polly raised her glass again. "To all of life's funny little surprises."

CHAPTER TWENTY-ONE

Rather than hurrying home, they'd all stayed late at Pizzazz talking about the many changes happening in everyone's lives. Sylvie and Camille cut out first, complaining about their early morning. Sandy had taken off around nine thirty, worried that Benji hadn't called her yet. She couldn't help herself.

Joss knew that Nate had put the twins to bed and was watching television, so she didn't need to hurry home. Mark was taking care of the dachshunds, giving Sal the opportunity to spend time with her friends.

They realized they were the last ones in the restaurant when the tables had been wiped clean and the kitchen staff was leaving. Instead of calling it a night, the three headed for the Jefferson Street Alehouse, not ready to leave each other yet. They'd talked about all of the changes on their horizons. Sal had asked Joss question after question about taking care of babies. She was another young woman who had never really spent much time around children throughout her life and Polly was glad Joss was there to give Sal some down-to-earth advice.

They talked about Joss's new house and her absolute panic

over the process in front of her. She felt as if she hadn't spent nearly enough time making decisions about all of the different appliances and paint, carpet and trim colors.

As Polly listened to her friends fret over the things coming at them, she realized how much she'd changed in the last few years. Most of that was because of Henry. If it had to do with something practical, he'd help her figure out how to deal with it. If it was emotional, he just held onto her while she worked through it. And through all of the mess this last weekend with Heath, he'd stepped up in a big way. He made a great dad. That didn't surprise her. Bill Sturtz was the same type of man and you couldn't be any more calm and sensible than Henry's mother, Marie.

She'd tiptoed up the back steps well after midnight. The house was quiet as she crossed into her bedroom. Hayden wasn't in the living room, so she hoped that meant Heath was feeling well enough for them to put the air bed up in his room.

Obiwan lifted his head and thumped his tail when she pushed the bedroom door open and Henry flipped on the light.

"Did you have a good evening?" he asked.

"Sal's pregnant," Polly replied. "Due in July."

He sat up. "Sal Kahane? Your Sal is having a baby?"

"I know. Imagine that. But she is and they're looking forward to it."

"When are they getting married?"

Polly sat down on the edge of the bed beside him. "Now, how old-fashioned are you? What if they don't want to be married?"

"You're right," he said. "So they aren't?"

"I didn't say that."

He creased his forehead. "What are you doing to me? You woke me up and now you're messing with my poor brain."

"I don't know what they're going to do. If they get married, they'll probably run away somewhere. But first they have to tell her parents." Polly rolled her eyes. "That is not a time I'd want to be a fly on the wall. Her mother is going to flip out. She'll want Sal to move back to Boston, with or without Mark."

"So she can raise Sal's baby?"

"Exactly. It won't be pretty. How were things around here this evening?"

"Quiet. Hayden had a pile of homework, Rebecca and Heath watched a stupid movie and I worked in my office."

"Hayden's in Heath's room?"

Henry nodded. "I hate that we only have three bedrooms."

"Me too. I need to get back into the Bell House so we can start working on it."

"Patience, dear Prudence. I told you it was going to take a long time."

"But this place didn't take that long." Polly poked his arm. "And it's much bigger."

Henry pulled her back to lie in his arms and kissed her lips. "Remember, you paid me to do the work on Sycamore House. You'd be amazed at how motivational that can be."

"I have other ways to motivate you now."

He chuckled and helped her sit back up. "Yes you do. However, Sturtz Construction has gotten busier these last few years. It's amazing what falling in love and wanting to build a life will do for a man."

"Would your dad build a crib for Sal?"

"He'd love to. He said something to me once about not getting to make baby room furniture for us. It would mean the world if you asked him."

Polly reached over, turned his light off and walked to the other side of the bed, slipping out of her clothes and dropping them on the floor. She felt around for her night shirt and pulled it over her head before climbing in under the covers.

"You're a slob, you know," Henry said, laughing.

"I feel guilty about it sometimes. Then there are those other times when I just can't put one more thing away because I ran out of cleaning mojo. But at least I try to contain it to our bedroom now." She snuggled up close to him. "With people in and out, I'm always having to tidy up. It's just easier to keep after it."

"It's a good thing you have Rebecca around."

"Have you seen her room?"

"But she helps you."

Polly nodded. "Most of the time, and so does Heath. Henry, what am I going to do in that big house? There's no way I'll be able to keep it clean."

"You'll hire someone."

She sputtered a laugh. "That will kill me."

"No it won't," he said. "You grew up with Mary in your house. She kept things clean and your Dad paid her."

"I suppose."

"And you're always good about finding people who need jobs and then putting them to work. I have confidence that you'll manage this."

"I have to talk to Heath tomorrow about the boys that beat him up," she said quietly. "I've put it off for two days, making the excuse that he wasn't healthy enough for the conversation."

"Do you want me to talk to him for you?"

"No. I told him I would. He's expecting it. Do I wait until Hayden's gone back to school?"

"See how it plays out in the morning," Henry said. "It might not be a terrible idea to have his brother involved in the conversation."

"Has Hayden said any more about where he wants to go to school?"

Henry chuckled. "No. Apparently our conversation stirred up more questions than answers. Now he isn't even sure that he wants to go to medical school."

"What?"

"If he goes straight research, he can stay at Iowa State."

"He shouldn't make life decisions based on staying close. He should feel like he has the option to do anything he wants."

"We'll keep talking. But if he wants to stay in the Midwest, that's his decision."

"Yeah, yeah, yeah. His decision. Just so he makes it based on what he wants to do for his own life, not what he thinks he should do for Heath."

"Sometimes that's hard for people to separate."

"It kills me that young people let so many things press down on them. They have so much potential and so many possibilities. Grab them all."

He pulled her into a hug. "I love you."

"I love you too," she mumbled into his shoulder. "Are you shutting me up?"

"We need to get some sleep."

"I miss having hours to talk to you about things."

"When did we do that?"

"You know, back before we had kids."

He laughed. "I don't remember hours of conversation, but we did get more sleep."

Polly took a long, deep breath and slowly exhaled.

"What are you doing?"

"I'm relaxing so I'll go to sleep."

"Goodnight, sweet girl."

~~~

Polly woke with a start. It was still dark out and Henry was pulling on his jeans. Then she realized she was hearing an alarm.

"What in the hell is that?" she yelled.

"It's the house alarm. I don't know what's going on." He turned on the lights as he left the room.

She jumped out of bed, put her jeans on and pulled a sweatshirt over her head.

Hayden was standing in Heath's bedroom door and Rebecca had come out of her room.

"What's going on?" Rebecca asked.

"We don't know. It's the house alarm," Polly said. "Have you guys been in your rooms all night?"

Rebecca nodded.

"Yeah. We haven't moved," Hayden said. "I told Heath to stay put."

"Take Han." Henry grabbed the dog's collar, picked him up and handed him to Hayden. "Shut the door."

Rebecca picked up Leia and held her close. "Are the police coming?"

At that moment, Polly's phone rang. "Hello?"

"Is this Polly Giller?"

"Yes it is."

"Do you have an emergency?"

"I don't know. I'm assuming we do."

"Should we send the police?"

Polly looked at Henry. "Police?"

He nodded.

"Yes, please."

"Stay on the line while we contact them," the voice said. "Is someone in your house?"

"I don't know," she said. "This is a big building. They might be downstairs."

"Lock all of your doors and remain inside."

"Don't go out there, Henry," she said as he put his hand on the front door handle.

"I'll be fine."

Polly realized that the fear she felt as he opened the door was probably the same thing she'd put him through so many times and she held her breath.

He silently closed the door behind him and all of a sudden she couldn't breathe.

"Are you okay, Polly?" Rebecca asked.

It took a moment for her to regain her thoughts. "I'm fine," she whispered.

Hayden came back out of Heath's bedroom and shut the door. "I think it's safe now. Whoever was here is gone now."

"How do you know that?"

"I saw him run down the driveway. He had a car parked on the other side of the barn."

"Would you recognize him if you saw him again?"

Hayden shook his head. "He was in a dark hoodie and jeans and the car was parked too far away for me to see it. I'm sorry." He started for the front door.

"Where are you going?" she asked.

"To help Henry."

When had she become the weak female? "No. You stay here with your brother and Rebecca. I'll go. Come on, Obiwan."

The alarms switched off and Polly took a deep breath. "That's better."

Hayden stepped toward the door and opened his mouth as if to protest, but Polly put her hand up. "My house. My rules. When things settle out, I'll let you know."

She met Henry as he was coming in the front door. "He's gone," Henry said.

"Hayden watched him from the bedroom window."

"I'm sorry I couldn't see him very well," Hayden said.

Henry turned around to go back downstairs. "He broke the window into your office, Polly."

She chuckled as she followed him down the steps. "I didn't know those were all alarmed."

"Jeff and I had a conversation last year."

"And you didn't talk to me about it?"

"What would you have said?"

"That it was a waste of money. Who would want to break in?"

"Look at all that time we saved," Henry said with a smile.

"It's a good thing I'm thankful for the alarm tonight or you'd be in trouble. How bad is the mess?"

"Bad. He went ripping through the boxes of Beryl's things."

"I'm so glad we took her aunt's tote bag of papers over to her house." Her head shot up. "You don't suppose he'd try to break into her place, too, do you?"

"What was he looking for? If he found it here, probably not."

Polly patted around for her phone and realized she'd left it upstairs. "I'm calling the police back. They need to send someone by her house just in case."

"You don't know who did this," Henry said.

"I have a good idea and he knows where Beryl lives."

They looked up at flashing lights in the driveway and Henry headed for the main door.

"You folks have a lot of excitement in your lives," Bert Bradford said when he came in. "We've talked about adding new staff just to handle the Polly Giller wing."

"Stop it," Polly said.

Bert walked around outside and looked in the window. "He couldn't have made any more of a mess of this. Did anyone see who it was?"

"Hayden saw him leave, but he was in the upstairs window and didn't get any details. The guy parked on the other side of the barn."

"Smart," Bert said. "Do you know what he was looking for?"

"It has to have something to do with the death of Ethan Carter," Polly replied.

"The boy you found down on the Des Moines river?"

"Yeah. And I'm worried that this person will go over to Beryl's house next if he didn't find what he was looking for."

"What's he looking for?"

"Evidence of buried gold from a hundred and fifty years ago."

Bert got a bemused look on his face. "Gold, eh. In Bellingwood. Well, I never."

"Is there anyone that can drive past Beryl's house and make sure that she's safe?"

He looked at his watch. "Misty's out on patrol. Let me contact her. She'll do a couple of drive-bys if you think it's a concern."

"That would make me feel better."

"I'll be right back." Bert went outside and Polly could hear him talking to someone. It made her feel better knowing that even in Bellingwood, people were awake at all hours to make sure they were safe.

He came back inside and pointed at the office. "Do you want to see if anything's missing?"

"I haven't been in there yet," Polly said.

Bert looked at Henry. "How'd you keep her out?"

"Stop it. Both of you," Polly said. "We only just got down here before you arrived." She opened the main office door and flipped the lights on, then went on into her office and let her head fall forward in disappointment. She looked up and turned to Bert. "If you weren't here, foul curses would come out of my mouth. Would you look at this mess?"

"At least it's not raining?" he said, trying to be helpful.

"At least. Why would he have felt the need to push all of the things off my shelves? He didn't hardly have time, especially if he was going to dig through boxes."

Bert stepped over glass and looked at the floor. "He brushed past them as he tried to get out, probably bumped the shelves pretty hard." He pointed at the boxes which had been opened, upended and spread across the floor. Several folders of things were spread out on Polly's desk. "I don't suppose you know what's missing."

"There's no way," she said. "Beryl picked these up from her brother this week and we were planning to sort through and catalog them, but we'd only begun. This is all just her family's history stuff."

"And it's important because of gold, right?" Bert asked.

"Beryl's ancestor, Jedidiah, was one of the Bellingwood's founders. But he was also a gambler and apparently he robbed his brother's bank. There are letters from Cyrus Carter saying that Jedidiah died before he could spend the gold. Cyrus told his other brother, Lester, in those letters, that he thought Jedidiah had probably buried it somewhere. Ethan Carter found the letters and came up here to look for that gold."

"And Ethan Carter is..." Bert waited for Polly.

"A descendant of Lester, the brother who moved out west. Cyrus was the owner of the bank."

"So Miz Watson's ancestor robbed his brother's bank."

She giggled. "Uh huh."

"She comes from some prime stock," Bert said with a laugh. "You have descendants of Jedidiah and Lester in Bellingwood right now. What about some of Cyrus's? Surely they still live around here."

Polly shrugged. "I'd guess so, but Beryl doesn't know who they are. She and Ethan's sister, Tallie, were going to dig through genealogy information she'd picked up from an aunt of hers to see if they could find names."

"And the sheriff is dealing with this case?"

"Aren't you glad you don't have to?" Henry asked.

Bert's cell phone rang. "It's Misty. Just a minute. Yeah, Misty?" He nodded and grunted a few times and then hung up. "She says she saw taillights turn a corner when she pulled up in front of Miz Watson's house, but thought it might be smarter to check things out at the house instead of chasing down some poor soul who was getting up early to go to work. She drove around a few times and didn't see the car anywhere else. We'll run by there a few more times tonight, just to make sure."

"Thank you," Polly said.

"Do you need help boarding up this window tonight?" Bert asked Henry.

"I'll take care of it. I need to run over to Dad's and get some plywood."

"Your thief won't be back again tonight, I'm sure," Bert said. "We'll get the alarm re-set, though. Could I speak with the young man who saw this person?"

Henry headed for the door. "I'll send him down to you. If I'm leaving, I'd rather he was here with Polly." He stopped himself before he got too much further.

Polly grinned. "Because I'm a feak and weeble woman," she said.

"I didn't say that," Henry protested. "I didn't even think that. I swear. Tell her, Bert."

Bert put up his hands. "I don't even know what it was she said. I'm not involved in this conversation."

"Hayden will be right down." Henry left and Bert turned to Polly.

"Do you have a broom? I'll help you sweep up the glass."

"You don't need to check for fingerprints or anything?"

"Not on the glass, but we should get it swept up so nobody tracks it out of here. If you aren't in a real hurry, I'll send someone over in the morning to process the rest of the office."

"No footprints?" she asked.

Bert looked down at the floor and shook his head. "No, I'm not too worried about footprints. The ground outside is too hard and they wouldn't tell us enough anyway."

"I'll get a broom then," she said with a smile. "And I was messing with ya. I figure you know what you're doing."

"Most of the time, ma'am. But you do tend to bring crime to an entirely different level in this town."

Polly walked out of the office. "I don't even know what to say to that."

Hayden was coming down the steps as she turned to the basement door. "Hey Polly. Henry said I should come down."

"Do you know Officer Bradford?" she asked.

He swallowed. "Yeah. I do."

"Is something wrong?"

"No. I haven't seen him since he ..."

"Since what?"

"He's the one who came over to find me in Ames to tell me that Mom and Dad had been killed. He's a good guy, but ..."

"Wait here a minute. Let me get a broom. I'll go in with you."

Eliseo kept an extra broom and dustpan just inside the basement door and Polly was able to put her hands on them without turning on the light. She came back out, hooked her arm through Hayden's and walked with him to the office.

Bert looked up when they came in and walked forward, his hand extended. "Hayden Harvey. It's good to see you. I've been paying attention to your game this year. You're doing a good job with those Cyclones."

"Thank you, sir."

"I'm glad you and Heath found a home with Polly and Henry. They're good people." Bert placed his hand on Hayden's back and Polly realized how young Hayden still was. He'd stepped back in time a few years at the sight of Bert.

"I just want to ask you a few questions about what you saw earlier, Hayden. Would you have a seat?" Bert gestured to the chairs in the front office and Hayden sat down, then leaned forward, his elbows on his knees.

"I didn't see much, sir. The man wore a dark hoodie and jeans and he never looked up."

Polly let them talk and went into the office with the broom. She picked up large pieces of glass and dropped them into her trashcan, then worked to sweep up as much broken glass as she could. What a mess he'd made.

CHAPTER TWENTY-TWO

"You'd think people would rather sleep than traipse around terrorizing friendly folk like us in the middle of the night," Henry complained as they trudged back upstairs.

"This happens a lot?" Hayden asked.

"It's always something." Henry opened the front door to the apartment. "It looks like we have an audience waiting for us."

"Heath, what are you doing out of bed?" Polly asked. "Are you okay?"

"I'm fine. It aches a little. Rebecca wouldn't let me go downstairs."

"Good for her. At least someone up here has a little sense." Polly pointed at him. "Put him back in bed right now," she said to Henry and Hayden. "And you, little girl, to bed with you. Tomorrow morning will be here in a couple of hours."

"But we want to know what happened," Rebecca protested.

"You know what happened," Henry said, putting his arm out to help Heath up. "Somebody broke in, they got away. The police came, I boarded up the window and now I want to get some sleep before this week starts."

Polly shooed Rebecca toward her bedroom.

"Was your office a real mess? What did they steal? Who was the police officer? Did Hayden tell them anything more?" Rebecca stopped in her doorway, placing her hands on the frame. "I have questions that need to be answered or I won't be able to go to sleep.

"Let's see," Polly said. "Yes. I don't know. Officer Bradford. I don't know. There. I've answered your questions. Now go to bed and we'll talk more at breakfast."

"But what if he comes back?"

"Then the alarm will sound and we'll play this game all over again, but I don't think he'll be stupid enough to do that. The police will patrol the area tonight. We're perfectly safe."

"I know we're safe," Rebecca said. "That's why you and Henry are here, but a girl shouldn't be left without answers. She makes things up in her head and has bad dreams."

Polly laughed and gave Rebecca a small push into the room. "No she doesn't. I love you, crazy girl. Climb into bed. Go on." She stood in the doorway while Rebecca took her robe off and climbed up into her bed. "Do you want an animal in here tonight?"

"Just leave my door open a little so the cats can come in if they want," Rebecca said. "Can you tell me what this was about?"

"Whoever broke in was digging into the boxes that Beryl left here. I suspect they're looking for information about the gold that her ancestor, Jedidiah, stole."

"Oh!" Rebecca slowly nodded. "I can't wait to go to sleep now. I want to dream about that."

"Good." Polly flipped the overhead light off. "Then, sweet dreams." She pulled the door closed, leaving a small gap and looked around the living room. Hayden and Henry had gotten Heath back into his room and were still talking with him, so she wandered around the house, turning lights off. Rebecca had taken out cookies and milk for her and Heath. What a good little sister she was. Polly set the glasses into the sink and looked out the kitchen window to the street.

"Keeping an eye out?" Henry's voice made her jump.

"I guess. Really, I was wondering if I'd miss living on a main street when we move to the Bell House. It's going to be so quiet over there."

He chuckled. "The house backs up to a cemetery. Of all places in Bellingwood, you are going to be near a cemetery. Something tells me that nice, quiet, serene setting will be regularly disrupted after you arrive."

"Stop that, you rotten man," she said, putting her hand on his chest. "It's not my fault. This tonight? Not my fault at all."

"Except that those boxes of Carter family history are here at Sycamore House and not at Beryl's."

"Wouldn't you rather that person break in downstairs than at her place?" Polly simpered. "She doesn't have two strong men around to protect her."

"Now you're just being a brat. Will you be able to go back to sleep?"

Polly looked up at the time. It was nearly four o'clock. Tomorrow morning was going to be painful. She opened the freezer and pointed at the extra breakfast sandwiches. "This is why I make so many. We're totally set. Now I can sleep."

Henry took her hand and they walked through the house.

"Thank you for taking care of things," she said. "I know that I give you trouble, but I'm glad you're here."

"Just call me your hero and we'll be good." He shut the door to their room and turned the overhead light off. Enough light came in through the windows for them to see.

Polly stripped back down to her night shirt and slid under the blankets, patting the bed for Obiwan to jump up and snuggle in beside her. Han leaped up, circled the base of the bed three times and dropped before Henry could climb in.

"I need room for my feet, you mutt," he complained.

~~~

Polly sat at the dining room table after Rebecca and Henry left for the day and took a deep breath.

Hayden and Heath had gone back to their room so Hayden could help Heath get showered and ready for the day. Heath insisted that he was doing better, but Polly was glad his brother was still here to give some assistance and let the boy retain dignity. There was no way she was prepared to be that close to her teenaged son.

Her phone rang and she glanced down.

"Good morning, Beryl. You're up awfully early."

"I just got a call from Lydia. Did you really have a break-in last night?"

"Yes I did. And I sent the police over to your house to make sure whoever did this didn't try to break into your place."

"Well aren't you just the sweetest pot of strawberry jam in town," Beryl said. "I appreciate how you take care of me. What do you think he wanted?"

"I'm guessing something from those boxes of family history that are here. Several were opened up and papers scattered around. I don't know if the person found what he was looking for, though."

"Maybe the first thing I should have asked was if everyone was safe there," Beryl said.

"Absolutely. Henry and Jeff had all of the downstairs windows alarmed last year, so that's what woke us up." Polly paused. "I hope it was just the downstairs windows. Maybe I should ask."

"Hard to believe you missed that going on right under your nose."

"Tell me about it. Did you have fun with Tallie?"

"We talked until we couldn't keep our eyes open, Polly. She's a terrific young lady. I've invited her to come back to Bellingwood this summer. She said she would love to. Can you believe that?"

"Of course she did. You're pretty wonderful."

"I'm just me, but we have so many things in common. We're spending today in the studio. Just us and paint and kittens. She loves my kittens, too."

"I'm glad she went home with you yesterday. Did you find anything in the research you were doing?"

Beryl laughed. "We found so much. Nobody tells me anything, though. Cyrus Carter's family lost their surname right off the bat. He had one son who only had daughters."

"That makes sense. Do they live around here?"

"It looks like there is one family who lives just outside of Bellingwood, but the rest have spread out across Iowa. I could round them up in a day or two ... if I was desperate. I'm not that desperate."

"Who is it that lives in Bellingwood?" Polly asked.

"The Dykstra's. Do you know them?"

Polly thought and then it came to her. "I know Jeanie. She plays flute in the summer band with me. I think she's a piano teacher here in town."

"That's their youngest daughter."

"You don't suppose they know anything about the bank robbery."

"The family has had that farm for as long as I can remember," Beryl said. "It wouldn't hurt to ask."

Polly waited and when Beryl remained quiet, she coughed.

"What?"

"Are you planning to make the call?"

"Since you know Jeanie, maybe you could do it?"

"Beryl Watson," Polly scolded. "You're going to make me call her? She's your family."

"She isn't any more my family than the man in the moon," Beryl said. "And I'm taking care of Tallie today." Her voice turned mock-whiny. "Please? Please? You're the only other person who is involved in this little mystery and if you did this I would love you forever."

"You're serious, aren't you!"

"I'm pretty much maxed out on my stranger-quotient for the month. You know I'd much rather be in my quiet little studio where no one can find me."

"Fine," Polly said. "I'll call Jeanie. Maybe I can talk her into meeting me at Sweet Beans before she starts her afternoon lessons. But you owe me."

"I owe you so much already," Beryl replied. "You're a special, wonderful, gorgeous, supercalifragilisticexpialidocious friend. Do I need more adjectives? I thought the last one pretty much encompassed them all."

Polly heard the boys moving around in the living room. She wanted to put this conversation with Heath behind her. The moment she thought about it, her heart jumped.

"Did I lose you?" Beryl asked.

"No. Sorry. I need to go talk to my boy."

"Which one? Henry or Obiwan?"

"Heath." Polly lowered her voice. "I need to make him tell me who beat him up and I'm nervous about it."

"Oh. Well, good luck. Let me know if you get anything from Jeanie Dykstra. And I know, I know. I owe you big-time. You can bet that pretty little bippy of yours that I'll find a fun way to make this up to you."

"Just enjoy your time with Tallie. That's enough for now."

Polly put the phone back down on the dining room table and took another drink of coffee. It was time.

"Boys," she called, walking into the living room. "Would you come out here?"

Hayden came out and turned around. "Come on. She won't bite. You know that."

Heath followed him and the two sat down on the sofa. Heath braced himself as he sat, then leaned back gingerly.

"Do you feel better now that you've showered?" Polly asked.

"A lot." He dropped his hand to rub Obiwan's head. The dog stuck his nose between Heath's leg and the edge of the sofa.

"Heath," she said. "I don't want to have this conversation with you any more than you want me to have it, but we must talk about Friday night. I've put it off long enough."

"Okay."

She glanced at Hayden, who wouldn't take his eyes off his brother. "Buddy, you've got to tell her."

"He's right, you know," Polly said. "You have to tell me. Who did this to you?"

Heath shook his head and looked down. "I don't know."

"You do know." Polly sat forward. "Look at me."

He looked up.

"You haven't looked me in the eyes any time I've asked you this question. When you tell me that you don't know, you're lying to me. Why is this such a big deal?"

"It's not a big deal. I don't know," he said, taking an interest in Obiwan's collar.

"You did it again, Heath," Hayden said. "Talk to her."

Heath rolled his lips between his teeth and refused to look up.

"I don't know what I'm going to do with you," Polly said. She put her elbows on her knees and dropped her head into her hands. "You frustrate the heck out of me." Then she sat up. "But I will tell you this. I have all day. If that's what it takes to get you to talk, I will sit here on this couch until you're ready."

She sat back and tucked her legs up underneath her.

"That's it?" he asked.

She gave a startled bubble of laughter. "What?"

Heath looked at his brother.

Hayden picked Luke up off the back of the sofa and put him into his lap. The cat pulled away, jumped back where he'd been and perched himself. "What's your end game, Polly?" he asked.

"My end game? All I want is the truth. We need to know who did this."

"And if you don't get an answer?"

"Like I said. I'll sit here until I do."

"But what if you don't?"

"I will," she said.

"But what if you don't?"

Polly peered at him. "I don't understand what you're asking. I insist that we talk about this. We aren't going anywhere until there is a good response." She smiled. "Okay. If we're here too long, you're going back to school, but Heath and I can stay like this as long as it takes."

"What if you don't like the answer?"

"We'll deal with it. At this point, I can't imagine that I'll like it.

You've turned this into something immense and it doesn't need to be. Obviously, the answer makes Heath uncomfortable. What are you asking me?"

"What happens if you don't like what Heath has to tell you?"

"I don't know," she said. "It depends on what it is. But it can't be as bad as the two of you are making it. So far, the worst thing that I know is that Heath and Libby went out to the trails when they aren't supposed to be together. And oh, by the way, her mother has made it quite clear that you aren't to see her again. That was a big mistake in your relationship with her. You couldn't obey the rules and now you'll have to face the consequences."

"Consequences?" Heath asked.

"Yes. You are no longer allowed to spend time with her outside of school. You screwed up. I can't punish you any more than that for making that mistake. That is, if she's someone you wanted to be with."

Heath nodded and looked down at the floor.

"That's a lesson you'll want to learn right away," Polly said. "If a girl's mother sets out rules, you follow them. Because when you don't, she will make it impossible for you to see her daughter. And oh, by the way, I'm fine with that."

He looked at her. "I thought you liked Libby."

"I like her, but you two disrespected her mother and I will support her decision." Polly wasn't about to tell him the rest of what Libby's mother had said. The woman was scared for her daughter and furious that they'd been sneaking around behind her back.

She took a deep breath and let it out in a sigh. "So what's the rest of the story."

Hayden glared at his brother and then turned to Polly. "He thinks you'll kick him out."

"What?" The word exploded out of her mouth, startling everyone in the room. Han jumped down from where he'd been sitting beside her, Luke leaped off the back of the sofa, Leia sat up, and Obiwan turned to look at her. The two boys were startled as well.

"Sorry," she said in a normal tone of voice, but then she stepped it up again. "How in the world could you believe something like that about us? Why would you even think that?" Polly stood up and then sat down on the coffee table in front of Heath. She was beside herself. She grabbed his knee. "After what you went through last summer, why would you think that there is anything you could do that would make us let you go? We are committed to you, for as long as you want to be part of our family." She sat back. "No, that's not right. It's not up to you. We're committed to you. That's all there is to it. There's not a damned thing you can do to change that."

Polly turned to Hayden. "And you, too. We might not have signed papers declaring that you're part of our family, but you are. Henry and I love you two. Both of you. And Heath..." She reached over and touched his face, forcing him to look at her. "You can't make us stop loving you."

Tears streamed from his eyes. Polly pointed at a side table on the other side of the room. "Tissues."

Hayden's eyes were full as he stood and went to get the box. He put it on the table beside her and she pulled out a handful and put them in Heath's hand. "I keep this nearby for just such occasions as this. I'm always crying."

He nodded.

"Is that a 'yes, you're always crying' nod?" she asked.

He smiled through the tears and nodded again.

"Have I cleared up your biggest fear about this conversation?"

Heath blew his nose and nodded one more time.

"I'm going to need a few more words," she said. "We are going to finish this today. And maybe it won't take quite as long as I worried it would. Are you ready to talk yet?"

He put his head in his hand. "I screwed up so bad. It's just so bad."

"There's nothing so bad that you can't recover from it," Polly said. "That's one of the great things about having a family. We act as a buffer between the really bad stuff and you. But we have to know what we're dealing with. You need to talk to me."

"It was Ladd," Heath said.

"I'm sorry, Ladd Berant?" she asked. "He's in prison."

Heath nodded. "Yeah. He is, but his crew isn't and they blame me."

"And they waited six months to retaliate?"

"I've been at work, home or school most of the time," he said. "I should have known something was up, but I thought maybe they'd finally forgotten about me."

"How did they know where to find you?"

"Libby is friends with one of their girlfriends and she was bragging about how we were going to sneak out of school and go for a walk."

"Yeah," Polly said. "I forgot about that. We'll need to deal with the whole sneaking out of school thing, too." She grinned at him. "I'm not too happy that you're laid up. It would have been a perfect time to get your shower scrubbed down."

"I'll do it when I'm better," he said.

"You're right," she agreed. "You will. Now, tell me what really happened Friday afternoon."

"I didn't think anything about it. Libby and I skipped last hour and went down to the trails. And they jumped us. They told Libby that if she didn't do anything, she wouldn't be hurt. I told her to just let it happen to me. All I could think was that I had to get her home in one piece. I'd just take the beating and it would be over before school let out and then she could get on the bus and no one would ever know."

He stopped.

"And then?" Polly pressed.

"And then it got worse. They wouldn't stop hitting me and then…" He touched his cheek. "He cut me and told me that was what was happening to Ladd in jail and that I needed to feel it because it was my fault he was there."

Polly took another deep breath and looked first at Hayden and then at his brother. "I'm sorry," she said. "I'm sorry that you are still dealing with this. We're talking to the sheriff."

"No," Heath said. "That will just make it worse."

"No way. I'm not letting these bullies hurt you like this and get away with it."

"But I can't go through any more with them. There's always another one who wants to prove that he's part of the crew. I'm a target."

"Not today you aren't. Not this week, in fact. We aren't finished talking about how to handle this, but the last thing you want to do is let a bully think he has won. This is assault with a weapon. Heath, we're calling the sheriff."

He slumped back on the couch and Hayden reached out to him. "She's right."

"I know," he said. "It just sucks."

"Today looks really bad," Polly said. She put her hand on Heath's knee. "That bit about your family being a buffer is true. We will discuss all of the options you have before you have to face any of those boys again. I promise."

"Like what?" he asked.

"Like I don't know yet," she said with a smile. "This will require more research. Now, is there anything else you need to tell me?"

The two boys looked at each other and grinned.

"What?"

"We had a bet," Hayden said. "I bet him that you wouldn't kick him out and he took it. He owes me ten bucks."

"Sucker bet," Polly said. "And if you didn't hurt so bad, I'd squeeze you."

Heath moved away from her. "Ouch?"

CHAPTER TWENTY-THREE

Leaving the boys in the living room, Polly called Aaron. When she gave him the names of the boys who had been involved, he groaned.

"What's wrong?" she asked.

"It's nothing. They are trouble."

She heard him breathing.

"Aaron?"

"Sorry. Is Heath willing to accuse them of beating him up?"

"I don't know," Polly said. "He's certainly fearful of reprisals. He didn't want me to tell you and I think he hopes this will just go away."

"This is one of those things I hate about my job," Aaron said. "I want to nail these delinquents, but Heath is right. It won't be easy for him at school. They have their claws dug in pretty tight and as you can see, they're more than willing to make a statement with their fists, feet, and now weapons."

"Doesn't that change things?" she asked.

"That a knife was used? Yes, for one of the boys. But the others will still be around to torment Heath and his friends. What a strange sense of loyalty they have. But it's worse for Heath because he was once part of them. He sighed. "We'll round them up and see what we can shake out, but I don't know what we'll be able to do. How is he doing?"

"He's getting better," she said. "I'm not sending him back to school this week. If he has to face them, I want him to at least be healthy. You know, Aaron, I can totally get helicopter parents. I want to yank him out of there and put him into a completely different school system so he never has to see those boys again."

"I understand," Aaron said. "Let me ask more questions at the school before you make any decisions. This beating is an escalation, but they've hurt kids before. From what I understand, Ladd Berant has become a hero to some of the kids that knew him."

"How does that even happen?" she asked.

"The world is a scary place for our young people some days."

"Can I open a little home school in my back yard?" Polly asked. "How can I send Rebecca into that type of environment?"

"Most kids don't even realize this is going on. She might never see any hint of it."

"This is Rebecca we're talking about," Polly said. "You know better than that. Say, by the way, have you gotten any more information on Ethan Carter's death?"

"Your friend Beryl and young Tallie gave me some names this morning. Anita is checking to see if any of the other cousins are in Iowa, just in case they came up to check on his progress."

"Finding a treasure that no one knows whether it even exists?" Polly was incredulous. "After all of these years, why would they think it's just going to pop out at them?"

"It's the only thing we have to go on."

"Did you talk to Beryl about her half-brother, Darien?"

"The English boy?"

Polly laughed. "He's not a boy. But yes. I'd almost bet that he was the one who broke into Sycamore House last night. It's the only thing that makes sense."

"What do you think he was looking for?"

"That's where we're stumped," she said. "Maybe it was the list of family members so he could reach out to Lester Carter's descendants or get in touch with some of the boys he'd talked to last fall when he contacted Ethan. Or maybe he was looking for the research Andy had done on land that the early Carters owned around here."

"This is all pretty convoluted," Aaron said with a chuckle. "I'm glad you reached out to Bellingwood police rather than me, though."

"That was the alarm company. I would have called you."

"Dead bodies, Polly. All I want is dead bodies from you."

"And beaten up sons?"

"I will always take care of your family. We do need to talk to Heath, though. Stu is up in that neck of the woods. Can I have him stop by?"

"Sure. Heath's brother is here for a while. It might help if Stu talks to both of them. Hayden is good support."

"I'll give him a call. Thanks, Polly."

"Thank you," she replied.

Polly wondered if she still had Jeanie Dykstra's contact information in her phone. They really didn't see each other outside of summer band rehearsals and performances, but they'd exchanged numbers the first year. She scrolled through the list until she found it. Blast Beryl anyway. This wasn't Polly's job and here she was doing it just because Beryl asked.

She frowned, then swiped the call open and waited as it rang.

"Jeanie Dykstra, how may I help you?"

"Hi, Jeanie. This is Polly Giller. How are you?"

"Polly! I'm fine. What can I do for you?"

"Well," Polly said. "Apparently you are descended from Lester Carter, one of the founders of Bellingwood."

Jeanie laughed. "Yes I am. Are you on the committee for the sesquicentennial? I guess you can't get started too early on this."

"No. That's not it. It's something else entirely right now. I wonder if your family has any old family letters or pictures or information from the days of Lester and Jedidiah Carter."

"I'm sure we do. They're all out at Mama and Daddy's house, though. What are you looking for?"

"That's just it," Polly said. "I'm not sure. Apparently, descendants of the third brother, Cyrus, found letters that Lester had sent to him regarding Jedidiah's robbery of the bank."

"Oh that," Jeanie said. Polly could hear the smile in her voice. "That's old news."

"What do you mean?"

"I don't know about the gold, but I know that it was all paid back to the bank. Jedidiah's daughter cleared his name. We have the bank ledgers. That's kind of a family legend that's been passed down."

"But you don't know if they found the gold?"

"I suppose not. You've heard about Pearl, though, right? How she wrote under a man's name? Cyrus was very proud of her. If she hadn't done what she did, he would have lost the bank because of her father. The regulators were coming in to audit the accounts and Cyrus didn't know what to do. Pearl sold more stories that year than ever before so that she could pay him back for her father's wrong doing. Old Jedidiah had died by that point. She wouldn't have had to take responsibility for it, but she did."

"So Cyrus didn't have any idea where Jedidiah might have buried the gold?"

"Buried it?" Jeanie laughed out loud. "He was such a thief and a gambler, it had to have just dribbled out of his hands."

"But as I understand it, he died before that could have happened."

"Hmmm," Jeanie said. "I suppose. It might not be a bad idea to look through that little box of goodies we have at the house. Maybe I should give Mama a call. Would you like to see it, too?"

"I would love that."

"Polly?"

"Yes."

"There's someone at the door." Jeanie paused. "Well, he's a handsome fellow."

"Tall? Dark hair?"

"Yes, do you know him?"

"Jeanie, don't answer the door."

"What do you mean?"

"If he's who I think he is, you don't want to answer the door. He's looking for the same information that I am, but I don't know what his motives are."

"What should I do?"

"I don't think he'll try to break in," Polly said. "Is your front door locked?"

"No," Jeanie said. "I never lock my door during the day. Do you think he'll come in?" Her voice dropped to a whisper. "He's opening the door."

"Halloo, is anyone here? Jeanie Dykstra, are you home?" It was a distinct British accent.

"That is who I thought it was," Polly said. She ran out into the living room. "Heath, do you have your phone?"

He held it up.

"Call the police and tell them that Jeanie Dykstra has unwanted company." Polly said to Jeanie. "What's your address?"

"Two-oh-four East Polk," Jeanie whispered. "I'm in the back bathroom. I don't think he came in the house, though."

Heath handed Polly the phone. "Hi, this is Polly Giller and I think the man who broke into Sycamore House last night might be over at Jeanie Dykstra's house."

"Is she safe?"

"I think so. Could you send someone by there, though?"

"Right away. Are you on the phone with her?"

"I am."

"Tell her to remain quiet and we'll be right there. Do you believe he's a threat to her?"

Polly pursed her lips and thought. "Not really. It's the middle of the morning, so probably not, but I'd hate to be wrong."

There was a knock at Polly's front door and she nodded at Hayden. She felt like an octopus with a telephone in each hand and now this. He stood up and opened the door, then stepped back as Deputy Stu Decker came in.

Stu took in Polly's situation and smiled at her, then extended his hand to Hayden.

"Stu Decker."

"I'm Hayden Harvey. Do you know my brother, Heath?"

Stu nodded. "How are you feeling today Heath?"

"Better."

"You still look pretty rough. Polly called the sheriff and said you have some names for us. Can we talk?"

Heath looked at Polly just as Jeanie said, "I think he drove away. Would he go out to my parent's house?"

Polly turned away from the conversation in her living room. "I don't know that, Jeanie. The police are on their way to you. If you're worried, call your mother and talk to the officer about it."

"Ms. Giller?" the dispatcher asked. "The officer is pulling up in front of her house right now. He says there is no one there. Will she answer the door for him?"

"Jeanie," Polly said, thinking she deserved a headache after this. "There's an officer coming to your front door. Do you feel comfortable letting him in?"

"I do. Can I call you later?"

Polly chuckled. "Of course. I'll stay on the phone until you tell me that it's okay."

"It's okay," Jeanie said. "I know him. Thank you."

With that she was gone. "She knows the officer that's at her front door," Polly said to the dispatcher. "Thank you for your help."

"Thank you."

Polly turned back to the men in her living room and Stu raised his eyebrows. "Officer? What's going on?"

"Too much," Polly said. "There has not been enough coffee in my morning for all of this."

"Is everything okay?"

"I think so. That was Jeanie Dykstra. There was a man at her front door that shouldn't have been there. I'm pretty sure it's the same man who broke in here last night. So, we called the police." She handed Heath's phone back to him. "Thanks."

Stu chuckled. "There's always something when you're around, isn't there?"

"Stop it. This is not my fault. When will you people get that through your head?" she asked with a laugh. "You got here faster than I thought you would. I haven't had a chance to talk to Heath yet."

"I see," Stu replied. "Heath, I just need you to tell me what happened Friday night and who was involved. How did they know where to find you?"

Heath looked up at Polly again and she nodded at him. "Tell him everything. You aren't in trouble here. He needs the whole story."

"Go ahead," Hayden said. "Just tell it. It's the right thing to do."

Heath told his story, this time with more confidence. Stu quietly took notes as the boy spoke, asking questions only to encourage him to continue. When Stu asked Heath if he feared for his life, Heath shook his head.

Then he stopped, looked down and then back up. "I do now. I don't want to be a drama queen, but they told me I'd die if I talked to you."

Polly sucked in a breath and held it. This couldn't be happening. Heath was finally participating in life again. He couldn't shut himself back inside the shell he'd built before coming to live with her.

"Would your friend, Libby, corroborate your story?" Stu asked.

"I think so," Heath replied. "She was pretty scared, though. I don't know what she remembers." He looked at Polly. "And her mom hates me now, so she might not help."

"What about other kids at school. Are these same boys threatening anyone else?"

Heath huffed a derisive laugh. "All the time. Nobody does anything about it, though. I even heard them threaten one of the teachers. Nobody did anything about that either."

"I see. Just four of them?"

"Yeah. I suppose," Heath said.

"What does that mean?"

"There's those four and then there are some hangers on. You know, kids that will do whatever they say so there isn't any trouble. Those kids are freshman, but they think they're big-time."

Stu reached over to shake Heath's hand. "Thank you for talking to me. I'm sorry this happened to you. We'll do what we can to make it safe for you to return to school."

"And if you can't?" Hayden asked.

"I don't know, son," Stu said. "We will do our best for your brother, though."

Polly walked Stu to the front door.

"I'm not sure what to say here, Polly. But don't hurry to send him back to school, okay? Give us some time to talk to people."

"He needs to heal anyway," Polly said. "Thanks for coming over."

She stood in the doorway and watched Stu walk down the steps. It made her angry that there was nothing she could do. It made her even angrier that there were more kids than Heath who didn't feel safe in school. My goodness, were people's priorities messed up. She took a deep breath, walked back inside and shut the door.

"I'm calling the school this afternoon to get your assignments. You're off for at least this week. We'll take this one step at a time," she said.

Hayden looked at his brother. "I need to head back to Ames. Is there anything else you need from me?"

She smiled at him and gave him a hug. "I'm glad you were here this weekend. Home game again next week?"

"We're on the road," he said. "But maybe I can come over Sunday night again?"

"You know you're welcome any time."

Polly wanted to talk to Jeff. She was sure Henry had contacted him about fixing the window, but she wanted to see him face to face. "I need to go down to the office," she said to Heath. "How about we move you into the media room before I go?"

He pushed the blanket off his lap and dislodged Han from his feet. "I can do it on my own."

"Of course you can," Polly said. "But how about you just let me keep an eye on things so I feel better about where you are. Please let me take care of you."

"You've already done more than anybody ever has for me."

"Hey," Hayden said, coming out of the bedroom. "I'm your bro. What about me?"

"That's right. You take care of me. Sorry." Heath tossed a pillow at his brother's feet. "Pick that up, please?"

"Punk."

"Dirtbag."

"Stinkyfeet."

Polly smiled. No matter how bad things looked, the truth was, you just had to manage your way through it.

"You gonna move into the other room?" Hayden asked.

"Yeah. What's it to you?"

"Let's make sure you can walk without my help. You don't want to lean on Polly and break her back." Hayden stood in front of Heath, held his forearm out and stiffened it so Heath could use it to pull himself up.

The two boys walked slowly through the dining room into the media room. Hayden dropped his duffel bag to the ground and took Heath's hand, allowing his brother to hold on as he braced himself on the arm of the sofa and finally dropped into place.

"Ask for help," Hayden said. "Don't hurt yourself because you're being stupid, okay?"

"Just go," Heath retorted. "I'll be fine."

"And thank you, big brother, you've been a big help this weekend," Hayden said.

Heath looked up at him. "Thanks."

"I'll see you later, Polly. Don't let him kid you, he still hurts."

"I know," she said. "Thank you for all of your help."

Hayden headed down the back steps and Polly looked at Heath. "What do you need?"

"A pain pill," he replied.

She looked at the clock on the dining room wall. He was well past the time for his medication. "We're running late. I'm sorry."

"I was trying to see if I could go without."

"Good for you," Polly said. "But rather than doing without, just plan to extend the time between pills." She put the remote in his lap and pulled the coffee table out of his way, then tugged the side table out so he could easily reach it.

After he took his medication, Polly sat down at the dining room table. The morning had already been more exciting than she'd expected. And all of that on very little sleep. A rhythmic noise from Heath told her that he had fallen asleep. If he was out, she had time to go downstairs.

Polly walked out the front door, shutting it on the dogs who wanted to go out and play. She ran down the steps and walked into the office.

"Good morning," Stephanie said. "How are things upstairs? Is Heath okay?"

"He's hurting, but he'll be fine. Have you heard from the police yet?" Polly nodded toward her office.

"They've been here and are gone already," Stephanie replied. "You can have it back. Eliseo came in and ran the vacuum again. We picked things up and tried to put them back in some kind of order, but you'll probably want to reorganize the knick knacks. Can you believe it? How crazy was that?"

"Pretty crazy," Polly said. "I had never heard the alarm before. I don't like it. I don't want to hear it again."

"But aren't you glad we installed it," Jeff said, coming out of his office.

She chuckled. "Nice of you to tell me."

"You signed the check. The description was on the invoice."

Polly didn't know what to say to that. "Oh."

"We're replacing a lot of windows these days," he said. "Somebody will be here to take care of this on Wednesday."

"What about out at Sycamore Inn?"

"Windows are replaced there, door sills are fixed, the rooms have been cleaned and we're repainting them this week."

Polly dropped into a chair in front of Stephanie's desk. "I just hit a wall."

"You've had a crazy week," Stephanie said.

Polly grinned. "I thought I was going to get out and meet someone at the coffee shop. But that didn't happen and I feel a little guilty leaving Heath alone upstairs." She sighed. "What kind of fun coffee did Rachel make this morning?"

Stephanie turned and glanced at Jeff and he laughed at her. "Go. You've been begging me all morning. Take a break."

"Do you want something from Sweet Beans?" Stephanie asked Polly.

Polly sat straight up. "What? Really?"

"I've been dying this morning. For some reason I didn't get enough sleep either last night." She giggled. "And I really want a raspberry scone, too."

"You're a lifesaver," Polly said. She reached into her pocket for her wallet and came up empty. "I think I have some money in my office."

Jeff took his billfold out and handed a bill to Stephanie. "It's on me. If she's drivin', I'm buyin'."

"Your mail is on your desk," Stephanie said, picking up her purse from under her desk. "I'll be back before you know it."

Polly leaned back and kicked her feet out in front of her. "This is the best news I've had all morning. Bless your little pink soul."

CHAPTER TWENTY-FOUR

Polly took another pan of chocolate crinkle cookies out of the oven and hesitated before putting them on the counter. She loved the smell of freshly baked cookies, no matter how often she baked. She shook her head and laughed. There had been more baking lately and she considered that it might be her way of managing stress. She checked out the kitchen window and saw Kayla, Andrew and Rebecca crossing the street. Perfect timing. Heath was feeling enough better that he was looking forward to company.

She slid the cookies off onto a cooling rack and walked out to the living room to open the front door. Much to her surprise, Jason was standing there when she pulled it open.

"Hey there," she said. "I wasn't expecting you."

"Can I come in?"

Polly stepped back. "Of course. You're always welcome. What's up?"

"Is Heath here?"

She pointed to the media room. "What's going on?"

"I have some stuff for him."

"Homework? I didn't expect them to send it back with you."

Jason shrugged. "I volunteered. The guidance counselor knew that we drove together, so she asked if I could bring it with me."

"Thank you. Do you want me to take it?"

"Nah. I'll give it to him. Do you mind?"

"Not at all." Polly watched him walk away and then was distracted by the three kids running up the steps and into the apartment.

"Was that Jason?" Kayla asked, her face red from running and her eyes bright with curiosity.

"It sure is. He brought Heath's homework."

Andrew and Rebecca ran into the dining room, dumping their bags and coats along the way.

"Jason," Andrew said. "What did they say at school today about Heath?"

Kayla took her coat off and put it and her backpack on the sofa, then stopped to straighten her hair. "Do I look okay?" she asked Polly.

"You look fine, honey."

"Really?"

"Really."

Kayla walked into the other room and Polly pushed the door closed. What was that about? When she got into the dining room, she realized what it was about. Kayla hung back, but couldn't take her eyes off Jason.

Jason and Heath were talking low enough that Polly couldn't hear words. Andrew and Rebecca had taken seats on the floor in front of Heath's sofa and watched the conversation raptly.

"Go on," Polly said to Kayla. "Cookies can wait."

"I can help you," Kayla said.

"Who wants cookies?" Polly asked, loudly enough for everyone to hear.

Andrew looked up at her, but didn't move.

She glanced at Kayla and filled a plate with cookies, then walked into the media room. "There's something interesting going on over here and I seem to be missing out."

"Jason's telling Heath what happened in school today. The cops were there and everything," Rebecca said.

Andrew nodded. "Because Jason almost hung with those guys last year. Remember?"

Polly looked down at Jason. "Not really," he said.

"How did it go then?" she asked.

"At school?" Jason responded.

"Yes. At school. With the cops."

"They took Shawn out. He was so stupid," Jason said. "He thought he'd get all up in the cop's face. Told him that he didn't have any right to harass him on school property. It's like these guys *want* to go to jail." He reached for the plate of cookies and took one, then handed it to Heath. "When they told him to back off, he pulled a knife. His life is oh-ver."

"What about the rest of the boys?" Polly asked.

Jason laughed. "They're nothing without their main guy. But it got pretty funny. Somebody made a poster. Like five hundred copies of it and spread it all around school. They stuck one in every locker and they were on the tables in the foyer and in the lunchroom."

Polly looked around at the kids, waiting for someone to ask. "Okay, I'll bite. What did it say?"

He dug down into the backpack and pulled a piece of paper out and handed it to her.

In large letters across the top were the words, "United We Stand, Divided We fall."

"Don't let bullies run our school.

Be proud. Be strong. Be a friend.

Name them by name, call them out.

Report their behavior, defend their victims.

Stand up for each other.

BE A FRIEND.

Someday it could be you who needs a friend."

Polly read the words and looked down at Rebecca. "Do you know something about this? The handwriting on that last line looks awfully familiar."

"I just thought it was a good idea," Rebecca said.

"When did you do this and how did you get these into the high school?"

"We put it together Saturday when you were gone," Andrew said. "And Rebecca called Jen who has an older sister that's a cheerleader. We scanned it and sent it to them and then I saw Jen at church and gave her money for copies. Her sister thought it was a great idea and was going to make the copies tonight, but I guess she did it early."

Jason nodded. "All of the cheerleaders got in on it and then a bunch of football players and some of the guys from the basketball team. They were all stuffing lockers."

"I can't believe the administration let them do this," Polly said.

"What were they going to do?" he asked. "There's nothing controversial or mean on it. They want the place to be good for us and if the kids are going to work together, the teachers think it's a great idea."

Polly bent over and hugged Rebecca's neck. "I'm so proud of you."

"It was Andrew's idea, too," she said.

"Not likely," Andrew said. "I just agreed when you brought it up."

"What do you think, Heath?" Polly sat down on the sofa by his feet.

"I don't know. It's weird. Nobody ever cared before."

"Nobody got beat up like you did," Jason said. "That sucks, man." He laughed. "And I'm supposed to give you these." He dug down into the bag again and pulled out several slips of paper.

"What's this?" Heath asked.

"Phone numbers." Jason grimaced. "You freakin' got phone numbers. A little cut on the face and some bruised ribs and girls wanted me to give you their phone numbers."

Heath's face grew bright red and he put them on the table. "Don't they know I'm with Libby?"

"She says you're not," Jason said. "She was telling everybody about how her mom freaked out because you disobeyed her rules and she can't go out with someone who used to be associated with those guys."

"But her friend, Jean, dated Dooley."

"The girls figured that out and told Libby she was being stupid. Apparently you're..." Jason held his hands up and made air quotes. "Cute. And the scar will give you..." He stopped and rolled his eyes. "I'm not kidding you when Selena Morris said it would give you a rakish quality."

Polly couldn't help herself. "Where did she get that?"

"You should see the books she reads," Jason said. "They're embarrassing." He shuffled the slips of paper around. "Here's her number. She was the most interested." He patted the rest. "Any of these you'd like to pass on to me, I'd be willing to take them off your hands."

"This is weird." Heath moaned and leaned back on the couch.

"Well, you're some kind of hero. You stood up for a girl, took a beating and then Rebecca, here, made it all about honor and friendship." Jason put his hand up. "Don't give me any trouble. I've been reading too. Andrew keeps putting those books beside my bed."

Andrew looked up and gave them all a not-so-innocent smile.

"Miss Jennet said that none of your homework was due tomorrow, but I can bring things back on Wednesday if you aren't in school by then. I'll pick up more assignments from her tomorrow after school."

"Thank you, Jason," Polly said.

"Yeah. I'd better get down to the barn. Eliseo doesn't know I'm up here." He looked at his phone. "Yep. There's a text. He doesn't let me get too far away. Can I take some cookies?"

"Come with me into the kitchen," Polly said. "I'll pack them for you."

"You'll be fine when you come back," Jason said to Heath. "I've got your back."

Heath just stared at Jason as the younger boy walked into the kitchen. Polly put cookies onto a paper plate and slipped them into a zipper-bag, then walked with Jason to the front door.

"What was that about?" she asked.

He shrugged. "What?"

"You haven't had a decent word to say to him until now. What changed?"

"I don't know. Whatever."

She put her arms around him and hugged him. "I like it. And thank you."

"He's okay."

"And so are you."

"Hello up there!"

Jason looked at Polly and she grinned. "That's Beryl. Send her up."

"Oh Polly," Beryl called. "I saw your door open. Are you up there?"

He hurried down the steps and before Polly knew it, Beryl and Tallie were standing in front of her.

"Why don't you come in?" Polly asked. "I have cookies."

"I knew you would," Beryl said. "Didn't I say that, Tallie? I told her that you knew we were coming and would have baked cookies. I felt it in the wind."

"You are a nut," Polly said. "I didn't feel anything. I just made cookies."

"But you made them for us." Beryl gave her a little push. "Now get out of the door and let us in. We have much to tell you."

Tallie carried two canvas tote bags and grinned at Polly as she followed Beryl into the dining room.

"Ahoy, young people," Beryl announced. "If you want to be part of the adventure of a lifetime, cast an eye and lend an ear."

She stood at the end of the dining room table and passed her hand across it. "Clear the decks and attend to the battlements." Beryl affected a pirate's accent. "We've gold to discover. Arrr."

Polly picked up the papers and debris that generally found its way to the far end of the table. She and Henry had a bad habit of keeping one end clear so the family could eat, but that only meant that the other end of the eight-foot table soon grew out of control. Every once in a while, she sat down to dig through the piles, but it had been well over a week. She looked around for a place to quickly place them and settled on the floor under the far corner of the peninsula.

"Hop to it, wench," Beryl said to Tallie. "Yer holdin' up the attack. Arrr."

The kids found places on either side of the table, while Polly stood next to Beryl. "Where be the treasure, matey?" Polly asked.

"Aye, that there's the question. But d'trusty bos'n has maps and charts. We jes need ta find the spot marked with an x."

"Are we doing that all afternoon?" Tallie asked, waggling her hand at Beryl.

"Only till I'm fed swill and grog by the serving wench."

Polly put a cookie in Beryl's hand and rushed to the fridge to pour a glass of iced tea. "Will this assuage your inner beast, Cap'n?" she asked.

Beryl took a long drink of the tea and sighed. "The beast has been tamed. Thank'ee."

Rebecca, Andrew, and Kayla giggled, caught up in Beryl's fun.

"What did you find?" Polly asked.

"Tallie and I spent the morning going through some of the things that Andy had collected, then believe it or not, Jeanie Dykstra's mother called me. She had a small tin box filled with photographs and old papers and she also had two really old ledger books. I think they're from the bank." Beryl shrugged. "Maybe I should recommend she give those back. They'd probably like to have the history." She took a bite of the cookie. "Wow, these are great. The beast is nearly completely under control. I will need at least one more and my bos'n should have one or two as well."

"Then we came over here," Tallie said. "I picked up some of Andy's research, and when the library opened, I stopped up there to see if they had any old plat maps of the county. There was even more information on those. But we haven't put it all together yet."

"I thought we should share that fun with you," Beryl said. "And besides, I was tired of worrying about whether or not that Limey bast-." She looked at the kids. "The British jerk was going to show up again."

"Did he try to go out to the Dykstra's?" Polly asked, ignoring the slip. Rebecca and Andrew giggled again, but she gave them a look and they stopped.

"I asked Marybelle and she wasn't too worried. Jim was in the house with her and Elbert was guarding the door."

"Elbert?"

"Her Remington shotgun."

"I see," Polly said with a nervous laugh. "In other words, be careful if you visit the Dykstras."

"Oh honey," Beryl retorted. "You should be careful if you intend to frighten most of the farm families around here. They know how to take care of themselves and their property."

"Okay, okay." Polly waved her hand at the papers that Tallie had been spreading out. "What's all this?"

Beryl looked at the table, then at Tallie and then at Polly. "You're so boorish."

"What?"

"You brought tea and cookies for me and didn't offer anything to my bos'n. How coarse."

"I'm so sorry," Polly said. She reached for Tallie's forearm. "That was rude of me. I just wanted Beryl's terrible pirate accent to stop. What would you like to drink?"

Tallie laughed. "Tea would be fine."

Rebecca put her hand up. "We haven't had anything to drink either. Could I get it?"

"I'm the worst host ever," Polly said. "Yes, please, Rebecca. See if Heath wants anything."

After everyone was settled back at the table. Polly sat down beside Andrew and Tallie sat across from them between Rebecca and Kayla. Beryl had definitively claimed her place at the head.

"Heath is okay over there?" Polly asked Rebecca quietly.

"He said he's tired. He can hear us."

"But you think he's okay?"

Rebecca nodded. "Just tired."

Polly glanced over to see that Heath had shifted himself so he was lying on his side watching television. She hoped he would let her know if he needed anything, but more than likely, he'd tough it out until she pressed. Now was not the time, though.

"Tell us what we have here," she said.

"This is a plat map of the area from 1930," Tallie said. "That's the earliest one we could find. We also found an atlas of the county from 1909." She pushed both maps toward Polly.

Polly set the atlas aside and opened the plat book. "There's still some land marked as belonging to the Carters here in the Bellingwood township."

She pointed at one section. "This says it was owned by the Bellingwood National Bank. But that's not in town. See, these grayed out blocks are Bellingwood."

"That's why we have the atlas," Tallie said. "So we can figure out where everything is. "And here's a current state map. I thought maybe this might help, too."

"Okay, now what?" Polly asked.

"Now we identify the most likely spots that Jedidiah would have buried his gold," Beryl said. She opened the tin box and took out a small stack of photographs.

"I've seen this one," Polly said. "It's Jedidiah and Cyrus in front of the bank."

Beryl slid her fingers into the stack and slipped out another photograph. "This is Pearl Carter with Cyrus. I wonder if she was writing him a check for her father's debts."

The photograph showed a young woman seated at a desk, with pen poised to write, while an older gentleman that Polly could now identify as Cyrus, was looking over her shoulder at the papers in front of her.

"And then there's this," Beryl said and handed Polly a small book.

"What is it?"

"Look inside."

Polly opened the book and in tight, precise letters, someone had listed all of the property owned by the Carter brothers. As Polly turned the pages, she saw various parcels of land being sold off and others purchased by Cyrus from Jedidiah.

"You have everything here," she breathed. "Now what about that big red X to mark the spot."

Tallie leaned across the table and tapped the book. "We know when Jedidiah robbed the bank, so we can eliminate property that was sold prior to that date. And honestly, if there was any property sold between then and his death, that can be eliminated, too."

"Yeah," Polly said. "He wouldn't be so stupid as to sell land where he'd buried his loot." She peered at Beryl. "Speaking of which, how much do you suppose he took?"

"That's right here," Beryl said and took out a newspaper clipping that had been folded up for many years. "I don't want to unfold that again. Tallie took a picture of it when I did earlier. Do you have that?"

"It's right here." Tallie swiped through her photos and showed the image to Polly.

"Three thousand dollars," Polly said. "What does that work out to?"

"We looked it up. Show her, Tallie."

"I can't find it that fast, but we'll say that an ounce of gold was around nineteen dollars."

Polly ticked on her fingers. "I'm calling it twenty dollars. I can do the math. He stole one hundred fifty ounces, or a little over nine pounds. What is gold worth now?"

Beryl grinned. "About thirteen hundred dollars an ounce."

Rebecca slapped her hand down on the table. "That's almost two hundred thousand dollars."

"No wonder there's such a fuss," Polly said. Then she slumped. "Can you imagine what it took for Pearl Carter to pay that back? That poor girl had to work hard. She could have done so many different things with her money, but her father flushed every cent of it away. And not just once, but over and over again."

A strange sound rang through the room and Beryl jumped out of her seat. "That's my phone. Where is it?" She patted the papers on the table in front of her and looked around, pushing the bags with her feet. "What did I do with it?"

"It's in your sweater pocket," Tallie said.

"Oh silly me." Beryl patted her pocket, took the phone out and said, "Hello, Beryl Watson here."

They watched as her face brightened, then grew serious, then grew even more serious and then she laughed out loud. "Good for you," she said. "I'm sorry you didn't get an opportunity to do permanent damage." She nodded and smiled and then said, "We're just getting into it. I'll let you know." She was quiet again and then said, "Thanks for calling."

"That was Marybelle Dykstra," Beryl said. "She scared the daylights out of our British gentleman and then told him she was calling the police to let them know that he was in town. I guess I'm the police."

"But we should call them," Polly said. "They'll want to know that he's still around."

Beryl flitted her hand at Polly. "That's your job. You have relationships with all the local law enforcement."

"Uh huh."

"Okay, so he's my best friend's husband. But trust me, I don't like having to call him professionally. He gets a little testy."

"Can I look at that book?" Rebecca asked.

Polly held out the property listings. "This?"

"Yeah. Andrew, Kayla and I can go through the pages and figure out what property Jedidiah Carter owned when he died. That sounds like fun."

"Sure." Polly glanced at Tallie and Beryl for their approval. Both seemed happy not to have to do the work. "There's paper in the middle left drawer of Henry's desk."

"I know where it is," Rebecca said. "Can we take that plat book too? I think the numbers correspond to it."

Beryl pushed the book to her. "Be careful with that stuff. It isn't mine."

"Of course we will," Rebecca replied. "Don't worry."

The kids took off for Henry's office and Polly took out her phone. She wasn't really sure whether to call Aaron or the police station. Aaron was used to hearing from her, but Bellingwood police had been tracking Darien Blackstone. It wasn't yet five o'clock, so she hoped that Mindy was still answering the phone.

"Bellingwood Police," a familiar voice answered.

"Mindy, this is Polly Giller."

"Hello there. It sounds like you had a rough night again last night."

"Yeah. And I'm calling about that guy. He's still in town and was just out at Marybelle and Jim Dykstra's house. She ran him off with a shotgun."

Mindy laughed. "Oh she did! I'm not surprised. There isn't much that scares her. Thanks for the call. I'll let Bert know. And I'll tell him to call before he gets there."

"Not a bad idea."

"There," Polly said after she put the phone down. "I've made yet another call for you."

Beryl bowed and rolled her hand. "Thank you, oh my wonderful master. Where would I be without you?"

"I have no idea. Show me what else you have going on in those totes while the kids are working on the real estate. Anything that pertains to this?"

"Not really," Tallie said. "It's fascinating stuff, but I don't think it will help us."

"Let's look anyway. Is there anything from the early nineteen hundreds? I'm looking for information about Bellingwood when the Bell House was built."

Tallie lifted a tote bag onto the table and pulled stacks of paper out. It was all still disorganized, but at least Polly knew that she could look through it without desperately trying to solve a mystery.

CHAPTER TWENTY-FIVE

Returning the kids to their homework had been no easy task, but after Beryl and Tallie left, Polly took the real estate sales information away and sent them to the dining room table. The treasure had waited this long, it could continue to wait.

On Henry's way back from Boone, he picked up supper and they ate in the media room. After the last few days, it felt good just to sit in front of a movie as a family. But by nine thirty, Polly was done. Heath was asleep, Rebecca had long since lost interest in the movie, and Henry was squirming and fidgeting in his chair. She told Heath and Rebecca that she didn't care if they went to sleep, but everyone was going to their bedrooms. Polly collapsed onto the bed and tried to read, but after Henry picked the book up off her chest the second time, she turned her light off and fell asleep, hoping that they'd get through the night without a crisis.

She turned over and looked outside to see the gray of pre-dawn.

"Good morning," Henry said. "Did you sleep well?"

"No dreams and nobody woke me up with alarms or phone calls," she replied. "I want a few more of those nights."

"Han and I are taking off early this morning. We won't be here for breakfast."

She sat up in bed. "What's going on?"

"Nothing abnormal, just a lot of work. But today will be a good day for him to go with me. Will that help you?"

"I guess. I like having him around, though."

Henry smiled. "So do I." He twisted around and rubbed his dog's head. "Hey buddy, wanna hang out with me?"

Han wagged his entire body and tried to climb up Henry's body in his joy.

"Silly dog." Henry swung his legs over the dog and sat on the edge of the bed. "What's up with you today?"

"I don't know," Polly said. "I'll check in downstairs. It feels like I haven't been there in a month, but I really want to get back to Bell House. We'll see what Heath thinks about being alone. Otherwise, I'll just stick close."

"Mom said that she and Molly would be glad to come over and spend the day with him if you had things to do."

"She's a wonderful woman," Polly said.

"She likes our kids."

Polly thought about that for a minute. No wonder Henry was so comfortable taking in whatever kids she found. His parents had taught him well. "I love her."

"She loves you, too." Henry leaned back and then tapped his lips so she would bend over and kiss him. "And so do I. Very much." He took a deep breath. "Okay, into the breach. Han, old buddy. I'd best get moving if I'm going to start this day."

"Do you want me to whip up some breakfast for you?" Polly asked before he disappeared into the bathroom.

He turned back to her and gave her a guilty laugh. "Please don't hate me for wanting to pick up coffee and a donut at Sweet Beans."

"You're a rat," she said. "I want to go with you."

"I'll take Obiwan outside and send him back upstairs before we leave. Does that help?"

"You're still a rat. But it's fine."

"Do you want me to call Mom?"

"If Heath needs a babysitter and I need to leave, I'll call her," Polly said. "No worries. And by the way..." She waited for him to turn around. "Cute butt."

Henry waggled it and went on into the bathroom to get ready.

Polly was in the kitchen when he came through. He stopped to give her a kiss and then took the dogs out with him. She had extra time before she had to get Rebecca moving, so she opened the cupboard doors and held on to the handles, leaning back. Surely there was something interesting she could make for breakfast. When nothing caught her eye, she moved to the refrigerator and then the freezer. This was pathetic. Hayden truly spoiled her on the weekends he came home.

She lifted the aluminum foil on a casserole dish and smiled. Leftover breakfast casserole it was. If she was lucky, there was a container of sausage gravy as well. After pulling both out, she started the coffee pot and lifted herself up to the counter top. She'd kill the kids if they did this, but who was going to catch her?

The morning continued to brighten. If this kept up, it was going to be a great day. Scrabbling toenails on the floor alerted her to Obiwan's return and she jumped down to fill his food dish.

After sending Rebecca to school, Polly tapped on Heath's door. "Are you awake?" she asked, chuckling. Because he was now.

"Come in."

She opened the door to find him sitting up on the edge of his bed, wearing a pair of sweatpants and his t-shirt around his neck. "Were you going to ask me for help?"

He groaned. "I should be able to do this, but I can't get my arms to go where I want them to go. It hurts too much." He looked down at his feet. "And I can't bend over to put my socks on."

"One arm at a time, then," Polly said. She helped with the t-shirt first and then knelt down. "Foot up." She put one sock on, massaged his instep, and did the same for the other foot.

He wriggled his feet away. "That tickles."

"Just checking," she said with a laugh. "Are you ready for breakfast?"

"Let me see if I can get out there by myself. I really am better. I don't want any pain pills today, either."

She stood and stepped back.

"Don't watch me," he said. "Just go away. I'll be there in a few minutes."

"You're sure?"

Heath glared at her.

"Got it. You're sure." Polly left the room, but hovered outside his door. He moaned and groaned, his breath hitched a couple of times, then she finally heard a first step and another. Before he got to the doorway, she made her way to the dining room.

"Polly?"

She ran back to him, worried that something terrible had happened.

"What?"

"I'm sorry. I forgot to get my backpack and phone. And I can't go back for it now."

"Phone on your bedside table?" she asked.

"Yes, and the backpack is on the floor on the other side of the bed. I was going to work on homework last night, but I fell asleep."

"Go on out to the sofa and I'll bring it."

Heath's room was much cleaner than Rebecca's. She picked up the things he might need and went back into the dining room. "How are your wounds?" she asked.

He was standing in front of the sofa. He leaned forward, grabbed the arm, then stood back up. He turned around and grabbed the arm again, then stood back up. Finally, he lifted his leg and dropped himself onto the seat cushion and groaned.

"I could have helped," she said.

"I have to do it myself. I didn't know how much we used those muscles to do everything."

"Are you going to be okay?"

"Just a minute."

She listened to him breathe in and out raggedly until his breath finally slowed. "Better?"

"Yeah." He peeled back the gauze from the wound on his arm. "Do you want to see it?"

"Not really. Do I need to?"

He gave her a wicked grin. "It's kind of gross."

"Gross, I need to get you to a doctor or gross, this is pretty cool."

"It's pretty cool."

"Then no, I don't need to see it. But I might ask Evelyn Morrow if she has time to check your bandages."

Heath moaned again.

"Something hurt?" she asked.

"No. You don't need to bring Mrs. Morrow over. Rebecca will help me tonight."

Polly chuckled. "Okay, then. What do you want to do today?"

"My homework. Sleep. Go to the bathroom. Watch television. Text my friends."

"Eat breakfast?" She'd warmed up a plate of casserole and gravy for him and put it on the table beside the couch.

"Thank you." He took the fork she handed to him. "Are you going to hang out here all day?"

"Do I need to?"

"Will you be mad if I tell you no, that you should go?" The pleading look on his face was priceless.

Polly sat down beside him. "Got some big date coming over?"

The look of shock was even better. "No! It's just that it takes me forever to move around and I don't want to make you worry. I'm really fine."

"Okay," she said. "But you have to promise me that you'll text me all day long and tell me you're okay. At least every hour. If I don't hear from you on the hour, or close to it, I'll be calling you. And if you want to take a nap, text me before you do that so I don't worry."

"Really?"

"Really." Polly put her hand on his thigh and rubbed his knee. "I worry about you. It's what a mom does."

"Thanks."

"I'm going to bring cookies and a couple of those travel bottles filled with water over to you," she said. "Do you want me to worry about lunch?"

"I'll find something. I have to start taking care of myself again."

She desperately wanted to hug him, but knew that would give him pain rather than comfort. "You're doing fine," she said instead. "The pain pills are on the kitchen counter if you decide you need one. Okay?"

He nodded.

Polly went downstairs after making sure that things were as easily accessible to Heath as possible. Stephanie smiled and greeted her as she passed through to her office. The plywood panel was still attached to the window. Polly laughed at herself. When the vandals had flung paint on Sycamore House, the one thing she'd worried about was what people would think. How young *was* she way back then? If people wanted to comment on this, that was their problem.

"The window people are going to be here this afternoon," Stephanie said. "They came up to measure things yesterday."

"Thanks," Polly said.

"Mrs. Watson called for you."

Polly frowned. "She called down here?"

"Yeah. She said she didn't want to bother you, but if you came to your office maybe you could call her." Stephanie smiled. "I was going to tell you even if you didn't come down."

"That woman is a nut," Polly said.

"She's really fun. The girl who is staying with her is nice, too. Kayla says they're trying to find where Jedidiah Carter buried the gold. Is it really worth two hundred thousand?"

"If it exists, it will be," Polly said. "But I don't have a lot of confidence about that. Too many years have passed and a lot of people could have found it between then and now."

"But it's still fun to think about. What would you do with it if you found the gold?"

"It's not mine," Polly said. "It probably belongs to Beryl's family since Jedidiah's daughter paid the bank back."

"Wow, that would be so lucky."

"Yes, it really would."

Stephanie looked as if she wanted to say something more, but she nodded and went back to her desk.

Polly decided two could play the game and dialed Beryl from the business phone on her desk.

"Hello, this is Sycamore House," Beryl said.

That didn't work. "Good morning," Polly replied. "You rang?"

"Tallie got a call from Aaron last night. They found Ethan's car down in Perry."

"Anything interesting in it?"

"Not a thing. Well, his clothes and personal items, but nothing that has to do with the treasure or might give them a clue as to who killed him."

"How in the world did it take so long for them to find it?" Polly asked.

"Aaron wouldn't say. But I don't know why he'd be embarrassed. Perry isn't even in Boone County. It's not like his deputies missed it. He did mention that it was disappointing you weren't involved in finding it."

"He did not."

Beryl laughed. "Yes he did. Maybe that's why it took them so long. You didn't have any reason to be in Perry, so it languished until the universe decided it had been long enough."

"Stop it," Polly said, laughter bubbling up.

"Do you want to do something fun today or are you busy?"

"What do you mean, fun?"

"Lydia offered to skip out on her church meeting this morning if we wanted to see the Reiman Gardens. If you go, you can keep her company while Tallie and I act all artsy-fartsy. I haven't been there in a long time, and there might be something interesting that I desperately need to paint."

"So your pleasurable day is dependent on my attendance?" Polly asked.

"Are you going to hold me hostage or will you be good to your poor friend?"

Polly chuckled. "No. I just need to change my clothes. I planned to work at Bell House again."

"You can do that any day. How often do you get an invitation to go somewhere beautiful with me?"

"You're absolutely right. Where are you taking us for lunch?"

Beryl snickered. "Hickory Park?"

"That would be foolish. You'd have to leave early because a crisis would call me home."

"That's what I hear. We'll find something. Lydia's driving. She always pulls into places that serve food on plates."

"As opposed to...?"

Beryl paused. "I've got nothing. How about we pick you up at ten forty-five, have an early lunch and then we can spend the afternoon at the gardens. We'll have you home by five o'clock."

That was a long time to spend looking at plants and flowers, but Polly knew that if necessary, she and Lydia could leave and do something else. However, she needed to wear her comfortable shoes.

"Great. I'll see you in a while." Polly walked out to Stephanie's desk. "Where's Jeff?"

"He's over at Sycamore Inn with Grey. They're interviewing somebody to help out at the front desk since Denis can't be there."

Polly had completely forgotten about that. She hadn't been much help to Grey this last week and felt guilty. She hated having her life explode to the point where she lost track of her friends and what they needed. "Is Grey okay?"

Stephanie nodded. "He's fine. You shouldn't worry."

"I promised to help him."

"Polly," Stephanie said patiently. "Everybody knows what you've been through. You hired us to do a job. We'll figure it out. You don't have to take care of things all the time."

"Yes I do," Polly grumped.

"Uh huh. You're really good at putting the right people in place to do their jobs. Would you heft hay bales if something happened to Eliseo?"

"Of course I would."

"Oh," Stephanie said. "Bad example."

"But I get it. Grey is doing his job and so is Jeff."

"Exactly."

"Since everyone is doing their jobs, I guess I'll go to Ames and wander around the gardens with Beryl and Lydia."

"That sounds like fun."

Polly nodded. She wasn't going to take the time to explain that it would be fun for an hour, maybe two, but four hours of gardens might just kill her. "I need to change. I'll talk to you later. And thank you."

Her phone buzzed with a text from Heath. "I'm fine."

She ran up the steps and walked in the front door. "It's just me. I'm changing my clothes to go to Ames with Lydia and Beryl," she called out. "I'm not checking up on you."

It took a few minutes to decide what to wear. The indoor exhibits would be warm, but there was still a chill in the air. She settled on a lightweight blue sweater over her jeans and she'd take her jacket.

Heath had managed to get his breakfast plate to the peninsula and had the television on and books spread out on the table in front of him. "Did you get my text?"

"It was perfect. Thank you. I'll be out of town today and that makes me nervous for you," she said. "So you have to promise me again that you'll keep texting. And if you need anything, call down to the office. Stephanie will be glad to help."

"I'll be fine. I'm not broken."

"You very nearly were," Polly said, patting his head. "And my heart can't take much more of that. The kids will be here before I get home. I'll take Obiwan outside one more time and he should be good until they show up. Then, you can run those three around. Make them take care of you." She pointed at his cheek. "And make Rebecca check that."

He nodded.

"That makes me a terrible mom, doesn't it," Polly said.

"It's okay. You do other stuff."

"You keep thinking that. Obiwan and I will be right back."

Polly stood in the doorway of the garage, shivering while Obiwan ran down to the tree line. He was going to miss this place if they decided to move into Bell House. The back yard there was huge and she'd feel much more comfortable letting him and Han out to run on their own with the fence that encircled its entirety, but he'd miss the horses and donkeys. The fence there needed to be replaced and Polly wondered what it would look like without it closing the land off from the rest of the world. Surely it hadn't been part of the original plans. She wondered when the cemetery had opened. What a draw for the fancy hotel. *"The upstairs rooms look out on our lovely, well-kept cemetery."*

Lydia's Jeep pulled into the driveway, startling Polly out of her reverie.

"Are you waiting for us?" Beryl asked after rolling down the window.

"No, you must be early," Polly said. "I was just waiting for Obiwan."

"Hurry that boy up," Beryl said. "We have places to be today. Aren't you as excited as I am?"

Polly looked at Lydia, who just shook her head. "Of course I am," Polly said. "Let me take the dog back up to Heath and I'll be ready to go."

Obiwan had wandered over to see who was visiting and Polly reached down to touch his head. "Come on in, boy. It's time for me to be going." She took him inside, opened the door to the apartment and ran up the steps. "They're here to get me, Heath," she said, walking into the media room. "Are you sure you'll be okay by yourself?"

"I'm sure," he replied. "And I promise to text you."

"Thanks. I'll see you later." He might be sure, but Polly was still nervous. Then she told herself to stop it and headed out.

CHAPTER TWENTY-SIX

After all the focus on Beryl's English half-brother, Lydia told them about a British Pub in Ames. Beryl thought it would be the perfect place to eat. The first time she said that she was eating bangers and mash, Polly must have giggled, because Beryl kept repeating it, changing the emphasis on the words until everyone was laughing.

They talked about many different things on the ride, but then Beryl would simply say "bangers and mash" and the laughter started again.

When Lydia pulled into the parking lot, she stopped the Jeep and turned in her seat. "You girls will be good. Do you understand me?"

"What, Mom?" Polly asked.

"I'm not kidding. The first person who giggles over bangers and mash is going to get a talking-to."

Polly had found the menu online and smiled sweetly. "Haggis and mash?"

Beryl snorted with laughter and Tallie put her hand over her mouth.

"I'm taking you to McDonald's," Lydia said.

"We'll be good. I promise." Beryl reached over and covered Lydia's eyes, then turned to the back seat and mouthed, "Haggis and mash."

Lydia slapped the hand away. "I heard that."

"Don't worry," Polly said. "We'll try not to embarrass you." She looked at the front door and grinned. "Whoops. Famous last words. Who will take a picture of me entering the Tardis?" A dark blue police call box had been painted on the door, letting everyone know that they took their British food seriously.

"I'll do it," Lydia replied. "Just play it cool for me, okay?"

Pictures took only a few minutes and Beryl opened the door. Then she pushed it closed and swore. "Damn it. That little..." She pursed her lips. "I won't call him what I want to call him."

"What?" Lydia asked.

"Is he an idiot?"

"Is who?" Lydia's eyes grew big. "Oh. He's in there now?"

Beryl nodded. "What are we going to do?"

"I should call Aaron."

"We're not in Boone County. There's nothing he can do here."

"He knows people," Lydia said. "Do you think he saw you?"

"No. He was facing away from the door."

"Well, we look like idiots out here," Lydia said. "What do you want to do?"

Beryl looked at Polly. "You're the criminologist. What are your thoughts?"

"Me? I'm just along to keep Lydia occupied while you and Tallie paint flowers," Polly protested. "Is he alone?"

"Yes. All by his lonesome."

"If we were adventurous, we'd sit in the Jeep and wait until he came out, then follow him. Do you know which car is his?"

Beryl looked around the lot and pointed to a white Camry. "I think that's it."

"Well?" Polly asked. "Are you up for an adventure?"

"No," Lydia replied. "Aaron would not approve. I will call him and he will call someone over here."

"Let's get back in the Jeep, though," Beryl said. "What if he comes out?"

Tallie laughed as they hopped back into the Jeep. Lydia pulled out of the parking space and parked a few spots away from the door and Darien Blackstone's car.

"You ladies are crazy," she said. "This was just supposed to be lunch."

Polly turned to watch the Camry. "We were asking for it. A British pub and all."

"That's only because you're with us," Beryl said. "If you hadn't come, we never would have run into this."

"It's not my fault. Nobody ever listens to me."

Beryl turned to watch as well. "We have to follow him. I don't want to lose him because we're waiting for you to make a call and Aaron to make a call and then for the police to get here." She opened her door. "I'll be right back."

"What in the world is she doing?" Lydia asked.

They watched Beryl creep along behind the cars until she got to the Camry. She tested each of the car doors and looked up at them when she discovered the driver's door was unlocked.

"She wouldn't," Polly said.

Sure enough, Beryl unlocked the doors and climbed into the back seat of the Camry.

Polly's phone buzzed.

"What are you doing?" Polly asked.

"Don't tell Lydia, but I'm tired of this. He's going to answer to me once and for all."

"What if he's dangerous?" Polly asked.

"He's not dangerous, just a gold-digging idiot who thinks he can figure out where Jedidiah's treasure is. The only thing he's done is break into Sycamore House and take some papers. Marybelle Dykstra…" She stopped. "Shhh, here he comes."

They watched in shocked silence as Beryl disappeared from view.

Darien Blackstone triggered the locks and climbed into the driver's seat.

Polly giggled when his hands went up in the air. "Oh no," she said. "Beryl's holding him up. We have to help her."

"You stay right here," Lydia said.

Tallie looked at Polly. "We should all go. That will scare him."

Lydia shook her head. "My husband is going to have my head for this."

Polly jumped out of the Jeep and waited for the other two to join her. Then she approached the Camry and tapped on the driver's window. Darien Blackstone looked at her in a panic and she motioned for him to roll down the window. He shook his head, fear filling his eyes. She chuckled and pulled the car door open.

"Do you recognize me?" she asked.

"No. Why would I recognize you?" Then it hit him. "You're the lady from the hotel."

"He thinks I'm a lady," Polly said to Lydia. "Isn't that sweet."

"What is this?" he asked. "Are you holding me up? I don't have very much money on me."

Beryl sat up and using the same low growly voice she must have been using before said, "You held us up. And now you're going to pay."

He looked in the rear view mirror and dropped his hands.

"Put 'em back up," she said, jamming her fist in the back of his seat. "I'm not done with you and I'm pissed."

"What are you going to do with him?" Lydia asked.

"I haven't made up my mind," Beryl replied. "Killing him right here would be wrong."

"I didn't do anything," Darien whined. "I'm innocent."

"My sweet American ass, you're innocent," Beryl snapped. "You are a lying, thieving jerk who deserves to waste away in a dark and dingy dungeon, far, far from your poor sweet family. You know that's what our prisons are like, don't you? We took our cues from old English castles. It's almost as good a deterrent as killing people on the spot."

He started to turn to look at her, but she slapped the back of his head. "Don't you turn around and look at me, you punk."

"Seriously, Beryl. What are you planning to do with him?" Polly glanced around, looking for something ... anything. "Tallie run back to the Jeep and get Lydia's scarf and anything else we can use to tie him up."

"My scarf?" Lydia asked. "Oh no you don't. I have rope in the Jeep. We aren't messing with my scarf." She followed Tallie.

"Here's what we're going to do," Polly said. "We'll tie you up. I'll drive your car and Beryl will stay in the back seat with her gun trained on you so you don't get stupid. Lydia and Tallie will follow us and if you do try to get stupid and jump out, I'll just have Lydia run over you."

"You people are crazy," he screamed. "Help! Help! I'm being kidnapped."

Beryl slapped the back of his head again. "Stop that or I will drop you where you sit. Imagine the headache that will bring when you wake up on the dirt floor of a cold, damp cell."

Polly was having the hardest time keeping a straight face, especially as she kept watching the front door of the restaurant, hoping no one else would come out until they were gone.

Lydia and Tallie came back with two lengths of rope.

"What in the world do you carry this for?" Polly asked.

"I don't know. Aaron made me put it in there. I have all sorts of things that I don't understand." Lydia held up a container of Mace. "But I thought you could use this, too."

Polly laughed. "I suppose I can. Here, you hold the Mace while I tie him up. Lean forward and put your hands behind your back," she ordered.

When he could go no further because of the steering wheel, she pushed his torso to the passenger side. "Give me your hands."

He obeyed and she tied his hands together. "Now scoot over to the passenger seat. We'll wait." She turned to Lydia. "I'm going to drive to Aaron's office in Boone. Will you call him?"

"He won't believe this," Lydia said.

"If you tell him that it's me and Beryl, he will." Polly waited while Darien negotiated the gear shift. He finally landed in the passenger seat. "Keep an eye on him."

She walked around, opened the passenger door and with the second length of rope, tied his feet together and then wrapped the rope around the seat release bar. "There, that should do it. Are you comfortable enough?"

"I can't sit back. This hurts," he complained.

"Too bad. It's a short drive to Boone. You can suffer."

"This is brutality."

"We ain't the coppers," Beryl snapped. "Quit 'cher complainin'."

"I want to get out of here before anyone else sees us," Polly said. She walked back to the driver's side, got in and adjusted the seat, then looked for the keys. "Where are they?" she asked.

His eyes darted to the console before he said, "In my pocket. Wanna try to get them?"

Beryl leaned forward and picked up the key fob. "Liar. You aren't helping your case any. Just push the button, Polly."

Polly started the car and pulled out onto Duff to head for Highway 30, checking the mirror to make sure that Lydia and Tallie were following.

"You really are an idiot, you know," Beryl said. "A silly woman and her friends just got the drop on you."

"I wasn't doing anything," he said. Polly was now quite tired of his whiny British accent.

"Why did you leave my kitties alone Saturday night?" Beryl asked. Before he could speak, she continued. "Why did you break into Polly's office? Why did you go out to Marybelle Dykstra's house? Why did you ever contact me in the first place? Why did you have to hurt me like this?"

"I didn't mean to hurt you," he said.

"How did you even know those papers were in my office?" Polly asked. "Henry put them there Sunday afternoon."

He nodded toward the back seat. Beryl picked up a pair of binoculars. "You've been watching everything, haven't you?"

"You went on and on about how you had all of that information. I didn't get enough time to look at it before you drove off Saturday night and I knew you wouldn't bring it back. You weren't any use after that."

"Any use? But we're family. I'm your family!"

"No," he spat. "You're part of the chosen family. Our father..." he growled out the title. "Our father was a piece of work. He thought he could buy my mum's silence with pretty gifties and money. Then one day he just didn't show up. But he had told me stories when I was a little boy. About three brothers who had come to Iowa. Two of them stayed and the other went west to get his fortune. Oh, he loved those stories. He knew about the gold, you know."

Beryl looked up in shock. "He what?"

"He said it was a legend and tried to make me believe that it wasn't true. But he knew that his ancestor had robbed his own brother's bank. That's the kind of stock that we come from. Bank robber, horse thief and gambler. Don't you feel special?"

"You're a horrible man," Beryl said. "But how did you get hold of Ethan Carter?"

Darien laughed. "He found me."

"How could he find you without finding me?"

"Ask your brothers. He found them first."

"They didn't tell me that."

"They've known that I existed for a long time," he said.

Beryl crumpled. "Why wouldn't they tell me?"

"Young Ethan wanted to find out where his family had come from, so your brother, Melvin, put him in touch with me, hoping that I could help him with genealogy in England. That was the beginning of a very interesting relationship."

"What about your wife and sons."

He gave her a sneering grin. "Lies. She lives in the flat next to mine and agreed to play you up for a fee."

Polly watched Beryl's face in the rear view mirror. Emotions played across it as the man spoke. Tears leaked from her eyes until the last bit of the conversation when she realized there wasn't anyone back in England who was waiting for him. Then, her eyes got hard. Polly had never seen that look on Beryl's face. Steely fury had taken over.

"Did you kill that young man?" Beryl asked.

He shook his head.

"Are you lying to us?"

"I'm not saying anything more. I believe that in your country I'm entitled to a lawyer."

"You aren't talking to the police," Polly snarled. "You aren't entitled to anything in this car." She was gripping the steering wheel so tightly, her fingers had lost their color. Relaxing a bit, she glanced back at Beryl who had sagged into the seat.

"Why in the world are you still in Iowa?" Polly asked.

"You haven't found the gold yet."

"There is no gold," Beryl said. "It was just a legend. It was a fun story, but there's nothing there."

"No one ever found it," he replied. "If you can just figure out where Jedidiah Carter buried it, we could all be rich."

"You'll be in jail," Beryl said. "We'll never find where he buried it. There are too many possible locations."

Polly's heart broke as she watched her friend deflate. "You're a contemptible, despicable man."

"You do what you have to when you grow up without a father," he replied.

"Bah," Beryl said, sitting up. "People grow up with single parents all the time and don't do what you did." She leaned forward. "Why did you shoot up the hotel?"

Polly snapped her head to look at him. "You shot up my hotel?"

He shrugged. It wasn't easy with his hands behind his back, but he still managed to look as if he didn't care. "I had to get into Beryl's house somehow. I was running out of money. And it had the added bonus of throwing suspicion off of me and onto a random person that didn't exist."

"You could have hurt someone," Polly said.

"I heard the girl get into the shower. I didn't want to hurt her and nobody else was staying back there. All I had to do was shoot out her car windows and into the wall of her room away from the bathroom. Then I shot at my car and my room, tossed the gun into the ditch behind the trees and showed up looking shocked and upset."

"You're going away for a very long time, you filthy SOB," Beryl said.

"It was your father who was the filthy SOB," he retorted. "My mother was not a bitch. She worked hard to make sure I had food and a place to sleep."

"And she'd be so proud of you now." Beryl sat back again.

Polly turned north on Story Street into Boone. Lydia was still behind her and wouldn't believe the story they were hearing. She wished they had a recording. Blackstone remained mute for the rest of the trip and looked up when she pulled into the parking lot of the sheriff's office. Lydia must have called her husband, because he and Stu Decker walked out to meet them.

"What have you two girls done?" he asked when Polly opened her door.

She chuckled. "We brought you a prisoner."

"Lydia told me what happened. You're lucky no one saw you and reported the kidnapping."

"I know," Polly said. "But once we started, we couldn't stop."

"Get him out, Stu," Aaron said.

Stu opened the passenger door and stepped back, his eyes wide and a smirk on his lips.

"He can't get out of the car," Polly said.

Aaron looked across at him. "What did she do?"

"She tied his feet to the seat release bar, boss." Stu said, laughter rolling out of him. "I've never seen anything like it."

"I was afraid he might try to jump out."

"Oh Polly," Aaron said. "This is too much."

"It was a citizen's arrest," she said. "And he told us everything on the way over. Except he hasn't admitted to killing Ethan Carter. He said he tossed the gun in the trees behind the hotel after shooting up the rooms and the cars."

Blackstone shook his head in disgust.

"We already have it," Aaron said.

She looked at him and raised her eyebrows. "What?"

"Show her, Beryl."

Beryl put her phone in his hand and he showed it to Polly.

"We're still connected. She called before he got in the car, but she wouldn't tell us what she was doing, just told Anita to record it."

"I can't believe you did that," Polly said.

"It's not admissible," Darien said.

"Are you going to deny all of the things you admitted to?" Aaron asked. "We'll just call Polly and Beryl as witnesses."

"Hearsay," he said as he climbed out of the car.

Stu snapped cuffs on him and untied the rope.

Beryl got out of the back seat and strode over to him. "Hearsay, you say? You're an idiot." She spat on the ground. "The next time I see you will be in a courtroom. I'll do all in my power to make sure you spend the rest of your life surrounded by the biggest, burliest, meanest men you've ever met."

He looked over at Aaron. "I won't talk until I have a lawyer."

"That's fine with me," Aaron said. "I'm not particularly interested in spending the afternoon with you anyway. Go ahead and take him in, Stu."

Stu led him away and Aaron crossed over to Beryl and took her in his arms. "I'm so sorry, honey," he said.

"You heard everything, didn't you?"

He nodded. "Would you like me to talk to your brothers?"

"No," she said. "I'll do it. They have some strange belief that they have to protect me. I want them to understand that all they did was make things worse."

Lydia had pulled in behind them and was out of the Jeep and standing beside the two as fast as she could. Aaron released Beryl into her arms. "We have it now," he said. "Take care of her."

He handed Beryl's phone to Polly. "When I realized what you had done, I nearly came down the highway after you. You've got to stop this. My heart can't take it."

"It's not my fault," she protested again. "Beryl started this and all I could do was get here as fast as possible."

He breathed a deep sigh. "You're going to be the death of me. Please stay out of trouble before you get back to Bellingwood."

She smiled. "I'll do my best."

CHAPTER TWENTY-SEVEN

"Yes," Polly said to the dogs as she walked down the steps. "I know, I'm leaving again. Sorry."

The week had zipped by in a blur. Darien Blackstone admitted to killing Ethan Carter at the height of an argument when the young man admitted to not knowing where the gold was. Ethan told Blackstone that he wanted to reach out to other descendants of the three Carter brothers and the older man had gotten furious, frightened that they would have to further split the wealth. Darien Blackstone had come this far; he could finish the task on his own.

During the fight, Blackstone shoved the kid backwards. Ethan's head had slammed against the stone as he fell and he died immediately. The gun they found behind the hotel was actually Ethan's and Blackstone had seen it as serendipitous. You never know when you'll need a gun. Tallie didn't know where her brother might have gotten it. He'd never carried one before. The whole treasure thing had been blown way out of proportion.

Andrew, Kayla and Rebecca had come up with three properties owned by Jedidiah Carter prior to his death. Two of the properties were dead ends. The elementary school sat on one and the grain elevator on the other. Nobody was digging for gold in either of those locations. The third, however, was the family farm where Melvin Carter and his family resided. Beryl was still upset that her brothers hadn't been honest about a prior relationship with Darien Blackstone and knowledge of Ethan Carter before his death. When Lydia reminded her that she hadn't told them anything either, Beryl just stopped talking.

She and Lydia had gone out to meet Melvin and Harold Thursday evening and the conversation had gone as poorly as everyone expected. Melvin's wife had been furious that people in town might be digging up their property looking for buried treasure. Melvin and Harold thought the entire story was hooey. When Beryl confronted them about withholding information regarding Darien Blackstone and Ethan Carter from her, Melvin tried to tell her it was none of her business. They weren't going to budge from their beliefs and she'd finally done what she always did and walked away, frustrated with her immediate family. It was going to take time for her to restore those relationships again.

This morning, though, Polly was helping two friends move into their new house. Camille had closed on her little home the day before and even though they intended to paint walls and replace carpet in several rooms, she and Elise were ready to move out of Sycamore House and into a place they could call their own.

When Polly had gotten up, the sky was grey and threatening, but it soon gave way to a beautiful, bright sunny day. She pulled her truck around to the other side of the building and went inside and up the elevator of the addition.

Noise and general chaos greeted her as she exited the elevator.

"Is Elise here?" she asked a young man, carrying a box. He shrugged.

"Elise?" Polly called out.

Camille poked her head out of the door. "Hi Polly. Elise is already over at the house. She didn't have very much stuff, so we packed it into her car. She'll direct traffic on that side of the move."

"Miss Polly." Abigail Specht, Camille's mother came out of her room.

"Hello, Mrs. Specht," Polly said. "This is a great day."

"It is," the woman replied. "We're very proud of Camille. She's finally putting down roots."

Three more young people passed Polly, carrying boxes and clothing on hangers.

"Do you need my pickup truck?" Polly asked. "Can I help you?"

"I think we have it, but if you want to go over to the house, we could find something for you to do. There is so much more heading that way," Camille said. "My father and brothers are bringing things from Omaha and I believe that Elise's cousins should be here this morning. They're unloading the storage unit she had in Ames as well as bringing things from her parent's home in Chicago."

"Are her parents coming?" Polly asked.

Camille shook her head. "Not this trip. Her dad's been sick."

Two girls came out of Camille's room, each carrying a box.

Camille chuckled. "It's a veritable parade. I didn't realize how long I've been living here. The room keeps getting bigger minute by minute."

"How many kids are here?" Polly asked.

Abigail stepped back as yet two more exited Camille's room. "Camille's nieces and nephews all wanted to see her new house."

Polly raised her eyebrows.

"They're not all our family," Camille said.

"Of course they are," her mother retorted.

"Yes, mama."

"I'll run over to the house and see what I can do to help Elise," Polly said.

Camille walked down the hall with her. "Could you do me a huge favor?"

"Of course. What do you need?"

"Sylvie has boxes of baked breakfast items for me. Could you pick those up before you head over to the house? I thought I'd have time, but..." she glanced behind her. "It would be easier."

"Well, shucks. I don't know," Polly said with a grin. "Forcing me to go up to Sweet Beans where there is coffee. That's rough."

"Thank you," Camille said.

Polly went back down to her truck and took out her phone to call Henry. She'd just left him, but he was caught up in paperwork at his desk and hadn't paid much attention. Rebecca and Heath were still in their rooms, so she'd slipped out.

"Hello?" he said, still sounding distracted.

"Hi there. It's me."

"Yeah?"

"You remember that you're taking Rebecca over to Beryl's for her lesson this morning, right?"

"Uh huh."

"And you're going to wash all of the windows with my panties, too."

"Okay."

"When you're finished with that, spin around three times and do a flying somersault, but make sure you stick the landing."

"What? What are you talking about?" he asked.

"You haven't been paying much attention to anything this morning."

"What was that about your panties?"

Polly laughed. "I'm just calling to remind you that Rebecca needs to go to Beryl's for her lesson this morning."

"Do you think Heath can do that?"

She thought for a moment. "I don't see why not. The doctor said his ribs are much better. He was cleared to go back to normal."

"That's great. He'll be glad to get out of the house."

"Bet me," she said with a laugh. "The last couple of days have been fun for him."

Henry laughed with her. "I didn't think I'd ever see that many high school girls in our house."

"At least not for a few more years. It was pretty cute, though."

"I'll make sure they're up and moving in time. Thanks for calling. When will you be home?"

"Hopefully by lunch. It sounds like they have plenty of help. I just wanted to show my face and do what I can."

"Okay, gotta go."

"Henry?"

"Yes."

"Do I need to call again to remind you?"

He chuckled. "Might not hurt, if you think about it."

Their house had been full of people the last two days. Jason had asked if Heath was up for company and warned him Wednesday night that he might want to get showered and shaved because some kids wanted to come see him. After school on Thursday, several girls had knocked on the front door, asking to see Heath. They oohed and aahed over his wounds and told him how badly they felt that he had to go through such a traumatic event. One of the girls told him she was glad he and Libby had broken up because a lot of girls wanted to go out with him.

When had girls gotten so forward? Polly kept an eye on him, wanting to make sure that he wasn't overwhelmed by all the attention, but he lapped it up.

Last night had been an entirely different story. Heath had gotten a call after school from one of the Thursday night girls - Polly couldn't remember her name - asking if he could come out Friday night with them. Polly said no, but suggested that maybe his friends could come over. And they had. Kids had started drifting in about seven thirty, then a few more came after the basketball game was over. The final count was twenty-two kids spread throughout the apartment. They'd brought games, junk food and soda, and Henry picked up pizza for the crowd. There wasn't a single slice left over this morning.

Heath hadn't known what to do with all of the attention. He introduced Rebecca around and she kept him involved in the party, moving him around the house, in and out of different groups. Polly was so in love with that little girl. She knew Rebecca was going to cause her annoyance and pain while she grew into herself, but when she was thinking about someone else, she was wonderful.

The first young girl that called Polly Mrs. Sturtz had elicited a giggle from Rebecca and Heath, but the kids had been pretty respectful. After Henry brought the pizza back, he hid in their bedroom with the cats and watched television. Polly spent time in there with him once she realized Rebecca had things well in hand.

Polly parked in front of the coffee shop and went inside.

"Hey there, chick-a-dee," Skylar called from the counter. "Your regular this morning?"

"Yes please," she said as she got closer. "I'm going to talk to Sylvie."

"I've got you covered," he responded.

"Good morning," Polly said to Sylvie from the doorway of the kitchen, nodding at the two girls working with her this morning.

"Hi, what's up?" Sylvie asked.

"Camille asked if I'd pick up her breakfast order."

Sylvie pointed to four boxes on the counter. "She must have an army."

"That's a good word for it," Polly said. "And Elise's cousins will be here, too."

"Those girls can't have that much stuff," Sylvie said.

Polly nodded. "Not in town, but it sounds like they have furniture and things coming in from all over the Midwest."

"Jason said he had a good time last night at the party."

"What a riot that was," Polly said. "Did you have a lot of parties when you were in high school?"

"No," Sylvie said, shaking her head. "Not at my house. I went to a few, but things are different these days. Kids just congregate and hang out together."

"I loved every minute of it," Polly said. "Now I really want to get Bell House finished so we can do this all the time."

"That would be a good location for parties like that. Lots of room to spread out. Jason said your house was packed."

"There were only twenty-two, but they were definitely everywhere."

Sylvie chuckled. "You counted."

"Well of course I did. And I was glad that Jason came up. I didn't know if he and Heath would ever be friends."

"That was kind of weird," Sylvie said. "But I wasn't going to get involved. I know my boy and if he thinks that I want him to do something, he'll not do it just to make me mad. It was best that I left it alone."

"They figured it out on their own," Polly said. "The next party is at your house."

"I'm glad to." She winked at Polly. "You can keep Andrew for the night and I'll take Heath and all their friends."

Polly stepped back. "You're kidding?"

"Kinda," Sylvie said, laughing out loud. "We're going to have a time with those two. They're trying so hard, but they are going to keep getting older. And bolder."

"Shut up, shut up, shut up," Polly said, putting her hands up. "I don't want to think about it. No, no, no, no, no."

Sylvie picked the up boxes and put them in Polly's arms. "You take these and go play with your friends. We'll worry about the stupidity of kiddos later."

"Are you working at Sycamore House this afternoon?" Polly asked.

"Yeah. It's a big one. The cake is already there. As soon as we get everything moving for the day, I'm heading over."

"Maybe I'll see you later, then." Polly left and headed back to the front.

"Whoa," Skylar said. "That's too heavy for a lovely lady like you. Let this burly knight relieve you of your burden."

Polly raised her eyebrows.

He shrugged. "At least let me help you so you can get this and your coffee to your truck without spilling everything on the ground."

"That's better." Polly put the boxes on the counter so he could pick them up. "That's mine?" She pointed at a cup.

"Mixed to perfection as always," he said.

Sal met them while they walked out to the truck.

"What are you doing up this early?" Polly asked.

"My doctor and I agreed that I could have one cup of coffee a day. If that's all I get, then I'm having the good stuff," she said.

"Okay, but it's still way early for you."

Sal scowled. "Apparently my hormones and my sleep cycle are no longer in agreement. I fall asleep earlier and get up earlier these days. If this baby thinks that it is going to be a morning person, we're going to have a long talk."

"You'd better start talking now," Polly said.

"Where are you going with all of that?" Sal asked.

Polly had opened the back seat of her truck and waited for Skylar to deposit the boxes.

"Camille and Elise's new house. There's a whole passel of people showing up for this move-in event."

Sal lit up. "That sounds like fun. Can I come with you?"

"Sure."

"Your regular?" Skylar asked, his hand on the front door handle.

"I'll be right in for it," Sal responded.

"No worries. I've had a lot of caffeine this morning, so I'm on high speed." He winked at them and went inside.

"I just love him," Sal said. "He's adorable."

"And he knows it." Polly opened the door of her truck and reached in to put her coffee in a cup holder. "Do you want to ride with me?"

"Unless you're planning to be there all day."

"This will be quick. Camille has a lot of family in town and we'll probably just be in the way."

"Her mother scares me," Sal said.

"Me too. I think she takes pleasure in intimidating us."

Skylar came back outside with Sal's coffee. "Just the way you like it." He turned to Polly. "Now you be careful with her today. Future generations depend on her, you know. She could be carrying the child who will save us all from termination at the hands of Skynet."

"Sal Kahane. Sarah Connor." Polly grinned. "It works for me. Are you going to help her up into my truck?"

He gave Sal a sideways glance and she glared at him. "Not on your life," she said. "Go back to work."

"Have a good day, ladies." Skylar went back inside, waving at them as he left.

"Not only are you up early, but you're awfully bright and chipper this morning."

"Shhh," Sal said. "I'm about to enter Nirvana." She sipped from the cup and moaned. "Oh, that's the stuff. Now let's do this thing. I'm ready to meet the family."

"Pregnancy suits you," Polly said.

Sal climbed into the truck and pulled the door shut, then took another drink. "I don't know what it is, but I've never felt so good." She laughed. "That will all change in two hours and I'll be madder than a wet hen." Sal giggled. "Why does a hen get mad when it's wet? I've never seen a wet hen. Oh Polly, I feel almost drunk with happiness right now."

"Did you have a good night with Mark last night?"

"I'll never tell. But being pregnant has made that a lot more fun, too. I can't tell you why, but it has."

Polly turned a corner and then put her hand up. "Stop right there. I'm sorry I asked."

"Yeah, because I'll probably tell you."

~~~

Hayden's basketball game was out of town this week, so Henry and Heath were home that evening. Instead of cooking, Polly was ready to go out and celebrate. After convincing her family to dress up, they went to Davey's for dinner.

Polly watched Heath as they walked in the front door. Davey's was where she'd first seen him as someone other than a hoodlum. He'd been miserable that night with his aunt and uncle; shut down and existing in as small a space as possible. Now, even after the beating, he was a much happier young man. He smiled and laughed with Rebecca and stood as straight as his healing ribs would let him.

The hostess took them into the main room and Polly laughed when she saw a large table filled with her friends. Lydia glanced up from her menu, then stood and waved them over.

"We can make room," Lydia said. "Please join us."

Polly looked at Henry and he smiled. He shook Aaron's hand, then stepped around to greet Len Specek. Beryl and Tallie scooted over so Polly and Rebecca could sit with them, while Aaron made room for Heath.

"We didn't want to bother you tonight," Lydia said. "I know you were busy with Elise and Camille this morning."

"We are celebrating," Polly said.

Beryl leaned across Tallie. "Celebrating what?"

"I guess everything. Aaron has the murderer, Heath is better, you and Tallie have found each other. Everything," Polly said. "I feel…" she looked around the table. "Content."

"That's a good word for it," Beryl said. "It's been a strange couple of weeks, but I've learned something."

"What's that, dear?" Lydia asked.

"You were right."

Lydia grinned and tipped her water glass at Beryl. "Of course I was. Is there ever a question about that? But what was I right about?"

"When we were kids, family was defined in very limited ways," Beryl said. "We never would have considered our friends to be family. Tonight, I look around this table and this is my family. Sisters that I could never have hoped to have, men who care for me as brothers should, and then out of the blue, a young woman shows up who, though our DNA is linked, I might never have gotten to know. And she's family to me. Love is kind of unexpected when it shows up, isn't it?"

Polly smiled and took Rebecca's hand in hers. She knew exactly what Beryl was saying. She risked a glance at Heath and gave him a small smile.

Aaron had leaned back while Beryl spoke and put his arm around Heath's chair, rubbing the boy's shoulder. Heath swallowed twice and looked down at his lap. One of these days Polly would quit thinking of him as having had a rough life in the past and they would fully focus on his present and future. But for now, she was still so grateful that he was in their lives.

Beryl caught the waitress who had been quietly taking drink orders around the table. "Who's the bartender tonight?" she asked.

"It's a new guy," the waitress said and then she grinned. "I forgot about that. What are you ordering?"

"Well," Beryl said. She bit her upper lip and grinned around the table. "Old Jedidiah Carter, who was one of the founders of Bellingwood was a bank robber."

The young woman nodded.

"He stole gold from his brother's bank and that legend has disrupted many a family this week."

"I heard he buried it in town somewhere," the waitress said. She glanced at Aaron. "But nobody knows where."

"They may never find it," Beryl said. "But some of us found something even better than gold." She grinned at Tallie. "Are you game?"

Tallie nodded.

"How about the rest of you?" Beryl asked. "None for the kids, of course, but I promise it will be fun."

Henry and Polly smiled at each other, then nodded. Soon everyone was agreeing.

"Bring a Gold Rush for everyone here," Beryl said. "And tell your bartender to make up something fun to match for the kids, okay?"

"What's a Gold Rush?" the waitress asked.

"If he can't figure it out, tell him to come ask me himself," Beryl said. "Go on now, I can't wait to hear what he says."

The waitress left the table and Beryl turned back. "It's just bourbon, lemon juice and honey syrup. It should be tasty."

"When are you going back to New Mexico?" Polly asked Tallie.

"She's leaving Monday morning," Beryl interrupted. "I'm going to miss her. We've had a wonderful week together."

Lydia smiled. "I'm so glad for you. Are you ever coming back for a visit?"

Tallie looked at Beryl, as if waiting for the woman to answer for her. Beryl scowled at her and Tallie replied. "This summer for sure. I want to be here for the sesquicentennial. And we're talking about a more long-term arrangement in the future when I can spend some time studying with Beryl."

"She's a wonderful teacher," Andy said.

Beryl shrugged. "We'll see. I'm thinking about scheduling a trip to Taos this spring. Tallie tells me that the colors are so different in the Southwest I won't believe it until I actually see it. An old lady has to be willing to learn, too, doesn't she?"

"That sounds cool," Rebecca said quietly.

"Maybe I'll wait until school's out and take you with me, little thing," Beryl said. She winked at Polly. "Would you let her travel with me?"

"As long as you don't lose her," Henry said. "We know about you."

Beryl cackled. "I'm much better on planes than I am in a car and Tallie promises me that I won't have to drive anywhere once I get there. She'll be in charge of our travel.

The waitress returned carrying a tray of drinks. She was followed by a young man who carried a second tray. She walked around the table, but not before nodding to Beryl.

"We have your Gold Rush, Ms. Watson," he said. "I've heard about you and did my best to be prepared, but this one required a little research." He placed a glass in front of her and smiled.

Beryl picked it up and took a sip, then turned to look at him. "Very good," she said. "You've earned your stripes."

They passed out the rest of the drinks and Beryl stood up, lifting her glass. "We might not have found Jedidiah Carter's gold, but I've found something worth so much more. Families come in all shapes and sizes. I am the richest woman in town because I have you."

~~~

Polly snuggled into Henry's arms on the couch in the media room. Heath had taken one overstuffed chair and Rebecca was curled up with Han in the other while they watched a movie.

"Will you two stop it," Rebecca said. "You're embarrassing us."

"Are we embarrassing you, Heath?" Polly asked.

He put a hand over his eyes and turned toward the television.

"We're an odd little family, aren't we," she said. "Beryl said she was the richest woman in town, but I'd have to disagree. I'm thankful for my riches. I never expected to find any of you, but then, there you were, filling up my life. Thank you."

Henry reached over and squeezed Rebecca's foot. She wiggled it. "You're still embarrassing us," she said softly.

THANK YOU FOR READING!

I'm so glad you enjoy these stories about Polly Giller and her friends. There are many ways to stay in touch with Diane and the Bellingwood community.

You can find more details about Sycamore House and Bellingwood at the website: http://nammynools.com/

Join the Bellingwood Facebook page:
https://www.facebook.com/pollygiller
for news about upcoming books, conversations while I'm writing and you're reading, and a continued look at life in a small town.

Diane Greenwood Muir's Amazon Author Page is a great place to watch for new releases.

Follow Diane on Twitter at twitter.com/nammynools for regular updates and notifications.

Recipes and decorating ideas found in the books can often be found on Pinterest at: http://pinterest.com/nammynools/

And, if you are looking for Sycamore House swag, check out Polly's CafePress store: http://www.cafepress.com/sycamorehouse

Made in the USA
Columbia, SC
07 September 2021